FROM THE
NANCY DREW FILES

THE CASE: *Bess is being held hostage to save a landmark theater—in a bungled kidnapping that could cost her her life.*

CONTACT: *Young film star Brady Armstrong is Bess's old school flame—and the intended victim.*

SUSPECTS: *Nick Falcone—he's leading a losing fight to save the Century Cinema.*

Simon Mueller—Brady's manager never misses a publicity opportunity.

Deirdre McCullough—the beautiful young actress has a jealous streak.

COMPLICATIONS: *Developer Bart Anderson is determined to raze the lovely old theater—even with Bess still trapped inside.*

Books in THE NANCY DREW FILES® Series

Available from ARCHWAY paperbacks

THE NANCY DREW FILES CASE · 38

THE FINAL SCENE

Carolyn Keene

AN ARCHWAY PAPERBACK
Published by POCKET BOOKS

New York   London   Toronto   Sydney   Tokyo

AN ARCHWAY PAPERBACK *Original*

An Archway Paperback published by
POCKET BOOKS, a division of Simon & Schuster Inc.
1230 Avenue of the Americas, New York, NY 10020

ISBN: 0-671-67490-0

First Archway Paperback printing August 1989

10 9 8 7 6 5 4 3 2 1

Printed in the U.S.A.

IL 7+

Chapter

One

BESS, WILL YOU STOP messing with your hair? You look great! And what's more important, Brady will think you look gorgeous."

Nancy Drew struggled to make her voice heard above the screams of hundreds of teenagers crowded outside River Heights's Century Cinema Theater. Her blue eyes were twinkling with amusement as she watched her friend Bess Marvin toy with her long blond curls.

Bess's cousin, George Fayne, was gently lifting and dropping one of Bess's curls. "You must have a whole can of mousse on your head," George said, running a hand through her own short dark hair. "A hurricane couldn't budge your hairdo."

Bess fiddled with the clip-on rhinestone earring that kept slipping off her right ear.

"Come on, guys," she said. "The last time I saw Brady Armstrong I was just a chubby little freshman and he was a handsome, sophisticated senior. Now that he's a famous movie star, I want to look really good for him."

"I can't believe you're still in love with him after all these years," George teased.

"Ninety percent of the female population is in love with Brady Armstrong," Nancy said as the three friends headed for the front of the theater.

"And the other ten percent is blind," Bess observed, staring at the life-size movie poster at the side of the main entrance.

Nancy watched Bess take in the photo of Brady, dressed as the space knight, Jonathan Ryder. He was wearing the white space suit and holding the glistening laser sword that he had become famous for. *Night of the Venus Moon* was his latest movie, the third in a series of sci-fi adventures starring Brady and a beautiful redheaded actress named Deirdre McCullough.

"Don't you wish you were Deirdre, just for ten minutes?" Bess continued to gaze enraptured at the poster.

George laughed and nudged Nancy. "Bess has it bad."

Nancy nodded. "She does, but can you blame her? He *is* gorgeous. Just look at his green eyes and all that wonderful black hair. Still, he isn't as cute as Ned."

"Now, that's loyalty," George teased.

Bess and George laughed, but Nancy found herself missing her boyfriend, Ned Nickerson, terribly. He was the only guy she had ever truly loved, but she didn't get to see him too often because he was a student at Emerson College. She could hardly wait for his next break.

"Ned's cute, but Brady's what I'd call a hunk!" Bess said, her eyes still riveted to the photograph.

"Apparently you're not the only one who thinks so," George added, eyeing the crowd of girls behind the police barrier that let out a single scream as a van and two cars slowed down in front of the theater. One of them was carrying a sign that read, Marry Me, Brady!

The three girls turned to see what had

caused the latest commotion. The local news was arriving.

"But—" Bess fingered her curls again and straightened the scoop neck of her teal blue sweater dress. She looked perplexed and sad.

Nancy guessed what was bothering Bess. She linked her arm through her friend's. "It looks like everyone else read the same issue of *Teen World* that you did."

"And I thought I was being so smart." Bess looked as if she were about to cry.

"Don't worry, Bess," George said, trying to reassure her cousin. "Just because everyone else read that Brady always arrives early for a personal appearance doesn't mean they've got you beat."

"Sure," Nancy added. "I'd guess we've still got a little time before Brady gets here. It should be enough."

"For what?" Bess asked.

"To find a way in!" Nancy said with a laugh. "After all, I am a detective. Right?"

Bess gave her a wan smile. And before Nancy could turn her attention to finding an entrance that wasn't blocked by fans or police, George elbowed her in the side.

"What's that all about?" George asked, nodding toward a dozen or more people carrying large pieces of cardboard mounted on sticks—

picket signs. But the signs were down, and the girls couldn't read them.

The group was gathering in a circle off to the side of the ticket office. One good-looking, dark-haired young man seemed to be in charge. He was giving directions and pointing to a clear stretch of street in front of the theater.

"They don't look like your run-of-the-mill Brady Armstrong groupies to me," Bess said with a note of concern in her voice.

"Quick," Nancy said. "We can use the diversion to sneak around to the back of the theater. We'll try a side door."

She led Bess and George past the pickets. As the girls rounded the theater, they saw a large, dignified-looking private guard standing in front of the old stage door. Luckily he didn't see them.

"Well, maybe not," Nancy said, sizing him up. "Let's check out the back door."

That door was unguarded but locked tight.

Nancy cast a sympathetic look at her friend. "Sorry, Bess. I don't see how we're going to get inside."

Bess was determined. "I *have* to get in there," she said. Suddenly her eyes lit up. "Wait a minute. I just remembered something!"

She led them to the parking lot and then behind a row of thorny bushes.

"Why are you taking us through these weeds?" George glanced around to see if anyone was watching their suspicious behavior, but there was no one in sight.

"I just remembered something from when I worked here as an usher two summers ago." Bess stooped down to gingerly brush away some dry twigs, soda cans, and candy wrappers from a rusty metal door buried in the ground.

"Working here did have its advantages. This is our way in," she said proudly.

"Here, let me do that," Nancy offered. "We wouldn't want you to meet Brady looking like you've been playing in the dirt." She smiled as she took over the job of pulling at the door.

"Have you been sneaking into movies for free?" George teased Bess with a quick grin.

"No, of course not," Bess replied indignantly. "But I could have. And I think my honesty is about to be rewarded."

The old, rusted lock came free in Nancy's hand. With a final grunt, Nancy lifted the heavy steel door and revealed a dark staircase below.

Nancy smiled and shook her head. "Love is

funny," she said. "You wouldn't break into the theater to save the price of a ticket, but you'd do it to get a look at a guy you think you love."

"Does that make this a crime of passion?" George asked innocently as Nancy led them down the dark stairs.

"Oh, stop it, you guys," Bess said, carefully choosing her footing. She was wearing high-heeled, sling-back pumps for the occasion, and with all the excitement, she wasn't too steady on her feet. "I just want a chance to see him alone for two minutes. I have to know if he remembers me after all this time."

Nancy reached into her purse and pulled out a small but powerful penlight. They were in the basement of the theater, a dark, damp, musty place that smelled of mold and decay.

Nancy cut a path with her flashlight through the maze of boxes, old trunks, and stage props that had collected over the years from community theater productions. On the far side of the room was a staircase.

"Oh, Nancy," Bess said as she looked up the stairs. "I'm so excited, I think I'm going to faint. Just think—a chance to see Brady Armstrong again!"

George glanced at Nancy and slowly rolled her eyes as they trailed Bess up the stairs. Bess

7

nudged the door open and peered up and down the hallway. "The coast is clear," she said. "Let's go!"

With Bess in the lead, they sneaked down the hall to the dressing rooms. Two doors were marked with gold stars.

"Well, this must be the place," Nancy said, pointing to the letters that spelled out Brady's name. She glanced over at Bess and saw that her friend's face was pale beneath her pink blush. "Are you okay?" she asked.

"Sure," Bess said and forced her breath out in one long stream. "Just a little nervous, I guess. Do you think he'll remember me? Do you suppose he'll get mad at me for barging in on him like this?"

"I don't think he'll get mad," Nancy said. "Brady was always a nice guy. Besides, you look great."

Bess smiled at the encouragement. Then she lifted her chin, her eyes bright with determination. "I came this far. I'm not going to chicken out now. Besides, I blew half my fall wardrobe budget on this dress. I want him to at least see it."

"We'd offer to come in with you," Nancy said, "but I'm sure you'd like to be—alone."

Bess grinned and waved her hand to motion

them away. "Thanks, anyway. But I'll sink or swim on my own. Will you wait for me? I'll come find you when I'm finished. Wish me luck."

George looked her cousin up and down, appreciating Bess's teal blue sweater dress with its silver sequin and gold bugle bead trim. "You don't need luck. You look great. Knock on his door, and knock him dead."

Nancy and George walked farther down the hall toward the women's dressing room, giving their friend a chance to be alone with her nervousness and her heartthrob.

Halfway down the hall, Nancy and George turned to watch as Bess knocked once, then again. No one answered. As she was raising her hand to knock once more, they all heard voices floating down the hall from the stage.

The shuffling of feet and droning of voices sounded like eight or ten people moving toward them. Nancy knew Brady and Dierdre had to be at the center of the group.

"Bess is ducking into his room," George said, shaking her head. "Boy, she's really got nerve when it comes to guys."

Nancy looked on in disbelief. "She actually went inside."

"Well, I don't want to get caught hanging out

here, either," George said as the voices moved closer. "I'm just an admirer, not the president of his fan club."

"Come on." Nancy and George slipped into a room marked Women's Dressing Room. She flipped on the wall switch, and the room was instantly bathed in bright light. Makeup mirrors lined the far wall. To their right costumes hung on a long rack: flapper dresses, Victorian gowns, Roman togas, and cowgirl outfits with leather fringe.

The girls listened at the door to hear if the group had moved closer toward them, but there was no more movement. Nancy eased the door open, and they peered out through the narrow slit. Brady was at the center of the stationary group, and there was the mayor, and . . . Nancy closed the door, not wanting to get caught.

"He's even more gorgeous in real life," George said, and moved over to investigate the costumes. "What do you suppose that protest outside was all about?" she asked as she fingered the fringe on a cowgirl outfit.

"That was Nicholas Falcone in charge," Nancy said. "I recognized him from pictures in the paper. He leads campaigns to save old buildings from demolition."

"That's right! And Bart Anderson's going to

tear down this beautiful old theater to build one of those impersonal movie complexes."

"So Brady's premiere is the last big event to happen here," Nancy said sadly. "No more movies, no more community theater productions."

The girls waited and listened, and in a few minutes they heard the group start their goodbyes and begin to move off. Then the sound of screaming teenagers filing into the auditorium masked all other sounds. The chants of "Brady! Brady! Brady!" that had started outside the theater were now louder and more impatient. Finally a voice over the PA system began the introduction for Brady Armstrong's new movie, and everything became quiet except for a couple of goodbyes in the hall.

"Maybe Bess's visit with Brady has started and is going better than she hoped," Nancy said with a smile. "Maybe that new dress did the job and he's on his knees this moment proposing."

"I hope not," George replied playfully. "If he even touched her hand, she'd faint. If he proposed she'd drop dead in her tracks of heart failure."

"On the other hand, she might be—"

The sound of a single male voice crying out in the hallway interrupted Nancy.

11

"Help! Somebody help! Get the police!"

Nancy and George ran out of the dressing room and straight into the object of Bess's affection. Brady Armstrong—in the flesh—was standing in the middle of the hall. His normally tan face was white, and his green eyes were wide with shock. He was having trouble breathing.

"What is it?" Nancy asked, a sick feeling in her stomach. "Are you all right?"

"In there!" He pointed back to his open dressing room. "I walked in and someone attacked me. Someone wearing a ski mask. I was grabbed around the throat," he finally got out.

George and Nancy looked at each other. Their faces quickly turned as white as Brady's.

"There was someone else in there, too," Brady added, gasping to catch his breath. "A blond girl. And she's still in there with that maniac!"

Chapter

Two

B<small>ESS</small>!" George and Nancy raced for the dressing room door, but Brady pushed ahead of them and ran into the well-lit room first.

Nancy blinked, but not from the bright light. She couldn't believe what she was seeing, or rather what she wasn't seeing. The mystery strangler wasn't there—and neither was Bess!

Nancy turned to Brady. "Where are they?"

Brady looked thunderstruck. "I—I don't know. They were right here a minute ago, and—"

George was already searching for her cousin. She looked behind the leather sofa, under the heavy oak dresser, and behind the antique dressing screen.

"Bess!" Nancy and George cried out together. "Where are you?"

Only thick silence answered them.

"I take it she's your friend. I should never have left. But I was so dazed that I just . . ." Brady couldn't finish his sentence. Nancy could tell he was as upset as they were.

"You couldn't know," Nancy said. She tried to be as reassuring as possible.

"Aren't you Nancy Drew? I remember you from school," Brady said.

"Uh-huh, and our friend is Bess Marvin. Do you remember her?"

Brady nodded and looked even more devastated.

Nancy searched the room once again. There had to be a logical explanation.

"Look, she's got to be here," George said, trying to be her practical self. Still, her shaky voice told Nancy how worried she really was. "You said she was in here with the person in the ski mask. You never left the hall, and we joined you almost instantly. There's only one door leading out of this room. Therefore—"

As George turned to point at the door, Nancy saw three people standing on the threshold: Deirdre McCullough; Joseph Hughes, who had worked at the theater for years; and another man in a burgundy sports coat, whom Nancy had never seen before.

Behind this threesome stood an even larger crowd of people: two men with cameras slung over their shoulders; a woman with her hands full with what Nancy knew were makeup cases; and a teenage boy, a suitcase in one hand and two garment bags in the other. They looked bored and quickly set their equipment down and talked among themselves. Apparently they were used to waiting and hadn't heard Brady's screams for help.

Brady rushed over to the man in the burgundy sports coat. "You're not going to believe what just happened! Someone in a ski mask tried to nab me, but he or she got this girl instead. Now we don't even know where they are, and—"

Deirdre gasped and put her hand over her mouth. "Oh, no!" she managed to say.

"What!" The man's face turned a deep shade of crimson that nearly matched his jacket. "What are you talking about?" he asked.

Joseph looked over at Nancy and George, whom he knew, and said, "What's going on here, girls?"

"We don't really know, except that Bess is missing," Nancy said to Joseph. He looked shocked.

"Missing?"

Nancy nodded and went over to Brady to put a comforting hand on his arm. "Brady, can you tell us exactly what happened?"

Before Brady could begin his story, the man in the burgundy sports coat cleared his throat and pointedly addressed Nancy. "I'm Simon Mueller," he said. "Brady's and Deirdre's manager. Not that it's actually any of your business. Now, what I want to know is, who are you and why are you asking all these questions?"

"This is Nancy Drew," Joseph said, coming to the girls' assistance, "and her friend, George Fayne. You may have heard of Nancy. She's River Heights's best-known detective."

Simon didn't seem impressed. He ignored Nancy and turned to Brady. "Okay, Brady. What you're saying is that while I was escorting those local dignitaries to their seats for the movie, someone in a ski mask tried to kidnap you?"

Nancy caught Deirdre looking at Simon quizzically.

Brady nodded. Nancy was about to ask another question when Simon interrupted her again.

"And just how did that happen?" Before Brady could answer, Simon went on. "Well? Let's get this story over with."

Nancy couldn't believe the way Brady's manager was talking to him as if he were a kid. And Brady was letting him! Also Simon wasn't taking any of it the least bit seriously—and Bess was missing. Not able to wait any longer, Nancy spoke up impatiently.

"What happened when you got to the theater?" she asked.

Deirdre stepped forward and put a hand on Brady's shoulder. "We came inside with a lot of local politicians and dignitaries. We stood around and chatted, then Brady said he had to change. I escorted our guests to their seats. Simon was outside still," she said pointedly, looking at Simon.

So that was it. Simon hadn't been with them, Nancy thought, filing away the information. "And when you let yourself into your room, exactly what did you see, Brady?" she asked.

"The lights were off, so I turned them on. And that's when I saw her—the blond girl—sitting over there on the sofa. She had a gag in her mouth."

Out of the corner of her eye Nancy saw George shudder slightly. Bess's situation was even worse than she imagined.

"I think I asked her something, like what was she doing here," Brady continued. "That was when the man in the ski mask attacked me."

"Was this person a man?" Nancy asked.

"Well, no . . . I mean, I don't know, actually," Brady said after considering. "With that mask on I didn't see a face, but I thought it was a man.

"He grabbed me around the throat, but I pushed him back and he lost his balance. Then I ran into the hall to get help."

Brady shook his head and dragged his fingers through his thick black hair. "I wish I had done something to help that poor girl. She looked so scared. But I thought I needed help." He gave Nancy and George a long look. "You don't know how rotten I feel about this."

Nancy found herself staring into Brady's green eyes. He really did look upset.

"So this person in a ski mask still has your friend?" Deirdre asked. Tears glittered on her long lashes. Her famous green eyes were wide with concern as she patted Brady with a perfectly manicured hand.

"It looks that way," Nancy said. "And who knows where he's got her!"

"We've got to do something, Nan," George said.

Joseph shook his gray head. "She's such a sweet child. Worked here one summer, you know. I got to be really fond of her—"

Nancy cut him off. "I know, Joseph, but just standing here isn't going to get her back. Every minute counts in a kidnapping case."

"So what's the plan?" George asked. She looked at her friend expectantly.

"Well, there's only one door leading out of this room and no windows," Nancy observed. "First we have to figure out how they left this room."

"Well, actually . . ." Joseph walked over to the large closet and carefully opened the door. "This old theater has secret passageways everywhere. And here's one of them."

He pulled back the clothes that were hanging in the wardrobe, including Brady's white space knight costume, to reveal a small sliding door in the back wall.

"Where does this door lead?" Nancy asked.

"To the leading lady's dressing room," Joseph replied. Then he grinned sheepishly. "In the old days, when this was still a full-time theater for plays, there was usually a romance going on between the stars who played this theater. I'd say there was quite a bit of traffic through this door over the years."

"So the kidnapper had to have taken Bess out this door after Brady left the room," George said excitedly.

Nancy took a deep breath and realized she and George were thinking the same thing. "And they could still be in the leading lady's dressing room!"

"Well, let's have a look," Joseph said. And he slid the door open.

One by one they slipped through the narrow door and entered the other room. Joseph stumbled through the darkness to the opposite wall. Nancy held her breath, hardly daring to hope as he flipped on the light.

One quick glance around the room told her everything. Bess wasn't there. This room was the same size as the leading man's, but it was decorated with a white satin sofa, a pink chaise longue, and a delicately carved dressing table with a gilded mirror. It had been a beautiful, glamorous room. Now it was a little worn and threadbare.

"This room is as empty as Brady's," George

said, sounding defeated. "We don't know any more than we did."

"Yes, we do," Nancy replied. "Now we know how he got her away from us."

"How?" Brady looked completely puzzled. "I mean, I know how he got her out of my dressing room, but how did he get her out of here. Since Bess obviously isn't here."

"While Brady, George, and I were searching Brady's dressing room, the abductor probably sneaked her out into the hall. Before Deirdre, Simon, and the crew got here, it had to be empty."

"But where are they now?" Joseph asked.

Nancy exhaled out loud as she realized, "They could be anywhere. From here she could have been taken to the basement or upstairs or out an exit or they could still be here in the theater." She finished slowly.

"Look, I'm sorry about your friend. But I honestly think she'll turn up. It's probably just a stunt to meet Brady. Brady and Deirdre have to get dressed to greet their fans during the intermission, and they've got to do it now."

"Mr. Mueller, this is no stunt, I can promise that," Nancy said, giving Simon a hard look. "And I'm going to find her even if we have to cancel your premiere."

"Go right ahead and try, young lady,"

Simon said. "You'll have a lot more than me to contend with. You try to tell all those fans why Brady and Deirdre won't be showing." He pulled on Brady's arm and started toward the door. "By the way, Ms. Nancy Drew, private detective, your friend is still in the building," he threw over his shoulder.

"Wait a minute, Simon," Brady said, stopping short. "What makes you think she's still here?"

Simon answered Brady sincerely. "The theater is full of people right now. It's surrounded by cops. It would be simpler for him to hide her than to try to leave with her. Now, come on, Brady. Let's go."

"I think we'd better call the police," Nancy said. "This is a kidnapping, after all."

"Can't we just go and get a police officer from outside the theater?" George wanted to know.

"No, I think we've got to call headquarters and make it official."

"You can use the phone in my office, Nancy," Joseph said, "and I'll go alert the theater's ushers and guards to what's happened. They can all help look for her. Don't worry, girls. If Bess is in this theater, I promise you, we'll find her."

Nancy looked at George and saw tears

pooled in her friend's eyes. Nancy couldn't remember the last time she'd seen George cry.

"I guess we have a new case, Nan," George said. Her voice was thin and choked.

Nancy nodded and swallowed down the knot that kept rising in her throat. She had a case all right—one she had to solve right away. Her friend's life depended on it.

Chapter
Three

NANCY AND GEORGE hurried across the marble lobby accompanied by very loud movie music. It sounded like a chase scene before the intermission when Brady and Deirdre were to be introduced quickly.

Who was the figure in the ski mask? Why did he kidnap Bess? Nancy wondered. Was he really after Brady, or did he settle for her friend?

"Nancy," George stopped short before they reached the office. "You don't think he'd hurt her or anything, do you?"

Nancy pushed the thought away. It wouldn't do Bess any good for her to panic. If she was going to help her friend, she needed a clear head.

"No way, George," Nancy said firmly. "Besides, we're going to find her before anything could happen."

From the auditorium, they could hear the music swell one last time, then wild applause sounded and finally the crowd chanted, "Brady! Bra-dy!"

"It sounds like his fans have finally gotten the chance to meet their hometown idol," George said with the shadow of a smile. "Too bad Bess is missing this."

The two friends opened the door to the manager's office. They heard Simon Mueller in the inner office, talking on the phone. Nancy heard enough through the half-open door to know that he was talking to someone from an international press agency, telling them about the attempted kidnapping of his hottest star. A moment later he dialed another number, arranging with the Tudor Hotel for Brady and Deirdre to stay on through the weekend.

"What do you think he's up to?" George asked in a whisper.

"My instincts tell me that Simon Mueller

has figured out that this kidnapping is a golden opportunity for publicity."

"That's right," Mueller was talking to yet another person. "It's just like I told you. Your paper will love the story. Local boy, teen heartthrob, nearly gets kidnapped and comes this close"——Simon held his index finger and thumb together as if the reporter were in the room with him——"to catching the guy who took another hostage. He feels so bad about it, he's going to stay in town the whole weekend just to help find the guy."

"Nan, you're right. Why else talk to the press?" George asked, sitting down in a chair beside the desk.

Nancy lifted the phone and used the free outside line to call her friend Detective Ryan. As quickly and efficiently as possible she filled him in on the details of Bess's kidnapping.

"He'll be right over," she told George as she replaced the receiver.

Both George and Nancy jumped just then as the door to the office was opened and Nicholas Falcone burst into the room. Locks of his dark, wavy chestnut hair were sticking out from his head and there was a wild look in his amber eyes. Despite his youth—it couldn't have been more than a year since he graduated from college—Nancy knew that Nicholas's energy was what made him so good at getting people stirred up to fight for a cause.

"What's happened?" he demanded. "I just met Joseph Hughes in the lobby, and he said something about a missing girl. Something about a kidnapping?"

"That's right," Nancy answered. "A guy in a ski mask tried to nab Brady Armstrong, but he got our friend Bess instead."

Nicholas slammed his fist down on the desk. "It figures that something like this would happen here, in this theater. As if the place didn't have problems enough of its own without this."

"Excuse me, but it is my friend whose life is in danger," Nancy replied dryly, thinking that Falcone's concern for the building was just a little misplaced.

"I'm sorry," he said, his dark eyes reflecting his remorse. "It's just that we're trying to save the theater from being torn down, you know."

"We know," George spoke up. "I mean, I've seen your picture in the paper, and we know about Bart Anderson."

"Anderson! When I think of what he'll do to this place." A fiery light appeared in Nicholas's eyes again. "My great-grandfather and my grandfather, as a young apprentice, helped to build this theater. Most of the ornate plaster-work on the ceilings and around the stage is theirs. I can't bear to think of it all being destroyed."

"I don't blame you," Nancy said, her feelings toward him softening. "I hope you win your fight."

"And I hope your friend is found safe," Nicholas answered.

Nancy was about to thank him when Simon Mueller came out of the inner office. He looked awfully pleased with himself, and Nancy found herself resenting him. One of her best friends had been kidnapped, and this man was using her misfortune to promote his star.

"Any word yet?" Mueller asked.

"No. But the police are on their way," Nancy answered as she headed to the door. "I'm going to start looking for Bess. If the two of you," she said, indicating Falcone and Mueller, "want to join us, we could use the help. After all, that person in the ski mask was trying to kidnap your star."

"I ... ah ... have things to do here," Simon said. "I'm expecting several phone calls, and—"

"I'll help," Nicholas said, "but first I have to try to call my grandfather again. He was supposed to meet me here, and I'm a little worried that he hasn't shown up. I tried to reach him, but there's no answer."

"I'm sure Joseph wouldn't mind if you want to use this phone," George said to Nicholas. "We'll meet you in the lobby."

As they were on their way out the phone rang and Simon rushed back into the inner office to pick it up. Nancy waited with her heart in her throat, hoping that it might be some news. But from Simon's side of the conversation, she could tell it was only another reporter.

She put her arm around George. "Come on. Think of it as a treasure hunt, with Bess waiting for us at the end." George didn't answer, but gave Nancy a weak smile in return.

As they left the office, it occurred to Nancy that for right now, Simon Mueller had to be her prime suspect. He was the only one really benefiting from this ordeal.

Moments later Nancy, George, and Nicholas met in the lobby near the refreshment counter to plan their search of the building.

Nancy was acutely aware of every passing minute. Time was running out. The movie would be over soon, and then the theater would be so full of screaming teenagers that it would be impossible to search the main areas.

As they were ready to start looking, Joseph came running down the stairs from the projection booth overhead. He had been running the film. His wrinkled face was flushed with excitement.

"I just got a phone call from the kidnapper!" he said. "It came through on the house phone in the projection room."

Nancy's heart leapt into her throat. "The kidnapper!" So the man in the ski mask really was a kidnapper. But what did he want with Bess?

"What did he say? What does he want?" George grabbed Joseph's sleeve.

"Well, he isn't asking for money like most kidnappers," Joseph said, rubbing his chin.

"What *did* he want, Joseph?" Nancy asked.

"It was really very strange. . . ." Joseph said slowly.

"What was?" From the abrupt way she asked the question, Nancy saw that George was getting impatient.

Joseph met Nancy's eye. "What he said." He paused.

"Which is?" Nancy prodded. The old man seemed to need to have his memory jarred.

"He said, 'I have the girl, and she's safe for now.'" George sighed with relief, and Nancy waited for Joseph to go on.

"And?"

"Then he told me . . . let me make sure I have this right." He paused again. "Yes. He said, 'If you let them tear down the Royal Palladium, I guarantee you'll never see her again.'"

Chapter

Four

"THE ROYAL PALLADIUM?" Nancy echoed. "What's the Royal Palladium?" she asked, her eyes searching Joseph's face.

"That was the name of the theater before it became a movie house," Nicholas said. "My grandfather told me," he explained. Even so, he seemed as confused as they were.

Nancy turned back to Joseph. "Did you recognize the caller's voice?"

"No. It was kind of muffled, like he was talking out of the side of his mouth."

"Was his voice deep or high?"

"In the middle, I'd say. I'm sorry I can't be more help, Nancy."

"That's okay, Joseph. You've helped a lot," Nancy said, laying her hand on the old man's arm.

"Well, it isn't much. I just wish I'd been there when that scoundrel nabbed young Bess. Unfortunately, I must have been up in the projection room, making the introduction over the PA and getting ready to run the film. You know I have to do everything around here these days—set up the movies, clean, run the office. . . ."

"That's okay, Joseph," George said. "We know you did everything you could." She took Nancy aside.

"What's wrong, George?" Nancy asked.

"I don't know, Nancy," George began. "But Joseph's so old, do you think he got the message right? What if he missed something, like some clue about where Bess might be?" She bit her fingernail absentmindedly. "I just wish we'd been there when the kidnapper called."

Nancy was about to answer her friend when the front doors of the theater opened, and a half-dozen uniformed police officers rushed into the lobby.

"Thank goodness they've arrived." Nancy breathed a sigh of relief. She turned to George and said with as much confidence as she could muster, "With all these men and women I'm sure we'll find her."

After Joseph had explained to the police about the kidnapper's message, Detective Ryan turned to Nancy.

"Okay," he said. "The first thing we do is try to find the girl."

"What about the phone call?" Nancy asked. "Shouldn't we be trying to follow that lead, too?"

Ryan smiled. "We should, but only after we find Bess. Then we can worry about who made the call. My officers and I will search the dressing rooms upstairs and the basement. Why don't you concentrate on the auditorium and backstage? We'll all meet back there to report what we've found."

"I'm really sorry to do this to you," Nicholas Falcone said. "I wanted to help search for your friend, but I have to drive out to my grandfather's house. He doesn't answer, and I'm a little worried about him."

"I'm afraid you won't be allowed to leave without an escort, friend," Ryan said. "Henry"—he motioned to a young police-man—"please accompany Mr. Falcone and bring him back here. I have a few questions for him."

"Why?" George asked when Nicholas was out of earshot. "Isn't he okay? He seems so concerned and nice, and he doesn't even know Bess."

"Yes," said Nancy. "That's the problem. Why was he hanging around? To see *where* we're going to search, or did he really want to help us? If the kidnapper wants to save the theater, who would benefit more from taking Bess than Nicholas? He's got a great big motive."

Ryan looked at her, tapped the side of his head, and winked. "That's my girl," he said. "Come on, let's get going."

Several hours later the girls collapsed into two of the plush front-row seats in the auditorium. The floor beneath their feet was sticky from spilled soda. Popcorn and candy wrappers lay everywhere, discarded by the screaming throng that was now long gone.

Nancy and George were too tired even to appreciate the gracious old-world beauty of the elegant theater around them. They were dirty, exhausted, and discouraged. They had searched and searched, but they had uncovered no sign of Bess.

"Come on, girls, you have to eat something," a tall, handsome police officer said as he shoved a bag of hamburgers and french fries under their noses. "Here, one of the guys brought these back for you."

"No, thank you," Nancy said. Just looking at food made her think of Bess, who was constantly dieting to lose the same five pounds.

"Come on," the officer said, pulling a cheeseburger from the bag. "You two have been crawling through every nook and cranny of this place for hours. You've got to eat."

"He's right," George said, taking a burger from the bag and unwrapping it. "We're not going to help Bess by starving."

Nancy absently took the bag from the officer, then handed it to George, who took out a bag of fries and began eating.

"Have you found your friend?" a male voice asked.

They turned around to see Nicholas standing behind them, a concerned look on his dark face.

"No, I'm afraid not," Nancy answered. "We've searched all evening, and the police are convinced that Bess isn't here. They're giving up the search for the night."

"And how about you, Nancy?" Nicholas

said, sitting down behind her. "Are you convinced that she isn't here?"

Nancy turned in her seat to face him. "Not at all. I'm sure she is here. There were too many people in and around the theater for them to get out of here. And no matter how much we've searched, there are still hundreds of cubbyholes in this old place that we haven't checked yet. This has got to be the best hiding place in town.

"Did you find your grandfather?" Nancy asked, changing the subject. Although her tone was casual, her blue eyes were searching Nicholas's face intently. He loved the theater, and he wanted to preserve his great-grandfather's and grandfather's art. Did he kidnap Bess?

Nicholas glanced away nervously. "I sure did," he said. "You know, I was worried for nothing. He was home all the time."

"Did the police question you?" Nancy asked.

"Yeah. When I got back, but I just told them I was outside protesting when she was taken. They'll check on my story, they said. I had lots of witnesses."

"How come your grandfather didn't answer the phone?" George wanted to know.

"He didn't hear the phone ringing because he was out in his studio."

"Your great-grandfather and grandfather did beautiful plasterwork." Nancy pointed to the embossed designs that framed the stage and the ceiling. Cherubs with trumpets in their hands flew on either side of the red velvet curtains.

"They don't build places like this anymore," Nicholas said sadly. "Artists like my grandfather aren't interested in the work, and even if they were, no one would pay them to do it. People don't want beauty and glamour anymore. Guys like Bart Anderson are only out for money."

They heard the side door of the theater open. Turning to see who it was, Nancy saw a large, beefy man with a bulldog face push his way past Joseph, who had opened the door.

"Speak of the devil and he'll appear," Nicholas muttered under his breath. "That's Bart Anderson himself."

The man walked straight over to Nicholas. Without glancing at Nancy or George, he stood and glowered at Nicholas, his hands on his thick waist.

"Just what do you think you're trying to pull, Falcone?" Anderson demanded.

"I don't know what you're talking about," Nicholas answered, meeting Anderson's look.

"The police called and told me that some idiot has kidnapped a young woman and won't let her go until we promise not to demolish the theater."

"That's right," Nancy interrupted. "And that young woman is my friend, Bess Marvin. She's still missing."

"Yeah, well, I'm sorry about your friend," Anderson said with a feeble attempt at sympathy. "But I'm not going to have my project jeopardized." He pointed to Nicholas with a jerk of his thumb. "Not by any crackpot or committee of do-gooders organized against me. This place is coming down on schedule, one month from today. And that's final."

"Mr. Anderson," Nicholas said, emphasizing the *Mr.* "No one on my committee had anything to do with this kidnapping. We wouldn't use your kind of tactics!"

Anderson ignored him and turned back to Nancy. "This building is coming down," he said. "But you don't have to worry about your friend. These clowns might be stupid enough to grab her, but I doubt that they'd actually hurt her."

"When it's my friend's life or anyone's life at

stake, I'm not willing to take that risk," Nancy said.

Anderson gave Nancy one final glare, then turned on his heels and stormed out of the auditorium. A couple of minutes later Nicholas followed him out.

"Okay, George," Nancy said, standing and crumpling what remained of her burger and wrapper. "Let's make one last search."

Half an hour later the two friends were going through the leading lady's dressing room.

"We'll just check this room one more time," Nancy said. "If we don't find anything, we'll go home for the night."

Nancy pulled the cushions off the sofa and ran her hands between the folds in the upholstery. George was on her hands and knees combing the floor.

"I found something jammed in the back of the sofa!" Nancy shouted. "Take a look." She held out a black ski mask with red trim around the eyes and mouth.

George shuddered. "Now we know for sure that he or she did bring Bess in here," she said. "But that doesn't take us any closer to finding her, does it?"

"I suppose not," Nancy said quietly, obviously thinking about something else.

"What is it, Nan? Something's bothering you."

"The mask. How could we have missed it earlier? I don't think we did. I think someone planted it so we'd find it. Someone wants us to know Bess is still here."

"But who, Nancy?" George asked, her voice strained and high. In her hand she was clutching the ski mask, a menacing reminder of their missing friend.

"It could have been Mueller—since the kidnapper was probably after Brady and not Bess. He could have done it as a publicity stunt."

"And he doesn't have an alibi. Deirdre says he wasn't with them during the time of the kidnapping."

"Exactly," Nancy said. "And then there's Nicholas. He loves this theater, and maybe he saw the kidnapping as a way of saving it."

"Maybe, but I can't believe it could be Nicholas. He seems so concerned about Bess."

Nancy shook her head. "That could be a cover-up. Still, he was outside picketing the whole time. Unless he left for some reason. We'll have to check it out."

They had reached the lobby. Joseph was in his office still. Nancy wondered briefly if he lived at the theater as she raised a hand to wave goodbye.

George was just about to push through the door when it swung in, almost knocking her down.

"I'm glad I found you," Nicholas said.

From the look on his face, Nancy knew he had bad news.

"What's wrong?" she asked.

"It's Bart Anderson," Nicholas said. "While you were searching again, he and I had a little 'chat' in front of the theater."

"And?" Nancy asked, pushing him to continue.

"And he got so mad at me that he's moved up the date," Nicholas said.

"What date?" George wanted to know.

"He's going to tear the theater down in three days!"

Chapter

Five

IT's BEEN twenty-four hours since Bess was kidnapped, and we still don't know anything," Nancy said in desperation. "We're running out of time. Something's got to give."

"How could Bart Anderson do this?" George said, dusting her jeans. "He can't tear this building down when Bess is still inside!"

"Maybe he's trying to pressure the police into stepping up the investigation and finding Bess," Nancy suggested. "I don't know. Maybe he knows something we don't know. It could be a ploy."

"You mean *he* kidnapped Bess, and he's using this whole thing as a way of getting the building torn down faster?" George asked.

Nancy ran her hands through her hair. "I don't know what to think, George. I feel so frustrated and helpless. I can't think logically with Bess missing. I know I should be checking out our suspects, but I keep thinking that Bess is here and we've got to find her."

"But maybe the police are right, Nan. Maybe Bess isn't here," George said gently.

"She's here," Nancy replied. "It just doesn't make sense to me that the kidnapper would take her out of the theater if he wants to guarantee that it doesn't get torn down. I'm staying here until they call off the demolition. But if we don't find proof, we're lost and the demolition won't be called off."

Just then footsteps and low voices sounded. Nancy and George turned to watch Bart Anderson's men trooping through the auditorium. Nancy had been seeing the crew off and on all day as they studied the building, deciding where to place their dynamite charges.

This time Bart Anderson himself was with them.

"I'll be back in a minute, George." Nancy stood up and hurried over to him. They met in front of the stage. "Can I have a word with you, Mr. Anderson?" she asked.

"I'm busy now," he answered. "This is important, and—"

"What I have to say is important, too," Nancy said politely but firmly.

"All right." He glanced at the heavy gold watch on his wrist. "You've got four minutes."

"Are you really going to go through with the demolition in three days? Even when a young woman's life is in danger?" Nancy fought with herself to keep the anger out of her voice.

He scowled down at her. "Look around you, Ms. Drew," he said sarcastically, pointing to his crew. "These men are specialists. They're paid by the hour. I wouldn't have them here if I didn't mean to bring this place down on schedule."

"But my friend is still here in the building," Nancy said, trying to control her feelings of frustration and rage.

"The police don't think so," he answered offhandedly. "And that's enough for me. Now, if you'll excuse me, I have work to do." Anderson moved away from Nancy, but she followed him.

"What about the kidnapper's threat?" she asked determinedly.

Anderson turned to face Nancy. He shrugged. "I told you yesterday that it's pretty obvious to me who took her—Falcone or a member of that stupid committee of his. They're crazy, but they aren't murderers. As soon as this place is leveled, they'll realize they've lost, and then they'll let her go."

"I wish I could be as sure of that as you seem to be," Nancy said, her voice rising. "To be honest, Mr. Anderson, I don't think you care what happens to Bess, as long as your project goes on uninterrupted."

Anderson lifted a bushy eyebrow. "Oh, is that so?"

"I'm afraid it is. Your new entertainment complex is more important than a girl's life!"

"Hey, what's going on in here?" Nancy turned to see Detective Ryan entering the auditorium. Behind him were Nicholas Falcone and Joseph Hughes. "We could hear you two all the way out into the lobby," the detective said.

"Nancy was only trying to reason with Mr. Anderson." George had come up to them and was defending her friend.

"You aren't really going to let him tear this building down after what the kidnapper said, are you?" Nancy asked Ryan as he walked down the aisle toward them. "Isn't there something you can do?"

Nancy knew Ryan didn't like Bart Anderson or what he was doing. He sympathetically placed a hand on Nancy's shoulder.

"There's not enough evidence to prove that Bess is in the theater," he said as gently as possible. "Unless we come up with something soon, we have to allow the demolition to proceed. Either way, it's late. I say we all get a good night's sleep and make a fresh start in the morning."

Nancy looked at George and knew she was thinking the same thing. They had to come up with proof that Bess was still in the theater—and fast.

The group gathered around the fireplace in the Drews' living room later that evening wasn't a happy one. Nancy, George, Carson Drew, and Hannah Gruen, the Drews' housekeeper, sat on the sofa.

"I just can't believe this has happened to Bess," Hannah said as she dabbed at her eyes with a tissue. "You've got to find her."

"We will, Hannah." Nancy put a hand on the woman's shoulder. "She'll be all right. She has to be."

47

"It's too bad you can't tell Bess's parents," Hannah said, looking across the room at the telephone.

"I know," Nancy answered. "Of all the times for them to be touring Africa." Her father had tried to reach the Marvins since Bess disappeared, but they were unreachable.

Mr. Drew walked over to the fireplace and held his hands out to the blaze. He was feeling chilled even though it wasn't cold in the house or outside.

Nancy watched her father and knew he was thinking how he'd feel if it had been his own daughter who was kidnapped.

She stopped herself thinking those thoughts. It wasn't the time to let her imagination or emotions take hold. The only thing she could do for Bess was to solve the case and find her.

"Dad, what do you know about Nicholas Falcone?" she asked.

"I've never met him, but I know his grandfather Louis Falcone. We've served together on the building preservation committee." Carson turned and looked at her curiously. "Why?"

"It's possible Nicholas may be behind the kidnapping. He loves that old theater, and I think he'd do almost anything to save it."

"Who else do you have on that mental list of

yours, Nancy?" Mr. Drew asked, his handsome face drawn in concentration.

"There's Simon Mueller. I think we told you about him, Brady's and Deirdre's manager," she said. She explained to Hannah and her father how Mueller had used the kidnapping for publicity.

"I know," Carson said. "I saw today's headlines in the papers. But do you think that's motivation enough to do something as serious as kidnapping?"

"Your dad's got a point there, Nan," George said.

"I don't know," Nancy went on. "I don't trust Bart Anderson, either, but he doesn't really have anything to gain from the kidnapping. Except that the demolition is now happening sooner."

"Hmm," Carson Drew said as he sat down in a leather wingback chair. He looked very tired. "I'm familiar with Anderson's dealings here in River Heights. He sometimes operates in the gray area of the law, but I've never known him to cross the line into illegal activity."

Nancy was about to ask her father what else he knew about Anderson when the doorbell rang.

"Who could that be at this hour?" Hannah asked, hurrying into the entrance hall.

"I'll get it, Hannah," Nancy said, following her.

When Hannah opened the door, they saw a young man standing on the porch with a wreath of flowers in his hands.

"Hi, I'm from Blossoms and Bows Florist Shop," he said. He wore a sheepish, confused look on his freckled face. "I'm supposed to deliver this to a Nancy Drew."

Nancy stepped forward to receive the flowers. A cold shock washed over her when she realized they were no ordinary bouquet.

"This is a funeral wreath!" she said. "Who sent this?" she asked, her voice tight with tension.

"I don't know," the boy said. "There was an envelope shoved under the shop door. It had some money in it and instructions about what kind of wreath to send, where, and when. I had to take it home with me and deliver it tonight."

"Look, Nancy," Hannah said. "There's a card with it, too." She pointed to a dark purple envelope that stuck up from the middle of the wreath.

Nancy plucked the card from the flowers and ripped the envelope open.

Everyone leaned over her shoulder as Nancy read the big block letters out loud.

I don't want to hurt the girl. But if the Royal Palladium dies, she will be killed, too.

The next morning Nancy couldn't stop thinking about that funeral wreath as she and George made their way past a small group of teenagers who had come to the theater hoping to catch a glimpse of their beloved Brady.

Nancy quickly scanned the line of picketers to her right, and she saw that Nicholas wasn't with them this morning.

Could *he* have sent that wreath? He had to be her number-one suspect because he had the strongest motive. But then, too, Simon Mueller had had the studio eliminate two stops on his stars' tour so they could remain in River Heights longer to capitalize on the publicity.

The security guard who was posted at the door allowed the girls to pass without question. He recognized them from the day before. As they entered the lobby, they saw Joseph Hughes polishing the brass handrail on the staircase up to the balcony.

Nancy's heart went out to him. The building

was scheduled to be torn down in two days, but he was still giving the place its usual care.

"Good morning, Joseph," she said.

He looked up from his work. "Good morning, young ladies," he said. "Heard anything new about Bess?"

"No," George replied. "We were hoping maybe you had."

"Not a thing. I slept in the office all night. Hoped maybe that fellow would call again and I could talk him into letting her go. But nobody called or came by."

"Thanks for staying, Joseph," Nancy said. "You're a good friend."

Nancy was about to look for Detective Ryan when Joseph stopped her with a raised hand.

"You know, I can't believe it, but I almost forgot to give you this." He reached into his pocket. "Last night when I was vacuuming in the leading lady's dressing room I found something on the floor. I don't know if it belongs to Bess or not."

He pulled something out of his pocket that caught the light and glistened like a miniature chandelier.

George gasped. "Oh, Nancy!" she said. "It's Bess's rhinestone earring!"

Chapter

Six

SHE'S HERE," Nancy said ten minutes later as she triumphantly dangled the earring and note from the wreath in Detective Ryan's face. "Here's all the evidence you need to halt the demolition."

"Where did you find these?" Ryan asked curiously.

"Joseph found the earring last night in the leading lady's dressing room," George said. "And the note was delivered to Nancy's house with a funeral wreath."

The detective shook his head. "I'm sorry, but all the earring proves is that your friend *was* here, not that she still is. And the note doesn't state that she's here, only that if the theater dies, she will, too."

Nancy, George, and Detective Ryan were standing in Joseph's office, all looking frustrated.

Nancy carefully put the card back into its purple envelope and shoved it back in her purse.

"I'm sorry, Nancy, George, but I need positive proof that she's here."

George turned her back on them and stretched. Nancy knew that the experience was beginning to take its toll on her friend. "So," George said, facing them again, "what you're saying is that we've got today and tomorrow to find Bess. Because after that this building is going to be torn down—with my cousin in it."

"Please," Detective Ryan said. "Believe me that I'm on your side. I understand your concern. But we've searched this place from top to bottom, and we can't find her. I have to assume she isn't here."

"And Bart Anderson is more important than one missing girl?" Nancy asked pointedly.

"Look, if we can find out who took her and

where she is, Anderson won't matter. But until then, well, yes." Ryan stood up. "I can't hold up his project without something more concrete than an earring and note."

Nancy sank wearily down into the desk chair. "But we don't have enough time!"

"We'll find her, Nan." George's voice was determined. "And maybe Nicholas will succeed in pulling strings at City Hall to stop the demolition."

"Nancy . . ." The detective's eyes were kind and full of concern. "I really do understand. And I'm sorry. I have to get back downtown now, but I will leave some people here to keep searching for your friend."

When Detective Ryan left the office, Nancy turned to George. "Okay," she said. "We've got to move into high gear. I'm going to try to find out more about Mueller. You learn all you can about Nicholas and keep an eye on him if he comes to the theater. See if he does anything suspicious."

"Nancy—" George began.

"I know what you're going to say, George, but we can't rule him out. Not yet."

George shrugged, and she and Nancy headed out of the office. George left the theater and joined the picketers to begin to ask questions.

Judging from the group of fans outside, Nancy figured Brady Armstrong was probably around the theater somewhere. They followed him wherever he went. Brady was the best source for information about Simon Mueller.

Nancy found Brady in the auditorium, sitting in one of the front-row seats, looking dejected.

"Hi, Nancy," he said as she walked down the carpeted aisle toward him. "Any news?"

"Nope, afraid not."

She sat down next to him. "What are you doing here?"

"I came about two hours ago. I couldn't sleep, thinking about Bess, so I decided to come and look for her."

He hung his head, and the golden glow from the wall sconces glittered in his dark hair. "I really feel responsible for what happened to her," he added. "If she hadn't been one of my fans—and if she hadn't come to my room just to see me, she wouldn't be missing right now. It's pretty obvious the kidnapper was after me, not her." He let out a long sigh.

"It wasn't your fault, Brady," Nancy said. But even as she was speaking, she wondered if he really felt that bad. His own agent could be the kidnapper. Was Brady the nice guy that he appeared to be, or was this the image that Simon Mueller had shaped for the public?

"I just wish that I could do something that would help," he said.

"Maybe you can," she replied. "Would you answer some questions for me?"

"I'll try." His green eyes sparkled eagerly.

"It's about Simon Mueller."

Suddenly the interest in his eyes died and he looked away. "What about Simon?" he asked distractedly.

Nancy took a deep breath. She could tell it wasn't going to be easy. "Do you think he would attempt a kidnapping as a publicity stunt?"

"Why would you ask a thing like that?" Brady asked defensively.

Nancy noticed how uncomfortable the question had made Brady. "Because he wasted no time in making the most of the opportunity."

Brady shrugged. "Simon's a good agent and manager. He's smart. That doesn't mean he's a kidnapper."

"That's true," she admitted.

"Look, Nancy, I'm not going to say anything bad about Simon. He's one of the best managers in the business, and I'm lucky he took me on as a client. He got me where I am today, and

I'm not going to cross him in any way." Brady set his lips in a firm line, obviously resolved not to support Nancy's theory.

"I understand," Nancy said, sensing Brady's mood and realizing she wasn't going to get any more out of him about Simon Mueller.

As though eager to leave, Brady stood and zipped up his leather jacket. "If you need anything else, just ask," he said, but his eyes were still guarded.

"Brady, just one more thing. Don't give Simon too much of the credit for your success. You're a very talented actor. You deserve to be at the top."

He smiled and said, "Thanks, Nancy. But the more I learn about this business, the more I realize it's more complicated than that." Brady stood up and put his hand on her shoulder. "Still, thanks for the good words." He turned and walked up the aisle toward the exit.

Nancy sat there for a minute longer, thinking. Out of the corner of her eye she saw a movement on the stage. One of the red velvet curtains had rustled ever so slightly.

Someone had been eavesdropping on their conversation.

Quietly Nancy stood and walked to the front of the auditorium and up the steps to the stage. Straining to hear the sound of footsteps behind the red velvet curtain, she waited. Slowly she pulled the heavy curtain aside and stepped into the darkness of the stage area.

She had the uncomfortable feeling that someone was watching her from the many black shadows.

"Who's there?" she asked, keeping her voice steady. No answer. Nancy felt a prickling along the back of her neck.

She turned to leave the stage. She had taken only one step when, overhead, an enormous light started to fall.

Nancy hit the stage floor and covered her head and face with her arms only a second before the light hit.

In another second, she felt a shower of glass rain down on her in hundreds of sharp needles.

Chapter
Seven

As soon as she was sure that the glass had stopped flying around, Nancy scrambled to her feet. With her eyes closed, she carefully brushed the tiny slivers of glass from her body and hair. Some of the shards pricked at her hands and made them sting.

Opening her eyes, Nancy looked around. But there was no one on the stage. Just herself and the shattered glass that glittered like tiny diamonds on the stage floor.

She was moving down the stairs off the front

of the stage when a deep male voice came over the PA system. It was distorted with a heavy reverberation.

"That was only a warning, Ms. Drew," the voice said. "If you want to see Bess Marvin again, you'd better not search for her any longer. If you persist, what happened just now was an indication of what you and your friend can expect."

Nancy whirled around and looked up over the rows of green seats to the sound booth, but it was dark and she couldn't see who was talking.

He was in there. In the booth. Now she had a chance to catch him.

Wasting no time, Nancy raced through the auditorium and out into the lobby. When she reached the stairs to the balcony, she took them two at a time. At the top she turned to the left and plunged into the small room that functioned as a sound booth.

He wasn't going to get away this time.

But he already had. The room was empty.

Whoever it had been had left the power on the soundboard. Six or seven tiny lights glowed like winking red eyes in the darkness.

As Nancy stood there in that empty room, she could still feel the kidnapper's presence.

She was completely discouraged. He had been so close, within her grasp, but she had missed him.

Fifteen minutes later Nancy walked into the Tudor, a posh hotel just around the corner from the theater. She was going to find Simon Mueller and get some answers from him.

She asked the front desk to ring his room, but Mueller didn't answer. Stalled again, Nancy thought. But, no, that meant Mueller could have been the one who dropped the light in the theater.

Just as she was about to leave the hotel, Nancy glanced through the large double doors to her left that led to the restaurant. She caught sight of a familiar head of copper red hair. Deirdre McCullough was sitting in a corner booth.

Several teenagers were crowding around her table with autograph books and bits of paper in their hands. Nancy waited for Deirdre to finish with her fans. If she could have a minute alone with the girl, she might get further with her on the topic of Simon Mueller than she had with Brady.

"Hi, Deirdre," Nancy said as she walked over to the booth. "Mind if I sit down?"

Deirdre gave Nancy a big smile. "Not at

all." She shoved her soft chocolate leather purse and jacket over so Nancy could sit down opposite her. Nancy noticed that the bag matched Deirdre's jacket and skirt perfectly. Her beautiful coppery hair was set off by a ginger-colored silk blouse.

"Actually, I love having the company," Deirdre said after Nancy was settled and had ordered a glass of juice. "I was just sitting here thinking how much I miss my sisters and girlfriends back home in Los Angeles."

"How long have you been on the road?" Nancy asked.

"Oh, this is just our first stop, with the movie premiering here and all," she said. "I've been away from home for less than a week. I just get homesick really quickly. You'd think I'd be used to it by now. I've been an actress since I was four years old."

Any other time Nancy would have been fascinated by this inside look at a famous actress, but that day she had other things on her mind.

"I came to the hotel to talk to Simon," Nancy said. She sensed Deirdre tightening up at the mere mention of Mueller's name. "I asked the front desk to ring his room, but he didn't answer. Have you seen him this morning?"

"No," Deirdre responded quickly. "No, I haven't."

"And how about Brady? Have you seen him in the past half hour or so?"

"Why do you ask?" Deirdre asked, lifting one delicate eyebrow. "Is Brady a suspect?"

"I'm just trying to check everyone's whereabouts," Nancy said offhandedly.

"I haven't seen Simon or Brady since breakfast," she said cautiously. "They were having a slight argument over their cereal and grapefruit, so I didn't hang around. I hate it when they fight."

Nancy perked up instantly. "Does that happen a lot?"

"More than I can stand. Simon is always pushing Brady to do things, and . . ."

Her voice faded and she looked as though she were afraid she had said too much already.

"What kind of things does he want Brady to do?" Nancy prodded.

"Oh, you know, publicity things. This morning Simon was telling Brady to ride around town in the limo."

"And Brady didn't want to?"

"No. Some stars thrive on attention, but Brady doesn't like having girls scream and yell and faint at his feet. Sometimes they grab at him and rip his clothes. He hates that."

"And how about you, Deirdre? Do you thrive on attention, or do you hate it?" Nancy asked.

Deirdre smiled, and Nancy was struck by how natural and easygoing she was. "I'm somewhere in between. I would probably be disappointed if I walked down the street and no one recognized me. But sometimes, like this morning, I just like to get away from all the fans and autograph hounds."

"And that's why you're sitting here?"

Deirdre nodded.

"They found you anyway."

"They always do," she said with a slight shrug.

"So, who won the argument this morning? Brady or Simon?" Nancy asked, sipping at the tall glass of orange juice the waitress had set down in front of her.

"Brady, I think. He wanted to go back to the theater to look for your friend and—well, for old times' sake."

"Old times' sake?"

Deirdre looked very uncomfortable, as though she had revealed something she hadn't intended to. "Ah, yes. Brady has some . . . uh . . . memories of the place."

"What kind of memories?"

"I don't know. Just memories."

"Did he ever work in a community theater production there?"

"I don't know," Deirdre said, suddenly quite agitated. "He might have. You'd actually know that better than I. Listen, I have to go now. I've got to get my hair done for a date that Simon has arranged for Brady and me this evening. Simon is determined that Brady and I act like an item for a while. You know, publicity and all."

Nancy's curiosity was aroused. "Then you and Brady aren't an item?" she asked.

Deirdre smiled her breathtaking smile. "Brady's a sweetheart, and I'm very fond of him. But there's this hunk back in L.A. He's the real reason I'm homesick." She stood and draped her purse over her shoulder. "I suppose you'll find out soon enough, but Simon has called a press conference for later this afternoon."

"Another one? Why?"

"He's going to offer a reward for information leading to the release of your friend." Deirdre sighed. "I'd like to say it's because Simon is such a wonderful human being, but . . ."

"You think it's just another publicity gimmick," Nancy offered.

Deirdre hunched her shoulders and shook

her head as though she were tired and slightly disgusted. "See you around, Nancy."

"Yeah, see you."

As Nancy left the restaurant and walked through the hotel lobby she realized that the motive for his reward fit in perfectly with everything else she had learned about Simon Mueller.

And perhaps the most disturbing bit of information was that Brady Armstrong might have a motive, too. He could have worked at the theater. Maybe he loved the old place also. But enough to stop it from being torn down?

That's stupid, Drew, she thought. Why would Brady engineer his *own* kidnapping and then not stop the "kidnapper" from taking the wrong person? It was impossible. Or was it?

As Nancy was about to walk through the large revolving door out of the lobby, she heard her name being paged.

"Ms. Nancy Drew. Pick up the courtesy phone, please."

She hurried to the white phone in the corner of the lobby. George was on the other end.

"Nancy, you've got to get to the theater right away!" George sounded breathless.

"What is it, George?"

"We were right all along, Nan. Bess *is* still in the theater!"

Chapter

Eight

W<small>HAT HAVE YOU FOUND?</small>"

"Meet me in Joseph's office. I'll explain everything when you get here." The sound of a dial tone told Nancy that George had hung up.

Nancy wondered what her friend had found. To save time, she entered the theater through a back door and wound her way through the maze of hallways toward the front of the theater.

As she walked past the stars' dressing rooms, Nancy thought of the day when she had seen

Bess knocking nervously on that door. Bess had looked so pretty in her new dress. And she had been so excited about the prospect of seeing the boy she had had a crush on four years earlier.

Nancy couldn't bring herself to dwell on it. What happened, happened. All that mattered now was rescuing Bess.

As Nancy neared Joseph's office, she heard voices, George's and Joseph's. They were discussing something in very excited tones.

"Wait until Nancy gets here. She'll be so excited to hear the news," George was saying.

"To hear what?" Nancy asked as she charged into the room. "What's up?"

"Joseph and I found the proof we need," George said. "Come on." Nancy followed George and Joseph as they led her around the auditorium and down the stairs that led to more dressing rooms.

"Where are we going?" Nancy asked her friend.

"Joseph and I were looking below the stage. First we heard a tapping noise, then what sounded like someone crying."

"Bess?" Nancy said.

George nodded, and Nancy saw her friend's eyes light up. "We thought it had to be her, so we went looking."

With a triumphant grin, George turned to Joseph. Nancy looked at him questioningly.

"There's a secret doorway here that leads straight into the orchestra pit," he explained. To prove his point, Joseph opened a closet door and pushed a rackful of costumes aside, revealing a small door.

Single file they passed through the narrow door and found themselves facing the open side of the orchestra pit.

George led Nancy and Joseph to a row of doors that were parallel to the pit's walls. "What are these rooms?" Nancy asked as her friend opened one of the doors into a tiny room no larger than six feet square.

"These were the musicians' warm-up rooms," Joseph explained. "Members of the orchestra could warm up in these rooms before each performance."

"I checked them out myself last night," George said as she neared the end of the row. "There wasn't anything then. Now—look!"

Nancy ran to the open door and peered inside. Joseph flipped the light switch, and a dim light came on.

"Nancy, she was here!" George cried as she pointed out a rumpled pallet that lay bunched in the corner of the cubicle. "There's her purse—and her shoe. We left them just the way we found them."

Nancy's heart wrenched as she looked at the pump lying next to the mattress. When she remembered how Bess had complained about those new shoes, she felt like crying. But she fought back her tears as she knelt down on the rumpled pallet.

Laying her hand on the blanket, she said, "She couldn't have been gone for very long. It's still a little warm. I can't believe we came so close to finding her."

Joseph knelt down beside Nancy and placed his hand on her shoulder. "At least the kidnapper has been feeding her," he said, pointing to a half-eaten pizza that lay in a box on the floor beside the pallet. Next to the box were three empty soda cans.

George laughed, but the sound was hollow and bitter. "Something's wrong with Bess," she said grimly.

"Why do you say that?" Nancy asked.

"Because if Bess was her normal self, she would never have left half that pizza uneaten. It's pepperoni and mushroom."

"Come on," Nancy said. "Let's go to the office and call Detective Ryan. He needs to know about this."

* * *

Early that evening the girls were standing in the theater auditorium. After Nancy had called Detective Ryan, he had brought his squad out to search the theater once again.

After a grueling three-hour search, they still hadn't found anything. Finally the police left, advising the girls to give up and go home.

But neither Nancy nor George could pull themselves away.

"Why didn't I find Bess when I searched that room yesterday?" George asked as she leaned back against the edge of the stage and massaged her aching back. "I swear she wasn't there then."

"I'm sure she wasn't," Nancy answered, stretching her legs out in front of her. "The kidnapper must be moving her constantly. She could be right under our noses and we wouldn't even know it."

"Well, we know he moved her just before I went into that room today, because the pallet was still slightly warm. I wonder where Simon Mueller and Nicholas Falcone were then?"

"I was thinking that myself," Nancy replied. "So when I came up to the office to phone the police, I called them, too."

"And?"

"And neither of them answered his phone. Brady and Deirdre were gone, too. Not that I suspect them, but I figured it couldn't hurt to check."

"It has to be Simon," George said with conviction. "Nicholas and Brady wouldn't do something like this."

"I'd like to think so, too," Nancy said. "But someone is moving Bess all over this theater. And whoever it is must know the place pretty well."

"Simon Mueller doesn't know the building," George said. "So, if it is him, he would have to have an accomplice. Joseph told me that Brady worked here in community theater productions in the summers when he was in junior high school. Joseph said that was when Brady first developed an interest in acting."

Nancy twisted a lock of her reddish blond hair around her forefinger. "What if Simon set it up? And Brady, because of his loyalty to Simon, went along with the stunt, never dreaming that anyone else would become involved and hurt by it?"

"By the time Simon grabbed Bess, it would be too late for Brady to back out," George added.

"Exactly."

"And it would be hard for Brady to come forward now that he's an accessory."

"That's all possible," Nancy said, still thinking. "But then, too, it could be Nicholas Falcone. Did you see the way he was looking around this place? Like someone he loved was about to die."

"He's very loyal to his grandfather. And he seemed uncomfortable when you questioned him, Nancy."

"I noticed," Nancy answered. Her eyes wandered around the auditorium. Then, tensing, she looked carefully at the stage.

"What is it?" George whispered. "What do you see?"

"Do you remember when I told you about the light that fell?" Nancy said quietly.

"Sure."

"Well, just before I walked up on stage, I saw the curtains moving, as though someone were eavesdropping on the conversation I was having with Brady."

"And?"

"Don't look now, but I'm pretty sure I just saw the curtains move again. Keep talking."

George feigned a yawn. "I'm getting pretty tired," she said loudly. "Do you suppose we should take Detective Ryan's advice and go on home?"

Nancy's sharp eyes caught the slightest ripple of movement in the stage right curtain.

"There's someone there for sure," she whispered. Then, louder for the listener's benefit she added, "We might as well go home and get some sleep. If she was here, we would have found her."

"Come on," George said. "Let's go."

The girls walked casually in front of the stage and orchestra pit toward the left.

"Should we go out the front door?" George asked, projecting her voice.

"I think Joseph already locked it. Besides, my car is parked in the alley. Let's take this side exit."

Nancy walked over to the side door, opened it, and let it close loudly, hoping the eavesdropper would think they had left.

She and George waited several quiet, tense moments beside the door.

"I saw the curtain move again," George whispered, her mouth close to Nancy's ear.

"Where?"

"Over on the far side of the stage."

Nancy nodded. "Come on."

Silently they crept up the stairs leading to the stage. Their sneakered feet made no sound on the thick, dark green carpeting. They slid behind the red velvet curtain and waited a second for their eyes to adjust.

A dark figure slipped behind an old scenery drop, and the girls silently followed, being careful to stay in the shadows. They trailed him through a maze of ladders, curtains, and props left over from the last community theater production.

"What's he doing?" George whispered when the figure paused at the foot of a ladder attached to the back wall.

"He's climbing up to the catwalk," Nancy said, pointing out the narrow metal grid that was about four feet out from the back wall and forty or fifty feet off the stage floor.

"I'll go after him." George was always ready for an athletic challenge.

"I'll wait down here and guard the other ladder, in case he decides to come down there," Nancy said. She took her position up behind the trunk of a giant prop pine tree.

Her heart pounded as she watched the man make his way across the catwalk until he was almost directly over her head. At the other end, almost fifty feet away, George was climbing up after him.

They had him trapped, whoever he was! In the darkness Nancy couldn't identify him. He seemed to be of medium height and build, wearing nondescript dark clothing. He was nimble footed and seemed at ease as he crossed the narrow, suspended walkway.

When he reached the other end, almost directly over Nancy's head, he stopped and knelt down. He was working on something. Nancy strained her eyes to see what he was doing, but there wasn't enough light.

She scanned the walk, looking for George. She had made it almost halfway across. What was she up to? Nancy wondered with a sharp pang of concern.

George wasn't going to confront him up there on the catwalk, was she?

While Nancy's mind raced, trying to decide what to do next, the man continued to kneel and work.

Suddenly Nancy realized the man had known all along that they were following him. He had deliberately lured George up onto the catwalk.

And just as quickly, Nancy figured out what he was doing.

"George, get down from there!" she screamed. "Get down! Hurry!"

But her warning came too late.

The man leapt and landed on the ladder against the back wall. In a flash he disappeared down the rungs.

Nancy watched as the catwalk beneath George's feet trembled as though it were being blown by a strong wind.

Nancy heard her friend scream.

As Nancy gazed in horror the catwalk started to collapse and fall, bringing George down to the concrete floor forty feet below.

Chapter

Nine

"Geowge!" Nancy raced across the stage. She saw George thrust out an open hand and grab one of the metal grids as she was tossed off the collapsing bridge. She was dangling by the fingertips of her right hand from the metal catwalk that was bouncing up and down like a diving board. Only one end was bolted to the wall now.

"I'm barely holding on!" George yelled. "I'm slipping! Can you get me down?"

Nancy jumped for the end of the walk,

which hung above her head, but she couldn't reach it.

"What's going on here?" a male voice behind Nancy shouted. From out of nowhere Nicholas Falcone appeared, Joseph right behind him.

"It's George!" Nancy yelled, pointing up at her friend. "She's going to fall!"

"I'll get her!" Nicholas said. He leapt for the end of the walk, and Nancy watched as he pulled himself hand over hand up the dangling catwalk grids.

"I'm on my way, kid!" he called up to her. "Hang on."

When Nicholas reached George, he braced himself well and wrapped an arm tightly around her waist.

"Okay, I've got you," he said, "and I'm not going to let go. Reach your hand through here and get a secure hold with both hands."

Nancy held her breath as George managed to work her way hand over hand down the sloping walkway. "That's it, George," Nancy said, encouraging her.

Nicholas carefully followed her down again. In less than a minute they were both jumping the last fifteen feet to safety.

Nancy was waiting for them when they reached the floor. She threw her arms around her friend. "I was worried there for a bit," she said.

"Me, too." George wiped her forehead with the sleeve of her rugby shirt. When she turned from Nancy to hug her rescuer, Nancy caught a look of gratitude and adoration in George's eyes.

"That was a fine job of climbing you did there, son," Joseph said, pounding Nicholas on the back. "You picked a fine time to take a break from the picket line." Then Joseph turned to George. "I'm glad he got you down in one piece, young lady. But I want to know right now what you were doing up there."

"We were chasing the kidnapper," Nancy said, coming to George's defense.

"The kidnapper?" Nicholas and Joseph exclaimed in unison.

"At least we think that's who it was," Nancy added. "We were here in the auditorium and saw some movement behind the curtain. George followed the eavesdropper up the catwalk, but he unbolted it and made one end fall while she was on it."

"Sounds like the kidnapper is playing hardball now," Nicholas said, smoothing his dark hair back into place.

George watched the gesture with rapt attention, and Nancy sighed to herself. Her friend had liked Nicholas all along, but now she owed him her life.

Nancy studied Nicholas as he, George, and Joseph continued to discuss the accident. She knew that she should be grateful to him for saving George's life. And she was. But she couldn't help being suspicious. Although she hadn't gotten a close look at that shadowy figure, Nicholas was about the right height and weight. And he was wearing dark clothing, too.

So, he had left the picket line at the right moment, she thought. Could Nicholas have collapsed the catwalk, only to risk his own life to rescue George? Maybe it had been his way of throwing suspicion off himself. She couldn't help remembering how nimbly he had moved as he had climbed up to save George.

As she watched George gaze up at Nicholas with gratitude shining in her eyes, Nancy knew that if she had any more doubts about Nicholas Falcone, she had better keep them to herself.

When Nancy and George stepped into the Tudor Hotel a little while later, they had no trouble finding Simon Mueller's press conference. He and Brady and Deirdre were in the middle of the hotel lobby surrounded by at least a dozen reporters and as many photographers.

Brady and Deirdre were dressed in evening clothes and made a stunning couple. Brady wore a winter white wool suit that contrasted handsomely with his dark good looks. Deirdre's red hair glistened against her black, beaded gown.

Apparently they were getting ready to go out on the "date" that Simon had fixed up. Nancy noticed that they were playing their parts well as they looked deeply into each other's eyes.

Simon Mueller stood a foot off to the side, merrily chatting, a broad smile on his face. He was obviously pleased with his stars' performances.

"I'm glad Bess isn't here to see this," George commented as Brady leaned down and gave Deirdre a quick kiss. "She'd be eating her heart out."

"They're only acting," Nancy said. "Deirdre told me this morning that she has a boyfriend in Los Angeles. This whole romance thing was Simon's idca."

Nancy and George stayed at the back of the crowd and watched as Brady and Deirdre answered questions and signed autographs.

Finally Simon said, "Excuse me, ladies and

gentlemen. I hate to interrupt our lovebirds, but we have a serious matter to discuss here."

Nancy and George listened while Mueller announced the reward that Brady's studio was offering for Bess's safe return. He played the role of philanthropist to the hilt.

"You'd think the money was coming out of his own pocket," George remarked dryly.

Nancy didn't answer her. She was watching Simon's movements as he made his way through the crowd. He was a large man, a bit overweight, and while he wasn't clumsy, he didn't move like an athlete either. Nancy just couldn't see him running around on that catwalk.

Then Nancy spotted Brenda Carlton, a local River Heights reporter. Brenda was more than a little spoiled and difficult. She and Nancy had locked horns more than once, but Nancy always tried to be civil to her.

"Let's say hello to Brenda," Nancy said, dragging George in her direction.

"Why?" George asked, confused. "She's one person I really don't feel like talking to right now."

"Because," Nancy explained, "Brenda has eagle eyes, and it's just possible she could give us a lead or two on whether or not Simon and

Brady were around the hotel when the kidnapper set that catwalk trap."

"Good thinking, Nan," George said with a smile.

Nudging their way through the crowd, Nancy walked over to Brenda. "Hi, Brenda," she said.

"Well, hello, Nancy, hello, George," Brenda said. "It's just awful about your cousin," she continued, trying to sound sympathetic. "I can't believe she still hasn't been found."

The idle tapping Brenda was making with her pen on her notebook while she kept an eye on Brady and Deirdre told Nancy how little Brenda really cared about Bess.

"Brenda," she said sweetly, "I just got here. Has this media event been going on long?"

Brenda shook her head. "No, it just started. It was scheduled to begin almost an hour ago, but Brady was late. He and his agent were out. They returned to the hotel just a few minutes ago and had to rush upstairs to change."

Brenda laughed as she gave Brady an admiring glance. "It was the quickest clothes change I've ever seen. From casual to gorgeous in four minutes."

Nancy looked over at George, and their eyes met in a meaningful exchange.

"Excuse me," Brenda said, standing on tiptoe to look over Nancy's shoulder at Brady. "You're blocking my view."

"Sorry," Nancy said. Taking George's arm, Nancy led her to a quiet corner behind some feathery palms that were planted in a marble urn. "So, Simon and Brady were out of the hotel when you were dangling from that catwalk," Nancy said. "Interesting."

George peered through the palms at Brady, who was putting his arm around an elderly lady's shoulders while the woman's husband took a picture.

"Just look at Brady," George said. "I can't believe he'd kidnap Bess or knock a catwalk out from under me. It has to be Simon. Look at him. Would you buy a used car from that man?"

Nancy studied Simon through the palm fronds, taking in his prissy, overly neat clothes. "Are you sure it isn't his taste in clothes that you object to?" she teased.

"It's his shifty, beady little eyes. But that tie doesn't help."

"Are you two hiding back here?" asked a woman's voice.

They turned around to see Brenda Carlton eavesdropping on their conversation.

"You'd be surprised what you can find out

while lurking behind a palm tree," Nancy said, laughing a little.

"Thanks for the tip." Brenda chewed thoughtfully on her pencil. "Tell me, what *do* you think about this so-called kidnapping attempt?"

"You sound as though you don't believe it," Nancy answered carefully.

"Well, considering Simon Mueller's track record, it's a little difficult to swallow. The man has cried wolf too many times to be taken seriously."

"What do you mean?" Nancy asked.

"You mean you don't know about Simon Mueller's other 'kidnappings'?"

Nancy could see that Brenda was wrestling with her desire to tell her all she knew versus her natural stinginess with information. "I'm surprised you don't know, Nancy. You're always on top of everything. Brady is the third star of Mueller's to have this particular 'problem.' The first was five years ago. One of Mueller's young starlets was snatched. Two days later she turned up safe and sound with some half-baked story about how she subdued her kidnappers and escaped."

"Oh, really?" Nancy said thoughtfully as she watched Simon whisper something into the ear of a reporter.

"And last year," Brenda continued, "another of Mueller's clients, an old silver-screen star who was trying to make a comeback, said that three men broke into her home and tried to grab her. The police proved her story was false, but they chalked it up to her age."

Brenda fingered the strap on her camera. "Gives one cause for doubt, don't you think?"

Nancy looked over at George, who raised one eyebrow. "It certainly does."

"Well, it looks as though our conference is breaking up," Brenda said as the other reporters began to file out the hotel door. "I guess it's off to the typewriter for me. I hope that one of us can solve this case, Nancy. Frankly, I hope it's me."

Nancy shook her head as Brenda walked away. "Leave it to her to get in the last word."

"Look," George said. "Brady and Deirdre are going into the Palms Restaurant. Do you want to ask Brady where he and Simon were earlier?"

"You bet," Nancy answered.

The girls followed the couple out of the lobby and into the elegant restaurant, Nancy leading the way.

Once inside, Nancy stopped abruptly, and George barreled into her.

"What is it?" George whispered.

Nancy pressed her finger to her lips, then pointed right ahead of them.

Brady and Deirdre had escaped the reporters and fans by retreating into a quiet alcove that led to the telephones and rest rooms. They were talking in urgent, hushed tones, but the girls were close enough to hear every word.

"I think we should tell her, Brady," Deirdre was saying. Her pretty face was drawn into an expression of deep concern, even fear. "It's too important."

"We can't say anything. It's not as though we have proof of anything."

Deirdre's voice rose in frustration. "Brady, if you don't tell Nancy, I will!" Her whole body was tense, her hands clenched into fists at her side. "That girl's life could depend on it!"

Chapter

Ten

Nancy's heart leapt into her throat. They were talking about Bess. One look at George told Nancy that her friend knew the same thing.

She stepped forward between Brady and Deirdre. "What is it, Deirdre?" she asked, glancing from her to Brady and back at Deirdre. "What did you want to tell me?"

Deirdre looked at Nancy, then at Brady, and then down at the floor. Her beautiful eyes filled with tears.

"I . . . I mean we . . ." she murmured.

"Deirdre, think about what you're doing," Brady warned. Nancy saw he was holding on to Deirdre's hand tightly.

"Brady," George said with a shaky voice. "If you know anything that might help us find Bess, please let Deirdre tell us."

Brady looked as tormented as Deirdre. "Don't you think we'd tell you where Bess was if we knew?"

"I don't know," George said. "Would you?"

"Of course we would," Deirdre said.

"But you do know something," Nancy insisted. They were close to finding out the truth. Now wasn't the time to go easy.

Deirdre opened her mouth to speak, but her eyes locked on something over Nancy's shoulder and she quickly swallowed her words. Deirdre and Brady looked like children who had been caught in some mischief. Nancy turned to see Simon Mueller hurrying into the alcove.

When he saw Nancy and George talking to his stars, his face flushed red.

"What's going on here?" Simon demanded, giving Nancy a dark look. Then he turned to Deirdre and Brady. "I've been looking all over for you two. The limo's waiting to take you dancing and—"

"Simon, I'm exhausted," Deirdre said. "I'm just not up for going out."

"But the reporters are waiting at the club. I've got it all arranged."

"So, unarrange it!" she snapped. "I'm tired, and I'm going to bed. Good night." The tears in Deirdre's eyes spilled down her cheeks as she turned and walked out of the restaurant, leaving everyone silent in her wake.

"Well!" Simon said with a snort. "That's gratitude for you. What got into her?" he asked Brady.

"She's tired, Simon, and worried," Brady said. His usually expressive eyes were empty, drained of emotion. "This thing is taking a toll on all of us."

"What are you talking about?" Simon demanded. Then he caught a glimpse of the glare Nancy was giving him. She found it hard to hide her distaste for the man.

"Oh, you mean the kidnapping," Simon said nonchalantly. "Sure, it's a rotten thing to have happen, but we've done what we could—offering the reward and all. Take it easy and realize why you're here. You're a star, Armstrong. This kidnapping doesn't involve you."

"I was there when he grabbed her! I could have stopped the whole thing. That makes me involved, Simon. Why do you have to be such an insensitive jerk?" Brady whirled around and stomped out.

"You kids have forgotten who you're talking to!" Simon bellowed, following Brady. "I put you on top and I can bring you down!"

Nancy watched as a photographer who was wandering around the lobby took the opportunity to snap some shots of a very angry Simon Mueller.

"I wonder what Deirdre wanted to tell us?" George mused.

"I don't know," Nancy said, "but whatever it was, Brady didn't want her to say it. Why don't you stay here. Keep an eye on Deirdre, Brady, and Simon. Try to get Deirdre alone. She's dying to tell us something. Pretty soon she'll get up the nerve."

"Gotcha. What are you going to do?"

"I'm going back to the theater," Nancy said. "I want to see if there's any news." Actually, she was hoping Nicholas would be there, picketing. She wanted to talk to him, but she wasn't sure if she should tell George. Better to keep it to herself, she thought.

As Nancy headed back to the theater she felt a rising tide of panic. Nothing in the case was breaking, and they were reaching the end of the line. In one day Bart Anderson was going to tear down the Royal Palladium, and she wasn't even one step closer to finding out who had wanted to prevent the demolition enough to kidnap her friend.

She scanned the picketers for Nicholas. No luck. A phone call to his grandfather was in order. Nancy could check out whether or not Nicholas had been to see him the day before.

In Joseph's office, Nancy found him lovingly dusting his old oak desk. When he looked up at Nancy, he wiped a weary look off his face and gave her a halfhearted smile.

"Hello, there, young lady," he said, sitting down. "What brings you back here?"

"Actually, I wanted to use the phone," Nancy said honestly. "And I'm finding it hard to stay away," she added simply. Nancy felt she could admit to Joseph, if no one else, how helpless she felt.

He nodded. "I understand what you mean. It's awful to think about what she must be going through."

The telephone rang, and they both jumped. Joseph grabbed for it. "Hello? Yes, she's right here." He handed the phone to Nancy.

Nancy was surprised to hear Deirdre's voice on the line.

"Nancy, I'm glad I found you. I have to talk to you," she said.

"Are you still at the hotel?"

"Yes."

"I'll be right over."

"No." Deirdre sounded very nervous. "I don't want anyone to see us together. I'll meet you in the theater's auditorium."

"I'll be waiting. And, Deirdre," Nancy added, "I should tell you that George is keeping an eye on the hotel lobby. Explain to her when you see her that you're coming to meet me." Nancy didn't know how to finish the sentence.

Deirdre caught the drift of what Nancy was telling her. "Otherwise, she's going to think I'm up to something suspicious, right?" she asked with a laugh.

"I hope you understand," Nancy said.

"It's okay, Nancy. See you in ten minutes."

As Nancy hung up the phone she looked up to see Joseph watching her anxiously.

"Good news?" he asked.

"Sort of." She wanted to tell him about the call, but she didn't want to break Deirdre's confidence. Deirdre had said specifically that she didn't want anyone to know they were getting together.

Nancy picked up her purse and tucked it under her arm. "I'm going to take another look around the theater before I go home," she said.

"I wish you wouldn't," Joseph said, concern registering on his wrinkled face. "After what happened to George this afternoon, I'm worried about you girls."

"I'll be careful, Joseph. I promise."

Joseph stood up from his chair. "If you're really going to do it, I'll go with you."

Nancy thought of Deirdre. "No, really," she said, trying to stop him. "You don't have to."

"I don't mind a bit. I'm going to lock up anyway."

Nancy could see that no matter what she said, Joseph was going to tag along with her. She hated to lie to him, but she couldn't see any way out.

"Well, if you're going to look around yourself," she said, "I suppose I'll just go on home."

He seemed relieved. "That's a good idea. You've been through a lot these past twenty-four hours. Some rest would do you good. Just leave the search up to me. I probably know where to look better than anyone else anyway," he said with confidence.

"Good night." Nancy hurried out the office

door across the lobby. At the front door she turned and looked back toward the office. Joseph was standing there waving goodbye. She returned his wave and walked out the door.

Once outside Nancy rounded the building and ran to the side door, hoping to get there before Joseph locked up for the night. She made it.

Nancy was surprised to see Deirdre already there, standing off to the side on the stage. Deirdre seemed nervous.

"How did you get in here?" Nancy whispered as she climbed the steps up to the stage. She motioned Deirdre back into the shadow.

"I sneaked in the back door. I didn't want anyone to know I was here. I told everyone I was going to bed early because of a headache." She pressed her hand to her forehead. "And it wasn't a lie—about the headache, I mean."

"Do you want to sit down?" Nancy asked, motioning toward a couple of folding chairs in the wings.

"No, thanks. I'm fine standing."

"So, why did you want to see me?" Nancy asked anxiously.

"I wanted to tell you this earlier, but Brady said I shouldn't," she said. "It's about Simon."

"Yes?" Nancy tried not to appear too eager.

"I think he may have kidnapped Bess."

"I think he may have, too," Nancy said. "Tell me why you think so."

"Because I heard him and Brady talking the other morning on the plane when we flew in. Actually, they were arguing."

"About what?"

Deirdre nervously bit the tip of her manicured fingernail. "I'm not sure, exactly. I heard Simon say something about a publicity stunt, but Brady violently shook his head. When I asked Brady about it later he said that Simon was only asking the two of us to pretend we were in love."

"But you didn't believe Brady?"

"No," Deirdre answered, looking down. She toyed with the fringed edge of the emerald green scarf that was knotted around her slender waist. "There had to be more to it than that because Brady seemed really upset. And the romance gimmick is done all the time. I don't think he would have objected so strongly to it."

Nancy chewed on her lower lip as she considered this new information. "But Brady wouldn't tell you the real story?"

"No. That's what he and I were arguing

about in the restaurant. I told him that if he knew something he had to come forward, but I think he's afraid that Simon will drop him as a client."

"Would that be so bad?"

Deirdre shrugged. "Brady seems to think so." She glanced around nervously. "I have to go. My mom will be calling from L.A. pretty soon, and if I'm not in my room, she'll call Simon."

"Thanks for your help, Deirdre. If you can get anything at all out of Brady . . ."

"You'll be the first to know. And, Nancy," she added. "I don't want Simon to know I've been to see you."

"Don't worry, Deirdre. He won't, I promise."

They said good night, and Deirdre left to go out the back door.

Nancy stood on the stage for a moment, thinking about what Deirdre had said. The more she heard about Simon Mueller, the more she thought he had to be the kidnapper.

Then she heard a creaking sound. She wasn't alone. From the wings to her left the noise grew louder. Metal screeching against metal.

Every nerve in her body tensed as she slowly made her way toward the noise.

Abruptly the sound stopped. Nancy stood, quietly waiting, straining her ears. But only thick silence greeted her.

A flash of silver above her made her flick her eyes up. Just in time to see a heavy object come falling from the ceiling. A movie screen hit her then, striking her on the head.

Nancy fell to the floor. As she lay there, she felt a suffocating darkness close in.

She tried to move, but her legs were pinned under the screen.

She tried to scream, but she couldn't make a sound come out of her throat. It was a nightmare.

Then the darkness became a black void that swallowed her, and she slipped into unconsciousness.

Chapter

Eleven

Nᴀɴᴄʏ ᴡᴏᴋᴇ ᴜᴘ to the sounds of breakfast carts being wheeled down the hall. A loud voice paged, "Dr. Evans. Dr. Evans, please come to I.C.U."

Blinking her eyes against the morning sun that streamed through a window beside her bed, she murmured, "Where am I? What happened?"

In an instant Carson Drew was at her side, holding her hand. "Nancy, it's me. Dad. Wake up," she heard him say.

"Dad?" she asked as the image of his face swam into view.

"Yes. I'm right here. And George is here, too."

Nancy lifted her head to look down toward the foot of the bed, but she groaned as a pain shot through the left side of her head. "Oh, wow," she moaned. "It feels like there's a team of hockey players going at it inside my skull."

"Don't try to move, Nancy," George said, taking her friend's hand. "You got quite a bump. The doctor says you should lie still."

"My arm—is it broken?" Nancy asked as she looked down at the sling on her right arm.

"No," her father answered. "Just sprained."

"It feels broken. What hit me? A semi truck?"

Nancy saw her father and George look at each other.

"Don't you remember what happened last night?" George asked.

"Last night?" Nancy closed her eyes and tried to think back. Then it came to her. "Something fell on me."

"It was a movie screen," Carson Drew offered. "Can you remember anything about it?"

Nancy shook her head and instantly regretted having moved as another pain shot through her. "No. I heard a noise and I decided to investigate. But I made it all the way."

George looked disappointed, but Mr. Drew reached out and gently patted her shoulder. "That's okay, sweetheart."

"Deirdre," she said, fighting to stay awake and gather her confused thoughts. "I met with Deirdre just before it happened."

"Yes, we know," George said. "She was the one who rescued you. She said she was just walking out the rear door when she heard a loud crash. She was afraid something had happened to you, so she went rushing back."

"She was the one who called the ambulance," Mr. Drew said. "If it hadn't been for Deirdre, who knows how long you might have been there before anyone found you."

"She came back to the hotel lobby to tell me about your accident," George said. "Then I called your father."

"I told her that you were staked out there in the lobby," Nancy said as her mind cleared, and she remembered her meeting with Deirdre. "She didn't want anyone to know that she had been to see me. Especially Simon. She suspects Simon of the kidnapping."

"Really?" Mr. Drew pulled up a chair and sat down beside the bed. "Tell us."

"There's not that much to tell. She said that on the plane here Simon was trying to talk Brady into some kind of publicity stunt, and Brady wasn't buying it. They argued about it."

"Well, that's all the proof I need," George said. "It's got to be Simon."

Nancy chuckled and turned to her dad. "George fell for Nicholas when he helped her down from that catwalk. Now she's determined to prove that it's Simon and not Nicholas."

"But you still suspect Nicholas?" Mr. Drew asked.

Nancy cast a sideways glance at George and saw her disapproving scowl.

"I have to suspect everyone," Nancy said carefully. "And, yes, he's still one of my prime suspects. The kidnapper is a man who's well-acquainted with the theater. Nicholas knows the place, and he has a strong motive for the kidnapping—family loyalty and love of the place."

"So," said a voice from the doorway. They all turned to see Nicholas standing there with a box of chocolates in his hand and a dark look of anger on his handsome face.

"Just because I'm loyal to my family and want to preserve that beautiful old building, that makes me a kidnapper?" he asked pointedly.

He walked across the room and tossed the candy onto the foot of the bed. "I heard about your accident, Nancy," he said. "I came to tell you that I hope you recover quickly." He walked back to the door where he stood with his hand on the knob. "I'm sorry that you think so little of me as a person," he said with bitter sarcasm. "But I still hope you get well soon."

He slammed the door behind him. The sound echoed for a long moment in the heavy quiet of the room. No one spoke.

Finally George broke the silence. "His feelings were really hurt," she said in a slightly accusing tone.

Carson Drew cleared his throat. "It was unfortunate that he walked in at that particular moment."

Nancy looked at her friend's troubled expression and felt terrible. "I'm sorry, George," she said. "And if Nicholas really is innocent—and I hope he is—I'm sorry I hurt his feelings."

At ten that morning George drove Nancy home from the hospital. Hannah had her tucked into her own bed in no time at all.

"I can't believe you disobeyed your doctor's orders and checked out of the hospital today," Hannah said, bustling around. "Did your father know you were going to do that?"

Nancy sighed and laid her head back on the pillow that Hannah had just fluffed. "No."

"Well, he's going to be very angry with you when he finds out," Hannah said, her hands on her hips.

"I know," Nancy said, reaching for the bedside telephone. "That's why I'm going to call him now and tell him myself before the doctor has a chance to get to him first."

"I'll make you some chicken soup," Hannah said as she left the bedroom. "And, George, make sure she stays in that bed!"

George smiled. "Hannah's famous chicken soup could cure anything from the common cold to bubonic plague," she said.

As Nancy dialed her father's office number, she knew that this time Hannah's soup would not stop her head and arm from aching.

Hannah had been right, of course. She probably should have stayed in the hospital. She would have stayed, but she couldn't help Bess from a hospital bed. And if she didn't break this case today . . .

This was the last day. In less than seven hours the theater would be a pile of rubble and

Bess would be dead. Time was running out, and Nancy was keenly aware of every passing minute.

When her father's secretary put her through to him, Nancy steeled herself for his reaction.

"You did what?" he roared into the phone when she told him.

"Dad, I had to. Please try to understand. You wouldn't stay in the hospital if it were me who was missing."

There was silence on the other end. Nancy couldn't tell if he was still angry or considering her point of view.

"Dad?"

"I understand," he said at last. "That doesn't mean I approve. Just promise me that you'll take it easy."

"I'll try." Nancy hung up the phone.

"So what's the plan?" George asked.

"Hmm?" Nancy bit her lower lip.

"When you get that look in your eyes, I can tell you're up to something."

Nancy got out of bed, and before slipping into a pair of jeans and a sweater, slipped out of her sling. Her arm was okay but felt a little stiff.

"Maybe I should be hit on the head more often. I just thought of something we should have done long ago."

"So, tell," said George.

"We need to go to City Hall to see if we can locate the blueprints of the theater. There might be a hidden room we haven't searched."

The telephone rang, but Nancy knew that Hannah would answer it. A few seconds later Hannah ran up the stairs and knocked on Nancy's door.

"It's for you, Nancy. It's some man, but he wouldn't say who."

"Thanks, Hannah." Nancy raced to the phone. "Hello?"

"I have a suggestion that might help you with your investigation," the voice said in a raspy whisper.

"Who are you? Are you the one who took Bess?"

Nancy frantically grabbed a pencil and began scribbling with her left hand on a nearby notepad. She wrote, "Trace call. Dad's study phone." Then she shoved the note into George's hand.

"It doesn't matter who I am or if I have her," the man said. "Do you want the suggestion or not?"

"I'll gladly accept any help you can give me," she said, trying to prolong the conversation.

"Okay. I'm only going to say this once. Take

another look at your list of suspects. You haven't considered everyone who has a vested interest in the theater."

"What do you mean?"

"Exactly what I said."

"Just tell me one thing," Nancy said breathlessly, "is Bess still in the—"

But he had already hung up.

A few moments later George came running back into the bedroom. "They got it," she exclaimed. "With that new equipment of theirs they traced it right away."

"Where was the call coming from?" Nancy asked anxiously.

George drew a deep breath. "From a telephone at five-twelve East Main Street."

The call had come from inside the theater!

Chapter

Twelve

WHAT DO YOU THINK it means, Nancy?"
George asked as Nancy rushed her from the
bedroom.

"Shh, George," Nancy said, putting her finger to her lips. "I don't want Hannah to hear
us. She'll have a fit if she even knows I'm out of
bed."

After silently sneaking down the stairs, Nancy opened the front door. She and George
quietly slipped out of the house.

"Whew. Okay," Nancy said. "There are two

possibilities. First, it was the kidnapper himself who called, and he's still inside the theater —with Bess."

"That's not logical," George said as she opened the passenger door of the car for Nancy. "Who would throw you onto his scent like that?"

Nancy thought for a moment. "You're right. But the second possibility is that someone inside the theater knows more than we do but doesn't want to come forward."

"Like Brady!" George said excitedly. "Or Deirdre!"

"That could be. I still haven't ruled out Simon Mueller. Still," Nancy said slowly, "the caller said we hadn't considered all the possible suspects. That implies it isn't Simon. And it means we're missing something important. But what?"

"I don't know, Nan. Whatever it is, we'd better find it soon."

"I told you they aren't here," said the young woman in the city planning office of the River Heights City Hall. "The blueprints you want simply aren't here."

The woman pursed her strawberry red lips and put her hands on her waist as she stared at Nancy and George.

Nancy leaned across the narrow counter and tapped her fingers impatiently on its scuffed surface. "Are you absolutely sure?"

"Of course I'm sure. And I'm as upset about it as you are," she said offhandedly while examining the chipped polish on the nail of her pinky.

"I doubt that," Nancy muttered under her breath to George.

"I trusted that man with those prints, and now look what's happened," the young woman said with a bored pout.

"What man?" Nancy exclaimed.

"Just some guy. He came in a few days ago and asked to see the blueprints. Then he asked permission to take them down the hall to photocopy them. Our copier was broken, so I let him take them. He brought the envelope back later and left it on the counter. Like a dummy I filed it without looking inside. Apparently he took them with him." She patted her carefully styled blond hair. "And he seemed so honest, too."

"What did he look like?" George asked eagerly.

"What?" The librarian squinted at George through her heavy blue mascara. "What did he look like? He looked—just regular."

"Did you notice anything about him? Like the color of his hair?" Nancy continued.

"I think it was kind of gray," she said. "But I'm not really sure. I think he was older, anyway."

Nancy was going to push for distinguishing features, but she realized there was no point. The woman seemed to care more about her own appearance than anyone else's.

"Why is everyone so interested in the theater all of a sudden?" the young woman asked. "Does it have anything to do with that kidnapping?"

Nancy looked at George, her pretty face reflecting her concern.

"Yes," she said, "it has everything to do with the kidnapping."

Nancy led George out of the office and down the hallway.

"We don't know much more than we did before," George said dejectedly.

"Sure we do. We know someone wants to stop us from finding those blueprints, and that someone may be older." Nancy looked at her watch. It was noon.

George must have noticed the nervous gesture. "We've got to think of something, Nancy."

"I'm thinking." Someone older. Haven't considered all the possibilities. Who would want the plans to the theater? Who else had a motive?

"Bingo!" she said. "I can't believe we didn't think of it before."

"Nancy," George said, grabbing her friend's arm, "would you care to let me in on it?"

"Louis Falcone." Nancy let the words sink in.

"Nicholas's grandfather?"

"We've never considered him as a suspect, but what if he's behind all this? It would make sense. There's no way he'd want that theater torn down, and he probably knows that building better than anyone." It was all falling into place.

"But, Nancy—"

"There's no time to waste."

Within a few minutes Nancy had looked up Louis Falcone's address and called Detective Ryan to arrange for him to meet her at the theater later.

After half an hour's drive out of River Heights, Nancy and George were in the middle of the country. They took several rural roads and finally turned into Louis Falcone's driveway. It was lined with plaster sculptures.

"Just look at this place!" Nancy exclaimed

as she and George stepped out of the car and walked across Louis Falcone's front yard. "Have you ever seen anything like it?"

"No wonder Nicholas is so proud of his grandfather," George said. "Can you imagine having the talent to create such beautiful things?"

Nancy pulled on her friend's arm. "Now, remember, we're here to ask him about Nicholas. Then we'll see if he reveals anything suspicious."

"I hate the idea of tricking him like that, Nancy," George said, shaking her head.

"It's the only way, George. Trust me. Besides, it's all for a good cause. If we don't figure this out soon, Bess is—"

"I know, Nancy," George said. "You don't have to tell me."

Together the girls strolled up the stone walkway to the door of a small cottage. In answer to their knock, the door opened, and the girls found themselves face to face with one of the handsomest older men that either of them had ever met.

Louis Falcone was tall, with a dark complexion like his grandson. He had a full head of snowy white hair and piercing blue eyes. "Yes?" he asked. His voice was rich and deep.

"Mr. Louis Falcone?" Nancy asked, though

she was sure she had found Nicholas's grandfather.

He nodded his silver head. "I am. And who are you?"

"I'm Nancy Drew, and this is George Fayne. We're investigating the disappearance of our friend, Bess Marvin. You may have heard about—"

"Oh, yes, of course." A guarded look crossed his handsome features. "My grandson told me all about you. How can I help you?"

"Could we possibly come in, Mr. Falcone? There are a few questions we'd like to ask you, if you don't mind."

"Certainly. Please, come inside."

He ushered them into his home, which was as charming and quaint inside as outside. Carved animals of all species adorned his mantle. On the coffee table was the figure of a young man sitting on a tree stump, his elbows on his knees, his chin resting in his hands. He looked very thoughtful and serious.

"That's a wonderful sculpture," George said. "It's Nicholas, isn't it?" Mr. Falcone nodded.

"I think you really caught his personality," she remarked.

Mr. Falcone studied the piece as though

seeing it for the first time. "Yes. I was pleased with it. Nicholas is such a serious, intense boy. Always has been."

It sounded funny to Nancy to hear Nicholas referred to as a boy when he was at least twenty-three years old. She supposed that to his grandfather he would always be a child.

"So, have you heard any news about your kidnapped friend?" he asked, motioning for them to take a seat on the sofa.

"No. Unfortunately not," Nancy said.

"And I'm now one of the suspects on your list," he said, looking at Nancy.

Nicholas's grandfather had guessed why they were there. She decided to be honest. "Your feelings about the upcoming demolition are a matter of public record," she said. "And none of us can blame you for wanting to preserve your father's and your art."

Louis Falcone said nothing for a long moment. He only walked over to a small table and picked up a chunk of wood that he had apparently been carving.

Walking over to the girls, he showed them the piece. "Do you see this?" he asked. "This is just a bit of baroque carving, a shell. It's only a fancy little curlicue. I've been carving on it for two hours. Like this—"

He took a sharp knife from his pocket, pressed the tip to the wood, and scooped out a small bit of the wood. "When I'm finished carving this," he said, "I'm going to use it to make a mold. From that mold I can cast dozens of these shells in plaster. Then I paint them gold or silver. Mixed with other shapes I can create those ornate borders that you see all over the theater."

He walked back to the table and laid down the wood and chisel. "I began learning my craft back in Italy when I was only six years old. By the time I was fourteen, I was here in the United States working as a master craftsman."

"You have a wonderful talent, Mr. Falcone," George said sincerely.

"Yes, I have," he said without pretending to be humble. "But a man only creates a few truly beautiful things in his life. That theater was one of my father's and my contributions to this world. I spent a long time creating the Royal Palladium. I don't want to see it destroyed in one day."

"I don't blame you," Nancy said. Then she asked him pointedly. "Did you kidnap my friend, Mr. Falcone?"

He returned her steady gaze as he said, "No, Ms. Drew. I didn't."

Nancy swallowed hard. George glanced at Falcone, then gave Nancy a sad and disappointed look.

"Do you believe me, Ms. Drew?" he asked with a half smile.

"I think you and your grandson would do almost anything to preserve that building," Nancy said, baiting him. Carefully watching his reaction, she saw his eyes flash with anger and determination.

"You're right, Ms. Drew, we would. And if that makes us suspects on your list, so be it."

He stared at her with such intensity that Nancy found herself having to glance away. Her gaze swept Mr. Falcone's studio, and a photograph, hanging among others on the wall, caught her attention. She stood up and walked over to the wall.

"This is a picture of you, Nicholas, and Joseph Hughes," she observed. "I didn't know that you were friends."

"I've known Joseph for years," he said. "He's a good man."

"Do you think Joseph is capable of kidnapping?" Nancy asked him.

"Joseph is a very capable man," he said without hesitation. "He has a deep love for the theater, and I'm sure that he would do anything he could to save it. But he's a kind soul. I can't imagine that he would hurt anyone."

Nancy turned to face him, her eyes trained on his face to watch his reaction to her next question. "George and I went to City Hall less than an hour ago to look at the blueprints of the theater. They're missing. Do you have any idea who might have taken them?"

He smiled a half smile and shrugged. "I can't imagine. Now if you'll excuse me, I'd like to get back to work."

Nancy looked at George in frustration. Another dead end, and it was getting later by the minute.

They said goodbye to Louis Falcone and headed back down the walkway to their car.

"I think he did it," George said with conviction.

"But he denies it, and we haven't got any proof." Nancy shook her head sadly.

"I know. I think if Bart Anderson had been in the room with us, he would have strangled him."

"Unfortunately, that's not enough." Nancy sighed. They were headed back to River Heights knowing no more than when they had left. "Hold it! Pull over, George."

George slammed on the brakes and pulled

into a gas station they were passing. "What's up?"

But Nancy was out of the car, heading toward the phone. Within two minutes she had Nicholas Falcone's address and was back in the car.

"Let's go. Fifteen-twelve Rampling."

"Why do you want to talk to Nicholas again?" George asked as she turned the car down Rampling Street.

"I want to try to shake him loose. If he knows anything or even suspects anything, now's the time for him to tell us."

They pulled up in front of a modern apartment house, got out of the car, and entered the building as one of the tenants opened the large glass doors. Nancy checked the directory for Nicholas's apartment number.

As the mirrored elevator quickly whisked them to the third floor, George looked at Nancy. "I hope he's home," she said. "And I also hope you're wrong. I like Nicholas."

"George, I'm sorry. But we can't afford not to question him," Nancy said through tight lips.

They made their way down the carpeted hall to his apartment.

"Here it is," Nancy said, pointing to the door on their left, which was slightly ajar. "Hey, look. It's open."

"At least he's home," George said, knocking on the door.

Nancy felt her heart quicken as she waited for Nicholas to answer the door. After a few seconds she decided to knock. Still no answer.

She glanced up and down the hall, then gently pushed the door open. "I hate to do this, but—"

The sight that greeted Nancy from inside Nicholas's apartment made her stop in her tracks.

Chapter

Thirteen

NANCY'S EYES TOOK IN the overturned coffee table, the broken lamp, the green plants that lay across the carpet in their spilled dirt.

"Nicholas!" George called.

"Nicholas, are you here?" Nancy echoed. But she knew, even as she called his name, that Nicholas wouldn't answer. She knew that something must have happened to him.

Nancy and George searched the apartment for him, afraid of what they might find. After a few minutes they gave up looking.

"I just hope he's not hurt, considering the fight he must have put up," Nancy said.

"How can you tell he was in a fight? This could have been robbery or someone searching for something."

"I don't think so," Nancy said. "The place wasn't searched. None of the drawers have been pulled out, and the cushions on the furniture are still in place. Besides, the VCR is still here. That's one of the first things a burglar takes."

"You're right," George agreed. "And since Nicholas is nowhere to be seen, I wonder if maybe we have a second kidnap victim."

Just then there was a knock at the door. Both girls turned and called, "Come in." Joseph Hughes entered, looking terribly worried.

When he saw the condition of the room, he turned even more pale. "What happened?" he asked.

"We don't know for sure," Nancy said, "but it looks as though Nicholas had some trouble."

Then Nancy found herself wondering what the elderly caretaker was doing there. "Is there some reason you're here, Joseph?" she asked.

"What?" Joseph stared at her as though in a daze. "Oh, I came here to check on Nicholas. The kids on the picket line were worried about him. He didn't show up."

Joseph looked around the room again, then began to murmur to himself. "This wasn't supposed to happen," he said. "Nobody was supposed to get hurt. I never meant for—"

"You never meant for what?" George asked, jumping on his words. "What wasn't supposed to happen?"

"Nothing." He closed his eyes and shook his head violently. "Nothing . . . I just meant that . . ."

He opened his eyes and looked around the room again, becoming more agitated by the moment. "Oh, Nicholas. If anything happens to that boy, it'll be all my fault."

Nancy walked up to him and caught him by the arm. "Why, Joseph? Why would it be your fault?"

Joseph looked at her as though seeing her for the first time. Then he seemed to realize what he had said. "Never mind," he said, pulling out of her grasp. "Just never mind."

He backed away from her toward the bedroom, his hands in front of him as though he were warding off an evil spirit. Nancy wondered what she had said to set him off.

Whirling around, Joseph raced into the bedroom, slammed the door, and locked it behind him.

"Joseph, open up!" Nancy shouted as she

pounded on the door. "George, get my purse. I need my picklock. Hurry."

George brought Nancy's bag, and in a minute Nancy had found her tool, jimmied the lock, and opened the door.

They raced into the room but found it empty.

"Where is he?" George shouted.

"Over there," Nancy said, pointing. "The window's open."

They ran to the window and squeezed through onto the fire escape. Far below they saw Joseph scurrying down the escape, nimbly jumping from one level to the next.

There was no point in chasing him. He had too great a head start. They both watched the old man as he hit the ground running and disappeared down the nearest alley.

They turned to each other, both of them thinking the same thing.

Nancy was the first to say it. "He sure is spry for such an old fellow!"

"Spry enough to climb around on a cat-walk," George observed.

"Definitely." Nancy ran back into the living room and grabbed her purse. "Come on. We've got to find Bart Anderson. We still can't prove anything, but when we tell him about

Joseph, he'll just have to postpone that demolition!"

Fifteen minutes later the girls stood in Bart Anderson's outer office.

"I'm telling you for the third time, Mr. Anderson is out. *Out.* You know, not in." His secretary bristled at Nancy and George as they stood in front of her desk, demanding to see her boss.

"So, why is a dark blue Mercedes parked out front in his space?" Nancy asked. She found that her voice came out sounding far calmer than she felt.

"I don't know," the secretary answered. "Maybe he went for a walk somewhere. But he isn't here. I'll have to ask you again to leave and stop pestering me. I have work to do."

To illustrate her point, she turned to the typewriter, slid in a piece of paper, and began to type furiously.

"Come on, George. She obviously has her instructions not to let anyone see him."

At the door Nancy paused and said over her shoulder, "When you see Mr. Anderson, please tell him that we were here. And tell him we'll be in touch again. Today."

As soon as Nancy and George were out in

the hall, Nancy looked at her watch. "The best we can do is wait in our car to see if he shows up. But only for a couple of minutes. We should get to the theater to confront Joseph."

Minutes later they saw Bart Anderson walk out of his office building toward his blue Mercedes.

"There he is," George said. She started to open the car door.

"Wait a minute, George," Nancy said. She watched as Bart Anderson glanced nervously around before getting into his car.

The girls ducked down, out of sight, below the dashboard.

"He definitely looks like a man with something to hide." Nancy peeked over the dashboard. "Let's follow him and see what he's up to."

George bit her lower lip. "You got it." They fastened their safety belts.

Ten minutes later, they turned off the main highway to follow the Mercedes down a narrow dirt road.

"Where do you think he's leading us?" George asked as she peered through the cloud of dust raised by the car in front of them.

"We'll find out pretty soon," Nancy said. "This road can't be very long. Wait, hold on. Look." Anderson had stopped his car.

"Let's wait here until we see what he's up to." Nancy reached into her purse and pulled out a pair of miniature binoculars. "He's going into a trailer," she said. "It looks like one of those little portable offices that builders move from one construction site to another."

Nancy lowered the binoculars and looked at George. "We have to know what he's doing in there," she said.

"Absolutely. Let's go."

The girls left George's car and sneaked up to the trailer. They circled the trailer until they came to the side where there was a tiny window.

"What's he doing?" George whispered as Nancy stood on her toes and looked inside.

"You're not going to believe this, George, but he's got Nicholas!" Nancy exclaimed in a hushed voice. "He has him tied to a chair."

George craned her neck to see in. Both girls winced as they heard Anderson's voice boom through the thin walls of the trailer.

"I know you've got that girl," he roared. "And if you don't tell me where she is right now, I swear I'm going to kill you!"

Chapter

Fourteen

W E'VE GOT TO HELP HIM!" George said, her eyes wide.

"We're going to," Nancy answered. She quickly climbed the two steps leading to the door. Taking a deep breath, she threw the door open and charged inside.

Bart Anderson was standing next to the tied-up Nicholas.

"What's going on here?" Nancy demanded.

"Yeah, what do you think you're doing to him?" George added indignantly.

Nicholas opened his eyes wide. "Nancy, George, what are you doing here?" he asked. "But, hey, never mind why you're here," he added. "I'm just glad you are. This man is a lunatic."

"How did you— You followed me here, didn't you?" Anderson said. "Why, I ought to call—"

"No, you really shouldn't," Nancy said flatly.

"Look, I was just trying to help you find your friend," Anderson protested.

"I don't think you can solve one kidnapping by committing another," Nancy said.

Nicholas looked extremely relieved as George worked on untying him. "That's what I've been trying to tell this guy. He had his goons grab me at home. Then they brought me here and tied me to this chair."

Anderson could see that he was beat. He turned and stomped out of the trailer, slamming the door behind him.

"That's crazy!" George said. "Why kidnap you? Why not try to help us find Bess instead?"

Nicholas shook his head. "I don't know, except that it looks to me like Anderson's running scared. He's got a lot of money riding on being able to demolish that theater *today*."

"But he can't if Bess is still in there," Nancy concluded. "I'll bet you anything that after I talked to Detective Ryan, he called Anderson to say there might be a delay."

"You're probably right, Nancy," George said, finally freeing Nicholas's hands.

He gingerly massaged his chafed wrists. "I don't know why everyone thinks *I* did it."

"Because you have the perfect motive."

Nicholas quickly looked away from both of them.

"Are you protecting someone, Nicholas?" Nancy asked. "Please, tell us."

She walked over to him and knelt beside his chair. "Is it your grandfather you're protecting? Is he the one who took Bess?"

Nicholas struggled with the words before he let them out. "I don't know. I hope not, but he might be."

"What makes you think he might have done it?" George asked. "Because he loves the theater so much?"

"No, it isn't that."

"What is it?" George asked, probing.

Nicholas took a deep breath. "Remember when Joseph got that phone call from the kidnapper? The one he told us about when we were all standing there in the lobby?"

"Yes, of course," Nancy said. "Go on."

"Well, Joseph said the kidnapper called the theater the Royal Palladium."

"And the theater hasn't been called that for years. No one would call it that except someone who had been around in the old days," Nancy finished for him.

"Like your grandfather?" George asked.

Nicholas nodded. "Like my grandfather."

"Or Joseph Hughes," Nancy said. The pieces were beginning to come together. "Joseph is an old-timer, too. He might have called it that himself. We only have his word for it that there was a phone call at all."

"But Joseph couldn't have kidnapped Bess," George said. "He was making the introduction for the movie over the PA at the time. Remember, we heard it in the women's dressing room."

"We heard Joseph's voice, so we just assumed that he was in the sound booth at the time," Nancy said. "But he could easily have made the tape ahead of time and rigged the PA system to play at the right moment."

"Do you really think Joseph would be capable of kidnapping someone just to save that building from destruction?" George asked.

"I know Joseph," Nicholas said. "He's a

good person." He thought for a moment. "But he loves that theater more than anything. It's possible he might do anything to save it."

"Of course," Nancy said. "I should have thought of it before. *That's* why Joseph's been staying in the theater night and day."

"And he's the one who found Bess's earring!" George added. "Not only that, but I just realized something."

"What?" Nancy asked.

"Joseph was the one who thought of searching the stage again yesterday, when we heard that tapping noise and found the room she had been in."

"He led you to it, George! He must have wanted us to know that she was still there!"

Nancy found herself excited, worried, and relieved at the same time. If Joseph was the kidnapper, then they were on their way to finding Bess. If they still had time.

The trailer door opened, and Bart Anderson stepped inside. He was wearing a broad grin that made Nancy uneasy. Anything that made Bart Anderson that happy had to be bad news.

"I've just been on my car phone," he told Nicholas, "and I pulled a few strings at City Hall. I had to cash in on some long-standing favors that I'm owed, but it was worth it."

"What was worth it?" Nancy asked, afraid she didn't want to know.

"I moved the demolition time up."

"You did what?" George exclaimed.

Anderson smiled and pointed to the thin gold watch on his wrist. "That's right. That building's coming down in fifteen minutes. I don't want any of this foolishness to interfere with my project. And the only way to stop it from interfering is to finally destroy the place."

"Fifteen minutes!" Nancy reached out and grabbed the front of Bart Anderson's jacket. "We just solved the case. We know who kidnapped Bess. And now we're sure that she's still in there!"

Anderson looked suspicious and doubtful. "Do you really? Or are you just trying to stall me again?"

"It's Joseph Hughes," Nancy said. "It has to be."

"The janitor?" Anderson asked.

"He's a lot more than the custodian. Joseph is the soul of that theater," Nancy said. Her heart was in her throat. She had to make him believe her.

"Please, Mr. Anderson," she continued, "I don't have time to explain all the details to you now, but we really do have very strong reasons to suspect him. You've got to stop that demolition. Our friend is in that building. If they tear it down, she'll die."

Not more than five minutes later Anderson's Mercedes was hurtling down the dirt road, sending a whirl of dust into the air.

"Can't you drive any faster?" George urged.

"It won't help your friend if we get ourselves killed before we get there," he said grimly. But from the passenger seat, Nancy saw him press the accelerator closer to the floor and the speedometer jump another ten miles per hour.

"Try to get your crew on the phone again," Nancy suggested. "Or better yet, let me try. You've got your hands full driving."

She dialed the number he gave her, but there was still no answer.

"That means they're at the theater already," Anderson said.

"Do you think we'll make it in time?" Nicholas asked, leaning forward from the back seat.

"I don't know. My crew is very efficient. Once they start, it won't take them long to level the place."

Ten minutes later the Mercedes screeched to a halt in the theater parking lot. As the group piled out of the car, Nancy reached down to Anderson's tape deck and grabbed a cassette tape out of it.

"What's that for?" Nicholas asked when he saw her shove it into her pocket.

Nancy didn't have time to explain that she would need it to bluff Joseph. She was already running toward the building. She followed Anderson as he raced toward his crew, who were assembled at the side of the building.

"Hey! Stop! Hold it, you guys," Bart shouted.

But they couldn't hear him above the noise of the machinery and the pickets' cries of protests. To add to the bedlam, Brady, Deirdre, and Simon chose that moment to arrive. Seemingly from out of nowhere twenty screaming girls appeared and surrounded the stars, waving bits of paper and pens.

Bart ran up to the man operating the wrecking ball. "Hold it, Charlie!" he shouted.

But he was too late. Nancy watched in horror as the huge steel ball crashed into the side of the theater and its wall collapsed in a cloud of dust.

Chapter

Fifteen

"YOU CAN'T GO IN THERE!" Bart Anderson shouted to Nancy, Nicholas, and George as they ran through the front door of the theater. "The building's unstable now, and it might—"

They didn't hear the rest of what he said. Their only thought was of their friend and her safety.

They paused for a moment in the lobby. Plaster dust swirled around them and drifted down, covering the white-and-black marble floor at their feet.

"We have to find Joseph," Nancy told them as she anxiously searched the empty lobby. "My guess is he's in here, going down with the ship, so to speak."

"I'll check downstairs," Nicholas said as he headed for the staircase. He ran up the steps, taking them two at a time.

"I'll search the office," George said, taking off in that direction.

Nancy ran into the auditorium. The deserted room was half-lit by the stream of light that poured in through the gaping hole in the side wall.

This was the heart of the theater. Something told her that he would be there.

He was.

Nancy hurried to the back of the dark auditorium where he sat huddled in a seat. His head was down between his knees, his arms wrapped over his head.

"They're going to do it," he said tearfully. "They're going to pull it down and kill us all."

Nancy sat down in the seat beside him and put her arm around his shoulders.

"No one's going to die, Joseph," she said as gently as she could. "They've stopped the demolition."

She looked over at the gaping hole in the

side wall. Through the space she could see Bart Anderson and his crew milling around outside.

Slowly Joseph lifted his head and looked around. He could see for himself that they had halted the destruction.

"How did you get them to stop?" he asked.

"We found out for sure that Bess is here in the theater, Joseph. And we know that you're the one who took her."

He looked at her in disbelief for a long moment. Then, suddenly his dazed look dissolved. He jumped to his feet, and before Nancy had a chance to grab him, he ran to the back door of the auditorium.

"Oh, no, you don't!" she cried out as she ran after him. "You got away from me once today, and that's enough."

She burst through the doors that were still swinging from his escape. As she ran into the lobby, Nancy caught a glimpse of Joseph as he disappeared down the steps leading to the lower level.

Oh, no, Nancy thought. If he gets down there into that maze of practice rooms, I'll never find him.

Instead, Joseph turned to the left and down the hall. Nancy chased him down the hallway.

It was a dead end with some dressing rooms and a costume room at one end.

I've got him now, she thought. She saw him jerk open the door to the wardrobe room and disappear inside.

But by the time she ran into the room, he was gone.

Nancy shook her head in disbelief. There were no other doors out of the room. The man came and went like a phantom in the old theater.

Then she caught a movement out of the corner of her eye. The costumes that were hanging on a rack to her right were swinging ever so slightly.

She ran to the rack and paused only a moment before sweeping the clothes aside with her hand. She expected to see Joseph standing there, huddled behind the costumes.

Nothing! He was gone again!

Nancy scanned the wall for a seam. Joseph couldn't have disappeared into thin air. There had to be another secret door here, just like the one Bess had disappeared through.

There was. Part of the wood paneling was several shades lighter than the rest, and one board in particular stuck out from the wall.

Digging her fingernails into the crack between the panels, Nancy pulled on the board. A thrill of triumph passed through her as the panel opened, but it faded quickly when she saw only darkness ahead of her. There was a musty, dank smell, like a basement that had been closed for a long, long time.

She reached into her purse and took out her penlight. Its golden beam pierced the darkness, and she saw a narrow staircase leading up into still more darkness.

Nancy carefully climbed the steep, rickety steps that twisted and turned, first to the right, then to the left.

There was no banister, only bare walls on either side. Nancy shuddered as a spider's web brushed across her face and down her neck.

As she climbed, she kept her ears open for any sound from above. She had to find Joseph and make him tell her where Bess was. If he got away, they might never find her.

With her flashlight pointed at the steps, Nancy followed the set of footprints that Joseph had left in the thick dust. In the distance, far above, she heard the sound of his feet pounding as he ran.

Then the footsteps stopped. Was Joseph lying in wait for her?

Nancy slowed her pace and tried to see into the darkness above her. Quietly she made her way to the top. Through the blackness, she saw a thin line of light streaming in. Another secret door!

Carefully she pushed the door open, bracing herself. Joseph could be right on the other side. But when Nancy opened the door, she saw that he had led her all the way to the hallway on the third floor. She was standing in the corridor outside the projection booth.

Joseph was at the end of the hall and heading for the stairs that led back down to the lobby.

Nancy's heart sank. He was about to get away again!

"Joseph!" she cried out.

He turned to face her. Then, hardly believing her eyes, Nancy saw George and Nicholas appear on the stairs right behind Joseph.

"There he is!" George shouted.

"Get him!" Nancy yelled. They raced toward Joseph.

Nancy saw the panic in the old man's face when he realized he was trapped. George and Nicholas were behind him, and Nancy was bearing down from the other side. Turning on his heel, Joseph darted into the projection room.

"We've got him!" Nancy cried. They all charged into the room after him.

They had him cornered. There was no way for him to escape now.

Joseph backed up against the wall, his eyes wide with fear.

"It's okay, Joseph," Nancy said. "We know why you did it. We understand, really."

"How did you find out?" he asked.

She reached slowly into her pocket and took out Anderson's cassette.

"We found the tape, the one that you recorded the movie introduction on."

Joseph's eyes darted from the tape in Nancy's hand to the projector. Nancy caught the glance. His eyes told her where the real tape was.

In an instant she was taking the projector case apart and looking inside.

"Here it is!" she announced proudly as she pulled a cassette tape out.

George ran toward the projector. She leaned over Nancy and reached inside. "Hey, what's this?" she asked. "There are some papers here, too."

"The missing blueprints!" Nancy exclaimed. "So Joseph was the old man who took them from the archives."

"Where is she, Joseph?" Nicholas asked.

Joseph looked more like a frightened child

than an old man as he stood there in the corner, trembling.

Nancy smoothed the wrinkled blueprints against her thigh and then held them out to Joseph. "Show us, Joseph. Please. Show us where you've hidden Bess."

Chapter
Sixteen

Nᴀɴᴄʏ ᴡᴀᴛᴄʜᴇᴅ as a variety of emotions played across Joseph's wrinkled face: fear, sadness, and finally, shame.

"I never meant to hurt young Bess," he said in a shaky voice. "I was going to hold Brady, but she was there and—"

"I know you didn't," Nancy said soothingly.

"I showed you the earring," he said, "and I told you that I heard her crying out. I wanted you to know for sure that she was here in the theater, but I couldn't take you to her. As long as I had her, there was some hope I might save the theater."

"But why did you try to scare Nancy off at the same time?" George asked, confused.

"You mean the flowers, the light, and the movie screen?" Joseph asked. "I never meant to hurt you, Nancy. I just thought that if things kept happening at the theater, you'd know not to stop looking there. You'd realize that the kidnapper—and Bess—really were still inside."

Nancy sighed. It was so illogical. But all of Joseph's thinking seemed confused and twisted. Obviously, his love for the theater outweighed all his reason.

"I think I understand, Joseph." She held out the blueprints to him. "But, please. Show us where Bess is. They've stopped the demolition. You can tell us where she is now."

Joseph blinked several times, holding back his tears. Then Nancy watched as he slowly reached out his hand. His finger trembled. Nancy held her breath. Finally, after a long pause, Joseph pointed to the spot where he had hidden their friend.

"An ice depository?" Nancy asked as she and George followed Nicholas up a steep, narrow flight of stairs toward the attic. "What's an ice depository?"

"It was the air-conditioning system in the old days," Nicholas said, panting from exertion. "There's this narrow space between the attic and the ceiling of the auditorium. They used to put big chunks of ice there in the summer to keep the audiences cool."

"Did it work?" George asked.

"I don't know. I wasn't around back then. I just remember hearing about it."

"So, where is it?" Nancy asked when they reached the attic.

Nicholas referred to the paper in his hand. "Somewhere about here." He dropped the blueprints and began examining the wide boards in the floor. "The opening where the ice was put in has been boarded over. But if Joseph has been in here, there should be some loose planks."

Suddenly a board came up at his prying. The girls caught their breath.

"Bess?" George cried.

They paused a moment to see if they could hear anything.

They did. A faint movement from the dark recesses that Nicholas had just uncovered.

"Bess, is that you?" Nancy called.

"She's in there," George said firmly. "I just know it."

Nancy knelt beside the hole and shined her flashlight into the darkness. That was when she saw the most welcome sight of her life—a patch of teal blue and the sparkle of sequins. And it was moving.

"It's her!" she cried. "And she's alive!"

"Here, let me get her out," Nicholas said, gently easing Nancy aside. "It would be my honor, really."

Nicholas slipped easily into the narrow space and disappeared for a while. In less than a minute he reappeared with a dirty, disheveled, but happy Bess in his arms.

He lifted her out of the hole and handed her to George and Nancy, who instantly smothered her with hugs and kisses.

"Oh, Bess, we were so worried!" George said while laughing and crying at the same time. "We didn't know where you were, or if he'd hurt you, or even who had you. It was awful."

Nancy grinned in relief. "Hold on, George. Before you have your reunion, let's untie her and take the gag off her mouth."

George quickly untied the towel from Bess's mouth, while Nicholas and Nancy unbound her hands and feet.

When Bess opened her mouth to talk her voice was hoarse and shaky. "What took you guys so long?" she asked.

With that one question, Nancy was reduced to tears. At last, they had found their friend.

"Just look at the two of you," George said, "lying there like ladies of leisure." She stood at the foot of Bess's hospital bed. In the bed next to Bess lay Nancy. Both of them looked more bored than ill.

"Hey, I'll trade places with you any time you're ready," Nancy said. "The only reason my doctor is making me spend the night is to get even with me for running out this morning."

"And what are you in for?" George asked her cousin.

"Five years to life," Bess complained. "Actually, just overnight like Nancy. They just want to keep an eye on me to make sure that I don't croak or something."

"Hey, is this slumber party for girls only, or are fathers allowed?" Carson Drew stuck his head through the door. Then he showed them a box of Hannah's chocolate-chip cookies. "I bear sweets and good news."

"Cookies!" Bess looked ecstatic. "Wow! I

feel like I haven't had a chocolate-chip cookie since my previous lifetime."

"Didn't Joseph feed you?" Mr. Drew asked, handing her the tin.

"Just pizza," she said, munching on one of the cookies. "He didn't want to leave the theater to get groceries, so he just kept ordering out for pizza. I'll never look at another mushroom and pepperoni in my life."

Nancy and George giggled.

"Sure—" Nancy said.

"You know, I still can't believe it was Joseph. I thought I recognized his voice at one point, but he kept me blindfolded the whole time. He must really love that old theater."

"He meant to grab Brady, you know. He never planned on taking you," George added.

"Yes, he told me that. Said he meant to get a boy because boys were sturdier and less afraid than girls. So, of course, I had to be a good sport and hang tough to show him how wrong he was."

"And you did," Nancy said with a grin.

"I'm just glad he didn't hurt you," she added.

"My wrists and ankles are a little sore from the ropes, but that's about it." She took another cookie from the tin.

"What's going to happen to Joseph?" she asked.

"After we put you in the ambulance, we handed him over to the police," Nancy said. "They arrested him on the spot. I suppose he'll be charged with kidnapping and extortion."

"That's too bad," Bess said. "Even though he put me through one of the worst experiences of my life, I feel sorry for him. Maybe my testimony will help him in court."

"I'm sure it will," Mr. Drew assured her. "And now for my good news."

"Oh, yes, he brought good news with his cookies," Nancy exclaimed. "Let's have it."

"Thanks to the efforts of Nicholas Falcone, his grandfather, and the Landmarks Committee, the demolition of the theater has been canceled—permanently," he announced proudly. "And the city has declared it a historical landmark."

"Bart Anderson must be livid!" George said, not bothering to hide her glee.

Mr. Drew cleared his throat. "Actually, Bart Anderson has other things on his mind. He was arrested, too, along with Joseph."

"He was?" the girls asked in unison.

"For what?" Nancy asked.

"Kidnapping. Remember, he had Nicholas

taken from his home and physically restrained him. He's in deep trouble with the law."

"Hey, this looks like a party! Can we join in?" Deirdre asked as she peeked into the room.

"The more the merrier," Nancy said. "But Bess wants to know if you brought pizza."

Bess groaned. Deirdre walked into the room, followed by Brady and Nicholas. When Bess saw Brady she gasped and pulled the sheet up to her neck to cover her ugly hospital gown. Instinctively she put her hand up to her hair, but it was a lost cause.

"Hi, Bess," Brady said as he walked over to her bed. "It's good to see you again."

"Do you remember me?" she asked breathlessly.

"Of course I do." His green eyes twinkled and he smiled his easy, heart-stopping smile. "And you're just as pretty as I remember you. Even prettier. I can't tell you how bad I feel that you were kidnapped instead of me. I would have traded places with you if I could have."

"Oh, Brady. How sweet. I didn't mind, really."

Brady pulled a bouquet of red roses out from behind his back. "These are just a small token of my gratitude," he said, handing them to her. "As soon as you're out of that hospital bed, I'd like to take you out for dinner, maybe some dancing if you're up to it."

"I . . . oh . . . sure. I'd love to."

"Thank you." He leaned down and placed a kiss on her cheek. Bess looked as though she were about to faint away. Then she blushed bright pink, and Nancy thought she had never seen her friend look more lovely. Bess put her hand to her cheek and drew a long, shuddering breath.

"Wow! A kiss from Brady Armstrong! I almost feel like it was worth getting kidnapped!"

Nancy's next case:

Nancy's summer vacation is going just fine—she can hang out and spend time with Ned. All that changes when Vanities, a teen boutique at the mall, is hit by a series of high-priced thefts. Nancy is convinced that it's an inside job, and she turns up the heat to smoke out the thief.

During Nancy's investigation, her next-door neighbor Nikki Masters lands in some hot water of her own. Her boyfriend, Dan Taylor, has turned up dead, and the police name Nikki as the prime suspect. But Nancy can't shake the suspicion that there's a hidden connection between the boutique thief and Dan Taylor, the thief of hearts. Nikki may have fallen for the wrong guy at the wrong time, but Nancy knows one thing for sure: Nikki Masters is not the kind of girl to be mixed up in murder . . . in *THE SUSPECT NEXT DOOR*, Case #39 in The Nancy Drew Files™.

Dear Friend,

I want to tell you about a terrific new series that's coming next month. It's called *River Heights*, and yes, it takes place in my hometown.

You already know there's plenty of mystery in River Heights, but now there's a whole lot more. You're about to discover an exciting new world of fun, friendship, secrets, and romance—starring the teens of River Heights High. (I'll be there too, from time to time.)

You'll meet Nikki Masters (my next-door neighbor) and Brittany Tate, the scheming leader of the "in" crowd. When these two get together, sparks fly! Then there's Tim Cooper, the sensational new guy in school, Jeremy Pratt, the king of the snobs, and lots of others.

Don't forget—a thrilling new book will appear every other month, all with the kind of intense, emotion-packed stories you love. So turn the page and meet the teens of *River Heights*. You'll also find a special preview of the very first book, *Love Times Three*.

I think you'll enjoy it!

Sincerely,
Nancy Drew

Introducing . . .

Nikki Masters: Blond, blue-eyed, and pretty, Nikki is a good student with a flair for photography. There's one major complication in her life: her classmate Brittany Tate.

Brittany Tate: Dark-haired, dark-eyed, and curvy, Brittany secretly envies Nikki. Through hard work (and lots of scheming) she's become the leader of the "in" crowd, but she has a few secrets of her own that she'd rather keep buried.

Tim Cooper: The gorgeous new hunk in school. Brittany has her eye on him, but Tim is looking only at Nikki.

Lacey Dupree: One of Nikki's best friends and junior class secretary. Quiet and dreamy, Lacey usually has a faraway look in her eyes. Don't be deceived: Lacey is not as naive as she appears.

Robin Fisher: Nikki's other best friend specializes in acting and dressing outrageously. Robin is also a dedicated athlete on the school swim team.

Jeremy Pratt: King of the snobs. With his upper-crust good looks and privileged background, Jeremy is Brittany's social counterpart.

Kim Bishop: Brittany's chief crony and major female snob. A real match for Jeremy Pratt—if she could stand him.

Samantha Daley: Brittany's number-two pal. She's a transplanted Southern belle with a talent for scheming that rivals Brittany's.

SHARE THEIR DREAMS, THEIR SCHEMES,
THEIR HEARTBREAKS, AND THEIR HUMOR IN
LOVE TIMES THREE

"Do you want my honest opinion, Nikki?" Nancy Drew tilted her head and gave her next-door neighbor a long, critical look. "I think you're going to knock the socks off every boy at River Heights High!"

Sixteen-year-old Nicola Masters—Nikki for short —shook her head. "I'm not so sure about that, but thanks for the compliment," she said.

Nancy spun her friend around so that she was facing the full-length mirror on the back of Nancy's bedroom door. "There," Nancy said emphatically. "Take a good look at yourself and then tell me I'm exaggerating!"

Nikki stepped back to study her image in the mirror. Shiny, medium-length blond hair framed her gently rounded face. Her azure blue sweater matched exactly her long-lashed eyes and made the most of her perfectly proportioned figure. So did her skirt, a straight shaft of winter-white cotton that stopped just short of her knees, revealing the rest of her slim, lightly tanned legs.

"Well?" Nancy asked.

"Well . . ." Nikki shrugged, then nodded at her reflection. "I might not turn the male population of

River Heights High into a bunch of raving maniacs, but you're right, Nancy. I look okay."

"You look great," Nancy corrected her firmly. "Listen, Nikki, I bet you're nervous about school because you're afraid people will still be gossiping." Nancy looked Nikki in the eye. "Just remember—your name is completely clear."

"I know," Nikki said, but she couldn't help sighing. It was bad enough that the boy she'd been dating, Dan Taylor, had been killed. But when she'd become the number-one murder suspect, her life had turned into a nightmare. If it hadn't been for Nancy, Nikki was sure she'd be on trial right now, instead of worrying about her back-to-school wardrobe.

"I don't really think anyone still believes I'm guilty," she added. "But people *do* give me funny looks sometimes." She laughed ruefully. "I guess it's not exactly the best way to start my junior year."

"Just remember," Nancy said. "You're not Nikki Masters, suspect. You're Nikki Masters, bright student, talented photographer, loyal friend. And don't forget," she added, her blue eyes sparkling, "great-looking girl."

"I won't forget," Nikki promised. "In fact," she said firmly, "I'm going to make my junior year the best year ever!"

"Nikki, over here!" Lacey Dupree waved and motioned for Nikki to join her. "I saved you a seat!"

Smiling, Nikki made her way down the aisle of the school bus toward her best friend on the first day of school.

Halfway toward Lacey, Nikki heard one girl say clearly, "Nikki Masters, well, *you* know."

Nikki raised her chin and kept on walking.

"You look great!" Lacey said, as Nikki sat down beside her and the bus lurched forward again. Lowering her voice, she added, "I know you were dying inside, but you acted as cool as a cucumber."

"Thanks," Nikki said, "but I didn't feel very cool. I hope I can keep up the act."

"You probably won't have to," Lacey told her. "By the time we get to school, everybody'll be too busy trying to figure out where the first class is to think about anything else."

The remark was typical of Lacey, who was always optimistic and a true romantic. Her light blue eyes usually had a faraway look in them, but Lacey's mind was in perfect working order.

Nikki felt her spirits rising. "We're juniors at last!" she said.

"It's going to be great!" Lacey agreed excitedly. "I still can't believe I'm class secretary. Between that and my job, I'm going to be swamped."

"You forget a few things, Lacey. Like trig and English and chemistry," Nikki pointed out wryly.

"And boys," Lacey added significantly. "I have a feeling this is going to be *the* year for love."

Nikki hoped so—for Lacey's sake, at least. For herself, well, love was just a word right now. After all, she had thought she was madly in love with Dan Taylor, but she'd been wrong. For now she planned to steer clear of romance and stick to her photographs for the *River Heights Record,* the student newspaper.

The bus lumbered up the last few feet of the school drive, and jolted to a stop. The first day of school was about to begin. Nikki stood up quickly, her heart thumping with excitement as she and Lacey joined the swirling crowd of students streaming toward the school.

The grass-covered quad was filled with hundreds of students shouting out greetings, catching up on news, and comparing class assignments. As Nikki and Lacey made their way through the noisy, milling throng, they spotted a tall girl with short dark hair, huge dark eyes, and a turned-up nose looking around anxiously. As soon as she caught sight of Nikki and Lacey, she grinned widely and thrust her hand into the air.

"Nikki! Lacey!" she yelled. "Over here!"

It was Robin Fisher, Nikki and Lacey's other best friend. She was the swim team's most dedicated member, and her great figure showed it. She also seemed to have an inside line on what was new and hot in fashion.

"Quick!" Robin said as Nikki and Lacey approached. "Tell me where your homerooms are. North or South?"

"North," Nikki said. "Mrs. Sheedy."

Lacey moaned. "*I* got stuck in South. And South is a complete maze," Lacey argued. "I'll need a map and compass just to find my way around."

"That's because you're such a space case, Lacey," Robin remarked, her dark eyes twinkling. "You'd probably need a map and compass to find your own bedroom."

"I would not!" Lacey tried to sound indignant, but she couldn't help giggling.

Nikki laughed, too, feeling much more comfortable now that she was with her two best friends. Then she took a quick look around the quad. There was DeeDee Smith, the editor of *The Record*. There was Jeremy Pratt, the rich, good-looking Snob King of River Heights High. And there, surrounded as usual by a big group of admiring boys and laughing girls, was Brittany Tate.

Sensational was the word for Brittany. She had long, lustrous dark hair, gleaming dark eyes, a pretty mouth, and a figure that curved beautifully beneath her clinging skirt and her silky, expensive-looking blouse.

Brittany always managed to attract a crowd. The school's social queen bee, she headed up what seemed like a hundred clubs and committees and wrote *The Record*'s widely followed column "Off the Record."

Nikki knew Brittany but not very well. Nikki sometimes got the feeling that Brittany was checking her out; other times, Brittany seemed to pretend she didn't exist. Nikki couldn't decide whether the girl liked her or not.

Meanwhile, across the quad, Brittany Tate dragged her eyes away from Nikki Masters and turned back to Ben Newhouse, the president of the junior class. "I'm sorry, Ben," she said sweetly. "What were you saying?"

"I asked if I could count on you," Ben told her. "You know, to help run the halftime show for the alumni football game. It has to be pretty spectacular."

"And *I* asked if you'd started your first 'Off the Record' column yet," DeeDee Smith put in. "The deadline's coming up fast."

"I know that," Brittany said. Actually, she had no idea what the deadline was. "Naturally, I've started the column." Another lie, but she could get the column done in a flash.

Brittany turned back to Ben. "The halftime show will be a knockout. I guarantee it."

With that settled, Brittany glanced back to Nikki Masters. She hated to admit it, but the girl was handling things beautifully. Suddenly Brittany frowned. Of course she's handling it, she thought irritably. With her background and upbringing, Nikki could afford to stay cool when the entire junior class was whispering about her. Brittany had worked and schemed hard to get to the top and it made her furious to think that Nikki Masters had been born there.

"Brittany!" Kim Bishop, Brittany's best friend, startled her from her thoughts. Blond and trim, Kim rivaled Jeremy Pratt for the title of School Snob. "When are you going to stop staring at Nikki?" she asked. "You're slowly turning green, and it's not your best color."

"That's right." Samantha Daley nodded. A transplanted Southern belle, Samantha was delicately pretty, with a lilting accent. There was nothing fragile about Samantha's mind, though. She could cook up schemes with the best of them. "Why don't you just forget about little old Nikki and listen to some really juicy news?"

"Okay," Brittany said. "I'm ready for some hot gossip. What is it?"

"There's a new guy in school," Samantha said, lowering her voice as if she were imparting a state secret. "I hear he's absolutely gorgeous!"

"From Chicago," Kim added briskly. "I haven't seen him, either, but his name's Tim Cooper. He wants to be an actor."

Samantha gave a throaty laugh. "Wouldn't it be fun to discover him?"

Brittany wasn't impressed. "If he's gorgeous, then he's probably conceited," she stated flatly.

"Suit yourself," Samantha said with a lazy shrug. "But I plan to keep my eyes—and my options—wide open."

The warning bell rang suddenly, and as everyone started heading into the building, Brittany and her friends were separated. Dashing across the quad, Brittany glanced briefly at her watch and ran headlong into someone coming from the opposite direction. She reeled backward, sprawling on her seat in the soft green grass.

"Hey, I'm sorry!" a low voice said.

Brittany saw a male hand reaching out to help her. She took it and looked up into the most startling gray eyes she'd ever seen. The guy's hand was warm and strong, his hair was dark and thick, and his build was sensational.

Brittany swallowed and finally found her voice. "It wasn't your fault," she told him with a bright smile. Who *was* this dream of masculine perfection? "I wasn't looking where I was going."

"Well, I wasn't either," he said. "I guess we're even."

They both laughed, and the boy turned away.

"Wait!" Brittany cried. She tried to sound casual, but her heart was thudding in her ears. "We might as well introduce ourselves. I'm Brittany Tate."

She held out her hand, and he took it. "Tim Cooper," he said. "I'm new this year—Brittany, you said your name is?"

She nodded, reluctantly letting go of his hand.

"It's nice to meet you. I guess I'd better get going," he added as the second bell rang. "But I'm sure I'll see you again, Brittany."

Oh, you *will*, Brittany thought as she watched him hurry off. Samantha and Kim had been right. And as of right now, Samantha's options were closed as far as Tim Cooper was concerned.

Brittany Tate was in love.

Nikki had only two minutes left to get to her homeroom. The halls were filled with jostling students as she joined in the mad dash to beat the bell.

Room 101 was in a state of barely controlled pandemonium. Nikki carefully smoothed back her hair and walked inside just as the final bell rang.

Almost instantly, the pandemonium stopped. Twenty heads turned toward the door, and twenty pairs of eyes fastened on Nikki. The silence lasted only a split second, but Nikki felt as if she'd been standing in the white-hot glare of a giant spotlight.

Nikki quickly spotted an empty desk in the last row, way over in the corner by itself. It would be the perfect seat to hide out in, she thought. Halfway to the solitary desk, Nikki stopped, suddenly furious with herself. She was acting like a coward. Straightening her shoulders, Nikki made a sharp turn, walked to the head of the classroom, and took a desk right in the middle of the first row.

The noise in the room rose to an ear-splitting level, but it didn't bother Nikki at all. She was busy writing her name in her notebooks when the noise suddenly dropped, then disappeared. Nikki raised her head.

This time, nobody was looking at her. Instead, they were all staring at the boy standing in the doorway. He was tall, with unusual, deep gray eyes and thick, dark brown hair. Nikki had never seen him before. She decided the boy must be new in school, then turned back to her notebooks.

Then Mrs. Sheedy bustled in. "All right, class," the

teacher began briskly, "let me take the roll and then we'll get on with business." She consulted her notebook and called out the first name.

"Hi."

Nikki looked up. The new boy had just sat down in the next seat and was smiling at her. "Hi," she replied.

"Timothy Cooper?" Mrs. Sheedy said.

"Here," the boy answered, then turned back to Nikki, still smiling. "Most people call me Tim," he added.

Nikki nodded, gave him a quick return smile, and opened her blue spiral notebook.

"I'm new in River Heights," Tim went on in a low voice. "We just moved here from Chicago."

"Christina Martinez?" Mrs. Sheedy continued.

"Here," a girl answered from the back of the room.

"What's your name?" Tim asked.

"Nicola Masters?" the teacher called.

"Here," Nikki replied. "Most people call me Nikki."

Tim laughed quietly. "I guess that answers my question."

"All right," Mrs. Sheedy said. "On to the announcements. Tryouts for the drama club's production of *Our Town* will be next Tuesday."

Nikki jotted down a reminder to herself.

"How is the drama club here?" asked Tim, who was also writing down the information. "Any good?"

"Very," Nikki told him. "There's lots of competition for roles."

"Great," Tim said. "I'm really interested in acting."

Mrs. Sheedy was reading more announcements.

"Students driving cars to school must have a parking permit," she intoned.

"I walked today," Tim told Nikki. "River Heights is a really nice-looking town. Have you lived here long?"

"All my life," Nikki answered distractedly. She knew Tim was probably a little nervous, but she wished he'd find someone else to talk to. Homeroom was almost over. Next came trig. Another class to face and another bunch of eyes staring at her. She hoped Tim didn't think she was rude, but she just didn't feel up to making polite conversation.

"One more announcement," Mrs. Sheedy was saying. The class gave a collective groan. "Your locker assignments are permanent. No exchanging with anyone else! You people!" she added loudly, pointing to a noisy group of talkers. "I suggest that you pay closer attention. Junior year is no piece of cake."

"Yeah," one guy chimed in. "It's a real killer!"

At the word *killer*, all conversation died. Nikki could feel everyone's eyes upon her, practically boring holes in her back.

Tim turned around, looking confused. "What—?" he began, raising his brows at Nikki.

But Nikki was already on her feet. She shot Tim one quick, despairing look, then raced for the door just as the first-period bell rang.

Tim checked his assignment card. He had one more class before lunch—honors English. Stuffing the card back in his pocket, he walked on, checking the room numbers. As he turned a corner, he collided with someone who was just straightening up from the water fountain.

"So," a soft voice said, "we meet again."

It was the girl Tim had run into outside earlier that morning. Beverly? Bethany?

"Brittany Tate," she said. "Remember me?"

"Sure," Tim replied with a smile. He might have forgotten her name, but her looks were sure easy to remember. Friendly, too. But she wasn't Nikki Masters. Nikki was the girl who'd really caught his attention.

"Well," he said quickly, "at least I didn't knock you over this time."

"Oh, don't worry about that." She swayed toward him so that he caught a faint whiff of flowery perfume. "I'm glad to see you again. How has it been going?"

"Not bad so far," Tim said. "Everyone seems pretty friendly."

"That's good," Brittany said. "Of course, I can't imagine you having any trouble making friends." She moved even closer and touched him lightly on the arm. "So, Tim, where are you headed?"

"Room 209, honors English. Mr. McNeil," Tim told her. "Am I heading in the right direction?"

Brittany's lovely mouth broke into a wide smile. "What a coincidence! That's where I'm going, too." Gracefully linking her arm through his, Brittany propelled him toward the door.

Tim saw Nikki the minute they walked inside. That soft blond hair, the nice blue sweater that matched her eyes. He'd been worried that he'd see her only in homeroom, but here she was. Now all he had to do was figure out a way to sit next to her.

Luck wasn't on his side this time. Mr. McNeil seated his classes in alphabetical order, and Tim wound up on the opposite side of the room from Nikki.

Of course, he didn't know her at all. Yet. She'd been

kind of cool this morning, not that he blamed her—he'd been babbling like an idiot. But he never expected that spark he felt the minute he laid eyes on her. She'd smiled at him—only once, but that was enough. Then that weird thing had happened. The place had gotten silent as a tomb, and Nikki had jumped up, looking like she'd been slapped in the face.

Tim had no idea what all that had been about, and he hadn't asked anyone. Sure, he was curious, but it didn't really matter. What did matter was getting to know Nikki.

"Good morning." Mr. McNeil spoke softly, but the class quieted down immediately. "I'm passing out the first semester's reading list," Mr. McNeil went on. "Look it over and then we'll talk about the first book, *The Scarlet Letter*. I want you to read the first fifty pages by Thursday."

He looked around the class and smiled. "I can tell that a lot of you already know the story," he said. "So let's talk. What is it about Hester Prynne that has kept Hawthorne's book alive all these years?"

Somebody mentioned loneliness; someone else suggested courage; and then Ellen Ming, the junior class treasurer, mentioned ostracism.

"Hester was shut out," she said. "Everybody can sympathize with her because everybody knows that feeling." Ellen looked around. "You know. Like Nikki." Then her face flushed. "Oh, I'm sorry, Nikki. I wasn't thinking."

Everyone stared in Nikki's direction. She looked quickly at the floor, as if she were hoping it might have a trap door she could escape through.

Mr. McNeil cleared his throat. "That's an interesting point, Ellen, but I think we should have Nikki's okay before we discuss it any further."

Nikki raised her eyes, started to shake her head, then shrugged and nodded.

Tim listened, shocked, to the discussion that followed. Nikki's story was completely different from Hester Prynne's, of course, but Ellen was right—they'd both been shut out.

The discussion was still going on when the bell rang. Shoulders back, eyes looking straight ahead, Nikki was the first one out the door.

Tim watched her leave, gazing intently after her.

Her own eyes narrowed to slits, Brittany watched Tim watch Nikki. His handsome face was serious. It was impossible to tell what he was thinking now. Earlier, she'd known *exactly* what he was thinking. And that had been maddening.

Tim hadn't taken his eyes off Nikki at the beginning of the class. Just her luck, Brittany thought miserably. Nikki Masters had to be in the same honors English class as Tim Cooper. Without lifting a finger, Nikki had Tim looking at her like she was the only girl in the world.

That was what really burned Brittany. Nikki Masters never had to try for anything.

For the first ten minutes of class, Brittany had felt like screaming. But then, thanks to Ellen Ming putting her foot in her mouth, things had brightened up. Nikki's whole awful story had come tumbling out, and Tim had heard it. Maybe now he wouldn't be so ready to throw himself at her feet.

The timing couldn't have been better, Brittany thought with satisfaction. Of course, she still wasn't sure how Tim felt. But she knew how she felt. She was crazy about him. She wanted him for herself. And she was going to get him.

Will Brittany break up Tim and Nikki's romance—before it even gets started? Find out in *Love Times Three*, the sensational first book in the new River Heights series, available in September.

IF THE SLIPPER FITS

"Filled with romance, breathtaking passion, and a dash of mystery that will leave you wanting more."

—*Night Owl Reviews*

"A dash of danger and a dash of fairy tale in the form of a very special pair of shoes add to the romance plot, filling out *If the Slipper Fits* nicely."

—*Romance Junkies*

"Cinderella knew it was all about the shoes, and so does master storyteller Drake as she kicks off the Cinderella Sisterhood with a tale filled with gothic overtones, sensuality, sprightly dialogue, emotion, an engaging cast, and a beautiful pair of perfectly fitting slippers."

—*RT Book Reviews* (4 stars)

"I was enchanted with this story as Olivia Drake took the residents of Castle Kevern *and* this reader on an emotional, delightful journey. A magical fairy tale deserving to be read and read again!"

—*Once Upon a Romance*

D0035366

ALSO BY OLIVIA DRAKE

THE CINDERELLA SISTERHOOD

Abducted by a Prince

Stroke of Midnight

If the Slipper Fits

HEIRESS IN LONDON SERIES

Scandal of the Year

Never Trust a Rogue

Seducing the Heiress

Bella and the BEAST

OLIVIA DRAKE

WITHDRAWN

St. Martin's Paperbacks

This is a work of fiction. All of the characters, organizations, and events portrayed in this novel are either products of the author's imagination or are used fictitiously.

BELLA AND THE BEAST

Copyright © 2015 by Barbara Dawson Smith.

For information address St. Martin's Press, 175 Fifth Avenue, New York, NY 10010.

ISBN: 978-1-250-06029-7

Printed in the United States of America

St. Martin's Paperbacks edition / November 2015

St. Martin's Paperbacks are published by St. Martin's Press, 175 Fifth Avenue, New York, NY 10010.

10   9   8   7   6   5   4   3   2   1

Chapter 1

Clarissa, the Countess of Milford, was sorely in need of a project.

Seated at the breakfast table, she buttered a slice of toast while reflecting on the dilemma. She had risen from the ashes to marry an earl. Then, as a young widow, she had enjoyed a scandalous love affair with a prince. She had led a full life as a doyenne of London society. Now, her fondest ambition was to give other women a chance at happiness, too.

Clarissa reached for the morning newspaper. Turning the pages to the gossip column, she scanned the names of notable debutantes who had attended the previous night's ball. Those pampered ladies, however, stirred no interest in her.

She was hoping to find mention of a lowly chaperone or a penniless companion. Such women were the forgotten of society, too often ignored or mistreated. They were wallflowers doomed to spinsterhood by undeserved misfortune.

Surely there had to be one in need of a matchmaker. In the few weeks since the start of the season,

Clarissa had searched in vain for the perfect girl. There had been several possibilities, but none had seemed quite right. None had stirred a flash of intuition in her. And none had inspired her to lend out the enchanted garnet slippers.

Sipping cream tea from a blue porcelain cup, Clarissa finished reading the news sheet. As she was closing it with a sigh, a man stepped into the dining chamber. Hargrove was the quintessential butler in a black tailcoat, pristine gloves, and cropped white hair. His harsh, stoic features masked his inner thoughts.

Clarissa set down her teacup and regarded him with great interest. He never disturbed her breakfast without good cause.

Hargrove reached the linen-draped table and inclined his head in a bow. "Madam, the one you were seeking has returned to England."

Clarissa gazed up at him in perplexity. Hargrove was a man of few words, and it took a moment to grasp his meaning. Then a frisson of interest prickled her skin. Pushing back her chair, she rose to her feet. "Isabella Jones? Are you quite certain it's she?"

"Indeed." Hargrove stepped forward to hand her a folded paper. "This arrived from Oxford not ten minutes ago."

The red wax seal had been broken, for the letter was addressed to Hargrove. The cheap paper felt rough to the touch. Opening it, Clarissa scanned the cramped penmanship, and the message brought a delighted smile to her lips.

"Most extraordinary," she said, returning the letter to the butler. "Miss Jones has been abroad for most of her life. For her to return now, and still unmarried at her advanced age . . . well, I must confess that I never

imagined your search would be so fruitful. Or so swift."

"Perhaps, my lady, some things are fated."

Not for the first time, Clarissa wondered if Hargrove knew more than he let on. Although he was her most loyal servant, she had never revealed to him the mystical power of the garnet slippers. That secret had been entrusted to her long ago, when Clarissa had been an orphaned girl, disinherited by her wealthy stepmother and ridiculed by her two stepsisters. At the lowest moment of her life, banished to the kitchen as a servant after her dear papa's death, Clarissa had taken pity on a Gypsy crone who had come begging at the back door. She had fed the old woman a hot meal, and in return, the Gypsy had presented her with the exquisite beaded shoes.

The slippers would fit only a girl who was worthy of true love.

Clarissa left the breakfast table and glided to the tall window overlooking the street. She gazed down at the carriages and pedestrians for a moment, then turned back to the butler. "I've another mission for you," she said. "This one will require considerable finesse. The Duke of Aylwin must be convinced that he is in dire need of an assistant. Discreetly, of course."

"At once, madam."

With a bow, Hargrove departed the dining chamber. Clarissa knew that she could depend on him to take care of the matter. He had a far-flung web of contacts worthy of a master spy for the Crown—indeed, that had been his vocation during the Napoleonic wars.

Her thoughts returned to the pleasure of the unexpected news. At last she had found the perfect wife for the reclusive Duke of Aylwin. Someone who could

entice him out of his beastly guise and back into the world of the living.

At least she hoped so.

Would the slippers fit? Would Miss Isabella Jones become the newest member of the Cinderella Sisterhood?

Clarissa could scarcely wait to find out.

Chapter 2

Bella Jones stopped to read the small card in the window of the dress shop in Oxford. She had been trudging along the busy street, not heeding the stylish gowns on display behind the glass panes, for such luxuries were far beyond her reach. Then her attention had been caught by the square of white pasteboard propped in the lower corner of the window.

SEAMSTRESS WANTED. EXPERIENCE REQUIRED.

A jolt of hope struck her heart. Bella desperately needed to earn a wage in order to support her brother and sister. She'd tried to be a tutor, but all of her inquiries had come to naught. Learned scholars abounded in this university town, men with advanced degrees in science and mathematics and literature. No one would hire a female whose education had consisted of studying archaic texts while trekking with her father through foreign lands. No one wanted a woman who could speak the Farsi language like a native Persian, or who could recite long passages from the *Ramayana* in the original Hindi.

When Papa had died in Persia nearly a year ago, he

had left his three orphaned children a cottage in far-away Oxford—and a promise of riches beyond their wildest imagination. So Bella had scraped together the funds to purchase passage to England. She and her siblings had left their tiny hut in the mountains, trekked by mule caravan across the Mesopotamian deserts, and sailed what seemed like halfway around the world in order to fulfill her father's last request.

Return to Oxford, Papa had gasped out on his death-bed, clutching at her hands. *Promise me. Find Aylwin. Find the map. You have half . . . the pharaoh's treasure.*

Amid her grief and worry, Bella had been sustained by a vision of gold and jewels. She had resolved to find Mr. Aylwin, ask him about the map, and demand Papa's half portion of the pharaoh's treasure. Then she would be free from the yoke of poverty. There'd be no more fretting about food or clothing or books or a dozen other household expenses.

Upon their arrival the previous month, Bella had made inquiries among the townsfolk of Oxford. She had questioned the postmaster, the butcher, the vicar. But no one had ever heard of a man named Mr. Aylwin, and finally she had been forced to conclude that Papa must have been rambling nonsense. He had been inco-herent from the high fever that had claimed his life.

They had journeyed to England for nothing.

There *was* no Mr. Aylwin. There was no treasure map, either. A pharaoh's riches would not save them from the poorhouse. That bitter truth lodged like a stone in her craw. Ever since, Bella had scoured the newspaper advertisements for work. She had gone to dozens of interviews, but to no avail.

Now, she lifted her gaze to the gold lettering on the window glass: FOTHERGILL'S FASHION EMPORIUM.

Perhaps no one here would deign to employ a woman who knew little of English style. With a single glance at her brown skirt with its gold-spangled trim and the crimson blouse belted in the traditional Persian fashion, they would scorn her as a foreign bumpkin.

Bella tugged the green knitted shawl tightly about her shoulders. Blast it, why should appearances matter so long as she could sew a straight seam? She certainly knew how to ply a needle—tedious though the task might be. Hadn't she always mended Papa's shirts and trousers? Hadn't she stitched every article of clothing for Lila and Cyrus until her sister had grown old enough to undertake the chore?

On that righteous thought, Bella pushed open the door of the dress shop and stepped into a beehive of activity. The buzz of conversation filled the high-ceilinged room. Swarms of ladies flitted from table to table, their lacy sleeves and kid-gloved hands fluttering over the displays of rich fabrics and lavish trimmings.

As busy as it was, however, the shop had an aura of refinement unlike the crowded bazaars of the East. Instead of shouting merchants and haggling customers, the black-clad salesmen here looked as elegant as the ladies they served.

Bella knew the moment one of those shop assistants spied her standing by the door. The scrawny man had dark beady eyes that narrowed directly on her. Beneath a long mustache, his lips pursed as if he'd bitten into an unripe pomegranate. He started toward her, but a lady stepped into his path and he turned with a pretentious smile to show her a tray of buttons.

Bella had no desire to be ejected by an underling. She needed to find the owner of the shop.

Keeping her head down, she slipped past the throngs of customers and made her way toward the rear where a door surely led to the offices. The variety of fine articles for sale dazzled the eye. Like women the world over, these English ladies liked to adorn themselves with myriad ornaments. There were boxes of colorful beads, cards of intricate lace, collections of ostrich and peacock feathers. Along the back wall, a display of multihued cloth drew her like a lodestone.

There she paused, unable to resist touching a sheer bronze silk. The fabric was so light that it slithered through her fingers like falling water. A distant memory stirred in her. As a girl, she'd entered their hut one afternoon to find her mother wearing a gown sewn of a similar fabric. The precious garment had always been kept tucked away in a trunk during their travels. But on that particular day, Papa had been off on an overnight exploration, and Mama had remarked wistfully that it was their wedding anniversary. So she had donned her bride dress, the only link to her life back in England.

A lump ached now in Bella's throat. Mama had never had the chance to return home to Oxford. She had died some fifteen years ago, shortly after giving birth to the twins . . .

"Remove your hands at once," a male voice hissed from behind. "That is French silk from Paris."

Bella dropped the cloth and spun around. It was the man in the black suit. From close-up, he had taut shiny skin like the carapace of a beetle. When he curled his lips in disdain, the ends of his long mustache waggled like antennas.

Bella lifted her chin. "I wish to speak to the proprietor."

The man snatched up the length of silk, turning it to and fro as if to assure himself it hadn't been soiled or torn. "*I* am Mr. Fothergill and this is *my* establishment. You must depart these premises at once. There is nothing here that you could possibly afford."

"I came to inquire about the position of seamstress."

His scornful gaze crawled over her foreign garb. "The post has been filled."

He was lying, she could tell by his shifty manner. "But the sign is still there in the window."

"Do you dare to question my word? Out with you now. Gypsies are not permitted on these premises."

Bella stiffened. Even abroad, Gypsies were regarded as tricksters and thieves. "Sir, you are mistaken—"

Her words broke off as Fothergill seized hold of her upper arm, his fingers biting like pincers. Without further ado, he hauled her toward the front of the shop.

Many of the customers turned to stare, whispering and exclaiming, some arching their necks to get a better view of the spectacle. One young blond lady in a pink bonnet said something to her friends and they all laughed aloud. From them, the tittering swept the large room in a wave that inundated Bella and completed her humiliation.

Heat burned her cheeks. During previous interviews, she had detected a certain suspicion in the faces of those to whom she had applied for a post. People had seemed wary of a woman in foreign garb. But none had been so scornful as these posh aristocrats who viewed her as an object of ridicule, as if she were dirt beneath their well-shod feet.

Their laughter sliced deeply into Bella's pride. The weeks of fretting and frustration already had eroded her confidence. A part of her wanted to cringe, to

scuttle away in shame. Yet another part, a fierce primitive core, imbued her with a volatile fury. The force of it rose in her like a tide of fire.

Nearing the front door, Bella reached beneath her robes and drew out an ivory-hilted dagger from its hidden sheath. The ancient metal blade emerged with a metallic snick.

She pressed the tip beneath Fothergill's chin. "Filthy dog! Release me at once!"

The shopkeeper halted, paralyzed. His dark eyes bulged. The manacle of his fingers let loose of her arm.

Gasps rose from the ladies. Several screamed. They shrank back in alarm, skirts rustling and feet scraping.

Fothergill's air of snooty authority had vanished. His face took on the paleness of a corpse. The trembling of his lips made his mustache quiver. "P-please!" he gurgled. "Don't . . . don't kill me!"

Bella kept the tip of the knife beneath his chin. She relished his fear. She wanted the insect to squirm. It proved he was no more her superior than the bandit who'd crept into her tent in the deserts of Chaldea, intent on stealing her purse.

That one had fled howling into the night, dripping blood.

One of the onlookers let out a sob of fright. A glance around showed the ladies were staring at her in wide-eyed terror. She had lingered here too long. "I'll spare your miserable hide this time," Bella hissed. "But the next woman you mistreat may not be so generous."

She slid the dagger back into its sheath at her waist.

Fothergill staggered sideways. He clutched at his throat, gingerly rubbed it, then examined his hand for blood. Seeing none, he drew himself up. "Blasted dirty

Gypsy!" he sputtered. "The magistrate shall hear about this!"

Magistrate.

The word cast a chill over Bella. She could ill afford trouble.

Turning, she yanked open the door and dashed outside into the cloudy spring afternoon. She took off down the busy street, zigzagging past housewives with shopping baskets, dons in black robes, and ladies peering into shop windows. Behind her, Fothergill alternately shouted for a constable and implored someone to stop her.

Several tried.

She evaded the grasping hands of a stooped old workman and then a white-aproned chemist who had stepped out of his apothecary shop. The other pedestrians gave her wide berth. Determined to elude arrest, she plunged into the heavy traffic on the cobbled road, dodging a wagon filled with large barrels. Too late, she spied a fancy yellow carriage coming along at a fast clip.

It almost ran her down. The skittish chestnut danced sideways. Despite the efforts of the driver, the animal veered too close to the foot pavement. A stack of wooden crates in front of the greengrocer's crashed to the ground.

Fruits and vegetables rolled in all directions. The proprietor shouted curses as the hapless gentleman reined in the wild-eyed horse. People went scrambling after the goods. Several urchins began stuffing their pockets with strawberries and oranges.

Bella seized advantage of the distraction by losing herself in the multitude of shoppers. She slowed her steps to a swift walk to avoid drawing attention.

Making a quick turn at the nearest corner, she slipped down an alleyway, hurrying along before emerging into a tree-lined neighborhood.

Clouds hung low, heavy and gray, swollen with rain. The cool air smelled of dampness and coal smoke. Bella cast a furtive glance over her shoulder to make certain that no one was following. There were only a few people outside, and thankfully, none paid her any heed as she headed rapidly past a row of brick town houses.

The stone buildings of the university were visible over the rooftops, along with the tall pointy spire of St. Mary the Virgin's Church. Though new to the bustling town, Bella had learned to orient herself by those landmarks to keep from getting lost during her hunt for work.

Work. She was still unemployed. Having made a spectacle of herself, had she ruined any chance at all of securing a post?

Her wild anger subsided, leaving a sick sensation in the pit of her belly. She should *not* have lost her temper. She should *not* have drawn a knife and threatened Mr. Fothergill, no matter how insulting he had been. If she were tossed into prison, how would Lila and Cyrus survive?

At fifteen, the twins deserved the chance to continue their studies. They mustn't be forced to labor for a living just yet. They would have the formal education that she herself had been denied. Bella had been the only mother they had ever known. She must not fail them.

Her spirits sank lower. She'd have to stay out of sight for a time, in case the constable had been ordered to search for her. Thank heavens Fothergill did not know

her name or where to find her. In a few days, perhaps it might be safe for her to venture out again to seek employment.

She had to hope so. Her nest egg had shrunk to almost nothing.

If only Papa's deathbed rambling about a pharaoh's treasure had been true. If only she had been able to find the elusive Mr. Aylwin. Then her troubles would have been over . . .

As if to mock her, a gust of wind blew cold raindrops at her face. Bella drew the green shawl up over her head. Wishful thinking accomplished nothing. Dreams wouldn't fill their bellies.

A steady drizzle began to fall as she made her way toward home. At least she and her siblings had a roof over their heads. They belonged here, she reminded herself. Papa had been a baronet. Their blood was as English as any of those nasty ladies in the shop.

Bella had been born in Oxford twenty-nine years ago, though she had no memories of the place. She had been very young when she'd gone abroad with her parents so that her father, Sir Seymour Jones, could pursue his interest in ancient civilizations. Her childhood had been an endless adventure of wandering through foreign lands, finding ruins in jungles, discovering giant statues carved into mountainsides, exploring old palaces from long-forgotten empires.

Yet always it was England that had captured her imagination.

By the campfire each night, Mama often had related stories of their native land. She would tuck Bella in at bedtime and describe a gently rolling countryside, a misty green place of forested hills and winding roads where you might spy a princess riding in a gilded

coach or a fairy peeping out from a clump of ferns. It had sounded far more fascinating than the turbaned natives of the East or the caravans of smelly camels.

Now, the cold rain made her shiver. The hem of her skirt grew sodden from the many puddles. Life in England was no enchanted tale. Though the surrounding landscape was indeed lovely, with cultivated fields and pastures of woolly sheep, she had not the leisure to admire it.

Near the edge of town, she quickened her steps along a dirt lane that was lined with small homes. She tried to boost her spirits by telling herself that it would be pleasant to spend a few days with Lila and Cyrus. She could help them with their chores and lessons.

As the rutted track meandered past a stand of oaks, Bella came to an abrupt halt. She blinked to clear the raindrops from her eyelashes. Straight ahead lay the house that had been her father's legacy. The ivy-covered cottage had glass windows and two upstairs bedrooms tucked beneath the thatched roof. Wisps of smoke drifted from the chimney. In the tangled garden, a few yellow roses provided splotches of color.

But that wasn't what held her attention.

Parked by the garden gate was the most magnificent vehicle that Bella had ever seen. The cream-colored coach had fancy gold scrollwork on the door and enormous gilt wheels. A burly driver sat on the high perch, rain dripping from the brim of his tall black hat as he held a team of four white horses. By the cottage door, a footman in a leaf-green uniform stood guard beneath a black umbrella.

Bella gawked. The carriage looked as if it had sprung straight out of a fairy tale. But why was it here, in front of *her* cottage? Had it taken a wrong turn? Then why wasn't the coachman asking directions of

the inquisitive neighbors who peered from their doorways?

Who was the owner of the vehicle? More to the point, where was this esteemed personage? Inside the cottage?

Her heart lurched. Had one of the customers in Fothergill's Fashion Emporium recognized Bella, perhaps from a prior job interview? Had the lady come to berate Bella for her deplorable behavior?

Surely not. She had seen no one familiar in the shop. Then who else could it be?

Perhaps some calamity had befallen Cyrus or Lila. Perhaps they had ventured into town against Bella's orders. Lila usually obeyed the rules, but her brother was prone to wandering off to explore the neighborhood. Maybe he had trespassed onto private land. Maybe at this very moment he was being taken to task by some royal grandee. A villain as horrid and judgmental as Fothergill.

Bella's fingers briefly touched the hilt of the hidden dagger. Her sturdy half-boots squelching through the puddles, she darted behind the coach and made haste toward the cottage.

The garden gate opened with a squawking of hinges. Her skirt caught on a bramble as she hurried down the flagstone path. As she stooped to disentangle herself, the shawl slipped from her head and plopped into the muddy garden. Brackish water stained the green yarn.

Bella rolled the soiled garment into a ball and stuffed it beneath her arm. The white-wigged footman by the door cut his gaze toward her. Though his young features remained impassive, she felt rattled, her nerves on edge.

She marched to him. "Who is your master? Why are you here?"

"It is not for me to say, miss." He stepped to the door and opened it. Then he waited like a marble statue for her to enter the cottage.

Bella's anxiety deepened. The visitor must be someone very rich and very important to have such a discreet, well-trained servant. How long had Lila and Cyrus been at the mercy of this stranger?

There was only one way to find out.

Chapter 3

As Bella stepped inside the cottage, the rainy day cast gloom over the tiny entry hall. Ahead lay a narrow stairway and, beyond it, the corridor that led to the kitchen. A lighted candle flickered in a sconce.

She hastily hung her shawl on a wall hook. Through the doorway to her left, the dining table was littered with abandoned books, as if the twins had been interrupted at their studies. Three wooden crates stacked in the corner held all of her father's scholarly papers. To her right lay the entry to the parlor where she and her siblings gathered in the evening to read aloud or to review lessons.

The murmur of voices tugged Bella in that direction. Her fingers on the sheathed dagger, she stopped just inside the doorway. A fire hissed on the stone hearth, warming the room with its scattered chairs and tables. Age-darkened landscape paintings decorated the walls.

Upon their arrival, the cottage had had a musty aura of neglect. Lila and Cyrus had taken the oversized Turkish rug outside to beat away a quarter century of

dust, while Bella had scrubbed every inch of the stone floor. They'd opened all the windows, knocked down the cobwebs, aired out the straw mattresses in the upper bedchambers, and polished the bookcases that flanked the fireplace. They had cleaned until the place took on the fresh smell of beeswax and lye soap.

Today, however, a trace of flowery perfume drifted in the air.

Bella's gaze swept the chamber. In one corner, rainwater leaked slowly into a basin from an unseen hole in the roof. Plop, plop, plop. Then she spied the visitor.

At a small writing desk, the lady sat on a straight-backed chair like a queen on her throne. A mulberry gown trimmed with lace hugged her slender figure. As she turned her head to regard Bella, the elegant bonnet on her coal-dark hair framed a face of delicate loveliness. She was an older woman, though it was impossible to guess her age, for her skin was smooth and lustrous.

A charming smile lit up her countenance. Her eyes were a deep violet beneath arched black brows, and despite Bella's unease, she felt oddly mesmerized. She couldn't look away. Never in her life had she seen anyone so exquisitely beautiful.

"Bella! You're home early!"

Her brother's voice broke the spell. Bella blinked to see that Cyrus stood beside the desk, a quill in one hand and a penknife in the other. Heaven help her, she hadn't even noticed him. His sandy hair was mussed and his shoulders were hunched beneath his blousy shirt, for he hadn't yet come to terms with the spurt in his height that made him tower over his sisters. At times, his awkwardness could make him ill-tempered.

Today, however, he appeared more excited than sul-

len, and the anxiety constricting her heart eased somewhat. Was it possible that he and Lila hadn't landed
themselves in trouble, after all?

Bella gave him an inquisitive look. "What is going
on, my love?"

"Lady Milford was about to write you a note,"
Cyrus said in a tumble of words. "I was sharpening her
pen. She's come from London to call on us. Did you
see her coach?" He glanced out the window, his boy-
ish face aglow with excitement. "Isn't it splendid?"

"Quite." Since the visitor didn't seem to pose an
imminent danger, Bella's fingers fell away from the
hidden dagger. Nevertheless, she felt a deep-seated
suspicion of this stylish stranger. "I don't understand.
Lady Milford, how do you know us? Why have you
come here?"

The woman arose from the desk and glided forward
in a rustle of silk. "I'll answer all of your questions in
due course. In the meantime, I hope you'll pardon my
intrusion. You must be Miss Isabella Jones."

Bella frowned. No one ever used her christened
name. Where had this lady heard it? "I prefer Bella,"
she said stiffly.

Lady Milford inclined her head in a graceful nod.
"As you wish. May I say, Miss Bella Jones, I'm delighted to meet you at last."

The lady extended a slim hand in greeting. Bella
surreptitiously scrubbed her fingers on her skirt before
shaking that pristine, kid-gloved hand. She was keenly
aware of the contrast between them, Lady Milford so
perfectly groomed, and herself with untidy hair and a
belted foreign robe that was soaked by the rain.

She lifted her chin. "What do you mean, *at last*?"

"I knew your father, Sir Seymour, quite a long time
ago, before your family left England." A somber look

turned down the corners of Lady Milford's mouth. "Sir Cyrus has informed me that your father passed away some months ago. Pray accept my sincerest condolences."

Bella inclined her head in wary acknowledgment of the woman's sympathy. How odd to hear her brother called Sir Cyrus. Yet he *had* inherited the baronetcy. The entire situation seemed very peculiar. What could her scholarly father have had in common with such a frivolous female? "How did you know Papa?"

"We were acquainted through a mutual friend—"

Before Lady Milford could expound on the connection, or explain her purpose in traveling to Oxford, they were joined by Bella's sister.

Carrying a large tea tray, Lila glided into the parlor. She was so much the image of a pretty English girl that Bella felt a swell of pride. Unlike Bella, Lila had a natural flair for fashion. She was quite clever with a needle and had altered her native robes into gowns that would not look out of place at Fothergill's Emporium. Today, she wore a dress of spangled sky-blue cotton that fit her slim waist to perfection. Her golden-brown hair was fastened with a blue ribbon that matched her eyes.

Beaming at their visitor, Lila said in a bubbly voice, "Do forgive me, my lady, the water took ever so long to heat."

She set down the tray on the table by the fire; then her eyes widened on her older sister. "Oh, my goodness, Bella! You're sopping wet! Come, let's go upstairs at once and I'll help you change your gown."

Bella reached up to smooth her damp brown hair. Half of her longed to tidy herself as a matter of vanity; the other half—her prideful half—resisted the notion of conforming to the standards of a noble-

woman. A lingering resentment toward the snobs in the shop only made Bella want to dig in her heels all the more.

"I'll sit by the fire," she said. "My garments will be dry in no time."

"But you'll catch a chill," Lila argued. "I'm sure her ladyship won't mind waiting for a few minutes. Cyrus can keep her company."

"Be happy to do so," their brother said, ambling closer to cast a ravenous look at the contents of the tea tray.

"No, my love, I'm fine," Bella said firmly, giving her sister a warning look. She stepped to the best chair, the only one without moth holes in the embroidered seat, and motioned to their guest. "Lady Milford, pray sit down. Lila, if you'll be so kind as to pour the tea."

The girl thrust out her lower lip in a pout. But she obediently took up the rose china teapot and began to fill the cups.

Lady Milford cast a pensive look at Lila before taking a seat and addressing Bella. "Thank you, Miss Jones. I daresay, you strike me as a very practical young woman. So long as you are comfortable, a little dampness won't matter."

"I'm quite comfortable," Bella affirmed, though the truth was, she did feel rather wet and chilled. She took a chair by the fire, arranging her skirt with its drenched hem to take full advantage of the heat. At least the brown fabric served to minimize any mud stains.

China clinked as Lila passed out the cups in saucers. Bella added a crumb of sugar and stirred the steaming tea with a spoon. Questions crowded her mind. Had Lady Milford come to call on Papa? It seemed she'd expected to find him here. But why would she think he was back in England after nearly

thirty years abroad? And why would she travel all the way from London to find out? Why not simply post a letter?

Before she could ask, Cyrus lowered his gangly form onto a stool and said bluntly, "How d'you know our father?"

Lady Milford smiled warmly at him. "Sir Seymour and I met some three decades ago. May I say, with your sandy hair and blue eyes, you resemble him quite remarkably. He was a charming man and an excellent dancer."

Cyrus nearly choked on a gulp of tea. "Papa, a dancer? But he was always out tromping the countryside or digging up antiquities—when he didn't have his nose buried in a book."

"Young men can be very eager to please when they're courting. You see, Sir Seymour hoped to win your mother's hand. Lady Hannah Scarborough was one of the most sought-after beauties of the season."

"Season?" Bella asked in confusion. "Was it winter or summer?"

"The season is always in the spring," Lila piped up. She was flitting back and forth, offering paper-thin slices of seed cake. "It's when the nobility goes to London for parties and balls."

Bella glanced at her sister in surprise. "How do *you* know that?"

"Mrs. Norris showed me drawings in a fashion book." Setting down the plate, Lila turned to Lady Milford and explained, "Mrs. Norris is our neighbor. She's the widow of a vicar, and she used to be invited to a great many parties. *She* said the ladies wear the most splendid gowns. Oh, how I should adore seeing all those pretty dresses."

Cyrus sneaked another piece of cake. "I'd buy you

plenty of gowns if only Bella would let me learn a trade."

"You know that's out of the question," Bella said sharply. They'd had this quarrel many times. Regardless of his young age, Cyrus viewed himself as the man of the house. "You're to focus on your studies."

"Then Lila won't have any new dresses," he said with a trace of sullenness. "So she might as well stop looking at pictures of them."

Lila wrinkled her nose at her brother. "Don't be a spoilsport. Someday I'll go to a ball. I'll dance the night away." Her blue skirt swishing, she whirled around the little parlor as if held in the arms of an imaginary partner.

Bella pursed her lips. Her sister was behaving in far too familiar a manner in front of their guest. Since the conversation had drifted too far afield, she said, "Lady Milford, you claim to have been introduced to our father by a mutual acquaintance. May I ask who?"

"He was a nobleman who shared your father's keen interest in antiquities." Over the rim of her cup, Lady Milford's violet eyes took on a keen look. "Perhaps you remember him. The Duke of Aylwin."

Bella froze with the teacup halfway to her lips. Her throat went bone-dry. *Aylwin!* The fellow was a duke? She could still feel Papa's bony fingers clutching at hers as he'd uttered that name.

"Return to Oxford," he'd gasped out, his face pale from the ravages of illness. "Promise me. Find Aylwin. Find the map. You have half . . . the pharaoh's treasure."

His worsening condition had alarmed her. The cholera had struck him swiftly, and she cared nothing for any treasure, only the need to restore him to

health. "Please, Papa, you mustn't strain yourself. Rest now, and we'll speak of it on the morrow."

But there had been no further opportunity for him to elaborate. In the morning he'd been dead.

"Aylwin," Cyrus said around a bite of cake, crumbs clinging to one corner of his mouth. "Papa never mentioned him to me. What about you, Bella?"

She mutely shook her head. Her heart was thumping very fast. She had kept their father's deathbed revelation to herself. Her brother and sister were only fifteen, and she'd been loath to fill their heads with dreams of treasure maps and a pharaoh's riches. They had no idea she'd been searching for Mr. Aylwin.

And no wonder she hadn't been able to locate the man. Aylwin wasn't a plain *mister*. He was a high-ranking aristocrat. What an amazing twist of fate that Lady Milford knew him. Now, Bella had to find out more without revealing her true purpose . . .

"A duke!" Lila exclaimed. "Does he live in a castle like a prince?"

"One might say so," Lady Milford replied. "Aylwin House in London is as large as Buckingham Palace where the Queen resides."

Lila's eyes grew even brighter. "Oh, my! Have you been a guest of Queen Victoria, too? She looked ever so lovely in her coronation picture! Pray tell, is it true that she's being courted by a prince from Germany?"

Bella wanted no more distracting commentary. She set down her cup with a click. "I'm sure Lady Milford didn't come here to gossip. Lila, Cyrus, do leave us now. I should like a word with our guest in private."

Protests erupted from the twins. "But we haven't finished our tea," Cyrus complained.

"I want to hear more about this duke," Lila added.

"To think that Papa never told us he knew someone who was almost royalty!"

Bella clapped her hands. "That's enough, both of you. Run along this instant. And kindly close the door on your way out."

They continued to grumble, though both reluctantly obeyed. Lila dipped a curtsy to their visitor and then flounced out of the parlor, her nose in the air. Cyrus snagged another slice of cake and followed his sister, shutting the door with a bang.

The fire crackled into the silence. In the corner, rain dripped in slow plops from the leak in the roof.

Lady Milford sat serenely sipping her tea, as if unperturbed by the twins' impolite behavior. Bella wanted to pepper the woman with questions about the Duke of Aylwin. Yet she must proceed carefully. Unlike her siblings, she knew better than to trust the nobility.

Bella released a slow breath. "I must apologize for their chatter, my lady. It has been difficult to teach them proper conduct while living abroad, among people with different customs."

"They are lively children with a keen interest in the world. I find that refreshing." With an enigmatic smile, Lady Milford regarded Bella. "Sir Cyrus mentioned that your mother died shortly after he and his sister were born, and that you raised them."

"Yes. They never knew Mama at all."

"You must have been rather young yourself at the time."

"Fourteen, my lady." Noting a slight arching of the woman's black brow, Bella felt compelled to add, "I was not without resources. My father hired a nurse who stayed with us for a good many years."

A pang stirred in her breast. It had been difficult to

say good-bye to Jaleh. They had all wept copiously, but Bella hadn't been able to afford to bring the old woman with them to England.

Lady Milford leaned forward. "And how are your resources now, my dear? I don't mean to pry, but did Sir Seymour leave you an inheritance? Or is this cottage all that you have left?"

Bella stiffened. "It's enough for us. We do not require fancy trappings."

"Forgive me, I've offended you. Pray consider my interest only as concern from an old friend of the family."

Her expression was so kindly that Bella felt an unexpected urge to blurt out all of her troubles, to unload the burden that had been weighing on her since the death of her father. But this woman was clearly a busybody, and Bella couldn't shake the odd sense of being maneuvered by her for some unknown purpose. It was time that she herself took control of the conversation.

"I hope you'll tell me more about my father's life here in England, my lady. Papa was so involved in studying ancient civilizations that he seldom spoke of his own past." Bella shaped her lips into a polite smile. "This duke . . . you said his name was Aylwin? Why did you think I might have heard of him?"

"The fourth duke was a scholar and an amateur Egyptologist. He engaged your father's assistance in excavating a tomb in Egypt." Lady Milford tilted her head to the side. "Do you truly not remember?"

"Should I?"

"You went to Egypt with your parents, though you could not have been more than five or six years old at the time."

Egypt. Bella had a sudden vision of herself digging in the hot sand, trying to widen a hole that kept refill-

ing, and an older boy laughing at her struggles. Then the fragment of memory vanished, leaving her disconcerted. "My family wandered far afield. We traveled to many different places throughout Asia and the Near East."

Picking up the teapot, Lady Milford refilled Bella's cup and then her own. "Nevertheless, you did live in Egypt for at least a year, I'm certain of it. You see, the Duke of Aylwin's expedition was the talk of the ton. Especially when he was killed in that dreadful attack."

Bella gasped. The news struck like a spear. "The duke is *dead*?"

"Yes, it was a terrible tragedy. He was set upon by grave robbers."

To conceal her shock, Bella turned her gaze to the dancing flames of the fire. If Aylwin had been murdered long ago, her father must have known. So why had he urged her to return to Oxford and seek out the duke?

Perhaps it was just the fever. Papa must have been hallucinating.

Her briefly resurrected hopes burned to ashes. Her father's confused mind had transported him back in time, that was all. He had merely fancied Aylwin was alive again.

Strange, how neither of her parents had ever mentioned the sojourn in Egypt. Had the memory of the duke's violent death been too distressing? Now she would never know. Nor would she ever find the treasure map . . .

Bella released a ragged breath. "I—I'm sorry to hear of it," she murmured, returning her gaze to Lady Milford. "Since he was a friend of Papa's, I should have liked to have met the duke."

A secretive smile touched the woman's lips. "Very

well. If you wish to meet the Duke of Aylwin, I'm certain it could be arranged."

"I beg your pardon?"

"The present duke—the fifth duke—inherited the title from his father. He also inherited his father's devotion to Egyptology, along with a vast array of artifacts that were shipped back to England many years ago."

Bella sat in stunned silence as Lady Milford set aside her cup and arose from the chair. The elegant woman glided to the window to peer out at the rain before turning back to Bella.

"For more than two decades," Lady Milford continued, "his son has devoted himself to organizing the collection. Alas, it is an enormous undertaking. I've long believed that His Grace needs to hire a curator."

"A curator?"

"Indeed, that is precisely why I journeyed to Oxford, Miss Jones. I'd hoped your father might have returned, and that I might convince him to lend his aid to the duke." She tapped her chin with one finger. "However, you seem a practical, intelligent woman. I do believe that *you* might apply for the post."

Bella's mind raced. The opportunity was nothing short of a miracle. Lady Milford could never imagine how desperately Bella wished to gain access to the duke's antiquities. Did Aylwin have the map in his possession? The one that proved Papa's claim to a pharaoh's treasure?

Perhaps it was the *son* that Papa had wanted her to seek out.

She struggled to contain her excitement. "But . . . why would Aylwin hire me? I've little knowledge of Egyptian history."

With a breezy flutter of her fingers, Lady Milford

dismissed the problem as if it were nothing. "You're the daughter of his father's business partner and surely that will be recommendation enough. The rest shall be left to your own resourcefulness."

Turning to the writing desk, she picked up a blue velvet bag that Bella hadn't noticed until now. The woman untied the cords and then reached inside the purse.

Bella paid little heed. She bit her lip, her mind intent on the problem of how to convince the Duke of Aylwin to engage her services. No doubt he would be prejudiced against females, especially one who lacked scholarly credentials. The interview was bound to be even more difficult than her job hunt here in Oxford. Only look at the disdain with which a lowly fellow like Fothergill had treated her.

A sense of urgency filled Bella. She *had* to secure this post. It was the only way to conduct a secret search for the missing map . . .

With a start, she realized that Lady Milford was standing directly in front of her. The woman held a pair of beautiful slippers. The rich garnet satin was frosted with tiny beads that glittered in the firelight.

She placed the shoes on the threadbare rug. "Since His Grace resides in a grand house, you must dress accordingly. Do try these on. If they fit, you may have them on loan for a time."

Bella stared down at the high-heeled slippers. How peculiar that Lady Milford would carry an extra pair of shoes in her purse. Even more peculiar that she'd offer them to Bella. "When would I ever have occasion to wear such shoes?"

"To your interview, of course. Aylwin is a man of high stature and great consequence. You do wish to look your best, do you not?"

Bella despised handouts. But if she were to claim

her half of the pharaoh's treasure, she had no other choice. This duke would not dismiss her as an unkempt Gypsy. He must not!

She bent down to tug off her half-boots. Scuffed and worn, they looked like lumps of coal beside the sparkly slippers. At least her white stockings hid the indelible tribal tattoos around her ankles. Lady Milford might withdraw her help if she were to spy such a foreign oddity.

Bella thrust her stockinged toes into the fancy slippers. At once, a sense of well-being lifted her spirits. The luxurious shoes enveloped her aching feet as if she'd stepped into a cloud. On a surge of vitality, she sprang up from the chair and paced the perimeter of the small parlor, marveling at how comfortable they felt.

"They fit perfectly, my lady. How amazing that we should wear the same size." Bella glanced down, raising her still-damp hem to admire the shoes. "But I fear they're much too fine for a drab spinster like me."

Lady Milford's expression had the satisfied look of a cat that had lapped up a bowl of cream. She stepped forward to lay her hands on Bella's shoulders. "My dear girl, never forget that you've noble blood flowing through your veins. With the proper wardrobe, you'd be the match of any well-born lady."

Bella choked on a dubious laugh. "A lady? Me?"

"Yes, and you'll need an English gown for the interview, too." Lady Milford took several coins from her bag and placed them on a side table. "Consider this a gift to the daughter of an old friend. There should be enough for you to purchase the necessities—and to hire someone to chaperone your brother and sister here while you travel to London."

Aghast, Bella stared at the woman. "I cannot accept your money!"

"You must if you wish to be hired as curator. In return, I've only one request. You must never mention my name to Aylwin. The duke is a proud, reclusive man who dislikes being maneuvered."

Bella felt like the one being maneuvered. It grated on her pride to take funds from this noblewoman. Yet how else was she to gain entry to Aylwin House? "As you wish, my lady."

"And be forewarned," Lady Milford added with a faint, mysterious stare. "Aylwin can be a difficult man. Some have even called him a beast. But never fear, I'll tell you exactly what to say to him."

Chapter 4

Miles Grayson, the Duke of Aylwin, was crouching before a massive granite stela when the doors of the ballroom banged open. The sound of footsteps echoed through the cavernous chamber.

Two sets of footsteps.

A curse hissed through his clenched teeth. In the afternoon sunlight from the wall of windows, he had been focused on the task of deciphering the chiseled inscription on the stela. He was close to identifying an unfamiliar hieroglyph. So close he could almost taste victory.

Now, his concentration had been shattered.

Miles glanced over his shoulder to see who had invaded his sanctum, but the vast collection of statues and other artifacts blocked his view. The servants knew better than to enter here when he was working. The ballroom was forbidden to all but himself.

Tossing his gold-rimmed spectacles onto the sheaf of papers on the floor, he straightened up and peered over a row of stone gods and goddesses. His scowl deepened when he spied the intruders. He should have

guessed their identity—they were two of the silliest, most worthless people in all of England.

His cousin and heir, Mr. Oscar Grayson, wove a path through the maze of ancient relics, his gold-topped cane tap-tapping on the parquet floor. He wore a dandified forest-green coat with a knee-length skirt, a crimson waistcoat with brass buttons, and checkered stirrup trousers. His dark curly hair was trimmed as neatly as his muttonchop whiskers.

A jovial smile tilted his lips. "Oh-ho, we've found you, cousin! Hiding out in this jumble pile, as always!"

Beside him, his wife, Helen, looked like a fashion plate in a rose-pink gown with narrow, ruffled sleeves and an impossibly tiny waist. Her outward beauty of golden hair and creamy skin left Miles unmoved, for he knew too well her shallow vanity. In contrast to her husband's dull-witted features, she had the cunning amber eyes of a cat.

Those eyes skimmed over the loose shirt and black trousers that constituted his work clothes. She glided forward, enveloped him in a cloud of perfume, and smacked an air kiss near his cheek.

"Dear Miles, how wonderful to see you again," she purred. "But we've caught you in dishabille. I trust we're not disturbing you."

"Of course you're disturbing me," Miles said, irritably clapping the dust from his hands. "It's the middle of a workday. I gave strict orders to be left alone."

"Surely that doesn't include your only relations," Oscar said. "Why, you spend every waking moment cooped up in this mausoleum. It would do you well to spare a few minutes for a visit with your kinfolk."

Miles had every reason to doubt their familial affection. They never came to Aylwin House without a scheme in mind. "If you've been gambling again, I

refuse to settle your debts. Nor will I grant you an advance on your quarterly allowance. There, I've saved you the trouble of trying to wheedle me."

Oscar's grin turned sour. "I had no intention of asking for funds. However, now that you bring up the topic, you certainly *could* afford to increase my payment. You, with this great pile of a house and five vastly profitable country estates."

"It shall all be yours someday. Perhaps then you'll be glad that I kept it from being squandered on frivolities."

"Frivolities, bah! We live nearly as paupers on the paltry sum you provide—"

"Now, darling," Helen said with an admonishing touch to her husband's forearm, "don't let yourself be goaded into another tiresome quarrel. That isn't why we came here."

A private look passed between the couple. A look that Miles knew not to trust. "Speak up, then," he snapped. "I'm extremely busy today."

She gave him a winsome smile, her lashes fluttering. "First, allow me to express our great disappointment that you refused the invitation to our musicale last week. Really, Miles, you missed a very lovely evening."

"Listening to the caterwauling of opera singers? God forbid."

"I warned you he wouldn't attend," Oscar said to his wife. "The fellow is a hermit. He has no interest in cultivating friendships." To Miles, he added, "*We,* however, have an extensive circle of acquaintances in society. We're invited to all the finest parties in London."

"And we always do our best to return their hospitality," Helen said. The corners of her mouth turned

downward. "But alas, our town house *is* rather cramped. Had you ever deigned to call on us, Your Grace, you would know that it lacks the space necessary to host a grand ball . . ."

Irked by their inane chatter, Miles stole a glance back at the stela. That unknown symbol nagged at him. Where had he seen it before? He had spent hours searching through Champollion's *Primer of the Hiero-glyphic System* as well as the dictionary he himself had been compiling for over a decade.

All of a sudden, Helen's voice intruded on his thoughts.

". . . holding our ball here at Aylwin House would be so very perfect. Why, look at this magnificent ballroom! It has been sorely neglected for too many years." She spread out her dainty, kid-gloved hands to encompass the long chamber with its hundreds of Egyptian artifacts. "Imagine, if you will, this chamber restored to its former glory, the chandeliers spar-kling with hundreds of candles, the walls draped with mint-green silk, the tall vases of pink roses on pedes-tals, the gentlemen and ladies dancing on the newly polished floor—"

"No!" Miles's thundering voice echoed off the arched ceiling with its painted cherubs and frolicking nymphs. "Absolutely not!"

Helen's eyes widened. "There is no need to shout, Miles. I assure you, I will personally see to all the ar-rangements myself. You won't be inconvenienced in the *least*. All of these"—she cast a shuddering glance at a large statue of the falcon-headed god Horus— "these *things* can be moved elsewhere. To a storage room, perhaps. A team of stout footmen could accom-plish the task in a day."

"I said *no*," Miles enunciated through gritted teeth.

The gall of her, to think she could banish these priceless objects in order to hold one of her inane parties. "Hear me well. There will be no ball at Aylwin House. Nothing will be moved. This chamber shall remain exactly as it is."

"Please, dear cousin, you mustn't refuse," she begged prettily. "Everything can be returned here afterward. The place will be restored to your satisfaction. At least give the matter some thought."

"There is no need for reflection. My decision stands."

The coquetry vanished from her expression and she pushed out her lower lip in a pout. "But this house is overflowing with dusty old relics. Surely you can work in another room for a week or so. Oh, do tell him not to be such a beast, Oscar."

"Don't be such a beast," her husband dutifully repeated, shaking his cane at Miles. "It's a small favor to grant to a family member. You've a hundred other rooms in which to play with all this rubbish."

That did it.

Miles pointed to the arched doorway. "Out. Both of you. *Now*."

"Oh, you're impossible!" Helen exclaimed. "It isn't as if we'd have forced *you* to attend the ball. We *know* how you despise society. But you shouldn't deny *us* the pleasure of entertaining!"

"He's selfish, that's what," Oscar declared. "Aylwin House is my heritage, too. My papa cut his teeth in the nursery upstairs. He was the son of a duke!"

"The second son," Miles clarified. "Now, you'll depart of your own accord or I shall summon a pair of footmen to toss you both out into the street."

He fixed them with a dictatorial stare. They were

like spoiled children. He had learned to handle them with a firm hand. Oscar had always been something of a sniveling brat while growing up, and marrying Helen the previous year had not improved his character. Where before he had merely been demanding, now he had been infected with her social-climbing disease, as well.

The two sulked and complained for another few moments. Then Helen said in a martyred tone, "Come, my darling. We are not wanted here!"

As they retraced their steps through the labyrinth of artifacts, Miles followed close behind. His fingers possessively brushed a granite sarcophagus dating from the Old Kingdom. He didn't trust those two not to damage one of these rare objects out of spite.

Offering a chilly farewell, Oscar and his wife minced down the wide corridor with its massive white marble pillars. They immediately began chattering in low, peevish tones that echoed off the stone walls. Miles watched until the couple disappeared around the corner. He didn't need to hear the conversation to know they were airing their grievances about him. Let them complain; he would not change his mind.

A blasted ball! No doubt the notion had been hatched by Helen. What was it with women that made them so hostile toward the priceless remains of an ancient civilization? His mother had not cared for them, either, preferring to stay in the country until her death ten years ago. Every lady who had ever crossed his threshold had gazed askance at the many Egyptian objects that were scattered throughout the house. Several had even hinted at the need to redecorate in the latest style.

He grasped the door handle. By damn, he'd turn the

key in the lock this time. There must be no more interruptions for the remainder of the afternoon. The tantalizing hieroglyph awaited his decryption, and the
prospect of identifying its meaning filled him with
vigor.

But as Miles began to close the door, he spied a
footman in crimson livery at the end of the long, stately
corridor. The servant was carrying a silver salver and
walking toward the ballroom.

Bollocks, Miles thought, clenching his jaw. Hopefully, it was only a letter. Surely he could not be plagued
with yet another visitor. It was high time the staff was
reminded of their duty in turning away all uninvited
callers.

The carpet muffling his swift steps, he met the footman halfway. "George, I need a word—"

It was then that Miles noticed the woman.

She was creeping down the corridor in a clandestine manner, slipping from pillar to pillar. A gold sash
cinched the waist of a gown the color of deep bronze,
and the wide brim of her straw bonnet formed a semi-
circle around her face, shading her features from his
view. Even as he narrowed his eyes at her, she ducked
out of sight again, apparently flattening herself against
the wall.

He took a step forward. "Who the devil is that?" he
bit out.

George glanced back over his shoulder. "Beg pardon?"

"The woman hiding behind the pillar. She was following you."

The footman's face went as pale as his powdered
white wig. He presented the salver. "Er—you've a
visitor, Your Grace. She was most insistent on an audience. I bade her wait in the antechamber."

Miles snatched up the pasteboard card. The neatly penned letters read *Miss B. Jones.*

The name meant nothing to him. But he had a grim suspicion of her purpose. Over the years, ladies of the ton had used a variety of excuses to worm their way into Aylwin House. One had conveniently sprained an ankle while strolling past the house. Another had claimed to bear a private message from the bailiff on one of his estates. Yet another had purported a friendship with his late mother. Their scheming minds shared one belief: that a bachelor duke must be in want of a wife.

"Shall I send her away, then?" the footman asked rather nervously.

Miles crushed the card inside his fist. "No. I'll deal with her myself."

Flinging the crumpled bit of paper back onto the salver, he stalked down the corridor to her hiding place. The thick carpet muted the sound of his footfalls. Miss B. Jones must not have heard his approach, for she peeked out from behind the colossal pillar.

Her widened gaze lifted to him. The crimped edge of the bonnet formed an oval frame for her features. In an otherwise unremarkable face, her dark blue eyes had the depth and richness of lapis lazuli.

He stopped, curiously stunned. His tongue felt incapable of producing speech. She was no naïve debutante, but a mature woman. For a moment they stared at each other, Miss Jones hugging the pillar and himself struck by the odd impression of a connection between them. He sensed a vague familiarity about her, something deep and mysterious, something that pulled at him.

What nonsense. Aside from her eyes, she wasn't even pretty.

"What are you doing here?" he demanded.

Her gaze flicked to his informal garb. Then she stepped out from her hiding place. "I am on my way to see the Duke of Aylwin. I have an appointment with him."

"Liar. I've no appointments on my schedule today."

"Oh! Surely you're not . . . but perhaps . . . *you* are the duke?" Her cheeks took on a becoming blush. "It's a pleasure to meet you, sir. I'm Miss Jones. Miss Bella Jones."

She dipped an awkward curtsy, then thrust out her hand, not in the limp, delicate manner of a lady, but like a man, brisk and purposeful. He found himself grasping her gloved fingers in his. They felt strong yet feminine, the fingers of a determined woman.

A devious woman.

He released her hand at once. "You were prowling through my home without invitation," he stated coldly. "I've no wish to speak any further with you. The footman will show you to the door."

George discreetly appeared at her side. "This way, miss."

She ignored him. Her blue eyes intent on Miles, she said, "Pray forgive me. I followed your servant only because I feared that you might refuse to see me. I've a matter of great importance to discuss with you."

"You've wasted your time. Leave this house. And never return."

Pivoting on his heel, Miles started back toward the ballroom. The audacity of her manner irked him beyond measure. And those eyes—gazing at him with such boldness. As if *he* were the one at fault for refusing to be duped by her scheme. He hadn't gone more than three steps when her voice called out to him.

"Wait, sir . . . Your Grace! I'm no stranger to your

family. My father was Sir Seymour Jones. He was a colleague of your father's in Egypt."

The bottom fell out of Miles's gut. He turned slowly around to face her again. Disbelief warred with astonishment. Was that why he'd sensed a connection between them? Because they'd met as children?

More than twenty years had passed since that tragic episode in Egypt. He tried to reconcile her features with the hazy memory of the six-year-old girl who had followed him everywhere in the encampment. Bella . . . *Isabella*. That was what she'd been called back then. The child he'd known had had blue eyes, too. But he recalled little else. He'd only been thirteen at the time and prone to ignoring pesky infant girls.

And Sir Seymour! He had seemed a friendly, honest fellow, always patient and helpful whenever Miles asked questions about the excavation of the pharaoh's tomb. He could still picture the man, his bearded face browned by the hot Egyptian sun, his white teeth flashing in a smile.

By God! Miles had naïvely trusted the rascal even after his own father had been murdered by grave robbers. Not twenty-four hours later, Sir Seymour had abandoned him. He had taken his wife and daughter and vanished into the night, never to be seen again.

Miles could still feel the crushing weight of despair and grief at being left alone and fatherless in a foreign country. Even worse was the burden of his own guilt. If not for the quarrel they'd had, his father would never have left the encampment that fateful night. He would never have died . . .

The memory threatened to suck him down into a black hole.

Miles drew a deep breath. He cautioned himself not to take this woman at her word. Her claim might yet

be a trick. A clever ruse concocted for the purposes of ingratiating herself with him.

But if Miss Bella Jones really *was* Sir Seymour's daughter . . .

Then Miles had to find out what she knew.

Chapter 5

"Follow me," the duke snapped.

Bella hastened to comply with the terse command. After being caught in a barefaced lie, she didn't dare risk incurring his wrath again. She half ran to keep pace with his long strides down the corridor. Her fingers clutched at her skirt to avoid tripping on the gown with its myriad stiff petticoats.

With the funds from Lady Milford, she had sent Lila to buy the bronze silk from Fothergill's shop. It had given Bella great pleasure to wear the very fabric that he had deemed too fine for her.

But now she longed for the comfort of her Persian robes. The whalebone corset pinched her ribs and the wide brim of the bonnet acted like blinders on a horse, restricting her vision so that she could only gaze straight ahead at the duke.

Where was he taking her?

She didn't know, but at least he hadn't ejected her from his house. A cautious elation lifted her spirits. She had crossed the first obstacle. She had convinced him to listen to her.

But oh, Lady Milford had not exaggerated. The Duke of Aylwin really *was* a beast. He was an imperious, high-handed autocrat who rejected even the veneer of hospitality. His rude manner only solidified Bella's distrust of the English aristocracy.

She glowered at his broad back. Never once did Aylwin turn around to make certain she was still behind him. He seemed indifferent to her presence as if he were accustomed to having underlings obey his orders at the snap of a finger.

Yet he wasn't quite what she'd expected, either.

On the coach ride to London, she had pictured in her mind an aging dignitary in rich, elaborate garb with a purple robe around his shoulders and a gold scepter in his hand. But Aylwin was no old codger; he was a man in his prime. He resembled a common laborer, all brawny muscles and rumpled dark brown hair. His linen shirt was open at the throat, and the sleeves were rolled up to expose his bare forearms. There was even a smudge of gray dust on his black trousers.

How could she have guessed that *he* was the duke?

The memory of his brown eyes boring into her caused a disturbing quiver inside Bella. The feeling resonated in her depths like an instinctive warning. Aylwin didn't appear to be the sort who could be easily deceived. He looked hard and tough, no one's fool. Yet somehow she had to convince the tyrant to hire her.

Bella followed him through an arched doorway and into an enormous oblong chamber. There, she stopped in amazement. Afternoon sunlight poured through the wall of windows at one end of the room. The formal style included cut-glass chandeliers, gilded wall panels, and an arched ceiling painted with cherubs and nymphs.

But that wasn't what held her attention. It was the contents of the room. Spread out before her lay a vast sea of Egyptian artifacts.

She advanced slowly, turning her head in the restrictive bonnet in order to view every piece. There were many strange figures carved in stone, some of them part human, part animal. Gods with jackal or ram heads. Women with kohl-rimmed eyes and snake crowns. Polished stone boxes that looked like coffins.

Bella reached out to trace the granite hand of a robed man with a curiously long goatee and a tall crown. A sense of wonderment filled her, the same excitement and interest she'd always felt when helping her father explore an old shrine in a jungle or excavate a crumbling monument in the desert: It was as if she stood inside an ancient tomb instead of a grand house in the middle of London.

"Don't touch."

Bella jumped at the gravelly sound of Aylwin's voice in her ear. Her hand flew to her bosom and she whirled around to find the duke standing directly behind her. "You startled me," she chided.

His lips thinned, he regarded her with distaste. "It's that wretched hat. It impedes your vision. I don't know why women wear such impractical nonsense."

Bella had done so because she'd wanted to play the part of a well-groomed English lady. Lila had assured her that the straw bonnet was the very latest style. Bella disliked the wide brim, but Aylwin's rudeness irked her into saying, "I thought gentlemen were trained to offer compliments, not criticism."

"I am no gentleman. Now, you really must take it off."

Before she realized his intent, his hand flashed out to yank on the ribbons tied beneath her chin. He

plucked the bonnet from her hair, pivoted sharply, and dropped the hat onto the head of a tall stone goddess with the face of a lioness.

"There," he said on a note of grim satisfaction. "Now I can see if you really are who you claim to be, *Miss Jones.*"

Shocked, Bella reached up to pat her uncovered hair. She felt exposed and outraged by his imperious action. The place where his fingers had brushed against her throat burned from his touch.

She checked the impulse to grab for the bonnet. How was she to retrieve it without looking like a fool? It was out of her reach, and anyway, she needed to remember that her purpose here was to charm the beast into employing her as his curator.

Nevertheless, the audacity of his action made her seethe.

With effort, she kept her voice modulated. "I am indeed Isabella Jones. Who else would I be? And I fail to see how removing my hat would prove my identity, anyway."

"That remains to be seen. Come with me."

On that cryptic remark, Aylwin wrapped his fingers around her upper arm and pulled her deeper into the labyrinth of artifacts. Bella drew in a breath to object, but a whiff of his alien masculine scent warned her to be cautious. Aylwin was nothing like her openhearted brother or her mild-mannered father. By stark contrast, the duke had an intimidating nature that complemented his superior height and physical strength. In less than ten minutes, he'd proven himself to be harsh, dictatorial, unpredictable. His thoughts were as incomprehensible to her as the strange symbols chiseled on many of the stone relics.

At least she'd had the sense to hide the dagger on

her person. If he tried anything untoward, she would make him very sorry.

But at the moment, he merely escorted her to the wall of windows and released her arm. Planting his hands at his waist, he surveyed her from head to toe and back up again. "Your hair is a middling brown," he pronounced. "Hers was lighter than yours, almost blond."

"Hers? Who?"

"Isabella Jones. Sir Seymour's daughter."

Bella blinked. How could he have known her hair color as a child? Understanding struck in a blinding flash. "Are you saying . . . *you* were in Egypt, too? At the same time that *I* was there?"

He inclined his head in agreement. "I accompanied my father on the expedition and helped out at the work site. Whether or not you were the nosy little girl sneaking around the camp, peeking into everyone's tent, remains in question."

She tried to absorb the news. How amazing to think that she'd met Aylwin already—although he had not been the duke then, only the heir. And she remembered the fragment of a scene that had come to her when Lady Milford had told her about the sojourn in Egypt.

"I was too young to remember very much," Bella said. "I only recall one incident. I was trying to dig a hole in the sand and it kept refilling. I remember hearing a boy laugh at my efforts. Was that you?"

He gave a quick, impatient shrug. "I've no recollection of it. I'm afraid I'll need better proof than that of your identity."

"How do I know *your* memories of *me* are accurate?" she countered. "How old were *you*?"

"Thirteen. And I shall conduct the questioning here.

Tell me, why should I trust that you're Sir Seymour's daughter when your hair color is different?"

"It isn't uncommon for blond hair to darken with age. Surely you know that." But he still looked skeptical, and Bella felt mired in frustration. The duke would never employ her if he believed her to be a liar. It didn't help matters, either, that he had already caught her in one fib. "Your Grace, I fail to see why you'd think I'm pretending to be someone else. What would be the purpose of such a deception?"

He stood before the backdrop of a lofty stone stela. His austerely handsome face appeared chiseled from granite, like one of the fearsome gods on display. "Ladies have a habit of trying to ingratiate themselves with me," he said. "They use trickery in the hopes of deceiving me into marriage. I'll admit your ploy is cleverer than most. It required some research into my family's past."

He believed her to be a husband hunter?

The notion was so absurd that Bella felt a trill of mirth bubble up into her throat. As a little choke of hilarity escaped, his face tightened and she clapped a hand over her mouth. "I'm sorry, I don't mean to laugh. It's just that . . . at my advanced age, I'm too set in my ways to think of taking a husband, let alone *trapping* one. Rather, I came here because . . . because of the connection between our families."

She paused, hesitant to make her application for curator while he looked so ill-humored. Better to flatter him first by asking questions about his Egyptian artifacts. Men always liked to talk about their particular interests. "You see," she went on, "my father died last year and I'd hoped to find out more about his work in Egypt. When I heard that you had inherited many of

the artifacts that Papa helped discover, I thought perhaps that you might show me some of them—"

"By damn," Aylwin broke in with a snap of his fingers. "There *is* a way to confirm your identity. Something I'd nearly forgotten."

"Oh?" A little bemused, Bella took a step toward him. "Do tell. I'm happy to lay your doubts to rest."

His shrewd gaze fixed on her, the duke prowled back and forth. "Sir Seymour's wife fell very ill while in Egypt. Her daughter's nursemaid was a Berber woman who held many superstitious beliefs. She had Isabella's legs inked with symbols designed to ward off the *jnoun,* the evil spirits that bring disease. The markings are indelible. If you are indeed who you claim to be, you should still have those tattoos."

A tremor quaked through Bella. He knew about the strange patterns on her ankles? When she had been old enough to ask, Papa had explained that the tribal woman had only meant to protect Bella from illness. He had led her to believe that the incident had occurred during a journey through Morocco . . .

But apparently it had happened in Egypt. Why hadn't Papa told her the truth?

Aylwin stood waiting, his arms folded across his broad chest. The directness of his stare increased her disquiet. Did he expect her to show him the markings? He must.

The very idea of letting this man look beneath her skirts revolted Bella. Not just for the assault on her modesty, but also because she had never revealed the tattoos to anyone outside her family. At one time, she had considered them a disfigurement. In her youth, she'd attempted to scrub them off until her flesh had turned raw. But the ink went too deeply into her skin.

Now, she seldom spared a thought for the markings. They were simply a part of herself that could not be changed. A hidden secret that no man—not even a duke—had any right to see.

"Yes, the designs are still there," she admitted stiffly. "But you will have to take my word on the matter."

He made a sound halfway between a snarl and a laugh. "Your word? I think not. You will verify your identity here and now—or I will know you to be a charlatan."

The gleam in his dark eyes spoke volumes. He expected her to refuse to comply with his command. The bully wanted to expose her as an impostor, to prove she was a husband hunter like those other women, so that he could toss her out of his house.

His ultimatum set her teeth on edge. But Bella could hardly refuse. If she didn't show him, she would lose any chance to convince him to hire her. She would never have the opportunity to search for the missing map—or to claim her half of the pharaoh's treasure.

"Turn your back," she ordered. "I'll need to roll down my stocking."

The duke cocked a haughty eyebrow, but did as she commanded. He swiveled to face the stone stela with its depictions of life in ancient Egypt. In an aggrieved tone, he said, "Hurry up. I haven't all day."

It was likely the first time that he had ever obeyed a woman, Bella thought tartly. For added privacy, she stepped behind an enormous granite statue of an Egyptian god with a falcon's head. There, she bent down to reach beneath her petticoats. The starched muslin rustled loudly, and she cringed to think that Aylwin must hear it. Filthy dog! Wishing all manner of curses on the beast, she untied the garters on one thigh and rolled the white silk stocking down to her ankle.

Her hand brushed the dagger strapped to her other leg. With the fitted gown, there had been nowhere else to hide it. She could only hope he wouldn't see it.

Letting her skirts drop, she stepped out from behind the statue. Aylwin still had his back to her. But he was hunkered down now, studying the pictorial symbols chiseled into the base of the stone stela. As she watched, he traced one with his forefinger as if attempting to decipher it. Could he read the hieroglyphic language?

Now was not the time to ask.

She cleared her throat. He turned in a crouch and stared pointedly at her lowered hem. His lips curled in a sneer. "So. You've realized the impossibility of deceiving me."

"Quite the contrary." His gloating assumption emboldened Bella. He needed to see that she would not be intimidated. She marched forward and stopped directly in front of him. Grasping her skirt, she lifted the hem slightly and thrust out her foot. "There is your proof."

From her vantage point, she could see the tiny crystal beads on Lady Milford's slippers sparkling in the sunlight. The rich garnet hue of the satin lining contrasted with the deep bronze silk of her gown.

"Fancy shoes for a spinster of such advanced age," Aylwin said.

Bella scowled down at him. Was he teasing? No, he didn't have a humorous bone in his brutish body. "Just look at the markings. They're right above my ankle."

"I can't see them. Your skirts are in the way."

She raised the hem another modest inch or two. "That should be sufficient to confirm that I'm . . . oh!"

Without warning, Aylwin sat back on his heels, took her ankle in a firm grip, and lifted her foot onto his thigh. The action caught Bella off balance. Gasping,

she was forced to steady herself by grabbing hold of his shoulders.

His very broad, very muscular shoulders.

Much to her consternation, she found herself leaning over the duke, so close that she could see each individual strand of his chocolate-brown hair. Her heart thumped against her breastbone as the heat of his skin seeped through the linen shirt. Again, she caught a whiff of his darkly enticing scent.

More startling than anything else, though, was the feel of his callused hands delving beneath her skirts.

Blood rushed through her body. She tried to pull away, but he kept a secure hold on her leg. "Excuse me, sir!" she said, her voice high-pitched. She drew a breath and strived for a firmer tone. "What do you think you're *doing*?"

Aylwin glanced up. His gaze flicked over her, lingering a moment on the low cut of her bodice, which was regrettably in his direct line of sight. The glance sparked a tingly warmth in her bosom that could only be due to acute anger at his boldness.

One corner of his mouth curled up in a half smile that made him dangerously attractive. "I should think it's obvious what I'm doing, Miss Jones. I'm checking your credentials."

With that, he pushed the petticoats up over her knee, exposing her lower leg to his view. Bella clenched her jaw. She didn't like this man. She didn't like him one jot. He was a tyrant who did as he pleased without a care for common decency.

Placating him, however, was a central part of her plan to gain employment in his house. For that reason alone, she forced herself not to move as Aylwin examined the markings on her lower leg. Cupping her ankle, he leaned closer, so close that his warm breath

feathered over her bare flesh. Her limbs went weak and she felt as if she might melt into his lap at any moment. How foolish!

"You've seen quite enough," she said curtly. "There can be no more doubt that I *am* Isabella Jones."

As if she hadn't spoken, he lightly rubbed his fingertip over the inked pattern that encircled her ankle. A corresponding prickle traveled up her leg and magnified her discomfiture. Never had she known that her skin could be so sensitive.

Or that any man could be so irksome.

"Fascinating," he murmured. "Do you know the meaning of these symbols?"

Bella shook her head. Perhaps she'd known at one time. But how was she to remember anything when his invasive touch engaged her entire attention? "Kindly release my foot, sir."

Aylwin ignored the request. "I've seen similar markings on tribeswomen. The circle with the line through it represents the sun and its healing properties." He traced one tattoo, then another. "The inverted semicircles around the stars are meant to ward off the evil eye."

"They ought to ward off impertinent dukes."

Looking up at her again, he let out a full-bodied laugh that made him appear almost . . . charming. A charm that threatened and allured at the same time. But any glimmer of warmth on his face vanished at once. His gaze took on a hard, analytical edge, and she wondered if the wretch had known all along that she was Sir Seymour's daughter.

It didn't matter; Aylwin couldn't possibly guess her game.

Bella gave her leg a hard tug to break his hold. This time, he let her go and she stepped back. Her skirts

tumbled back down, and with both feet planted on the parquet floor again, she felt fortified by the restoration of clear thinking.

At least until she saw the object in his open palm. As he stood up, the ivory-handled blade glinted in the sunlight.

"My dagger!" she cried out.

Angered by his theft, she rushed straight at him. Aylwin raised his arm to hold the weapon high. She stretched up on tiptoe, heedless of the need to press herself to his muscled form, her only thought to retrieve her precious means of defense.

It was no use. The duke had the advantage of his superior height.

She stepped back, drawing in large breaths to cool her ire. How had the beast snatched the dagger from its sheath without her knowledge? "That was a gift from my father. Give it back to me at once!"

Aylwin glanced at her heaving bosom before returning his hard gaze to hers. "No. This is my house and no one here carries a weapon. It shall be returned upon your departure."

He placed the knife atop the stone stela, out of her reach.

Bella fumed. The filthy dog! Only the requirement of her mission stopped her from voicing that slur on his character. She must remember her purpose here. The dagger could be retrieved later.

"Excuse me," she said rigidly.

She marched behind a tall granite statue. In relative privacy, she drew up the saggy stocking and refastened the garters beneath the voluminous petticoats. Residual anger made her fingers clumsy. Aylwin had gained the best of her several times already, with her bonnet, with his peek under her skirts, and with the dagger.

But now it was her turn. She would make him dance to *her* tune. Even if it meant swallowing her pride and—heaven forbid—charming him.

The gravelly sound of Aylwin's voice came from beyond the stone behemoth. "So, Miss Jones, where have you been all these years?"

"Been?" she asked over her shoulder while struggling with one of the ties.

"Your parents left Egypt rather abruptly. It was right after the death of my father. Where did you go?"

"I'm afraid I couldn't say, I was too young to remember." Bella strove for a mild, conversational tone—only for the purpose of her ruse. "We traveled a lot since Papa was very interested in studying ancient civilizations."

"Tell me where you traveled."

"Here and there through Asia and the Near East. My childhood was spent roaming in caravans, camping under the stars, visiting many archaeological sites. And then . . ."

Then the twins had been born and Mama had died and the family had stopped wandering like vagabonds. They had settled in the mountains of southern Persia near the ruins of Persepolis because even Papa had been forced to admit that it would be unwise to transport two infants on long expeditions through harsh and perilous territory.

"And then . . . ?" Aylwin prompted from the other side of the effigy.

Bella swallowed the lump in her throat. She must not reveal that she had a sister and brother living in Oxford under the watchful care of a neighbor, Mrs. Norris. The less the duke knew of her personal life, the better. She would never subject her siblings to his tyrannical nature.

Besides, she didn't want to complicate the story that Lady Milford had advised her to tell. Bella had come to Aylwin House for a specific reason. In order to achieve that purpose, it would be necessary to weave a few falsehoods and half-truths into the tapestry of her tale.

The time had come to hoodwink the duke.

Chapter 6

Impatient for Isabella Jones to reveal more of her past, Miles shifted from one foot to the other. The statue of Horus blocked his view of her. Only the edge of her gown could be seen as she bent over to finish tying her garters. What the devil was taking her so long?

He should have done the task himself.

Miles imagined sliding his hands beneath her skirts, this time all the way up to her thighs and beyond. She had a passionate nature, given her reaction to his seizure of her dagger. How enjoyable it would be to make a game out of tying the garters, caressing her smooth skin with its strangely erotic tattoos, reaching higher to brush her moist folds as if by accident, then using bolder strokes to make her cry out in ecstasy . . .

As heat clenched his loins, he pushed the fantasy from his mind. Lust was a pointless distraction. He wasn't stupid enough to bed a spinster lady, not even one who'd had such an eccentric upbringing. All he wanted from Miss Jones was information about Sir Seymour. To understand why the scoundrel had left Egypt in such a damnable hurry.

Miles had never been able to shake the uneasy notion that foul play had been involved, that someone had paid those grave robbers to kill his father. But if Sir Seymour had been the culprit, what had the fellow gained from it?

He had taken nothing of value when he'd fled into the night with his family. Miles might have been only thirteen at the time, but he'd known the excavation site inside and out. Every artifact had been engraved in his memory. And he hadn't been aware of any quarrel between the two men.

A knot tightened inside him. No, the only quarrel had been between Miles and his father . . .

At that moment, Bella Jones stepped out from behind the stone statue. A ray of sunlight made her blue eyes luminous and gilded a few golden strands in her otherwise mousy brown hair. As she took a deep breath, her bosom lifted, drawing his attention again to its shapeliness.

"You wished to know what happened to me next," she said, her voice somber. "Last year, Papa died of a fever in Persia. I'd always kept busy as his assistant by transcribing his notes and organizing his papers. But after his death, I lacked the means to live on my own."

Surprise pricked Miles. "Your father left you nothing?"

"Very little, I'm afraid. You see, we'd always managed to scrape by through selling a few small antiquities here and there, earning just enough to live on." She bit her lip, glancing out the window before returning her gaze to him. "With Papa gone, that was no longer possible. The local officials wouldn't allow a mere woman to engage in trade. And so, having nowhere else to go, I returned here to England in the hopes of securing employment. This is, after all, my birthplace."

"Have you no family to take you in?"

"None—either they are dead or they want nothing to do with a woman who grew up among foreigners. They're strangers to me, anyway. I'd much prefer to earn my own way."

No wonder she'd carried a dagger for protection. But Miles didn't want to think about her dire circumstances. Her life was no concern of his. All he cared about was information. "It was imprudent of Sir Seymour not to build a nest egg by selling more artifacts. There's a fortune to be made in the antiquities market."

Her lips pursed at the criticism of her father, Bella Jones trailed her fingertips over the statue of Horus. It was the only hint of the fierce woman behind the spinsterish façade. "With all due respect, Your Grace, not everyone has the means to bring such relics as these back to England where they fetch higher sums. My father sold to dealers for much lesser amounts. He was quite happy to do so, for he preferred to study ancient civilizations, not profit from them. And . . ."

"And?"

"And knowing one of those dealers has been quite helpful to me." She dipped her chin and gave him a wide-eyed look. "You see, upon my arrival in London, I went to visit a colleague of my father's, an antiquarian whom we'd met overseas. Mr. Smithers mentioned that he'd recently made your acquaintance."

Miles felt an unpleasant jolt. A dark-haired man with weathered reddish features and flashy garb, Smithers had called here out of the blue three days ago and had talked Miles's ear off before he'd finally ejected the fellow from the house. "You know that windbag? He visited me under false pretenses by claiming to have several rare Egyptian items for sale.

Then he tried to sell me a box of commonplace scarabs."

"Did he? Perhaps he didn't realize you're a premier collector." She tilted her head to one side. "I must confess, Mr. Smithers is the one who suggested that I come here to Aylwin House. He knew that Papa had once worked with your father many years ago. He also told me that you were interested in hiring a curator."

"Bollocks," Miles scoffed. "Forgive me, Miss Jones, but I'm afraid you have it all wrong. Smithers had the cheek to declare that I *needed* help. It was his idea, not mine."

She took a step closer, lacing her fingers together at her waist. "But surely there must be some truth to his observation, Your Grace. You've a great many artifacts, not just here in this room but elsewhere in the house, too. I saw them as I was—"

"Sneaking through the corridors?"

"I had to speak to you, Your Grace," she said firmly. "I couldn't take the risk of being turned away without an audience. Because you see, *I* would like to apply for the post of curator."

Miles's jaw dropped. So that was her game. He had suspected from the start that she had an ulterior motive in calling on him. She'd been far too determined to prove her identity. He had expected her to play on her father's connection to his family and beg for an artifact or two, something that she could sell for money on which to live.

But this? Surely there could be no fate worse than hiring a talkative, meddlesome female who would distract him from his work. A woman who gazed at him with the biggest, bluest eyes he'd ever seen.

Irked by that direct stare, he prowled back and forth.

"I'm sorry, but Smithers misled you. There *is* no job of curator to fill. I've always worked alone."

She fell into step beside him. "Have you organized all these artifacts? Do you have a complete written description of every piece in the house? Have you made a copy of the symbols carved on each relic? Those are all tasks that I can accomplish on your behalf."

He hadn't completed those chores and it would be useful to have them done—not that he intended to tell her so. "Don't be ridiculous. Employing you is out of the question. What do you even know about Egyptian history?"

"I know quite a lot about other ancient civilizations. That will give me a unique perspective. The rest I can learn." She stopped pacing and folded her arms. "Besides, I acquired many useful skills while assisting my father at his work. I know how to keep catalogues. I can copy paperwork and organize your writings. And I promise to be as quiet as a mouse. You'll hardly even know that I'm here. If it pleases you, I'll work in a different room so that I won't disturb you."

He bit back a harsh laugh. Bella Jones would disturb him all right. One look into those lapis lazuli eyes foretold trouble. He needed to eradicate the feel of her soft skin and shapely legs from his mind. His every instinct warned him to eject her from his house at once.

And yet . . . he had not completed his investigation into Sir Seymour. Miles itched to question her further, to pursue additional information about her father. There might be some nugget of truth that could be coaxed from her memory, something that would close the door on that terrible night once and for all.

Something that would ease the weight of his own guilt.

Her hand came down on his sleeve, a light touch that jolted him nonetheless. "Please, Your Grace, I shall be the most dedicated servant on your staff. At least allow me a trial period of a fortnight in which I might prove myself—"

"Fine," he growled, stepping back so that her hand dropped from his forearm. "A fortnight and then I'll reassess your usefulness." That ought to be time enough to find out what he needed—and then he would send her packing.

Her lips curved into a pretty smile that lit up her face. "Thank you, sir. You won't be sorry, truly you won't."

He was already sorry. Especially when his gaze dipped to the shadowed valley between the mounds of her breasts. "Run along and see Witheridge," he said gruffly. "You can't work while dressed like that. You'll need the proper garb." Hopefully, a drab costume that covered her up to the chin.

"Witheridge?"

"The housekeeper." He gave an impatient wave of his hand. "And don't return to this chamber until tomorrow morning at nine sharp."

Miss Jones nodded and made a move to depart, then turned back. "Might I . . . stay here at Aylwin House? A small room in the servants' quarters would be sufficient. It would be so much more convenient for working, you see."

She held her head high, and it struck Miles that she likely didn't have a place to live. Dammit! He didn't want her here as a permanent fixture, underfoot at all hours, disrupting the peace that allowed him to focus on his work.

He clenched his jaw. "Tell Witheridge to put you in

the east wing. Now for pity's sake, get out and leave me alone!"

His thundering delivery didn't appear to dismay Miss Jones in the least. Instead, she merely gave him that bright-eyed smile again and curtsied almost as an afterthought before turning around to make her retreat through the maze of artifacts.

Miles moodily watched until she disappeared through the arched doorway. Then he glanced down at the hieroglyph he'd been working on earlier, but found that he had lost the concentration required to solve it. Rather, he craved to unravel the mystery of Isabella Jones.

He had sensed all along that she was maneuvering him to her own purposes. And he now understood why. She was destitute and in need of employment. Nevertheless, he despised being manipulated—especially by a woman.

Perhaps the crux of his irritability was that she stirred his desires. Several weeks had passed since he had visited a certain discreet house in Covent Garden where he could take his pick from a host of nameless beauties. He should go there again. Very soon.

Yet he would prefer to bed Isabella Jones.

Not that *she* was any great beauty. But she had a bold vitality that gave her charm. Blue eyes big enough to drown a man. And slim, tattooed legs that lent her an aura of the exotic. How he had relished stroking her soft skin, tracing the delicate patterns that made her unique from any other woman he'd ever known. He had wanted to slide his hand higher, to explore her hidden depths . . .

Miles raked his fingers through his hair. Seduction was out of the question. One didn't seduce virgins—

and she was certainly that. The shock on her face when he had touched her leg had not been feigned. For that reason alone, he needed to purge her from his thoughts.

It was a difficult task when the signs of her presence lingered here. That damned bonnet still dangled atop the statue of Sekhmet, the lion-faced goddess of war. He could still detect a trace of her feminine scent, something light and intoxicating, alien to the familiar odors of dust and ancient stone. He plucked the dagger from the top of the granite stela and balanced it in his hand. From the carving on the ivory hilt, it appeared to be Persian.

Miles tossed it down onto his papers. The weapon would have to be secured someplace safe. He didn't put it past Isabella Jones to slide the blade between his ribs in a fit of anger over a grievance.

His jaw clenched, he crouched down in front of the stela and absently traced the unknown hieroglyph. What the devil had he done in hiring the woman? Ferreting out information about her father didn't require him to lodge her under his roof. He should have bombarded her with questions instead of allowing her to cajole him. Now he was stuck with an interloper in his sanctum for the next two weeks.

Or not.

He mulled over a possible solution. By God, if he could be quicker about finding out from her what he wanted to know, then the problem would be solved. He could oust her from Aylwin House and resume his well-ordered life so much the sooner.

A sudden brightness lured Bella from the depths of slumber. She cracked open her eyes to see the hazy outline of a figure drawing back the blue brocade draperies from a wall of windows.

Disoriented, she raised her head from the feather pillow and blinked to focus her vision. The blue and yellow décor and the fine furnishings momentarily confused her. Where was the tiny bedchamber where she and Lila slept? Where were the moth-eaten beige curtains and the little washstand with its chipped porcelain bowl?

Then the events of the previous day returned in a flood of lucidity. She had left her sister and brother in Oxford under the care of a neighbor. She had spent the night in London in a room large enough to swallow her entire cottage.

Approaching the canopied bed, the figure materialized into a sturdy, brown-eyed girl with a freckled face and red hair that peeped out from beneath her white mobcap. She wore a crisply ironed apron over her black gown.

"'Tis a fine morning, indeed," she said, bobbing a curtsy. "Mrs. Witheridge said ye was to be awakened at the dot o' seven. So's ye can be ready to help the duke."

Aylwin! Bella was to meet with him for instructions at nine o'clock.

A buzz of excitement jolted her fully awake. Her plan had worked. She had convinced the duke to employ her. And today, if the opportunity presented itself, she could start her search for the missing treasure map.

She sat up and threw back the covers. "Thank you ever so much for the reminder. Pray, what is your name?"

"'Tis Nan. I'm to be yer maidservant."

"My servant? Why?"

"I'm to help ye ready yerself. I brung yer gown and hot water for washin'. 'Tis in the dressin' chamber."

Bella swung her feet out of bed and shivered from

the chill in the air. Though it was late May, the huge room held the night cold. "But I'm in the duke's employ. Doesn't that make *me* a servant, too?"

"I dunno about that, miss," Nan said doubtfully. "Yer a lady and Mrs. Witheridge bade me wait on ye." She scurried to fetch a pair of slippers from the floor. Bending down to slip them onto Bella's feet, she gasped. "Oh! Yer legs!"

Bella realized that the tattoos were visible beneath her nightdress. She scrambled quickly out of bed, but the hem of her nightgown was a bit too short to hide the marks. Ruefully, she looked down and surveyed the inked patterns just above her ankles. "They're rather unsightly, I'm afraid. The designs were placed there by my native nursemaid when I was a little girl visiting in Egypt."

Nan's eyes were wide as saucers as she took another peek at the tattoos. "Cor! Did it hurt? Was there needles used?"

"To be honest, I don't remember. I was too young."

"Well!" Nan exclaimed, helping Bella into her old green wrap. "Them marks took me by surprise, they did. But I daresay they're handsome. Like bracelets round yer ankles."

The words warmed Bella's heart. "That's kind of you to say so."

Nan didn't smile back; instead, her coppery eyebrows lowered in a troubled look. "Mr. Hasani has such a mark, too, on the back of his neck. But that one gives me a fright, it does."

"Who is Mr. Hasani?"

"The master's valet. He's a foreigner from Egypt." She glanced around as if the walls had ears and continued in a lowered tone, "*His* mark looks like an eye . . . an eye watching ye from the back of his head."

Bella's skin prickled. "Don't be silly. No one can see out of a tattooed eye."

"If ye say so, miss."

But Nan looked unconvinced. As the maid knelt by the hearth to clean out the ashes, Bella headed into the dressing chamber to perform her morning ablutions. How interesting to learn that Aylwin had a manservant from Egypt. She hoped to meet the fellow, to see the tattoo that had so alarmed the maid. She herself didn't believe for a moment that it had supernatural properties. Just as she knew that her own skin markings lacked the power to ward off disease. After all, she'd had her share of minor illnesses.

Standing at the washstand while splashing water on her face, Bella had a vivid memory of the duke explaining to her the significance of those symbols. He had caressed the marks with his fingertips. He had bent his head close to her leg, so close that his warm breath had feathered over her skin. The mere thought of it caused an irresistible contraction deep in her core.

No other man had ever affected her that way. Of course, no other man had ever lifted her skirts, either. Aylwin had a virile quality that he'd used deliberately to intimidate her. He had stolen her dagger, a fact that still infuriated her. He was a cad and a despot, and she looked forward to the moment when he would be forced to hand over Papa's share of the pharaoh's treasure.

Lying alone in her darkened chamber the previous night, she had tossed and turned for a long time, mulling over every aspect of their encounter. The Duke of Aylwin was rude and blunt and arrogant. He had snarled and shouted at her, and paced the floor like the beast that he was.

But she'd had the best of him. And he didn't even know it.

She had lied through her teeth to get him to hire her.

Recalling those falsehoods, Bella reached for a linen towel to dry her face. She had never met Mr. Smithers. If ever the man had traveled overseas as a dealer in antiquities, she didn't know about it. Lady Milford had instructed her to say those things. For some reason, the woman had gone to great lengths to pave the way for Bella.

No, for her father.

Lady Milford had admitted that she'd originally come to the cottage in Oxford to tell Papa about the position of curator. Bella still didn't understand why. Had Lady Milford nurtured an affection for him all these years? If they were friends, why had Papa never mentioned the woman?

Regardless of the reason, it seemed an excessive action for Lady Milford to take. Perhaps it was due to some sort of camaraderie between aristocrats. With a sigh, Bella gave up trying to understand the eccentricities of the nobility.

But she didn't regret the scheme to dupe Aylwin. Not one whit.

Return to Oxford, Papa had gasped out on his deathbed. *Promise me. Find Aylwin. Find the map. You have half the pharaoh's treasure.*

Bella swallowed past the constriction in her throat. Now that she'd met the duke, and had seen for herself how cold and callous he was, she had a strong suspicion that he had cheated Papa out of his rightful share of the pharaoh's treasure. It made her all the more determined to find the map and prove her case.

Chapter 7

Bella was too edgy to do more than pick at the breakfast of toast and hot chocolate that Nan had brought on a silver tray from the kitchen. By the time the ornate gilt clock on the mantel had chimed the hour of eight, she was ready to start work even though there was still an hour left before the appointed time.

She checked herself in the pier glass one last time and turned around to view herself from all angles. The marine-blue gown provided by Mrs. Witheridge had a high neckline and long sleeves. Bella's reflection appeared sober and efficient, especially with her hair drawn back in a severe bun. How had Aylwin disparagingly described the color? *A middling brown.*

Pooh on him. Little did he know, it would serve her purpose to look ordinary, unremarkable, inconspicuous. To be the sort of female that no one noticed. By blending into the background, she would avoid attracting attention while she poked through Aylwin's possessions.

She left the dressing room to find Nan plumping the pillows on the large bed with the sky-blue canopy.

"Does His Grace have a library?" Bella asked. "I should like to see it before I begin work. If you don't mind, that is."

"Straightaway, miss. 'Tis easy to get lost in this grand house."

They left the bedchamber, the maidservant allowing Bella to precede her out the door. Their footsteps echoed through a long corridor with landscape paintings and myriad closed doors on either side.

"Are these *all* bedchambers?" Bella asked, boggled by the thought. "Do the servants sleep here?"

Nan giggled. "Oh, nay, 'twouldn't be fitting! Our rooms are in the attic. The east wing is reserved for noble guests like ye."

Bella decided that the English must have a caste system like the one in India, where a person was born into a certain position in life. That must be why Aylwin had put her on this floor even though she was his employee. Growing up abroad, she hadn't thought much about her father's title or her own blue blood. She had considered herself to be no different from the local peasants who labored for a living. Her only permanent home had been a stone hut in the mountains where she'd had to cook over an open fire and fetch water from a nearby stream.

Never had she ever imagined staying in a palace like this one.

Nan rattled on, "I heard tell that before the old duke died, he hosted many a grand ball here at Aylwin House. There was visiting lords and ladies in every one o' these bedchambers. I fear 'tis rather dull now, for no one comes to stay anymore."

Having arrived at a marble staircase, Bella placed her hand on the carved newel post. "So I'm all alone here? Mine is the only occupied room on this floor?"

"Aye." Nan's brown eyes widened in a look of dawning alarm. "Perchance did ye hear strange noises last night? There's some that say the east wing is haunted . . . by spirits."

Bella hid a smile. She didn't want to offend the girl by poking fun at her gullible nature. "I assure you, the place was quiet as a tomb. Now, why don't you help me remember my way around? I certainly don't wish to resort to leaving a trail of bread crumbs!"

As they headed down the stairs and through several more corridors, navigating twists and turns along the way, Bella paid close attention as the maidservant pointed out statues and busts on pedestals and other objects that could serve as landmarks. Many of them were smaller versions of the ancient Egyptian artifacts in the ballroom. As they passed through the entry hall, there was even an obelisk that towered toward the glass-domed ceiling.

They arrived at an open doorway framed by gilded woodwork. " 'Tis the library, miss. Around the corner and up the stairs is the ballroom where the master works most days." Nan pointed the way. " 'Tis easy to find, ye'll see."

With a murmur of thanks, Bella headed into the library. She would have to hurry; surely less than half an hour remained before her appointment with Aylwin. Yet the splendor inside took her breath away and she paused a moment to admire her surroundings.

In all of her travels, she had never seen so many books in one place. The huge room had tables for writing, comfortable chairs where one might curl up and read, and two enormous cream marble fireplaces at either end. The dark oak shelves held thousands of leather-bound volumes, and she longed for the leisure to peruse each and every one of them. In addition, a

small staircase led up to a narrow walkway that circled the walls and allowed access to the upper shelves.

She had come here for a purpose, to find a particular volume, but the sheer abundance of books overwhelmed her. How was she to know where to begin her quest?

"May I offer my assistance?" spoke a melodious voice.

Bella whirled around to see a short, stocky man standing in an alcove behind her. A loose white robe fell to his knees over a pair of dark trousers. He was middle-aged and balding with a laurel of salt-and-pepper hair, swarthy skin, and a broad, clean-shaven face.

His dark eyes were fixed on her. He appeared to be studying her as keenly as she was him.

She guessed his identity at once. "Hello, are you by chance Mr. Hasani?"

The duke's Egyptian valet pressed his palms together and made a slight bow of acknowledgment, though not low enough for her to spy the tattoo on the back of his neck. "You must call me Hasani, no mister," he said, a slight foreign accent lending a musical quality to his voice. "And you must be Miss Jones. His Grace informed me of your arrival."

She could only imagine Aylwin's withering description of her. His reluctance to hire her had been obvious. She still wasn't quite sure why he had conceded. Perhaps he'd merely wanted cheap labor for a fortnight. "I'm to help him with the cataloguing of his artifacts and any other tasks he might require."

"I see. He met you in Egypt many years ago."

"Yes, although I was just a little girl then. My father was Sir Seymour Jones, a noted archaeologist. He worked with Aylwin's father."

Hasani gave her a charming smile. "Ah, you are an old friend of the family, then. I am at your service. Were you seeking a particular book here?"

"I was hoping to find a comprehensive history of ancient Egypt. Something that would give me a good overview." Bella glanced wryly at the towering shelves of books. "But I confess to being rather stunned by the size of this library. I don't know where to begin my search."

"I am very happy to show you. Follow me, if you please."

He glided across the vast room, weaving a path through the maze of tables and chairs. Bella fell into step behind him. Intensely curious, she seized the chance to study his sturdy back, but regrettably, his robe had a high collar that concealed his neck. Nothing could be seen of the tattoo that had alarmed her maid.

Hasani stopped at a section behind a desk that held writing paraphernalia and a globe of the world. "His Grace owns many books written about my homeland, including a history written by the Roman, Pliny the Elder. But I believe there is one in particular that will be most helpful to you."

He bent down to retrieve a book from a lower shelf. As he did so, his collar shifted and she saw it: a single eye inked on the nape of his neck. A black brow topped the almond-shaped eye, while two lines swirled from the bottom.

Bella felt an involuntary shiver. She had to admit the tattoo had an eerie quality, for the pupil did seem to be staring straight at her.

Why did he have it? What was its meaning?

She wanted to ask, yet he was a stranger—a foreigner—and she didn't wish to offend him. There

were cultural taboos in much of the Near East, and Hasani might consider it an invasion of his privacy to be asked a personal question by a woman.

Besides, she liked his friendly, talkative manner, and she didn't want to jeopardize that. At some point, he might be a source of information in finding the missing map.

Hasani stood up, a thick tome in his hands. If he had noticed her scrutiny of his neck, he gave no sign of it. Instead, he reverently placed the book on the desk and opened it to an illustration of three triangular stone structures against a desert setting. "These are the great pyramids. They were built many thousands of years ago."

Bella stepped closer to examine the sketch. A robed man on a camel was dwarfed by the edifices. "How very enormous they look. Are these tombs?"

"Yes, they were the final resting place of several pharaohs. Under the rule of various dynasties, Egyptians were the first to discover the foundations of mathematics and science, arts and architecture." Hasani elevated his chin with pride. "My people could read and write when the rest of the world was still living in caves."

"That is quite a remarkable history," she said. "I look forward to learning more about it."

She reached for the volume, but Hasani picked it up first. "There is no time to examine it now, Miss Jones. With your permission, I will have the book delivered to your chamber. His Grace will be very angry if you arrive late to your meeting with him."

"Oh! Of course. It must be nearly nine already."

"Quite so, I will show you the way at once."

As they headed out of the library, Hasani cast her a sideways glance, his lips quirked in a rather sly smile.

"I have not been entirely forthcoming with you, Miss Jones. Perhaps it will surprise you to hear that this is not our first meeting."

Bella blinked at his olive-skinned features. She had been introduced to a bevy of the servants the previous afternoon while visiting with Mrs. Witheridge, the chatty housekeeper, downstairs in the servants' hall. But she didn't remember Hasani. "Oh?"

"You were a little girl when last I saw you, perhaps this high." He held out his hand, palm-down, at the height of his waist.

As they started up a grand staircase, Bella caught a startled breath. "So you knew me in Egypt! I should have guessed. Of course, the duke would have engaged your services there."

"Yes, I traveled to England many years ago. It is my home now." He paused, then added musingly, "So you do not have memories of your time in Egypt?"

She shook her head. "I'm afraid not. Nevertheless, I feel that I should apologize for not recognizing you."

"Bah, it is no matter. Perhaps some things are best forgotten. In particular, the violent murder of His Grace's father at the hands of grave robbers. They slit his throat and left him to die alone in the desert." With that unsettling statement, Hasani waved a hand toward an arched doorway. "There is your destination, and so we must part ways now. Good day, Miss Jones."

Bella watched the man stride away down the corridor, holding the history book that he had selected for her. She felt disappointed to have their conversation cut short. She would have liked to talk to Hasani further, to question him about Egypt. He was an interesting man, charming and helpful.

Unlike his master.

Her stomach clenched with nervous anticipation. At

last she would commence her quest by gaining access to Aylwin's private collection of antiquities. She smoothed her palms over her gown and then did the same to her tight bun, checking for any stray strands. She must look cool and efficient, a trustworthy assistant who could be permitted to work without supervision.

It was time to meet the beast in his lair.

Chapter 8

Bella found the duke in the exact spot where she had left him the previous day—hunkered down in front of the tall stone stela with the strange hieroglyphic carvings on it. Because her fine slippers had made no sound on the dusty parquet floor and the new marine blue gown no longer rustled without all the petticoats, he didn't hear her approach.

Or perhaps it was just that he was so engrossed in his work.

She paused to study him. He sat perched on a stool, angled to one side, affording her a view of the white shirt that stretched across his broad shoulders. He gave his full attention to the pile of papers in his lap. Much to her surprise, he wore a pair of gold-rimmed spectacles.

Beneath a tumbled lock of coffee-brown hair, his brow was furrowed in concentration. As his forefinger inched down the sheet, she could see that instead of words, there appeared to be symbols drawn on the paper like the pictorial writing on many of the artifacts.

She was struck by the notion that Aylwin seemed

less fearsome today. Perhaps it was the eyeglasses that somehow humanized him. Or the halo of sunlight that bathed his starkly handsome features. Whatever the reason, he looked like an ordinary man intent on analyzing a problem.

Then he shattered the illusion by snapping over his shoulder, "Come closer, Miss Jones. I won't bite."

Peeved that he'd been aware of her scrutiny, Bella walked forward and stopped in front of him. She was determined to be polite for the sake of her quest. "It would have been rude of me to interrupt your thoughts. My father often had that same expression of absorption while working on his notes. He preferred me to wait until he'd finished."

Aylwin swiveled on the stool, yanked off the eyeglasses, and glared up at her. As his keen brown gaze swept over her new garb, his scowl deepened. Bella braced herself for a misogynistic remark. She kept her expression calm and composed, and silently vowed to use diplomacy to deflect any criticism.

"What sort of notes did he keep?" Aylwin asked.

"My father?" she said, thrown by the question. "Well . . . at the end of each day, he recorded his thoughts and observations about whatever site he had been exploring. He wrote fast and his penmanship left much to be desired. Sometimes, when he filled up an entire volume, he would have me edit it and recopy it for him."

"You traveled with Sir Seymour for a good many years. You must have scores of these notebooks. Where are they now?"

Bella had no wish to reveal that her father's papers were still in crates at the cottage in Oxford. It was none of Aylwin's business. "They're in storage until such time as I can work on them again."

"You're still editing them?"

She hesitated to voice her future plans to this man. Yet perhaps it would make him see that she had a true interest in ancient civilizations. "Actually, I hope some-day to combine the best parts of his journals into a book suitable for publication. Scholars in particular would be fascinated to read about Papa's travels to re-mote lands. He knew a great deal about sites that are rarely visited by Westerners."

The duke set aside his papers and rose to his con-siderable height. "I'm curious. Did he keep a journal about his time in Egypt?"

As Bella tilted up her chin to meet his gaze, her heart skipped a beat. Aylwin had a dominant mascu-line presence that ruffled her composure. His eyes were like dark mirrors concealing his thoughts. To make matters worse, his probing questions held an un-dercurrent of intensity that she didn't quite understand.

"If Papa did keep such a journal, I never saw it. I've no idea what happened to his early writings—or even if he was making notes at that time. Why do you wish to know?"

"Because if you had read them, then at least you would have a rudimentary knowledge of Egyptian his-tory. But it appears you're a rank beginner."

He had that haughty look again. Bella privately dubbed it the Ducal Stare. "With all due respect, Your Grace, I never told you otherwise. And perhaps it will please you to know that I've taken the liberty of bor-rowing a history of ancient Egypt from your library so that I might begin to educate myself."

"How very reassuring," he said with heavy sarcasm. "Now, you've wasted enough of my time. I'll show you where you'll be working." As if she were a dog to be brought to heel, he snapped out a command. "Come."

Then he brushed past her and strode toward the door.

Following in his wake, Bella tamped down a blaze of irritation. Had no one ever taught him manners? She glowered at his muscled shoulders, the tapered waist and hips, the long legs encased in black trousers. Apparently he believed that his exalted stature as a duke granted him the right to lord over lesser beings. But these were not feudal times. She was an independent woman, not his serf. If he meant to intimidate her, he would not succeed.

He preceded her out into the spacious corridor, the same one where he'd caught her the previous day hiding behind one of the massive white pillars. Clutching the blue serge of her skirt, Bella hurried over the crimson carpet runner until she caught up to him. "Your Grace, I would very much like to familiarize myself with the scope of your collection. It would be helpful if you pointed out all the rooms where you keep any Egyptian items."

He aimed the Ducal Stare at her again. "No. You're not to wander about at will and poke into places where you don't belong."

She strove for levity. "I fear it will be difficult *not* to wander to some degree. There's a very real danger of me becoming lost in a mansion of this prodigious size."

"Then I would advise you to learn your way around very quickly. Or you will be out on your ear."

Bella pursed her lips. His cold manner didn't bode well for her mission. She needed to determine a likely location where he might store an antique map. She tried again. "But if you were to take me on a tour of the house, then—"

"There's no need. You'll be spending all of your working hours in the blue drawing room."

"The drawing room?" Bella instantly envisioned a chamber filled with sketch pads and easels, pencils and paints. How peculiar. What did he expect her to do in there? Draw pictures of Egyptian statues? Should she confess to him that artwork was not her strong suit?

As she pondered the dilemma, the duke turned abruptly in the passageway, pulled open a large door, and strode inside.

Trailing behind him, Bella found herself in a gigantic, dim-lit room with pale blue walls and a high ceiling. Only a few slivers of sunlight beamed past the dark blue draperies that covered the tall windows. There were no drawing materials in sight. Nor was there any sign of conventional furnishings like tables or chairs.

Instead, the entire room was piled high with crates and statues, vases and jars, and a thousand other bits of miscellany. The musty odors of dirt and stone permeated the air. Despite the gloom, she could see that the place was a considerable mess in comparison to the neat rows of stately sculptures in the ballroom. These items were smaller and many of them appeared to be broken.

Her heart sank. If there was a map in this chaos, it would take months, or even years, to find it. And Aylwin might well eject her from the house after a fortnight.

Or perhaps sooner. Already he seemed to regret hiring her.

"Your assignment is to catalogue every item in this chamber," the duke said, his stern gaze fixed on her. "I want a written assessment as to what is necessary for its restoration. And mind, everything here has historical value. You are to toss nothing whatsoever into the rubbish bin. Is that clear?"

"Yes, I'm aware of that from working with my father. Even the smallest shard of pottery can reveal clues as to how people lived in the past."

"Speaking of which, you can begin by sorting through those boxes of damaged pottery over there."

Aylwin pointed to a stack of wooden crates by the windows, then turned on his heel as if to depart. Desperate for information, Bella stepped into his path. She had to keep him talking. "May I open the draperies, Your Grace?"

He gave her a withering stare. "Of course. That goes without saying."

He made a move to brush past her, but she held her ground and blocked the doorway. "Perhaps it seems a foolish question, but I only wanted to be certain that the sunlight won't damage any of these relics. Documents, for instance. Did the Egyptians only chisel their writings on stone? Or did they also use some sort of paper?"

"Papyrus," he said curtly. "It was made from reeds. But you won't find any such papers in this room."

"Ah. Then you keep the papyrus elsewhere in the house."

His dark eyebrows hitched in a frown. "I've a collection of papyri, yes, mostly funeral rolls from tombs along with fragments of other documents."

"How fascinating that they've survived for thousands of years." Hoping that a humble plea might soften him, Bella laced her fingers together just below her bosom. "Might I have your permission to view the . . . papyri sometime?"

His moody gaze flitted to her breasts, which were covered by the modest gown with its high neckline. If anything, his expression grew even more hostile as he returned his eyes to hers. "Absolutely not. The papers are extremely fragile. No one touches them but me."

"I needn't touch them, Your Grace. My father taught me to take precautions around old documents. And just seeing the papyri would be an important lesson in ancient Egyptian history. Where are they kept?"

He cocked an eyebrow as if suspicious of her persistence. "In a storeroom in the west wing. It is an area of this house that you are strictly forbidden to enter."

"Forbidden?"

"You heard me."

Aylwin took a step so that a mere hairsbreadth of space separated them. His dark eyes revealed a fiery intensity that took Bella by surprise. Her heart thumped in response, and a sudden breathlessness made her giddy. She told herself to back away, but felt too transfixed to move. Especially when he lifted his big hand to cup her face, his thumb stroking over her cheek so that her whole body tingled.

He traced the curve of her lips with a featherlight fingertip. "The ducal apartments are situated in the west wing. It is *my* domain." Aylwin lowered his voice to a silken growl. "Heed me well, Isabella Jones. Should you dare to set even one pretty toe in my private quarters, I will presume that you have come to share my bed."

Late the following morning, Bella reached into a crate and extracted a shard of pottery from its nest of straw. Cradling the piece in her palm, she studied it by the filtered sunlight from the window. The faded black lines of a painted design allowed her to match it with a particular group of pieces.

She bent down to add it to one of the many small piles that dotted the dusty wood floor. Organizing the jumble of shattered bits was like assembling a puzzle, and Bella had found the work an enjoyable challenge.

After combing through numerous crates, she had identified a total of fifty-two broken terra-cotta vessels. When all the pieces of a specific pot or jar had been found, then she would carefully transfer them to smaller boxes in case Aylwin wished to have them glued back together someday.

Aylwin.

The mere thought of him made her quiver . . . with righteous indignation. She had not seen the duke since the previous morning when he had brought her here to this chamber only to unleash his beastly threat. Bella had tried her best to forget the incident. He would not drive her away from this house, not even by giving her the most menial of tasks.

She had worked diligently all day at sorting pottery, had eaten dinner on a tray in her room, and had spent the evening studying the book about ancient Egypt. But the moment she'd blown out the candle at her bedside, the memory had returned to haunt her: the carnal heat in Aylwin's eyes, the crowding of his large body against hers, the warmth of his callused fingers on her face—most especially her lips.

Even more outrageous had been that ultimatum. *Should you dare to set even one pretty toe in my private quarters, I will presume that you have come to share my bed.*

With that, Aylwin had sauntered out of the drawing room. Too late, a dozen retorts had leaped to her tongue. But she'd caught herself in time. To hurl insults at his departing back would have put her job in jeopardy. The Duke of Aylwin was not a man to suffer disrespect from an employee. Even if it was well deserved.

"Filthy dog," Bella muttered now, going to the crate to select another fragment of pottery.

She had resolved to labor diligently for a few days to prove her worth to him and to calm any suspicions he might have as a result of her questions. It wouldn't do to play her hand too quickly. But she was itching to search the storeroom where he kept his collection of ancient papyri. It was the most logical location to begin looking for the treasure map. The trouble was, the duke had expressly forbidden her to enter the west wing.

Should you dare to set even one pretty toe in my private quarters, I will presume that you have come to share my bed.

Did he really find her pretty?

No. No, of course he did not. What should it matter, anyway? Aylwin was a brute who enjoyed bullying women. It was his way of putting her in her place, reducing her to the lowly status of a serf who could be plundered at the will of an overlord.

But was his threat serious? If he caught her sneaking into the documents room, would he truly ravish her? Would he take her to his bed and force her to satisfy his lusts? What would it be like for him to haul her into his arms and kiss her passionately?

The notion caused a peculiar agitation deep in her core, and she took several deep breaths to calm herself. Aylwin had proven himself to be without scruples. He'd exhibited no qualms about touching her as he pleased, whether it was caressing her face or lifting her skirts to examine her leg. Therefore, she had to believe that he would indeed carry out his vile threat.

But she wouldn't back down. She couldn't give up the search. She would simply have to outwit him . . .

"Ahem."

Bella jumped at the sound of a clearing throat. In the doorway stood a very proper butler in a black suit,

snowy cravat, and white gloves. He was an elderly man with sparse white hair, his face devoid of expression save for puckered lips that made him appear in a permanent state of disapproval.

He bowed. "Do pardon the interruption, Miss Jones."

Bella put down the shard and then picked a path around the piles on the floor. "Pray come in, Pinkerton. You're not disturbing me in the least."

"I have located several additional spare boxes in the wine cellar. If you still need them, that is."

As a pair of stout footmen each carried a stack of small wooden boxes into the room, Bella gave the butler a brilliant smile. "Why yes, thank you, that was very thoughtful. You're a dear to remember my request."

A ruddy color spread from his starched collar up into his sunken cheeks. Bella wondered if no one had ever praised him before. It was her belief that behind his vinegary exterior beat the heart of an old softie. She had arrived at the conclusion that very morning upon catching sight of him tossing scraps to a stray dog outside the kitchen door.

Pinkerton cleared his throat again. "If I may also announce, you have visitors waiting downstairs. Mr. and Mrs. Oscar Grayson."

"There must be some mistake. I don't know anyone by that name."

"Mr. Grayson is the duke's cousin and heir to the title."

"Oh." Mystified, Bella cocked her head to one side. "But . . . why would they wish to see me and not Aylwin?"

"It is not my place to speculate about my betters." Pinkerton shifted his rheumy blue eyes back and forth,

then lowered his voice to a raspy murmur. "However, I suspect they are curious to meet His Grace's houseguest. Might I suggest tea in the morning room?"

Bella had no desire to endure an hour of chitchat with nosy aristocrats. She had too much work to do. Perhaps they wouldn't stay long if she gave them nowhere to sit. "No, send them in here, please."

"As you wish." With a creaky bow, Pinkerton disappeared out the door, the entourage of footmen in tow.

If only she too could disappear.

Vexed by the interruption, Bella shook the dust out of her wrinkled blue skirt. Then she hurried to the large gilt-framed mirror on the wall, a vestige of the décor before the drawing room had become a storage facility. A heap of fragmented statues hid the bottom half of the glass, and she had to stand on tiptoes to view her reflection.

Her hair looked a fright. Numerous wisps had fallen onto her brow and she puffed up a breath to blow them away. When that failed, she brushed at her face, but her fingers left a streak of dirt on her cheek that she had to scrub off with her sleeve.

Oh, bother. She should have run up to her bedchamber to wash before receiving the callers. Then again, what did she care of their opinion? Her purpose here was not to win acceptance by polite society.

Moments later, a gentleman and a lady swept into the drawing room. They stopped just inside the doorway and, with identical expressions of distaste, glanced around at the jumble of artifacts. Bella decided there could be no greater contrast to the clutter than this perfectly groomed couple. They looked as if they had never worked a single moment in their pampered lives.

Leaning on a polished black cane, Mr. Oscar Grayson had dark wavy hair that was artfully combed

around a rather ordinary face with muttonchop whiskers. As if to compensate for his bland features, he'd garbed himself in flamboyant clothing: a gold waistcoat beneath a jade-green coat, a cravat tied in grandiose loops, and black trousers with thin gold stripes. Beside him, his wife was willow-slender in a pale peach gown that enhanced her creamy complexion and fair hair. Those eyes of brilliant amber studied Bella in a critically assessing manner.

Bella knew at once that she had little in common with the couple. But as relatives of her employer, they deserved common courtesy.

Pasting on a smile, she stepped forward and held out her hand. "Hello, I'm Miss Bella Jones. You must be Mr. and Mrs. Grayson."

Oscar Grayson shook Bella's hand, though his wife kept her gloved fingers demurely folded at her waist. "Well, well," he said in a jovial manner. "So you are the infamous Miss Jones. The moment Helen heard the news from her maid, who learned it from one of the footmen here, we decided to pay a call. I cannot remember the last time when Miles had a female houseguest."

Bella raised an eyebrow at his rambling speech. "Miles?"

"My cousin, Miles Grayson, the fifth Duke of Aylwin." Uttering a chortle of laughter, he turned to his wife. "You see, Helen? You were wrong. She didn't even know his Christian name. So how can she possibly be his mistress?"

Bella had been reflecting on the fact that the Duke of Aylwin had a real name. *Miles.* It somehow made him seem less fearsome. Then the meaning of what Oscar Grayson had just said broke through her reverie.

"His mistress!" Aghast, she gripped the folds of her

skirt in an effort to hold back her temper. "Nothing could be further from the truth. Aylwin hired me to catalogue his collection of antiquities. Ask him yourself if you doubt me."

"So we are to believe you are merely an employee," Mrs. Helen Grayson said as she strolled around, careful to keep her pristine skirt from brushing against any of the grimy surfaces. "I certainly hope that Miles intends for you to clear out this drawing room. Then the place can be restored to its former glory."

"I'm afraid he gave me no such instructions," Bella said in a chilly tone. "Where else would he put all these artifacts?"

"Outside in the rubbish heap," said Oscar, aiming a smirk at the miscellany of statues and pottery. "That's where the whole lot will go someday when *I* am the sixth Duke of Aylwin."

His cavalier manner disturbed Bella. And not just because he would dispose of these ancient relics. He and Aylwin could only be in their thirties and already this man was anticipating his cousin's demise? "Your plan seems a trifle premature," she felt compelled to point out. "His Grace may very well marry someday and sire a son who will carry on with his work in Egyptology."

Oscar gave her a blank stare. "Aylwin, marry? What rot! Why, the fellow is leg-shackled to all this useless junk!"

Helen, however, narrowed her eyes and stepped closer to Bella. "Let us be perfectly frank, Miss Jones. Do *you* have designs on Miles? Do *you* intend to entrap him into marriage and give him a son? Isn't that the real reason why you've come here—to cheat my husband out of his rightful inheritance?"

A flush of incredulity heated Bella's skin. "No. No.

And no! There, I have answered all your absurd questions."

"By what ruse did you convince Miles to hire you?" Oscar asked, mincing forward with the cane to take a stand beside his wife. "Surely there are *men* who are far better suited to this work than a mere female."

Bella compressed her lips to hold back an irate retort. Never in her life had she been so insulted. She itched to order these two busybodies out of the drawing room, but what if they had influence over Aylwin? What if they convinced him to dismiss her?

Perhaps a little information would placate them. "My father was Sir Seymour Jones. He worked with His Grace's father in Egypt many years ago. So you see, I have a connection to your family."

"Sir Seymour Jones?" Helen made a little flutter of her gloved fingers as to dismiss the name as a sham. "*I've* never heard of the man. Who are his people? From where does he hail?"

"Oxfordshire. And I wouldn't expect you to have known him. He—*we*—lived most of our life abroad."

"In France or Italy, I should hope."

"No, ma'am. Rather, we toured extensively through the wilds of Asia and the Near East." Bella couldn't resist the chance to needle the woman. "We traveled by camel or mule in caravans and often stayed for months among the tribal peoples along the way. My last real home was a stone hut in the mountains of southern Persia."

Helen and her husband exchanged a look of revulsion. "You've lived among savages?" Oscar asked.

"Oh, but there is much to be learned even from those whom you consider barbaric. And it's truly liberating to escape all the strictures of English society. You should try it sometime."

"No wonder your knowledge of civilized conduct is sorely lacking," Helen declared. "It is a crime that a woman of your heathenish background should be living in the household of a duke!"

Stung, Bella retorted, "That is not your decision to make. Now, there can be no purpose in continuing this inquisition. If His Grace is satisfied with my qualifications, then you should be, as well."

Lifting her chin, Helen looked down her perfect nose at Bella. "Whatever Miles does also reflects upon his family. And if you are indeed a blue blood, where is your chaperone? No true lady would reside under the same roof as an unmarried gentleman."

"Touché, my darling!" Oscar said with an admiring glance at his wife. He turned to ogle Bella. "It would appear you are indeed a fallen woman, Miss Jones. And what do you say to *that*?"

His vilification of her character snapped the last thread restraining Bella's temper. "I would say that you've overstepped your bounds, sir. Now do be on your way—lest I be forced to cast an ancient tribal curse upon the two of you."

Switching to the Farsi tongue of the Persians, she launched into a diatribe about the cold, callous nature of snooty English aristocrats. The tirade was harmless, but it had the desired effect on Oscar and Helen.

The couple shrank back in horror at the sham curse. In great haste that had them half tripping over their own feet, they scuttled out of the drawing room.

Chapter 9

Only two hours later, Bella had to fend off another hostile visitor.

Her blood boiling after the encounter with the Graysons, she was unable to concentrate on the task of sorting pottery. She paced the drawing room for a time, walking up and down the narrow paths between the heaps of broken artifacts while penciling notes in her journal about how to organize the space. Gradually, her temper cooled and she could think rationally again. Yes, she had taken great satisfaction in watching Oscar and Helen beat a rapid retreat.

But what if those two snobs had run tattling to Aylwin? What would the duke think of Bella threatening his cousins? Would he use it as an excuse to dismiss her from his employ?

Her fingers tightened around the leather-bound notebook. Oh, she ought *not* to have lost control over herself again! That particular failing of hers often had earned a chiding from Papa in her youth.

She must not give vent to wild sentiments that might endanger her mission to fulfill his last wish. He had

wanted to give her the means to provide for her brother and sister. *Promise me,* he had gasped out on his death-bed. *Find Aylwin. Find the map. You have half the pharaoh's treasure.*

Thinking about those words, Bella confronted the notion that had hovered at the back of her mind since her arrival at Aylwin House. Perhaps she was wrong to expect a trove of gold objects and brilliant jewels. By "pharaoh's treasure," had her father been referring to the many artifacts here at Aylwin House? Had he been trying to tell her that she was entitled to half of Aylwin's collection of ancient Egyptian objects?

Surely not. If that were the case, Papa would not have been so adamant about her finding the missing map. Somehow, that map was the key to her quest. Once it was in her possession, perhaps she would understand the nature of the treasure.

She had only to exercise patience until then.

With a sigh, she knelt down to catalogue a box of scarabs. According to her studies, these small stone beetles were used as amulets to signify rebirth or to ward off evil. Each one was different, some with carved pictures of animals or birds, others decorated with colored stone like lapis lazuli. As she worked, a ray of afternoon sunlight fell upon an item half buried at the bottom of the crate.

Bella picked up a dainty alabaster jar that was some-what larger than her fist. With the hem of her gown, she gently wiped away the layers of dust. The pale stone vessel had only a minor crack in the lip. Nearby lay the carved head of a woman that had been broken in two. Carefully matching the pieces together, Bella placed the head onto the jar and saw to her satisfaction that it was a perfect fit.

Had Papa found this object—or others like it? Why

had he never mentioned his work in Egypt—or written about it in one of his journals? If only he were here to answer all of her questions.

A tightness in her throat, she imagined him working under the relentless heat of the Egyptian sun. Perhaps he had dug this very jar out of the sand, brushed off centuries of grime, and cradled it in his hands as she did now. So many times, in so many foreign locales, she had seen him treat ancient objects with great reverence . . .

Heavy male footsteps sounded out in the corridor.

Bella's heart gave a wild thump. *Aylwin*. He must be coming here to address her maltreatment of his cousins. Dear God, if she hoped to keep her position, she would have to find a way to mollify him.

She surged to her feet and turned toward the doorway. But to her surprise, a stranger stomped into the drawing room. He was a balding man of average height, sloppily dressed in a loose brown coat, saggy black trousers, and scuffed boots. With his jowly face and stocky form, he reminded her of an English bulldog.

He stopped and scowled at her. "That is a canopic jar of the nineteenth dynasty," he chided. "Have a care how you handle it!"

Bella realized she was still holding the little alabaster vessel. She was about to ask his identity when Pinkerton entered at a measured pace. The stooped old butler stopped just inside the doorway and intoned with a sour curl of his lips, "Mr. William Banbury-Davis to see you, Miss Jones. I'm afraid he refused to wait downstairs."

"You know very well that Aylwin has given me carte blanche to study his artifacts at any time,"

Mr. Banbury-Davis told him with undisguised irritation. "Now, run along with you."

The servant cast an inquiring gaze at Bella. Clearly, he would not depart without her consent, a fact that spoke volumes about his opinion of this visitor.

She set down the jar and dusted off her palms, then gave him a nod. "Thank you, Pinkerton. I'll ring if you're needed."

The moment the butler was gone, she stepped forward and offered her hand in greeting. "It's a pleasure to meet you, Mr. Banbury-Davis. I presume you are a colleague of the duke's."

Banbury-Davis glowered instead of shaking her hand. "Indeed, I am a noted scholar of Egyptology—unlike you. I could scarcely believe my ears when Mrs. Helen Grayson informed me that Miles had hired an assistant. And in particular the daughter of that scoundrel, Sir Seymour Jones!"

Bella bristled despite her vow to guard her temper. Curling her fingers, she let her fist drop to her side. "Enough, sir! First you are rude to the servants. Now you are rude to me. If you cannot speak civilly, then you may as well depart at once for I have no interest in conversing with you!"

He harrumphed and muttered something under his breath. Then he planted his hands on his hips and moderated his tone. "As you wish, Miss Jones. Tell me, have your parents returned to England, too?"

"My father died last year of a fever. Mama passed away some fifteen years ago. Did you know them?"

His pale blue eyes swept over her. "I attended Oxford with Seymour Jones. Tell me, where has he been all these years?"

"We traveled extensively throughout Asia and the

Near East. Most recently, we were in Persia, where Papa had been assisting in the excavation of the ancient city of Persepolis."

"And now here you are at Aylwin House." He took an aggressive step toward her. "Did Sir Seymour tell you to come here? Perhaps he instructed you to claim some of these artifacts for yourself. Did he say that you have a right to them?"

The accusation was perilously close to the truth. Nevertheless, Bella objected to his disdain for her father. What was the source of it?

"That is the second time you've denigrated Papa. He was a fine father, a hard worker, and an honest man. I wish to know why you would call him a scoundrel."

"Don't pretend ignorance. He abandoned Miles, that's why."

She raised an eyebrow at the strange accusation. "Abandoned him? How so?"

"The fourth duke hadn't been cold twenty-four hours when Sir Seymour took you and your mother away in the dead of night. He vanished without a trace. Miles regarded Sir Seymour as a second father—until the fellow left the orphaned lad to fend for himself in Egypt."

Bella pressed her fingers around the edge of a wooden crate. She couldn't believe such a thing of her father. "Did Aylwin relate these events to you? He was only thirteen at the time. Perhaps he had his facts wrong."

"No, Miss Jones. I witnessed it with my own eyes."

"Wait. You were in Egypt, too, back then?"

"Indeed so." As Banbury-Davis roamed in agitated steps between the rows of miscellany, he snatched up a scarab and rubbed it between his fingers. "*I* was the one who helped Miles in his time of need. *I* guided

his decisions as to which artifacts were to be transported back to England. *I* provided him comfort and assistance—because your father had shirked his obligations."

Bella hardly knew what to think. But it would explain Aylwin's hostility toward her, his probing questions about Papa and where they had gone after leaving Egypt. If this man's narrative of events could be trusted, then Papa had ignored his duty to the young duke. He had departed at a time when the boy had needed him most. How distraught the duke must had been at the shock of his father being murdered by grave robbers. And then to be forsaken in a foreign country by a man he had trusted . . .

No.

No, she could not believe her father capable of such infamy. Certainly Papa had been self-absorbed at times, wrapped up in his pursuit of knowledge, even to the detriment of his family. But he had not been deliberately cruel or unkind. Banbury-Davis must be exaggerating.

Crossing her arms, she stepped into the man's path and stopped his pacing. "Perhaps my father needed to seek new employment. He had a family to feed. You can't know for certain what was going on in his mind."

"Nonsense. Miles would have continued to pay his salary. I am sorry if this is news to you, Miss Jones, but your father was a cold, unfeeling villain. If you've any conscience at all, you will acknowledge that you do not belong here at Aylwin House!"

His attack made her stiffen. "I will acknowledge no such thing, sir. His Grace offered me the position of curator, and I have accepted it. I will not be driven away by you or anyone else."

Banbury-Davis uttered a snort of contempt. "Curator, bah! What is your experience? Have you lived and breathed Egyptian history for more than thirty years as I have done? Did you study under the finest scholars? Have you any academic credentials at all?" He snatched up the little alabaster vessel and thrust it into her face. "Do you even know the purpose of a canopic jar?"

She lifted her chin. Not for all the hidden treasure maps in Egypt would she admit her ignorance to this man. "You've no right to come here and interrogate me. These questions are insulting—"

"I must concur," Aylwin drawled from behind her.

Bella spun around to see Miles standing with one hand propped high on the door frame. No, not Miles, she corrected herself. The duke. She must not think of him in such a familiar manner.

Nor should she notice the way his stance stretched the white shirt across his muscled chest, or that his black trousers clung like a second skin to his long legs. His dark hair was rumpled as if he'd combed it with his fingers. He needed only her dagger clenched between his teeth to complete the guise of a pirate.

Her heart thrummed against her rib cage. She felt suddenly light-headed, breathless. Not because of any attraction she felt for him. He had startled her, that was all.

How much had he heard?

Aylwin strolled forward and took the vessel from Banbury-Davis, who had fallen silent, a disgruntled expression on his face. The duke turned the container in his hands. "A canopic jar was used during the embalming process to store the internal organs of a mummy. This one, judging by the lid, once held some-

one's liver. I'm sure Miss Jones is quite aware of that fact."

He was covering for her. Protecting her against the attack by Banbury-Davis. Why? His solicitude stirred a warm feeling inside her that she immediately squelched. Aylwin likely wished to reserve for himself the right to criticize her.

Their gazes met, though she could read nothing but severity in those dark eyes. She wondered if he had come here to confront her about insulting his cousins, only to walk in on a different quarrel. Oh, her foolish temper!

Aylwin handed the alabaster jar to her, and their fingers brushed, raising sparks over her skin and causing her to babble, "Yes, Your Grace. I am indeed aware of the purpose of this jar. Strange, isn't it, how the most beautiful artifact can sometimes have a rather morbid purpose."

Banbury-Davis harrumphed again. "I'll wager my last farthing she didn't know what it was until you told her, Miles. May I say, it is most imprudent of you to allow an inexperienced female to handle these rare items. No doubt she's as untrustworthy as her father . . ." His voice trailed off.

Aylwin had silenced him with a chilly frown.

It was the Ducal Stare, Bella realized, stifling an untimely tickle of mirth. She'd believed that he reserved it only for her. But apparently she was not the only recipient of his haughty displeasure.

"Come with me," Aylwin ordered the scholar. "Now." He turned on his heel and strode toward the door.

Clutching the canopic jar, she watched as Banbury-Davis trotted after the duke. The irritating man would

be forced to face Aylwin's censure, and she almost felt sorry for him. At least until he glanced back to give her one last resentful scowl.

A chill tiptoed down her spine. There could be no mistaking that glare. William Banbury-Davis despised her as he had despised her father. And she had no doubt he would do everything in his power to convince Aylwin to send her away.

Miles stalked into his study in the west wing. On any other day, the spacious chamber served as his retreat, a quiet place where he could concentrate on his work. The décor was exactly as it had been in his father's time: worn leather chairs, a mantelpiece of green marble, and dark gold draperies drawn back to allow a view of the garden. The floor-to-ceiling bookshelves displayed an array of select Egyptian objects, from ankhs to cats to goddesses. Another doorway led to a windowless storeroom where tall oak cabinets held his private collection of papyri in individual drawers, protected from the harmful sunlight until such time as he needed to study them.

He proceeded to the desk where a snowstorm of papers covered the polished mahogany surface. Only moments ago, he had been working there when Pinkerton had come to report that Bella was being harassed by another visitor. Miles could still feel the rush of fury that had propelled him to his feet. Not because he felt any concern for Bella. She seemed eminently capable of taking care of herself.

No, it was just that he was damned sick and tired of people interfering in his affairs. First, it had been Oscar and Helen, bursting into his study to complain about the indecency of an unmarried woman living under his roof, especially one who had been raised

among savages. He'd had a good chuckle over Bella's curse—clearly a clever fabrication—and had sent the disgruntled pair on their way.

But this time, the situation was more serious. William Banbury-Davis was a respected colleague, not a frivolous socialite.

Banbury-Davis followed him to the desk and cast a glance at the papers. In a too-hearty tone, he said, "How is the progress on your dictionary of hieroglyphics?"

"Never mind that. Sit down."

The man shot him a wary look and then settled his bulk into one of the chairs in front of the desk. Miles perched on the edge of the desk. Being higher gave him the advantage, a subtle reminder of his authority over the man who had once asserted *his* authority over Miles. But Miles was no longer a lonely, frightened child in need of a guardian.

He stared down at Banbury-Davis. "I've given you leave to come to Aylwin House and examine my artifacts as necessary for your own work. But I will rescind that permission if you ever again dare to behave as you just did."

A ruddy flush came over the man's rough features. "But . . . she's Sir Seymour's daughter! Have you forgotten how he betrayed you? What on earth could have induced you to hire her?"

Miles kept silent about the questions that he still had in regard to his father's death. Those doubts had never been expressed to anyone else, not Banbury-Davis, not even Hasani. Miles didn't know yet if Bella Jones might have the answers he sought. But she was a vital link to the one man who had known his father best— Sir Seymour, who had fled Egypt with his family without even saying good-bye.

"She needed an occupation," Miles said coolly. "So I gave her one. There's nothing more to the matter."

"I don't see why she came here at all. It's highly suspicious."

"Is it? After living abroad most of her life, she has very few acquaintances in England. It's only logical that she would seek employment from someone who had once known her father."

With stubby fingers, Banbury-Davis gripped the arms of his chair. "Nevertheless, *I* helped you bring the artifacts back to England all those years ago. *I* know more about them than anyone other than yourself. If you needed assistance, you ought to have engaged *my* services. Not this . . . this interloper!"

Miles held back a dark laugh. It came as no real surprise that jealousy was at the root of the man's resentment. William Banbury-Davis had always displayed a possessiveness toward the Egyptian artifacts. The man felt he had a vested interest in the relics because of his role in acquiring them.

He had appeared in Miles's life at a time when his father had just been murdered and Sir Seymour had vanished into the night. At thirteen, Miles had been in desperate need of guidance and advice—and he had been willing to pay for it. Banbury-Davis had been touring Egypt, and when he'd come to offer his condolences, Miles had convinced him to oversee the negotiations with local officials for the purchase of the antiquities.

For that reason, Miles had always allowed the man a certain latitude. Banbury-Davis had enabled Miles to fulfill his father's dream of bringing the vast array of objects back to Aylwin House.

But his service, valuable as it was, had been rendered over twenty years ago. It didn't grant Banbury-

Davis the perpetual right to dictate how Miles handled the artifacts.

He fixed the man with a cold stare. "Miss Jones can hardly be described as an interloper. She has an undeniable connection to the artifacts. So it would behoove you to accustom yourself to her presence in my house."

"You're intending to keep her on, then? For what reason? It can't be her skills. Or her ordinary face. Has she bewitched you with that comely figure?"

"Enough," Miles snapped, rising to his feet. "This conversation is finished. If you value the privilege of entering Aylwin House, you'll depart without uttering another word."

Banbury-Davis flinched visibly, a look of alarm on his flushed features. His mouth opened, then clamped shut again. He pushed himself out of his chair and stood up. After giving Miles one final worried glance, he plodded out of the study.

Miles stalked to the door. He took perverse pleasure in slamming it shut. Never in his life had he felt so affronted. Bella Jones had bewitched him? Bollocks!

Granted, she *did* intrigue him—but only because she was neither whore nor lady, the two types of women most familiar to him. Unlike them, Bella had a brain. She could match wits with him. She did not pander to him because of his damned title, either. In truth, his rank didn't seem to matter to her in the least.

Of course, he felt drawn by her physical attributes. He was a man, after all. And he found her anything but *ordinary*.

Besides the gorgeous blue eyes and womanly curves, she had soft lips that were made for kissing. He had relished the feel of them beneath his thumb the previous day. The entire time she had been asking questions about the papyri, he'd been consumed by the

awareness of how close they stood, by the way the high-necked blue gown had cupped her bosom, and by his strong desire to strip her naked and turn all of her prattling into moans of pleasure.

Should you dare to set even one pretty toe in my private quarters, I will presume that you have come to share my bed.

He had meant those words more as a taunt than a real threat. Bella Jones had an inquisitive mind and a bold disregard for rules. She was curious to view those old documents, and he half hoped that temptation would get the better of her. He would take great pleasure in claiming a penalty for her disobedience.

But he was far from *bewitched*, dammit. There were plenty of other women available to him, women practiced in the art of satisfying a man's lusts. They were far more skilled—and therefore more desirable—than a virginal spinster.

Tonight, he would select one of those women. He intended to ride her until his appetites were fully sated.

Having made that decision, Miles strode to his desk. He had wasted too much time on nonsense. All of these interruptions served as a detriment to his work of compiling a hieroglyphics dictionary. It was time to end the distractions.

And in particular, his dangerous craving for Bella Jones.

Chapter 10

The opportunity for Bella to hunt for the treasure map presented itself unexpectedly. Eating dinner from a tray in her bedchamber after work, she learned that Aylwin had gone out for the evening. Her gossipy maid had delivered the news while adding coal to the fire on the hearth.

Bella froze with a spoonful of mushroom broth halfway to her lips. "Out? Where did he go?"

"I dunno, miss. His Grace ain't one for fancy parties, though." Setting down the coal bucket, Nan cast an impish glance over her shoulder. "I hope ye don't think me a blabbermouth for repeating this but . . . George the footman says the master sometimes visits a bawdy house."

"Bawdy house?"

"A place where fallen ladies sell their favors to the gents." Nan waggled her rusty-red eyebrows. "If ye know what I mean."

Repulsed yet intrigued, Bella set down her spoon. A bordello! In her travels she had heard of such establishments where a man could hire a concubine. Did

Aylwin visit there often? How much did he pay the woman? Was she always the same one? Or did he choose someone different each time? And what exactly did those women have to *do* in order to please him?

Flushed at the direction of her thoughts, she banished her curiosity. Aylwin's private misdeeds were no concern of hers. Only one question truly mattered.

"How long is he usually gone?" she asked. "I'm curious because I wanted to ask him something about my work."

Propping the poker in its stand, Nan shrugged. "'Tis often past midnight when he rings for Hasani. Did ye need fer me to deliver a message . . . ?"

"No! No, it isn't important. I can speak to the duke in the morning."

To avoid further conversation, Bella pretended an interest in her dinner. But her insides churned with anticipation even as her mind focused on a plan. At last she could venture into the west wing without fearing to encounter Aylwin.

She could scarcely manage to eat more than a few bites of her roast beef and potatoes. English food was rather bland, anyway, and her throat was too tense to swallow. She dismissed Nan for the evening, assuring the maid that she could manage on her own.

Once the girl was gone, Bella paced the large bedchamber with its fine furnishings. Her mission would have to wait until the servants were all safely belowstairs or asleep in their attic bedchambers. Only then would the pathway be clear. As darkness gathered outside in the garden, she passed the time by analyzing the outrageous encounter with Helen and Oscar Grayson, and then reflecting on the troubling picture Mr. William Banbury-Davis had painted of Papa.

If only she had an explanation for her father's behavior!

According to Banbury-Davis, Papa had abandoned Miles shortly after the horrifying murder of his father. But surely there must have been extenuating circumstances, some rational reason behind her family's sudden departure from Egypt. And Miles had survived, after all. He had grown up to become the arrogant Duke of Aylwin, lord and master of this household. Was his beastly nature due in part to the anguish he had endured in his childhood?

Bella didn't want to soften toward him. He was a rude, vexing man—even if he *had* defended her against Mr. Banbury-Davis. She knew now that Aylwin was wicked, too, for he consorted with loose females. He had threatened to seduce her, as well, if she dared to enter the west wing.

Remembering the heat in his dark gaze, she felt a shamefully delicious shiver. Was it just an involuntary response to the allure of his masculinity? Having spent her entire adult life raising her twin siblings, she had had little experience with flirting. And she wouldn't start now, either. At nine-and-twenty, she was far too old to behave as a silly, moon-eyed girl like her sister, Lila.

Yes, an encounter with Aylwin must be avoided at all costs. Bella would have to be swift in her search. By the time he arrived home after midnight, she must be safely back in her own bedchamber. Hopefully, with the map in her possession.

The clock on the mantelpiece chimed the hour of half past nine. Judging it safe to venture forth, she took a silver candlestick and stepped out of her chamber. Immediately, a draft of cold air made the flame waver,

and she cupped her hand to protect it. The passageway lay in darkness except for the small halo of light around her.

As she began to walk, a muffled thump behind her broke the tomblike silence. She turned to look, but saw only shadows. The back of her neck prickled, and she had the eerie impression that someone was watching her. Nan had claimed that spirits haunted this floor.

What nonsense, Bella thought, shaking off her unease as she continued down the gloomy corridor. It was merely the settling of the old house. No one else resided on this floor—not even ghosts.

In truth, there was something sad and lonely about this enormous mansion with all of its empty guest chambers. A large staff of servants kept the place running smoothly—all for the comfort and privilege of one man, the Duke of Aylwin.

And he didn't even seem to be happy. By her calculations, he must be past his mid-thirties. Why had he never married and had a family? A flock of children playing hide-and-seek along these corridors would bring laughter and joy to the melancholy atmosphere.

An acute longing for the cottage in Oxford swept over Bella. It seemed much more a true home than this vast mausoleum. Despite her short stay in England, she had grown fond of the little house with its cozy parlor and the two tiny bedchambers upstairs. Were Lila and Cyrus asleep by now? Had they been keeping up with their studies? Had they been obeying their neighbor, Mrs. Norris?

Only four days had passed since her departure, yet Bella missed her sister and brother dreadfully. She did not even have the comfort of letters since she had cautioned her siblings not to contact her here at Aylwin House. In case of an emergency, they were to write to

Lady Milford, who would inform Bella if necessary. It was best that way, she knew. Best to protect them from becoming entangled in her clandestine search for the treasure map. She would not want their high spirits crushed by harsh criticisms from the duke.

Reaching one of the staircases, she made her way down the wide marble steps. She now had a better understanding of the layout of Aylwin House. Just that morning, Pinkerton had been obliging enough to sketch a map for her showing the location of all the major rooms.

She proceeded through several long, echoing corridors in the central portion of the house. There were numerous reception rooms here, many of them filled with Egyptian artifacts. As she held up her candle to one chamber, the meager light revealed tall stone monoliths like an ancient army looming in the shadows. At last she turned a corner and spied an open doorway framed by an elaborate, gilded arch.

The west wing.

Here lay the entry to Aylwin's ducal apartments, the private domain that he had forbidden to her. An attack of nerves made her pause. Bella drew a breath, reminding herself she would be long gone before he returned from his night of carousing.

She plunged boldly into a murky corridor with a high ceiling that was painted with scenes from mythology. In the silence, her footsteps sounded unnaturally loud. At regular intervals along the walls, niches held small statues of Egyptian gods and goddesses.

A series of closed doors presented a puzzle. Which of them opened to the storeroom holding the papyri? She would try them all if need be.

Just as her fingers curled around the brass handle of the nearest door, a movement in the gloom caught

her attention. She gasped as a ghostly form appeared farther down the passageway.

"Miss Jones?"

At the sound of that familiar male voice, she put her hand to her wildly beating heart. It was Hasani, not Aylwin, thank goodness. Dressed in his customary pale robe, the Egyptian valet glided toward her at an unhurried pace. His dusky face had a look of polite inquiry in the light of the small lamp in his hand. In his other arm, he carried a small pile of crumpled white linen.

"Oh!" she said. "You frightened me."

"I beg your pardon, miss," he said with a small bow. "Are you lost? I'm afraid that you have come to the wrong wing."

"Have I?" Bella glanced around in a pretense of befuddlement. "How foolish of me to have taken a wrong turn. This house is like a maze, especially after dark."

"It is no matter. I shall guide you to your chambers."

He made a smooth gesture with his hand, indicating that she should retrace her steps. Bella had no choice but to retreat with him at her side. "Thank you. That's very kind."

It was difficult to be polite when she felt horribly frustrated. Their footsteps scuffed against the marble floor as they went back out into the central section of the house. All the while she silently cursed her dreadful luck. Did Hasani intend to wait up for Aylwin's return? To return here to the west wing instead of going down to the servants' hall?

Oh, she hoped not. That would spell doom for her plan to find the map. And time was ticking; she had only two precious hours in which to conduct her mission.

Somehow, she had to get rid of him. But how?

"You needn't bother walking me all the way back," she said. "If you'll just point me in the right direction, I'm sure I'll be fine."

"It is no bother," he said in his melodic tone. "Indeed, I have been hoping to speak to you. I feel it my duty to apologize."

Bella looked sharply at him. In the lamplight, his face appeared quite solemn. "Apologize? For what?"

"For the rude behavior of Mr. Banbury-Davis. His Grace told me of his visit today."

"Oh, but that wasn't *your* fault."

"Nevertheless, I have known the man since our days together in Egypt. And I feel obliged to warn you that he bears a longtime grudge against your sire."

Her stomach twisted. "Yes, he accused Papa of abandoning the duke in Egypt. But it sounds so unlike my father. Do *you* remember what happened?"

"I am not referring to that incident," Hasani said, ignoring her question. "Rather, I speak of their rivalry, which began much earlier. You see, Mr. Banbury-Davis desired very much to be a member of the fourth duke's expedition to Egypt. But instead, the duke chose Sir Seymour to be his partner."

Bella stopped so abruptly that a droplet of hot wax fell from the candle onto her wrist. She absently flicked it away while searching Hasani's impassive features. "That certainly would explain why the man resented my father."

"Indeed. Mr. Banbury-Davis was sightseeing in Egypt at the time the duke was murdered. That is why he was able to offer his services in the absence of your father."

"I see." As they resumed walking, she tried to absorb the ramifications of the news. What did it all

mean? Why had Papa never spoken of it? Had he perhaps left a clue that she had missed? "I'll have to unpack his journals to see if I might have overlooked something."

"His journals?"

Bella realized that she'd voiced her thoughts aloud. How foolish of her when she hardly knew this man. "Papa kept copious notes about his travels, that's all. I never saw a journal about Egypt, but perhaps I missed one. I would very much like to understand his role in the sequence of events."

His gaze sharp on her, Hasani motioned her up a staircase. "Have you brought these journals here to Aylwin House?"

"Oh, no. There are far too many. I've . . . placed them in storage." Not wanting to mention the cottage in Oxford, she changed the subject. "Will you tell me about the night the duke's father was killed?"

As they mounted the marble risers, their footsteps sounded hollow, almost spectral. The lamplight cast half the Egyptian's face in shadow, making his expression difficult to read. "It is not my place to speak of that tragedy," Hasani said slowly. "You should ask your questions of His Grace. But perhaps . . ."

"Yes?"

"Perhaps he will not mind if I tell you this. The grave robbers who killed his father at the excavation site also attacked our camp that night. They set the tents on fire and young Miles saved you from being burned to death."

Bella stopped halfway up the steps. Instead of the darkened stairwell, she saw orange-yellow flames leaping against a black sky, heard wild cries all around, felt the clasp of arms dragging her back into the shadows . . .

The splinter of memory vanished as swiftly as it had struck. Shaken, she stared wide-eyed at Hasani. "I think . . . perhaps I remember that. There were flames and shouting and someone pulling me away from it all. Are you certain it was Miles?"

"Yes, for I was there, too. Your father had seized his gun to shoot at the invaders, and your mother was overcome by the smoke while trying to reach you. In the chaos, Miles rushed inside the blazing tent to snatch you from your bed and carry you to safety."

Bella shuddered to think that she would not be alive today if not for Miles's heroic action. Yet the revelation also made it even more reprehensible that her father would abandon him. If indeed it was true. "Why did the ruffians attack the camp?" she asked. "Wasn't it enough that they'd killed His Grace?"

"They were angry and desired revenge," Hasani said, as the two of them resumed walking up the stairs. "You see, when they attempted to rob the grave site, they found only stone statues, pottery, scarabs, the sort of artifacts that are common in Egypt. There was no sign of the legendary treasure trove."

Her mouth went dry. She hoped he didn't notice the hitch in her breathing. "Treasure trove?"

Hasani inclined his head in a nod. "The fourth duke went to the Valley of the Kings in the hopes of discovering the crypt of the Pharaoh Tutankhamen and the many golden artifacts rumored to be buried there. In his search, His Grace came upon the long-sealed tomb of a lesser pharaoh. Opening it, I fear, presaged his death."

"Why do you say that?" she asked as they reached the top of the stairs.

"There was a curse placed upon the site when the mummy of a pharaoh was laid to rest. The one who

breaks the seal of the tomb is doomed to die a violent death."

It sounded so melodramatic that Bella laughed. "You can't truly believe in such a curse."

Hasani's mouth tightened into a stern line. "You must not scoff, Miss Jones. The priests of the ancient Egyptians practiced a powerful magic. It is to be respected, not ridiculed."

Realizing that she'd offended him, she said quickly, "Pray forgive me. I meant no disrespect to your culture or your beliefs. I was surprised, that's all."

He acknowledged her apology with a nod. "We have arrived at your floor, so here we must part."

Her chamber lay at the far end of the shadowed passageway. Bella wanted to grind her teeth. She was back where she'd started. In desperation, she decided to plant a suggestion in his mind. "Will you be going down to the kitchen?" she asked. "It would be helpful if you would ask my maid Nan to awaken me tomorrow a bit earlier than usual."

"I am indeed going belowstairs, for I must see to ironing these cravats for His Grace." He indicated his armload of crumpled linens. "Good evening, Miss Jones."

As Hasani bowed, Bella hid a jolt of elation. He wasn't returning to the west wing, then. In a matter of moments, her way would be clear.

Then, as he turned to withdraw down the stairs, she caught a glimpse of the eye tattoo on the back of his neck. A chill crept over her skin. In defiance of all logic, she felt certain the eye was watching her.

The Duke of Aylwin savored the aftereffects of vigorous sex.

In a state of utter satiation, he lay sprawled between

a pair of supple thighs, his cheek pressed to a soft bosom. Every breath he pulled into his air-starved lungs held a trace of feminine perfume and the earthy musk of their joining. Every inch of his body felt replete from the force of his release.

Her golden-brown hair had come loose to spread across the pillows. He could feel the swift beating of her heart begin to slow in tandem with his. She had enjoyed their coupling as much as he had.

This discreet establishment trained their women well in the art of lovemaking. His partner was new and eager to please. Already her skillful hands were caressing him again, moving across his shoulders and down his back.

Miles was too drained to feel more than a mild stirring in his loins. But he intended to have her again—perhaps twice more before departing. He had paid well for the privilege. He let his fingers slide over the silken plumpness of one breast. There was nothing like an evening in bed with a beautiful woman to clear the tension from his body.

She moaned, her nipple puckering beneath his ministrations. Her tongue lightly lapped at his throat. In a playful tone, she said, "If I might ask, Your Grace . . . who is Bella?"

His hand stilled. He pushed himself up to regard her lovely features, the green eyes and the smooth skin. "What?"

"Bella. You spoke her name at your pinnacle."

He had done that? *Dammit!*

As if sensing the shift in his mood, she gave him a seductive look and moved sinuously beneath him. "It's quite all right, Your Grace. I'm yours to command. I'm happy to be whomever you wish me to be—even this Bella."

A coldness ran in his veins. He loathed hearing Bella's name on the lips of a harlot. He would not allow her to know of Bella's existence.

He curled a lock of her hair around his finger. " 'Bella' means beautiful in Italian."

"Oh! So I was mistaken, then. It was a compliment!" Her mouth formed a coquettish smile. "Allow me to thank you, Your Grace."

She slipped her hand in between them. But Miles pushed it away. Feeling a sudden distaste, he rolled out of bed and snatched up his trousers. As he stepped into them and fastened the buttons, the doxy sat up in the rumpled sheets. "Must you depart so soon? We were just getting started. I've plenty more tricks to show you."

Naked, she crawled to the foot of the bed, her large breasts swinging, her hips swaying. There, she wrapped her arms around the bedpost, rubbing against its crimson hangings like a cat seeking a scratch. With her tumbled hair and spectacular figure, she was every man's dream.

But Miles wanted no repeat performance. Not if he might speak Bella's name again in the heat of the moment. He yanked the shirt over his head and sat down on a chair to pull on his boots. Bloody hell! This night hadn't gone as planned.

It was early yet. The clock on the mantel showed the time to be just shy of ten. Now he was too damned restless to sleep. He'd have to return home and bury himself in work instead of feminine flesh.

The tall casement clock in the corner of the study bonged ten times as Bella began her search for the map. Two hours. That should give her ample opportu-

nity to poke into every nook and cranny of Aylwin's private sanctuary before his return at midnight.

She touched the flame of her candle to the three tapers in a silver candelabrum on the desk. The additional illumination enabled her to view the spacious room more clearly. The masculine décor included leather chairs, heavy wood furnishings, and tall draperies over the night-darkened windows. A collection of Egyptian artifacts on the bookshelves confirmed this was the duke's domain, as did the gold-rimmed spectacles lying atop the many papers strewn on the desk.

Examining the sheets more closely, she saw that they contained pictographic symbols, most with an English inscription neatly penciled beside them. There was a sketch of a waterbird paired with the word "fledgling." A seated Egyptian man pointing to his mouth opposite the words "to discuss." A picture of a young woman with the label "daughter."

Was Miles compiling a dictionary?

Bella tamped down her curiosity. She wanted to review all the pages and learn something of the hieroglyphic language. But not now.

Did he store the papyri in his desk? So that it would be handy when he worked on his glossary?

Seating herself there, she opened the drawers one by one. It made her vaguely uneasy to search through his personal belongings as if she were peeking into his private life. But the contents revealed nothing out of the ordinary: a sheaf of blank paper, writing supplies, string, wax for sealing letters, and other common paraphernalia.

Then a metallic glint in the dim recesses of the bottommost drawer caught her attention.

With cry of delight, Bella drew out her dagger. So this was where Miles had hidden it. She still resented him for issuing his arrogant decree. No one, he'd said, was permitted to carry a weapon in his house.

What nonsense! How were English ladies to defend themselves in the event of an attack? The duke probably thought they should cower in a corner and wait for a man to save them. Well, that wasn't the way *she* had been raised. Upon presenting her with the antique Persian dagger on her sixteenth birthday, Papa had declared that a strong woman must always be equipped to protect herself.

Bella's fingers tightened around the dainty ivory handle. She wanted to reclaim the dagger. But what if Miles noticed it was missing? He would realize at once that she'd been poking through his desk.

Blast him. The dagger was her property, and she felt safer with it in her possession. She placed it in the pocket of her gown. If necessary, she would argue her case with Miles.

No, not Miles. *Aylwin.*

She must cease thinking of him in so familiar a fashion. His first name had slipped into her mind too often since learning it today—though perhaps it was only natural. Even if she didn't quite remember him, they were linked by a shared childhood.

And he had saved her life. He had rushed into a burning tent and pulled her to safety. Only six years old at the time, she had been unable to save herself. His bravery on her behalf touched her heart.

She had Hasani to thank for telling her that story and for sparking her memory of the incident. The Egyptian had lifted the veil of the past and revealed a hidden part of her life. His other disclosure had been just as amazing, for it lent credence to her quest. He'd

told her that Aylwin's father had gone to the Valley of the Kings to pursue the legend of a fabulous treasure buried with a pharaoh named Tutankhamen.

Find Aylwin. Find the map. You have half the pharaoh's treasure.

The old duke must have discovered a map showing the location of the hidden tomb. A map that Papa had seen, too. Was it possible that Miles had never known of the map's existence, and the secret had died with his father? According to Papa, the map was here somewhere, perhaps stuck in a forgotten pile of old documents.

Rising from the desk, Bella picked up the candelabrum and surveyed her surroundings. There were no other cabinets or drawers in which to look. Where else might Aylwin keep the papyri? He had stated that the ancient papers were secured in a storeroom.

Perhaps she had been wrong to assume that meant his study.

Her gaze fell upon a closed door half hidden in the shadows. Proceeding there, she opened it and found herself in a somewhat smaller chamber, this one filled with row upon row of dark wood cabinetry. She pulled open a drawer at random and caught her breath.

Inside lay a yellowed, fragmented paper with hieroglyphic writing on it. The piece looked so fragile that she was afraid to touch it for fear it might crumble to dust.

Jubilation bubbled up inside her. *This* must be the storeroom that Aylwin had referenced. Yet the number of drawers boggled her mind. There must be several hundred at least, in cabinets that reached nearly to the ceiling. She'd have to conduct a systematic search.

From the open doorway to the study came the sound

of the casement clock bonging the half hour. Ten-thirty. She had squandered enough time already.

Seized by urgency, Bella crouched in front of one cabinet and opened the lowest drawer. She worked her way upward, discovering that each drawer contained more of the papyri, sometimes several documents in one. A few were so old that she had to bring the candles dangerously close in order to discern the faded ink.

All of them contained more of the pictorial writing. None, however, revealed the topographical features of a map.

At the bottom of the next row, tucked beside an ancient scroll, she was intrigued to discover something modern. It was a small packet of letters tied with a string. The topmost one was addressed to *The Most Hon. The Marquess of Ramsgate*.

The name sounded vaguely familiar, though Bella could not place it. But the distinctive penmanship caught her attention at once. With a gasp, she recognized that rough scribble. It was as if the author's thoughts moved swifter than his hand.

Papa had written these letters. When? And why had Miles preserved them in a drawer with his Egyptian papyri?

Just then, the click of an opening door came from the study. Someone had entered from the outside corridor. Jerking her head up, she froze, transfixed by the tramp of male footsteps.

Chapter 11

Bella's mind raced. Aylwin! It had to be him. But it wasn't even eleven yet. He had returned home early.

Dear God, he would notice the light in the storeroom. Even if she blew out the candelabrum, he would have already spied the candlestick from her bedchamber. She'd foolishly left it burning on his desk.

She was trapped. The storeroom provided no place to hide. Her only recourse was to brazen her way out of this disaster.

Bella stuffed the little packet of letters into her pocket with the dagger. Then she quietly closed the drawer and scrambled to her feet.

Just in time.

Aylwin stepped into the open doorway. The candlelight cast harsh shadows on his stern features. He wore a dark, fitted coat over his white shirt, and his untied cravat hung loose around his neck. His feet were bare as if he'd kicked off his shoes in preparation to disrobe for the night.

Despite the dire circumstances, Bella felt a pulse of attraction deep within her body.

He leaned one shoulder against the door frame and crossed his arms. A dangerous smile tilted one corner of his mouth. "Well, well. It appears I've caught an intruder."

She lifted her chin. He must not guess how swiftly her heart was thrumming. "My maid mentioned you were gone for the evening. It seemed the perfect opportunity to take a peek at the papyri without disturbing you."

"Even though I forbade you to do so."

"Pray forgive me, Your Grace, for I merely wished to expand my knowledge of Egyptian history." Striving for a sincere look, Bella took a step toward him. She stopped when he didn't budge from the doorway. "I would very much like to learn to read this hieroglyphic writing. Do you have a dictionary that I might borrow?"

His chuckle held an edge of sarcasm. "It's a far more difficult and complicated procedure than looking up the meaning of a pictograph."

"Perhaps you could give me lessons, then. I couldn't help but notice the papers on your desk. You seem to be quite the expert."

He fixed her with the Ducal Stare. "And you seem to be quite the little snoop, Miss Jones."

She met his gaze without flinching. "I'm fascinated by the hieroglyphs, that's all. If I can learn to read and write Sanskrit and Farsi, then why not ancient Egyptian?"

"Quite impressive," he said, cocking one eyebrow. "I can't claim to have ever known so educated a woman."

"My father always challenged me to learn the language of the places we traveled. He believed that

women have a better grasp of linguistics than men. But if you're too busy to help me, I understand perfectly. I'll just go now and leave you to your work."

Gripping the candelabrum, she marched toward Aylwin in the hopes that courtesy would induce him to move aside. Of course, he did not oblige. She stopped directly in front of him, close enough to see the faint shadow of a beard on his jaw. His dark hair was slightly mussed as if he'd just arisen from bed.

Which he had.

With a twist of her gut, she remembered that Aylwin had gone out to a bordello. He had spent the evening with a concubine. Why couldn't the filthy dog have caroused all night? Why had he returned so early?

He was eyeing her with the same intent look he'd had the previous day. As if he wanted to haul her into his arms and have his way with her. *Should you dare to set even one pretty toe in my private quarters, I will presume that you have come to share my bed.*

An inner tremor stole her breath away. They were all alone here. No one would hear her if she cried out. He could pull her against his muscled form, kiss her senseless, carry her into his bedchamber and ravish her. In a secret shameful part of herself, Bella wasn't entirely certain she wanted to stop him.

"Pray step aside, Your Grace," she said in her most frigid tone.

Aylwin regarded her for another long moment. The faint ticking of the casement clock filled the silence. Then, to her great relief, he moved slightly so that she could brush past him and enter the study. On wobbly legs, Bella went straight to the desk and set down the heavy candelabrum. Her fingers felt stiff from grasping it so tightly.

Intending to bid him a cool good night, she turned around with an excuse ready to make her escape. But he spoke first.

"Sit down, Miss Jones." He pointed at a pair of chairs by the unlit hearth. "Over there."

"I'm rather weary—"

"If you can peruse my documents without falling asleep, then you can certainly manage a conversation with your employer."

He stood with his hands on his hips like a king demanding obedience from a subject. Anxiety tightened Bella's throat. Her thoughts had been so centered on evading his seduction that she'd overlooked the very real possibility of being dismissed from his employ for her infraction.

She would lose any chance of finding the treasure map. And then how would she provide for her brother and sister?

She settled gingerly on the edge of the seat. "Of course, Your Grace. What is it you wished to discuss?"

Aylwin strolled to a table and uncorked a crystal decanter. As he filled a glass, he said over his shoulder, "For a start, your conversation with Hasani."

Bella blinked in wary surprise. Hasani had been the last person on her mind. Her gaze flitted to the door. Was the Egyptian nearby?

Cautiously, she asked, "When did you see him?"

"Upon my return half an hour ago." The duke approached with a glass in each hand. Towering over her, he thrust one into her hand. "I've dismissed him for the evening. You see, I had a suspicion I might encounter you here."

Distracted, Bella frowned at the amber liquid. "What is this?"

"Brandy. You look rather pale after being caught trespassing in my private domain."

"Of course! You startled me."

Aylwin's mouth crooked slightly as if he found amusement in her reactive reply. He settled into the chair opposite hers, crossed his bare feet on an ottoman, and took a swallow from his glass. "Drink up. It'll restore you."

Bella took a small sip. The liquor had a potent yet mellow flavor that slid down her throat to warm her insides. She took another sip and found that she did indeed feel somewhat better.

She looked up to find the duke watching her in that unnerving way of his. As if he were disrobing her with his eyes. Her insides clenched, and to deny her imprudent reaction, she said coolly, "I suppose Hasani told you that he saw me in this wing."

"He believed you were lost. But I knew perfectly well that your presence here was no accident. You were determined to view the papyri." Aylwin studied her over the rim of his glass. "I suspect that temptation is something that you find difficult to resist. Am I correct, Miss Jones?"

Her heart tripped over a beat. His silken tone of voice hinted at an erotic meaning. "I firmly believe in indulging my curiosity in regard to educational pursuits. It is a trait I learned from my father."

Aylwin's expression underwent a subtle alteration. His eyes became more secretive, his jaw tightening ever so slightly. He swirled the amber liquid in his glass and abruptly changed the subject. "Hasani tells me you had another memory of Egypt."

"Yes, I did." Peering down into her own glass, Bella experienced the scene all over again: the leap of flames

against the black sky, the wild cries, the clasp of arms drawing her away from it all. "The camp was attacked. I remember fire and mayhem—and someone pulling me to safety. Hasani said that *you* did so." She leaned forward, studying his features in a futile attempt to see him as the adolescent boy from the mists of her past. "Why didn't you tell me that you'd saved my life?"

"Frankly, I'd forgotten all about it."

Of course. He must have been caught up in the horror of his father's violent death. Bella ached to know every detail of what had happened that night—and to discern if the treasure map might fit somehow into the scenario. "Was it after the attack that you discovered your father was missing from the camp?"

A harsh mask tightened Miles's face. "No. I already knew he'd gone to the excavation site."

"How far away was it?"

"A quarter mile perhaps."

"It was nighttime. If there were bandits in the area, why did your father go alone to the tomb? What was so important that it couldn't wait until morning?"

Miles shot out of his chair and paced to the fireplace. "Good God, woman! *I* am directing this inquisition, not you. And you will tell me what else you remember about Egypt."

In the candlelight, his face was coldly authoritarian. Nevertheless, Bella felt the softening of compassion. The long-ago murder of his father must still be a raw wound in him. "I remember very little," she replied. "Other than a brief impression of the attack on the camp, there was only that one incident I told you about, digging in the sand and hearing a boy laugh at me."

He drained his glass and set it down with a sharp click on the mantel. "Surely if you gave the matter

some reflection, you could dredge up a memory of departing from Egypt."

"It isn't that simple."

"Then think, by God! Do you recall seeing your father talk to anyone? Did you perhaps overhear a snippet of conversation between your parents?"

Bella shook her head. "I'm afraid it's all a blank. I was just too young at the time."

He compressed his lips and glowered at her, and his expression of angry frustration only confirmed the accusation made by William Banbury-Davis. It pained her to admit it, but Papa had deserted thirteen-year-old Miles, and Miles had never forgiven him for that.

She set aside her glass and went to him, placing her hand on his sleeve, aware of the tension in his muscles. Gazing up into his hostile brown eyes, she murmured, "My father should have remained in Egypt to help you in your time of grief. It's important to you, isn't it, to understand why he left? That's why you're asking me these questions."

He subjected her to the Ducal Stare. "You were indeed an eyewitness to his betrayal. Though a rather useless one, it would seem."

Stung, Bella stepped back, letting her hand drop to her side. "Then why don't you prod my memory?"

"How so?"

"When Hasani told me about you saving me from the burning tent, it caused me to remember the incident. So tell me about that night and the following day. Give me all the details. Where was I? Who was I with? What was I doing?"

He made a dismissing gesture. "How the devil should I know? In case you've forgotten, my father had just been murdered. I was a bit too busy to pay heed to a pesky little girl."

His nettlesome temper exasperated her. "Then there is no way that I can help you, Your Grace. I'll bid you good night."

She brushed past him, intending to march out the door of the study. But his fingers clamped around her upper arm, dragging her around to face him. His eyes were intent on her, burning with anger and something else. Something that made her heart skip a beat.

"You aren't going anywhere," he growled. "Not until you give me my due."

"Your due?"

"I warned you not to enter my private quarters. Or there would be the devil to pay."

He hauled her close, molding her to the hard length of his body. With one strong arm locked around her waist, he used his other hand to tilt her face up to his. She caught her breath, inhaling a light, unfamiliar scent along with his masculine spice. Before she could identify it, his mouth came down on hers with raw, unbridled passion.

The speed of his assault momentarily disoriented Bella. Never in her life had she been kissed, let alone with such fervor. The jolt of pleasure she experienced when his tongue pressed between her lips was so startling, so unfamiliar, that she struggled in his arms and tried to turn her head away. His hand glided over her throat, cupping her jaw and holding her firmly in place.

As his mouth grew more coaxing, an irresistible desire swept away her resistance. His body felt like a bonfire that heated every inch of her. He tasted of brandy, and she felt giddy from the drink of his kiss. The pressure of his lips, the sweep of his tongue, ignited strings of pleasure that unraveled down into her core.

On the rare occasions when she'd wondered how it felt to be held by a man, she had imagined a chaste

peck, a brief embrace, not this wild seduction of her senses. The rough pads of his fingers traveled over her neck and upward to trace the curve of her ear, then slid into her hair to loosen her bun. A delicious shiver made her gasp, and she leaned closer, lifting her arms around him and returning the kiss with instinctive ardor.

Miles. This was Miles, whom she had known long ago, Miles who had saved her from certain death as a child. Now, it felt as if he were breathing new life into her once again, opening the door to forbidden pleasures, stirring an awareness of just how drab and colorless her existence had been without him.

When he kissed a path down to the hollow of her throat, she tilted her head back to accommodate him. The brush of his lips on her bare skin was pure heaven. Her eyes were closed, the better to savor the sensations he aroused. Her legs felt so shaky that if not for the support of his muscled arm, she would have melted into a puddle at his feet.

His fingers moved to her bosom, tracing the fullness of one breast and rubbing the peak. A moan rose from deep within her. Despite the gown and corset, she felt a flush of heat that radiated throughout her body and weakened her limbs. The vibrations stirred by his touch scorched her very center and throbbed in her veins.

"Bella," he rasped, nuzzling her throat. "I knew you had fire under all that ice. We belong together."

Her heart leaped at his stunning avowal. Did Miles truly think they were meant for each other? He was usually so aloof, so cold, so beastly. But perhaps that was merely the wall he'd erected around his emotions. Perhaps this kiss had made him, too, feel the deep connection between them, for their lives had intersected twice now.

Never before had she felt such an intense attraction to any man. The feelings he inflamed in her were new and exciting, and she ached to learn more about him, to become closer in mind and soul.

He nibbled on the lobe of her ear, feeding the fire within her. She felt his hands slide down her back to cup her bottom and press their hips together. The silken whisper of his voice tickled her ear. "I want you in my bed, Bella. Right now. Give yourself to me, and I'll make you the happiest of women."

In my bed.

Those words penetrated her sensual reverie, and she opened her eyes to the dim-lit study. She was gazing down at his dark head as he kissed her neck. At the chocolate-brown hair that was still mussed from his earlier tryst with a concubine.

He intended to use her as he had that other woman. Lust ruled him, nothing more. That thought flitted through her mind, yet she didn't want to believe it.

"Come with me," he murmured. "You're curious, aren't you? Allow me to educate you in the art of lovemaking. We'll have all night together, just you and I."

As he spoke, Miles drew her toward the door, his lips warm against her temple, his hands feathering over her throat and bosom. Her traitorous body responded to his touch, and Bella found herself tempted to succumb. To let him introduce her to the mysteries of fleshly desires.

The shock of her own weakness broke the spell. He wanted her to give to him what rightfully belonged only to a husband. This nobleman would take what he wanted and then walk away.

She writhed against his hold. "No," she said, her voice sounding far too unsteady. "No, let me go, Miles."

Instead of relenting, he brought his lips down on hers again, not in the wild manner of before, but sipping at her mouth in soft, persuasive kisses that sapped her of the ability to think. His fingers tenderly stroked her face. "Bella, darling. Please don't deny me. I want you so very much. You're a fever in my blood."

A gravelly sincerity vibrated in his voice. Miles meant every word. He desired her with all his being. The knowledge, rich and sweet, lured her beyond reason. It was flattering, enticing, enthralling, and nourishment to her starving heart.

Taking advantage of her vacillation, his nimble fingers shifted to the back of her gown, undoing the top few buttons, caressing bare skin while he murmured sweet nothings in her ear. As he touched a sensitive spot along her spine, she sucked in a quick breath. In so doing, she caught another whiff of the lighter fragrance intermingled with his masculine scent, and this time she realized what it was.

Flowery perfume.

The smell of his concubine.

A cold wave of revulsion doused her desire. In its wake, anger rose so quickly that it sickened her. *We belong together.* What a fool she had been to believe that—even for a moment! The Duke of Aylwin thought nothing of going from one woman to another, all in the same night.

He considered it his right. His due.

She must not be his next conquest. He would take her virtue, ruin her without a qualm. He was worse than a thief plotting to steal her last coin.

In desperation, Bella groped in her pocket and whipped out the dagger. Pressing the sharp tip beneath his jaw, she hissed, "Filthy dog! Release me at once. Or die."

Chapter 12

Miles froze as the blade pricked the underside of his jaw. His passion-hazed mind struggled to comprehend her threat. A moment ago, Bella had been kissing him. Responding to his caresses with passionate abandon. Granted, she had resisted him once or twice, but surely that was only to be expected from a virginal spinster.

What the hell had just happened?

He stared down into her ferocious blue eyes. Her breasts rose and fell with quick, angry breaths. The tip of the knife pressed into his skin. One hard upward thrust and she would slice open his jugular. He would bleed out in seconds.

The prospect chilled his ardor.

She wouldn't kill him, he told himself. She wouldn't dare.

Yet doubt held him motionless. Bella Jones lacked the prissy refinement of other ladies. She had been raised in a wild, uncivilized region of the world. The workings of her mind eluded and intrigued him.

Perhaps it was that very unpredictability that made

him mad for her. Even now. While she held a knife to his throat.

"I'll let go of you," he said. "Have a care with that blade."

It wasn't in his nature to retreat. Nevertheless, Miles stepped back, his hands raised, his palms open to show that he meant her no harm. His kiss had overwhelmed her, that was all. Bella was inexperienced, and for that reason, he should not have been so insistent in pressing his attentions on her.

But all logic and wisdom had fled him the moment he'd taken her into his arms. He didn't understand his own intense reaction. He usually kept a cool head even in the heat of the moment.

Bella's hostile gaze tracked his every move as he went to his desk and sat down on the edge of it. A few strands of glossy brown hair had tumbled down around her shoulders. Her mouth had the soft redness of a thoroughly kissed woman. There was nothing spinsterish about her now. She looked as fierce and untamed as the lion goddess Sekhmet.

He had never seen a more desirable woman. Or one more bossy and vexing. Rationality told him that Isabella Jones was the last female he should ever pursue. But his body spoke otherwise.

She lowered her arm, her fingers gripping the ivory hilt of a small knife. The blade glinted in the candlelight.

A nasty jolt of surprise struck Miles. That was *her* dagger, the one he had confiscated. Only a few days ago, he had stashed the weapon in the bottom drawer of his desk for safekeeping.

There was only one way she could have found it.

His temper flared, a vent for his physical frustration.

"I see that you searched more than my storeroom. You've also been rummaging through my desk."

She elevated her chin. "This dagger is my property, not yours. It was a special gift from my father. *He* trusted me with it."

Her devotion to Sir Seymour irritated Miles to no end. He had resented the man for so many years that he found it difficult to fathom her defense of him. At one time, he too had venerated Sir Seymour. Until he had vanished into the night and left Miles to fend for himself.

Bella Jones was the only one who might know why—even if that reason was buried in the recesses of her mind. There had to be some hidden clue that he could coax out of her memory. Until then, she would have to be placated.

"Keep the damned thing if you wish," he growled. "But if you ever draw that dagger on me again, it's mine for good. Is that understood?"

She gazed coolly at him. "I will use it as necessary for protection, Your Grace. That is why Papa gave it to me. To guard against villains."

Miles was livid. She had the audacity to label him a villain? It wasn't as if he'd forced himself on her— at least not much. And she had enjoyed his kiss, dammit. Maybe he'd taken it a bit too far for a virgin, but that was all he'd concede.

"May I remind you," he said icily, "you defied my explicit order to stay out of the west wing. I warned you there would be consequences."

"That doesn't give you leave to press your . . . your *lust* on me. You may be a duke, but I am not a serf to be used at your will!"

"Yet I *am* your employer." No one ever spoke to him in such an impudent manner. No one else dared. He

stood up, elevating his voice almost to a shout. "*I* make the rules in this house. It is your duty to obey them. For that matter, you are never to enter this room again without my permission."

"And *you* are never to touch *me* again without *my* permission." She raked him with a glare of contempt. "Especially when you reek of your concubine's perfume."

Bella spun around, her blue skirt flaring, allowing him a glimpse of the white stockings over her tattooed ankles and those fancy garnet slippers. Dagger in hand, she marched out the door of the study.

Miles stood riveted to the plush carpet. As he stared at the empty doorway, his anger receded and left him empty. He couldn't have moved if his life had depended upon it.

Bella knew where he'd gone tonight? That he'd been with a harlot? Had she merely guessed because of the perfume? Or had the servants been gossiping?

The answer didn't signify. All that mattered was that her words cast a whole new light on her rejection of him. Bella had been melting in his arms, ardent and eager, every bit as aroused as he had been. Then she had noticed the fragrance on his skin. And she had been justifiably furious. No lady wanted to be a man's second choice.

He ought to feel triumphant. She had rejected him out of jealousy, that was all.

Or was it something more?

An unfamiliar discomfort nagged at him, and it took a moment for Miles to identify it as shame. He was ashamed of his conduct tonight. He had been arrogant in assuming Bella would welcome the invitation to share his bed. Arrogant in thinking he had the right to seduce her. Arrogant in attributing her

reaction to jealousy, too. Rather, she was disgusted to be regarded as another conquest in his string of women.

Miles stalked to the window to stare out at the night-darkened garden. Yes, he had behaved badly. He had the sexual experience that Bella lacked, and he had wielded that power like a sword to cut away her defenses. He had been driven by his own desires without a care for her innocence. He had ignored the fact that Bella was an educated woman and a lady despite her unconventional upbringing.

She deserved better than to be treated like a paid whore.

The following afternoon, Bella brashly invited herself to tea with Mrs. Witheridge and Mr. Pinkerton. She had several questions to ask them about Miles and his past. Questions that might require a bit of diplomacy since they were two of his most devoted servants.

They all sat around a lace-draped table in Mrs. Witheridge's parlor, and Bella bided her time listening as the butler and housekeeper discussed whether Edna the kitchen maid should be reprimanded for flirting with George the footman, and who should bake the cake for Cook's birthday the following week.

Bella found this little room a welcome oasis in the vast desert of Aylwin House. As she sipped her steaming tea, she felt right at home with the china figurines crammed on the shelves, the overstuffed chairs, the vases of dried flowers. Lace curtains covered the high window, for the room was located belowstairs. To offset the chill of the cellar, a fire blazed on the small hearth, making the space warm and cozy.

Mrs. Witheridge did most of the talking while Mr. Pinkerton inserted a taciturn comment every now

and again. From time to time, he also slipped a crumb of biscuit under the table to the little scruffy dog that sat watching him with hopeful brown eyes and one ear cocked.

At last, the gray-haired housekeeper reached across the table to refresh Bella's cup of tea. The ring of keys at her thick waist jingled as she moved. "Now, now, will you listen to us go on?" she said with a kindly smile. "Have another slice of raspberry cake, Miss Jones, and then tell us what brings you belowstairs today."

Bella accepted the cake out of politeness. Her stomach had been tied in a knot ever since the previous evening when Miles had kissed her so passionately. She had not known it was possible to feel such desire for a man. But oh, he had made her so angry, too! He had wreaked havoc with her, body and soul.

But she mustn't think about that just now. A more pressing issue weighed on her mind.

After returning in a huff to her bedchamber, she'd remembered the packet of old letters in her pocket, the ones written by her father and addressed to *The Most Hon. The Marquess of Ramsgate*. Needing a distraction from the tangle of her emotions, Bella had stayed up very late deciphering Papa's untidy penmanship by candlelight.

Each letter had been written as if in reply to questions. Each was filled with practical advice on scholarly books to read, discussions of Egyptian dynasties, and detailed information about various artifacts found in Egypt. The overall tone of the letters was warm and friendly, and at times, oddly paternal in dispensing advice.

One passage in particular stuck out in her mind: *Aylwin can be a harsh fellow, but he wants the best*

*for you. Tend to your studies if you wish to prove your
merit. And pray be assured I shall speak to him about
your joining the expedition.*

To whom had her father been writing? Why had
Miles saved the missives? And why did the name
Ramsgate have a vague ring of familiarity?

Stirring her tea, Bella directed a pleasant smile at
the housekeeper and butler. She reminded herself to be
careful not to mention the pilfered letters. "I was hoping you wouldn't mind answering a few questions," she
said. "You see, while I was working, I came across a
name written on a paper. I wondered if perhaps either
of you might recognize it. The Marquess of Ramsgate."

Mrs. Witheridge chuckled. She and the butler exchanged an amused glance. "Why, of course we know
the name," the housekeeper said. "How could we not?
'Tis His Grace the duke himself."

Thunderstruck, Bella frowned at them. "Are you
saying . . . that Aylwin has two titles?"

"Several more than that, to be precise," the old but-
ler intoned, ticking them off on his knobby fingers.
"The Earl of Maynard, Viscount Silverton, and Baron
Turnstead, as well."

Mrs. Witheridge clucked her tongue. "Now, now,
you're only befuddling the poor girl. Growing up in
them heathen lands, she doesn't understand the ways
of the nobility." The housekeeper paused to take
a swallow of tea. "You see, at birth, the eldest son of a
duke is granted his father's next highest title. So young
Miles was the Marquess of Ramsgate until the death
of his father, God rest his soul."

Bella nibbled on a morsel of cake. How extraordinary. It all made sense now. Of course Miles had kept
the old letters. They had been written to *him*.

By her father.

The letters had been composed before the expedition to Egypt, so Miles must have been only eleven or twelve back then. How kind of Papa to have taken the time to correspond with a young boy, to offer guidance and advice. But why had Miles not sought the answers to his questions from his own father, the Duke of Aylwin? Hadn't he, too, been a scholar of ancient Egypt?

The conundrum made her even more curious about Miles's upbringing. She had been intending to ask about his childhood, anyway.

She looked at the gray-haired housekeeper with her rosy cheeks and the butler with his pinched lips and aged features. "You've both been employed at Aylwin House for quite a long while, have you not?"

"I came here as a scullery maid near forty years ago." The housekeeper's blue eyes twinkled. "Mr. Pinkerton was a high-and-mighty footman. But he liked to pull my braids, that he did."

The butler paused in the act of sneaking a bite of cake to the mutt under the table. A flush crept up from his starched collar. "I did nothing of the sort, madam."

Mrs. Witheridge reached over and poked him in the arm. "Come, come, Pinky. There's no harm in admitting it. You were sweet on me from the start. If I hadn't wed the head stable lad, who knows, I might've been Mrs. Pinkerton!"

The butler's sunken cheeks turned redder. "Marriage was never for me. My life has been devoted to serving the Dukes of Aylwin. It is my sole avocation!"

"Bah, you're devoted to Maisie as well," Mrs. Witheridge said, casting a good-humored look down at the ragtag pup, who wagged her tail on hearing her name. "One would think *she* was your wife!"

Seeing Mr. Pinkerton part his thin lips in protest of such an absurdity, Bella said quickly, "Since you've both been here for many years, perhaps you remember my father, Sir Seymour Jones. He was employed by the fourth duke during the expedition to Egypt."

Mr. Pinkerton inclined his head in a nod, revealing an age-spotted scalp sprinkled with sparse white hairs. "Sir Seymour did indeed visit Aylwin House several times. He seemed a good-natured fellow. Always had a smile and a kind word for the staff."

That sounded so like Papa that Bella felt a hollow throb of loss. How she missed his smile. "I hope you don't mind my asking, but what sort of a man was the fourth duke—the present duke's father?"

"A proud and notable lord, indeed," Mrs. Witheridge said, clasping her hands to the shelf of her bosom. "And ever so grand and dignified. Why, nothing could ruffle the man. On Boxing Day each year, all the servants would line up in the great hall and he would hand us each half a crown. One year, I tripped on me skirt while curtsying, fell flat on me bum, and he never even blinked an eye!"

"On the contrary," Mr. Pinkerton corrected, "His Grace glared at you for making such a spectacle."

The Ducal Stare.

Bella suppressed a quirk of humor. Miles must have learned it from his father. "He sounds rather forbidding," she said.

"Perhaps to some," the butler said, elevating his chin. "However, one cannot judge a duke by common standards. As a man of great consequence, he must carry himself with the strictest of decorum."

" 'Tis the way of the aristocracy," Mrs. Witheridge added with a sage nod. "Why, look at our present duke.

Such a splendid nobleman and every bit as admirable as his father."

Miles, admirable? He was a haughty, vainglorious beast. He bedded concubines and then came home and tried to seduce his employee. His notion of decorum was to kiss a woman senseless and then shout at her when she dared to thwart him.

Bella kept her opinions mum. It wasn't her place to shatter their illusions of his character. Especially now when she very much wanted to understand the role her father had played in his childhood.

"Is His Grace an only child?" she asked. "I presume he can't have any brothers since his cousin is his heir."

The housekeeper gave a mournful shake of her head. "Alas, his mother, the duchess, had a number of stillborn babes. She was sickly, too, poor thing, often confined to her chambers. His Grace was her only infant to survive."

Bella resisted a tug of sympathy. Being an only child and the heir to a dukedom, Miles likely had been pampered. He most certainly had been raised to believe himself superior to ordinary folk. "Was His Grace close to his parents? Did he ever quarrel with his father?"

"Quarrel?" Mrs. Witheridge said, looking at Bella as if she'd sprouted two heads. "Why, young Miles was in the greatest awe of his sire. He was obedient to a fault, too, for the duke expected the best behavior of him. He was a happy child, nonetheless, always smiling, especially when his father granted him permission to go to Egypt." She turned to the butler. "You were there, Pinky. Did you not say that he threw his arms around the duke?"

"I said that he looked as if he *wished* to do so," Mr. Pinkerton corrected with a sniff. "Of course, it

would have been unseemly for the heir to have shown any display of affection."

"Was my father present?" Bella asked.

"Indeed," the butler said. "As I recall, *he* clapped the boy on the shoulder and congratulated him."

Bella found the story sad and disturbing. Perhaps Miles had not been so spoiled, after all. His father sounded like a stern taskmaster, devoid of warmth, and Papa had been forced to intervene on Miles's behalf. What was it he had written in the letter to Miles? *Aylwin can be a harsh fellow, but he wants the best for you. Tend to your studies if you wish to prove your merit. And pray be assured I shall speak to him about your joining the expedition.*

Gazing down at the dregs in her teacup, Bella realized that Papa had been more of a father to Miles than his own sire. No wonder Miles had felt so utterly betrayed. In the wake of his father's tragic death, he had also lost Papa, his mentor and friend, perhaps the only adult he'd trusted.

The housekeeper heaved a sigh. "Ah, the poor lad's happiness was short-lived. When next we saw him, a year and a half later, he was no longer Lord Ramsgate. He was the Duke of Aylwin. 'Twas such a tender age to be taking on the weight of his duties. Sometimes I think 'tis why he lives the way he does now."

"What do you mean?" Bella asked.

Mrs. Witheridge leaned forward in a confidential manner. "He was always a sunny lad, but his father's death changed him, it did. Ever since, he's filled the house with those dusty relics, devoted himself to his work day in and day out, never courting any young ladies. There's some that find an excuse to call here, hoping to catch his eye. Yet His Grace'll have nothing to do with any of 'em." She eyed Bella speculatively.

"You're the first lady he's ever allowed to stay at Aylwin House. Mayhap he has his eye on *you,* miss."

Bella almost dropped her teacup. If only they knew, any designs Miles had on her had nothing whatsoever to do with marriage. Before she could formulate a response, Mr. Pinkerton spoke.

"It is not for us to speculate about our betters," he chided. "His Grace will marry if and when he sees fit."

"Humph," snorted the housekeeper. "No doubt he would benefit from taking a wife. A few youngsters in the nursery would brighten this house and bring a smile to his face again."

Bella had her doubts about that. She would not wish the Duke of Aylwin on any decent young lady. He was too dictatorial, too bad-tempered, too self-absorbed, and entirely too conceited.

Though perhaps he would be pleasing in the bed-chamber.

Without warning, Bella's imagination conjured a shadowy bed and herself lying beneath the covers with him. They would kiss and caress in that wildly wonderful way and his hands would roam over every inch of her body, touching her in the most wickedly intimate manner . . .

The tinny chime of the mantel clock shattered the fantasy.

Heat flew into her cheeks, and Bella hoped the servants couldn't tell the illicit direction of her thoughts. She pushed back her chair. "Oh, look at the time! I really must return to work now. Thank you ever so much for the tea."

As she hastened out the door and started up the narrow servants' stairs, she mulled over the conversation. It had given her a better understanding as to why Miles had turned to Papa as a mentor. Despite all his wealth

and privilege, the duke apparently had not enjoyed an idyllic childhood. He had been the sole surviving child of a sickly mother and a harsh father. How very different from her own upbringing, with Lila and Cyrus to enliven their mountain hut, and Papa with his cheery nature. Even without Mama, they had been a close-knit family.

According to Mrs. Witheridge, Miles had once had a sunny disposition, too. But Bella found that hard to credit. The housekeeper must be deluding herself out of loyalty to her overlord. Surely one unfortunate event—even as terrible as his father's murder had been—could not have so drastically altered Miles's temperament.

Well, at least one mystery had been solved. Bella now knew why the Marquess of Ramsgate had sounded vaguely familiar to her. She had encountered the name a long time ago in Egypt. As a six-year-old, she would have heard Miles addressed as Lord Ramsgate. Perhaps she herself had called him that. How amusing to picture herself as a little girl trying to pronounce such a fancy title . . .

As she neared the top of the staircase, the door opened suddenly. An elegant blond lady in a mint-green gown stepped into the doorway. Helen Grayson, the wife of Miles's cousin and heir.

Her lips curling, she stared down at Bella. "Miss Jones."

Bella hid her surprise and inclined her head in a nod. "Mrs. Grayson. Fancy seeing you here."

"I rang for Witheridge, but she never responded."

"She's taking tea in her parlor. I came from there just now."

"Tea with the servants, Miss Jones?" A tinkle of lady-like laughter floated down the steps. "Oh, but I quite

forgot. *You* are the hired help, too. Do excuse me now."

Helen did not withdraw from the doorway to let Bella out into the upper corridor. Instead, she barged down the narrow staircase, forcing Bella to squeeze back against the wall while shrouding her in a blanket of cloying perfume.

But that wasn't the worst of it.

As the woman surged past, she ground her heel down hard on Bella's instep. The sharp pain wrested a gasp from her.

Unmindful of any injury she might have caused, Helen continued blithely down to the cellars, leaving Bella no choice but to limp up the remaining few steps to the main floor.

She clenched her teeth against a throbbing soreness in the upper portion of her foot. Her mind reeled with astonishment and belated anger. What had been the motive for Helen's viciousness?

For one thing was absolutely certain. The woman's action had been no accident. It had been a deliberate attack.

Helen Grayson despised her.

Chapter 13

A short while later, seated on an overturned wooden crate amid the piles of broken artifacts, Bella was examining the welt on her instep when the door opened and Miles strode into the drawing room.

She tensed, her gaze riveted to him. A ray of late afternoon sunlight slanted through one window to illuminate his starkly handsome features. He looked as informal as usual in dark trousers and white shirt, the sleeves rolled to his elbows. No smile animated his taut expression. Yet his aura of masculine vitality seemed to enliven the entire room.

Her wayward heart leaped against her breastbone.

It was the first time she'd seen him since their passionate kiss, and the abruptness of his entry here irritated Bella. That had to be the reason for her sudden attack of breathlessness. She had just removed her shoe and stocking, and propped her ankle on her other knee in order to get a closer look at the bruise that was beginning to show. Her skirts were hiked up and Miles likely had a spectacular view of her petticoats.

She lowered her bare foot at once, flattening it on

the dusty wood floor. "Good afternoon, Your Grace. It would have been polite to knock first."

He ignored the testy comment and stopped in front of her. His frowning gaze dropped to her hem. "What's wrong? Have you injured yourself?"

Bella rearranged the blue skirt to hide her toes. "It's nothing."

"It's something, or you wouldn't have removed your shoe and stocking to examine it." He dropped to one knee in front of her. "Let me take a look."

She scooted back on the crate. "No! Leave it be."

"Don't be coy." One corner of his mouth crooked ever so slightly. "It's nothing I haven't seen before."

On that, he caught hold of her ankle and lifted it onto his knee. Just as the time when he had examined her tattoos, his touch on her bare skin sparked a flare of heat up her leg and straight into her core. Only now, her awareness of him as a man was even stronger. Now, she remembered the feel of his hands on other parts of her body, including her bosom. And now, she was plagued by the memory of his kiss.

As if oblivious to her inner turmoil, he held lightly to her foot, his large fingers cupping her heel as he turned her foot to and fro, studying the reddened welt. "It's already bruising. What the devil did you do? Drop a chunk of granite on your foot?"

His critical tone raised her hackles. Bella would rather choke than tattle to him about Helen Grayson. "Something like that."

"It may need binding. I'll summon a physician."

She wrested her foot from his hold. "You needn't bother, for I shall refuse to see him."

Bella stuffed the white silk stocking into her pocket rather than put it back on in front of Miles. Then she wriggled her bare toes back into the beaded garnet

shoe. At least Lady Milford's slipper hadn't been harmed by Helen's spiteful act. Bella had promised to return the pair when she left Aylwin House.

Anxiety vibrated inside her. Maybe she would be going home sooner than the agreed-upon fortnight. Maybe Miles had come to the drawing room to send her away. The previous evening, she had threatened to kill him. She had held the sharp blade of her dagger to his throat to stop him from seducing her.

The look in his eyes had been furious. Clearly, the Duke of Aylwin was not accustomed to being bested by a woman.

What if he had thought it over and decided to dismiss her?

As she rose rather unsteadily from the crate, he wrapped his fingers around her upper arm to provide assistance. "You'll need a crutch," he decreed.

"No. No, thank you, I won't." His nearness made her giddy and she quickly stepped away, shaking out her wrinkled skirts. Bella didn't want to give him any more ammunition to prove she was unfit for service. "See? I'm not even limping."

To demonstrate, she walked around the rubble of several broken statues, following a path past the box of scarabs. Her foot still throbbed, though not as much as initially. She caught his sharp gaze tracking her progress. Not for the life of her would she allow even a trace of a hobble.

To distract him, she said, "By the by, I passed Mrs. Grayson on the stairs a short while ago. Does she often visit here?"

Miles shrugged. "Helen sometimes takes it upon herself to check the menus or the linens or such. It matters naught to me so long as she stays out of my way. Why do you ask?"

"I merely wondered if she would be sending a maid in here to sweep up the dust."

"Absolutely not. The staff has strict orders to stay away from my artifacts." His hands on his hips, he stalked behind Bella as she strolled. "Enough with this blather. Where were you earlier? I came here twice. You were gone for the better part of an hour."

His cold dictatorial manner put Bella on familiar ground. It felt invigorating, too, as if they were gearing up for battle. A battle for her right to stay here and find the treasure map.

She turned to confront him. "I was having a cup of tea. Do you have a rule against your employees taking refreshment?"

He subjected her to the Ducal Stare. "Next time, leave a note. None of the servants knew your whereabouts."

"Actually, I was downstairs with Mrs. Witheridge in her parlor. Mr. Pinkerton was there, too. So at least *two* servants knew exactly where I was." Taking a deep breath, Bella crossed her arms. "I have work to finish before sunset, Your Grace. I presume you came here for a purpose."

His scowl deepened. "I want a report on your progress."

"My progress?"

"You've been here for several days now. All I can see is that a few crates have been moved around here and there."

Her worries lifted with the hope of a reprieve. Perhaps he wouldn't discharge her if he saw how hard she'd been laboring. "Then pray look more closely. I spent two whole days sorting broken bits of pottery. Those have all been individually boxed, fifty-two in total. Allow me to show you."

Bella proceeded to a corner where a number of small wooden boxes were neatly stacked. She pried off the top of one. "All of the pieces stored in here belong to a single vessel. They are now ready to be glued back together should you wish it."

She turned to find Miles directly beside her. The air snagged in her chest. He stood so close that he could bend his head and kiss her if he chose. Not that she would permit him, of course. And his attention wasn't on her, anyway. He was peering into the crate.

"Each box contains the shards of one pot or jar?" he asked.

"Yes."

He shot her a suspicious glance. "You're certain you put the correct fragments together?"

"Absolutely. I often helped my father sort bits of broken pottery such as these. It's like assembling the pieces of a puzzle." If only Miles with his tantalizing lips would move away instead of blocking her in the corner. Flustered by his proximity, she found herself babbling. "I have plans for the other artifacts in this room, too. Many of them could be cleaned and repaired. The scarabs in particular. I'd like to put them on display."

Miles straightened up to glower at her. "Display?"

"They oughtn't be all jumbled in a crate. No one can appreciate them that way. If you were to provide me with a length of fine white silk, I could lay them out neatly on a table so that people could view the individual scarabs. There are other small objects, too, that could be better exhibited—"

"No."

The duke stalked away, and she stalked after him. "Why not?" she asked, surprised that he would reject such a sensible suggestion. "If each scarab was labeled

with a description, then people could actually see and appreciate their beauty."

He turned to snap over his shoulder, "What do you want, that I should invite the public inside to tramp all over my house and gawk at my artifacts? No, absolutely not."

She gritted her teeth. How arrogant of him to think that one man had the right to own such treasures and never share them with ordinary folk. But that issue was none of her concern.

"Not the public necessarily," she clarified. "I was referring to scholars like yourself. Mr. Banbury-Davis, for instance. Surely there are others, as well."

Miles snorted. "What is it about women? They always want to move things into storage and redecorate. The next thing you know, they're nagging you to host fancy balls and society parties."

His reaction was so absurd that she laughed. "Who said that?"

"Helen, for one. My mother, too, before she died. And every other lady who's ever set foot in this house. There was a young chit just a few months ago who proposed to refurbish the place on half an hour's acquaintance with me."

Bella watched him pace back and forth. She could see why he had never married and it wasn't just his cantankerous nature. He valued the Egyptian artifacts above all else—even love and family. He guarded them as jealously as a child guarded his marbles.

Why? Granted, the ancient relics were priceless, but why keep them hidden away in this great mausoleum of a house?

Bella wanted to dismiss it as selfishness. Yet she sensed that a deeper motive ruled him. A motive that he kept locked up as tightly as the artifacts themselves.

Might it have something to do with the death of his father? She certainly wouldn't ask him, not in his present state of ill humor.

"Well," she said, striving for a lighter tone, "you may rest assured that *I* have no desire to redecorate Aylwin House. I know nothing of the latest styles, anyway. And as for putting these artifacts into storage, it seems to me that you've already done that yourself."

"What the devil does that mean?"

"Look at this scarab." She picked up a stone beetle, half the size of her palm, and gently brushed off the dirt and dust. "It's beautifully carved with an inlay of lapis lazuli. Yet you've left it forgotten in a box with a hundred others. It might as well still be buried beneath the sands of an Egyptian desert."

His dark brows lowered in a scowl. He looked so thunderous that Bella deemed it prudent not to add that he kept more than mere artifacts concealed. Miles also had barricaded himself from the outside world. He took no part in society and preferred to work alone, suffering company only when absolutely necessary.

Yet he had hired her—despite his animosity toward her father. Miles had allowed her to handle his precious relics, too, although only the broken ones. Most curious of all, he had not dismissed her from his employ even though she had drawn a knife on him.

She carefully replaced the scarab atop the pile in the crate. Perhaps it only went to prove how keenly he craved an explanation for Papa's abrupt departure from Egypt. Miles wanted her to remember something significant. If it would give him peace, Bella wished she could oblige him.

"Fine," he growled suddenly. "I'll grant you permission to rearrange this one room as you like."

A thrill eddied through Bella, for she had not ex-

pected him to yield. Her lips curved in an irrepressible smile. "Truly? That's marvelous."

His moody gaze dipped to her mouth as if he found her expression of pleasure objectionable. "Just leave the rest of the house alone," he snapped. "I won't have you creating an uproar by shifting things hither and yon. Is that clear?"

"Yes, of course, and may I say—"

In the midst of her speech, he turned on his heel and strode toward the door of the drawing room.

Bella was taken aback. Even for such a pigheaded nobleman, his behavior was exceptionally rude. Irked, she hastened after him, ignoring the twinge in her foot. "Wait, Your Grace! Please."

He turned, one dark eyebrow cocked, his displeasure palpable. "What is it now? Do you need a crew of footmen to help you move these things? Use the staff as you wish, just don't bother me about it."

She gritted her teeth. He was insufferable, a completely different man from the ardent lover who had whispered sweet nothings in her ear. The mere memory of his silken voice made her insides melt. *We belong together.*

What rot. He'd probably uttered that same hackneyed phrase to scores of women.

But none of his other women had ever stopped him with a knife to his throat. No doubt he was still smarting from the blow to his pride. And since they had to live together under the same roof, perhaps it was best to clear the air.

"I merely wished to thank you," she said stiffly. "And I'm sorry if you're still angry . . . about last night."

A muscle clenched in his jaw. He stared down at her, his dark eyes so stony that Bella instantly regretted

mentioning their thwarted embrace. Oh, why had she not kept her mouth shut? Why had she felt compelled to remind him of such a thorn in his conceit? Better she should lie low and stay out of his path—

With dizzying swiftness, Miles backed her up against the wall. His strong arms bracketed her on either side. He didn't quite touch her, but he stood so close that Bella felt scorched by his body heat. Her heart leaped and her mind raced. She should push him away, she should duck under his arm. But her limbs refused to move. She could only gaze up into his masculine features, his expression now ablaze with the same passion that had so enthralled her the previous night.

He glided the backs of his fingers down her cheek. In that seductive tone she remembered so vividly, he murmured, "So you think I'm angry, do you?"

His touch. It unfurled tendrils of pleasure that tangled her thoughts. "Of—of course. What else—"

"Bella," he said huskily. "You're far too adorably naïve for such an intelligent woman. Can you truly not guess why I'm short-tempered?"

"No. Why don't you enlighten me?"

He bent his head so that his warm breath feathered over her lips. "It isn't anger, it's frustration. Sexual frustration. Last night, you set me on fire and then left me to burn. I'm still burning for you."

Every part of her body thrilled to his avowal. She oughtn't be pleased to hear that he still desired her— so much that it made him irritable and snappish.

"Then it's your own fault for kissing me." As her gaze strayed to his lips, she felt a tug of longing that required an instant denial. "And should you ever dare to do so again, you'll regret it."

A chuckle rumbled from deep in his chest. His

mouth curved in a rare smile that made his handsome face even more devastatingly attractive. Bella might have melted into a puddle from the force of that smile if she wasn't a strong, sensible woman and capable of resisting his allure.

"Keep your dagger sheathed, darling. I've never forced myself on an unwilling woman—and I never shall." His lashes lowered slightly as he traced her lower lip with his thumb. "If you ever decide that you want me, you'll have to—"

He bit off his words and glanced back over his shoulder. Footsteps approached out in the corridor. He dropped his hand from her face. In one fluid move, he stepped away from her and turned around.

Just in time.

Mrs. Helen Grayson entered the doorway. Her keen amber gaze flitted from Miles to Bella and back again. Her lips tightened ever so slightly in her perfect face. "Ah, there you are, Miles. Have I interrupted something?"

"Nothing at all," Bella blurted out before he could reply. She willed strength into her wobbly legs and took a few unsteady steps. "His Grace and I had just finished talking."

Miles cast an enigmatic glance at her that suggested otherwise. Then he turned to his cousin's wife. "You were looking for me, Helen?"

"Yes. I should like a word in private, if you please."

"Of course."

He walked away from Bella without a backward glance. He and Helen strolled into the corridor and vanished.

Shaken, Bella headed to an overturned crate and sank onto it. The twinge in her foot reminded her of Helen's callousness. Blast that woman. It was just like her to

barge in here and lure Miles away right in the midst of a very intimate and enlightening exchange. *If you ever decide that you want me, you'll have to . . .*

Have to what? What had he been about to say? That it would be up to *her* to initiate their next kiss?

Bella resisted the leap of fervor inside herself. There must be no more kisses, no more embraces. Miles wanted her in his bed without the shackles of marriage. He would cause her to fall from grace and then saunter away, his own reputation safeguarded by his rank.

Nevertheless, she reveled in the knowledge that he desired her. The Duke of Aylwin craved her with an intensity that made him behave even more beastly than usual. Why? What did he see in a twenty-nine-year-old spinster? The bloom of her youth had faded. She had spent the past fifteen years mothering her twin siblings.

Yet Miles found her desirable.

A delicious shiver coursed through Bella, for she found him very desirable, too. There, she'd admitted it. Miles tantalized her—and not just in the realm of the physical. He stirred her curiosity, too. He kept himself as closely guarded as these artifacts, and she sensed there was much more to him than he showed the world. How she would love to uncover all of his secrets . . .

No! Spending more time in his company would be the height of folly. She had to put Miles out of her mind and concentrate on her mission to hunt down the treasure map. That meant finding a way back into the storeroom where he'd forbidden her access.

And if he caught her again, what would he do to her? Foolish or not, she could scarcely wait to find out.

"Miss Jones appeared to be limping a bit," Helen said as they headed down the corridor. "Did she hurt herself?"

"Yes." Miles spoke curtly, recalling how Bella had

refused his assistance. She was the most stubborn woman he'd ever known. And also the most intriguing. He had never before realized how stimulating the ordinary scent of soap could be . . .

"What happened to her?" Helen asked.

Miles intercepted her sharp glance. He hoped to God she hadn't guessed that he and Bella had just been caught up in the most erotic nonembrace of his life. "A piece of stone fell on her foot."

"Ah!" Helen's lips curved in an arch smile. "That explains it."

Miles found her reaction unsavory. It would be just like her to revel in someone else's injury. But today he didn't want to contemplate the strange workings of Helen's mind. He would rather reflect upon what had just happened in the drawing room.

He felt almost cheerful as they entered his study. The encounter with Bella had vented a portion of his pent-up frustration. He had enjoyed trading wits with her, watching those animated blue eyes react to his suggestive comments. His touch on her face had caused her expression to soften. Even as she'd vehemently denied wanting to kiss him again, her gaze had flitted to his lips.

Yes, Bella desired him, though maidenly scruples stopped her from admitting it aloud. Clearly, she was determined to keep him at arm's length. He was sorely tempted to test that resolve.

Miles had always avoided virgins. He had no interest in marriage, so what was the point? His women were the sort who tumbled into bed at a snap of his fingers. They could be had for the price of a few coins. Pursuit had never been necessary. Whores were always there, always available, an efficient and straightforward means of satisfying his lust.

Now, however, he found himself relishing the prospect of the chase. He wanted to tease Bella, to flirt with her, to stir her desires. Her wit and intelligence made him curious to learn more about her likes and dislikes, her childhood and her years abroad.

But he had no intention of taking her to his bed. None whatsoever. He had made a firm decision about that, and he wouldn't relent. Bella Jones was merely a novelty to him, an enjoyable pastime. As soon as she supplied the information he wanted about Sir Seymour, Miles would send her on her way.

"There must be something quite interesting in those papers," Helen said lightly from her chair across from him. "I do believe you've forgotten my presence entirely."

Miles hadn't even been aware of sitting down behind his desk. Or staring at the loose pages of the hieroglyphic dictionary spread across the polished mahogany surface.

He leaned back in the leather chair and regarded his cousin-in-law. She made an angelic picture, the mint-green gown a perfect foil for her fair features. But he wasn't fooled. As usual, Helen had some busybody purpose for wanting to speak to him.

She was damned lucky he felt magnanimous today, or he'd already have sent her packing. "I was thinking about all the work I have to finish," he said. "So tell me what you want and be quick about it."

She worked her face into a pouty expression, one that she'd no doubt practiced in front of a mirror. "I'm only here to help you, Miles. You see, I've been considering the situation you're in, and I'm very concerned for you."

"Situation?"

"Yes. With Miss Jones living here. I realize that you

felt obligated to hire her, given her father's connection to the family, but—"

"I was not *obligated,*" he corrected in irritation. "I needed a job done, and she is doing it for me."

Helen pursed her lips. "But you must realize that it's highly irregular for a lady to live in the household of an unmarried gentleman. People are already talking."

"Let the snobs gossip, it means nothing to me." He gathered a few of the papers into a sheaf. "Now, if that's all you've come here to say . . ."

She leaned forward, her hands clasped in a virtuous pose. "Please, Miles, I beg you to consider how your behavior reflects upon Oscar and me. That is why I would like to offer the perfect solution. Something that would be best for everyone."

"And just what might that be?"

"I am proposing to act as chaperone to Miss Jones. Oscar and I can move into Aylwin House for the length of her stay, and then there will be no hint of impropriety."

Miles snorted. He could think of nothing more irksome than bumping into her and his foppish cousin every day. "Good God. You can't be serious."

"I am, indeed. Only think of Miss Jones. Do you care so little for her reputation?"

"I doubt she'll be entering society anytime soon."

"But when she leaves here, she may seek a post as a governess among the ton. She won't be hired if you've allowed her good character to be ruined."

Miles narrowed his eyes. Helen was too selfish to make altruistic gestures. She had to have a reason to keep a close eye on Bella; he doubted she'd inconvenience herself for fear of gossip. Did she view Bella as some sort of threat? The most logical answer jolted him. Nothing could strike greater terror into Helen's

social-climbing heart than the prospect of losing her chance to become a duchess someday. She must fear he meant to propose marriage to Bella. That he might sire a son to usurp Oscar's place as heir to the dukedom.

For an instant, his blood heated at the notion of claiming Bella as his own, having her in his bed, making love to her each night for the rest of his life. But he rejected the notion at once. His life was already arranged exactly as he wanted it. He had no need for a wife. Especially a headstrong one who would be constantly underfoot, reorganizing his artifacts and disturbing his concentration.

And despite Helen's accusation, he hadn't *allowed* Bella's reputation to be harmed. Bella had *asked* to be housed under his roof. It had been her choice, not his.

He pushed back his chair and stood up. "The answer is no. Miss Jones is not a guest here but an employee. As such, she requires no chaperone."

Helen's expression turned petulant. "Well!" she said huffily. "I don't believe you can see what is going on right under your nose. Men seldom do."

"See what?"

"Isabella Jones has designs on you, Miles. A woman can tell these things in other females. And from the way she looks at you, it is quite clear she is angling for an offer of marriage!"

Miles bit back a dark chuckle. So he'd guessed right about Helen's purpose. "Poppycock."

"It's true, I swear it. She's extremely crafty—only look at how she insinuated herself into your household. Being so plain-faced, she will no doubt be forced to concoct a ruse in which to trap you into wedlock. Be forewarned of that!"

If only Helen knew, Bella had fended *him* off with a knife.

"Bella, plain?" he mocked. "Rather, I would say she has fine blue eyes, a pleasing smile, and a handsome figure. Should I ever choose to court her, it is no concern of yours."

Helen paled. "Court her? Why, she was raised among savages!"

Miles had had quite enough of the woman's smug commentary. He pointed to the door. "Better a savage than a meddlesome gossip," he said. "Now, begone with you!"

Chapter 14

The following morning, Hasani entered the drawing room with a large package in his arms. His robes swirling around him, he walked briskly forward and laid down the parcel on a crate. "His Grace asked me to deliver this to you, Miss Jones."

Bella had been sorting through a box of miscellany. Her eyes widening, she hurried to him. "For me? But what is it?"

"I do not know. His Grace went out himself this morning to purchase it." The Egyptian valet waved his olive-skinned hand at the parcel. "He said you were to open it at once."

Mystified, she untied the string and tore away the paper. Inside lay a generous length of white silk. With a sigh of pleasure, she stroked her hand over the soft fabric. "Oh, how lovely!" She glanced at Hasani to find him watching with polite curiosity. "Yesterday, I suggested to the duke that the scarabs should be displayed on a piece of cloth like this. How kind of him to remember."

"Kind" seemed too mild a word. Bella felt stunned

and amazed that Miles had listened to her. It gratified her to think that he might truly support her proposal to exhibit his artifacts to their best advantage.

"Such a plan is most admirable," Hasani said, his face warming in a smile. "I have long believed that even damaged treasures such as these deserve to be honored. Perhaps I might bring some tables down from the attic for your use."

"Thank you, that would be most helpful." She tapped her forefinger on her chin while glancing around at the piles of broken statues and other bric-a-brac. "I shall have to think about how to make room for the tables."

Hasani bowed. "I will leave you to your work, then."

"Please, wait," she said as he turned to go. "If I might ask you a question."

Bella had been mulling over her mission. She had assumed the treasure map was in the storeroom attached to Miles's study. But what if she was wrong? What if it was hidden in another location?

"I would like to identify all of the items in this room," she told the Egyptian. "Do you know if there are files somewhere describing them? Or paperwork relating to the expedition? Surely someone must have written out notes or lists before the articles were shipped to England."

Hasani gave her a keen look. "Have you not checked the archives, then?"

"Are you referring to the place where the duke keeps the papyri?" Bella asked cautiously. "I was told not to enter there for fear of damaging the ancient documents."

"No, there is another chamber. Come, I will be happy to escort you there. If now is a convenient time, that is."

"Of course! That would be perfect."

As she fell into step beside him and they went out into the grand passageway, Bella couldn't believe her luck. Her hunch had proven correct. The map didn't necessarily have to be stored with the papyri. It might just as easily be tucked in with old notes and shipping lists. And since Miles had not forbidden her to enter the archives room, she would be free to search to her heart's content.

All of a sudden, she realized they were approaching the arched entry to the west wing. Her steps faltered and Hasani looked inquiringly at her. "Is aught amiss?" he asked.

"I'm afraid His Grace may not approve of me entering his private quarters."

Hasani gave her a slight smile. "Then you will be relieved to know that the archives room is right here."

He proceeded a few more steps to a closed door directly opposite the entry to the west wing. Wrapping his fingers around the brass handle, he swung open the white wood panel and politely allowed her to precede him through the doorway.

Bella walked inside to find herself in a long chamber as large and spacious as the blue drawing room. Murals of cavorting nymphs and satyrs decorated the high ceiling, and panels in shades of green and gold covered the walls. Clearly, the space had once been used as some sort of reception room under previous dukes.

Sunshine poured through the tall windows and illuminated the many rows of dark oak cabinetry. So this was where the Egyptian archives were kept, she thought in rising excitement. All of the paperwork related to the long-ago expedition to the Valley of

the Kings had been filed right here. There appeared to be quite a lot of drawers, enough to keep her busy for days. Why had she not thought of asking about the records sooner?

Then she noticed that the chamber was divided into two distinct areas. The filing cabinets took up only half the space. The other half, at the far end of the room, had open shelves stacked with numerous long packages that appeared to be wrapped in strips of linen. One of the swathed bundles had been propped upright within a man-sized casket. Its form was eerily human.

Her heart jumped. Were those . . . mummies? The swaddled remains of ancient pharaohs?

She was about to ask Hasani when he abruptly pushed past her without an apology. His attention was fixed on something beyond her, and an icy mask of fury had replaced his pleasant expression. The sudden ferocity of his countenance chilled her to the bone.

What had wrought the change in him?

In a whirl of white robes, the Egyptian flew toward the far end of the chamber, and Bella felt compelled to follow. She quickly realized what Hasani had seen.

In front of one of the windows, a man was leaning over a wooden table on which lay one of the mummies. He was slowly unwrapping the linen strips that bound the body. Bella recognized his balding head and stocky form, the ill-fitting brown coat and sloppy trousers.

Mr. William Banbury-Davis.

"Stop!" Hasani commanded. "Stop what you are doing at once!"

Banbury-Davis lifted his head, annoyance on his bulldog face. He brandished a pair of shiny tweezers in one hand. "Why the devil are you shouting?" Then

he glanced at Bella and gave her a brief, disgruntled nod. "Miss Jones."

His fists clenched at his sides, Hasani stalked straight to him. "You are not to unwrap any of these mummies unless *I* am present to supervise."

"Oh, bosh. I'm the scholar here, not you. Besides, Aylwin has granted me permission to work in this room for a few days."

Hasani stared coldly at him. "You have misunderstood, then. His Grace would never cede my right to oversee the process. These are sacred remains and they must be blessed before being unwrapped."

Banbury-Davis grunted a sound of skepticism. "What, do you fear the consequences if you fail to mutter your mumbo jumbo over it? As if Ra or Anubis might curse us all!"

"Perhaps you would prefer that I summon the duke to determine which of us has authority here."

The two men stared at each other for a few moments. Dust motes danced in a beam of sunshine, a benign contrast to the palpable tension in the air. Then Banbury-Davis tossed down the tweezers and stepped back. "Just get it over with, then. And for pity's sake, don't take all day."

The Egyptian stepped forward and placed both of his hands, palms down, over the wrapped face of the mummy. Bella watched in fascination as Hasani bowed from the waist in a pose of supplication. With his head bent, she could clearly view the stylistic eye tattooed on the back of his neck. But she couldn't quite make out the words he spoke, foreign words uttered in a musical murmur.

A little shiver raced over her skin. She was reminded of an image she'd seen chiseled on a granite stela in the ballroom, the depiction of a religious ceremony

with a pharaoh. Hasani might have been an Egyptian priest performing an ancient ritual.

Many hours later, trudging up the staircase to the east wing, Bella felt pleasantly weary. She had enjoyed a productive day in the drawing room and had worked late, forced to stop only by the loss of light at dusk. In her arm, she carried a sheaf of papers from the archives.

After the brief altercation with William Banbury-Davis, and the subsequent blessing of the mummy, Hasani had grown calmer. He had regained his natural friendliness and had escorted her to the section of cabinetry that contained the shipping lists. He had gathered the appropriate papers for her and then shut the drawer. Having no excuse to linger, she'd left him and Mr. Banbury-Davis to their work.

Bella fully intended to return to the archives in the dark of night. She itched to conduct a thorough search through all of the records. And she certainly didn't wish to do so under the watchful eyes of Hasani or Mr. Banbury-Davis.

Or the Duke of Aylwin.

Reaching her floor, she started down the long, shadowed corridor. Twilight shrouded the windows at either end, but she could still see her way through the gloom. As she walked, a sense of isolation settled over her. How peculiar to reside in the same house with Miles and yet not encounter him the entire day. She had not seen him since the previous afternoon when he had pressed her up against the wall and told her how much he burned for her.

The memory caused a throb of pleasure deep inside of her. She didn't understand how he could have such a powerful effect on her. He was far too domineering

and forceful. Yet he had given way to her wish to reorganize the artifacts. He had even gifted her with the white silk on which to display the scarabs. And he had agreed not to seduce her without her consent.

Not that she would ever grant him such permission, of course, for nothing could come of this attraction she felt for him. He would never offer marriage, and she would never allow him to ravish her. If he was expecting her to initiate their next kiss, he'd have to wait until he was as ancient as those mummies in the archives.

No, she must concentrate on finding the map. Then she could claim her half of the pharaoh's treasure from Miles, go home to Oxford, and resume her quiet life with Lila and Cyrus. All of the wild, inappropriate passions inside her would soon be forgotten . . .

Nearing the door to her bedchamber, Bella suddenly spied a movement in the gloom ahead. A wraithlike figure flitted through the shadows at the end of the passageway.

It hovered there for a moment, whitish and insubstantial. A faint unearthly moaning drifted down the corridor. Then the figure glided onward and vanished as swiftly as it had appeared.

Bella stopped dead and blinked. Gooseflesh prickled down her spine. What had she just seen? Nan had claimed this floor was haunted, but Bella had scoffed at the notion of ghosts.

She still scoffed. This apparition had looked like a person. A maid in her white apron, perhaps? No, Bella had had the impression of a pale, hooded robe.

Only one person in the household wore robes. But why would he moan like that? Why not come forward and greet her?

Perplexed, she hastened toward the place where the

figure had been. She looked around and spied a door at the end of a short passageway. There was nowhere else that a flesh-and-blood person could have gone to hide. Marching forward, she opened the door to peer into the blackness of a small staircase used by the servants.

"Hasani?" she called. "Are you there?"

Only the echo of her voice answered. Silence hung heavy, as thick and dense as fog. No tapping of footsteps gave evidence to the presence of any servant.

Disquiet raised the hairs at the back of her neck. Bella had the uncanny sense of being watched by someone in that stygian darkness. She craved to know who it was. But without a candle, she might stumble and fall. By the time she returned with one, whoever it was would be long gone.

Still holding the sheaf of papers, she walked slowly back to her bedchamber. One thing was certain. She had not been dreaming. Someone had been there. Someone had moaned, too, then had deliberately hidden himself from her.

It was almost as if the unknown person had *wanted* to frighten her.

Chapter 15

Nan was kneeling in front of the hearth, her mob-capped head bent almost to the floor as she blew on the glowing coals on the grate. Spying Bella entering the bedchamber, she hopped up and curtsied. "'Evenin', miss. There's a bit of a chill in here, so I thought ye might like a fire. I brung yer supper, too."

"Thank you." Bella laid down the papers on the bedside table, on top of the book about Egypt that she'd borrowed from the library. In the cheery brightness of the room, the spectral figure at the end of the corridor seemed less disturbing. Surely there was a logical explanation. "Did anyone come here looking for me a short while ago?"

"Why, no, miss. I been here this past quarter hour, turnin' down yer bed and lightin' the candles and the fire. Was ye expectin' a visitor?"

"Not really. I thought perhaps Hasani might have dropped off some papers, that's all. It isn't important."

So the robed apparition could not be explained by so simple a means, Bella thought as she went into the

dressing room to wash away the dust of the day's work. It was probably nothing more than a servant. She wouldn't waste another moment fretting over it. Better she should turn her mind to the expedition into the archives tonight.

She scrubbed her hands with a cake of lavender soap. As before, she would wait until past nine o'clock. Even though Miles hadn't forbidden her to go into that room, it would be best not to encounter him in the corridors. She had already ascertained from talking to the servants that he usually retreated to the west wing after dark to work in his study before retiring for the night.

Bella dried her hands on a linen towel. One problem nagged at her. Somehow, she needed to return the little packet of letters that Papa had written to the Marquess of Ramsgate. Sooner or later Miles would realize they were missing, and he was sure to guess who had taken them. The last thing she wanted was to give him a reason to seek her out. Especially since their last two encounters had resulted in kisses and flirting that had stirred the untamed sensual desires inside her . . .

Bella went back out into the bedchamber, intending to tuck the little packet of letters into her pocket. If the opportunity arose, she would slip them back into the storeroom and no one would be the wiser. Keeping the letters made her feel like a thief. They surely had a special meaning to Miles, or he wouldn't have saved them all these years. They were probably a reminder of her father's treachery, but she liked to think that perhaps he'd wanted to preserve the happy memories, too.

Opening the drawer to the bedside table, she reached into the shadowy interior. But the space was empty.

She brought a candle closer and stooped down to see only the bare wood interior.

The packet of letters was gone.

At precisely nine-thirty, Bella slipped into the archives and quietly shut the door. The room was pitch-dark save for the lighted taper in her hand. She looked around for a table on which to set the candlestick. Since the front half of the chamber held only rows of cabinetry, she proceeded to the back section.

There, shadows cloaked the numerous mummies that rested on the wall shelves. The sight that had stirred only scientific interest in her during the daylight hours now raised an uneasy quiver in her. She scoffed at the involuntary reaction. It was strange to come here at night when no one else was around, that was all.

The only table present was the one on which lay the mummy that Mr. Banbury-Davis had been unwrapping. He had not completed the process, and a cloth had been draped over the upper portion of the body.

Bella walked slowly forward. Compelled by curiosity, she grasped the square of pale linen and lifted it. A shriveled face stared back at her, the eyelids sunken over empty sockets, dried flesh clinging to the nose and cheeks, and yellowed teeth visible between withered lips.

She dropped the cloth back into place and took a deep breath. How silly to feel unsettled by the sight. As Papa always said, the dead could do no harm. The table was long, and she could work at the other end of it. Yet she balked at the notion of sharing space with a long-dead Egyptian.

Feeling a trifle foolish, Bella retreated to the cabinets and set the candlestick on the floor. Then she opened one of the file drawers and removed a thick

stack of papers. Sinking down, she sat cross-legged on the wood floor, her skirts tucked beneath her as she began the task of examining the documents by the light of the candle.

These appeared to be shipping manifests, nothing of particular use to her. As she paged through them to check for a hidden map, her thoughts strayed to those missing letters. She distinctly remembered tying the string around the packet and placing it into the bedside table two nights ago. She had questioned Nan, but the girl had vehemently denied ever seeing them. Bella had hunted all over the bedchamber in the vain hope that she'd absentmindedly misplaced them.

But the letters were gone. Vanished without a trace.

It seemed especially telling that she'd made the discovery shortly after seeing the phantom figure at the end of the corridor. There must be a connection. Had that person stolen the letters Papa had written to Miles? Why? If it had been Hasani, why would he have been searching her chambers anyway?

Bella had no answers. The mystery would have to wait until later. At the moment, she must make full use of her time here in the archives.

She returned the shipping manifests to their proper place and then gathered another armload of papers from a different drawer. Resuming her place on the floor, she quickly found this set to be far more interesting. So interesting that she moved the candle closer in order to better view the pages by the flickering light.

In her lap lay a series of sketches executed in bold strokes of black ink. Each page contained another unique and fascinating depiction. An obelisk rising from the ruins of a temple. A statue of a jackal-headed god at the entry to a tomb. A plowman in Egyptian garb behind two long-horned cattle.

She came upon a drawing of a fishing boat on a river. Palm trees lined the bank, and reeds grew thickly at the water's edge. A frog perched on a flat stone, its tongue flicking out to catch a fly.

All of a sudden, the scene came alive with the blue sparkle of the river, the blinding brightness of the sun, and the sensation of rushing forward to catch the green frog, only to see it plop into the water and disappear beneath the rippled surface . . .

She blinked and the color vanished. The sketch once again became black ink on white paper. Had that been a flash of memory from her childhood? It must have been, though she could recall nothing else beyond that brief fragment.

All of a sudden, she grew aware of the distant sound of footsteps. Someone was approaching out in the corridor. That heavy tramp could only belong to a man.

Her fingers tightened around the pile of sketches in her lap. She glanced over her shoulder, but the row of cabinetry hid the door from her view. She had closed it, Bella felt certain of that. And no one could possibly spy the feeble light of the candle back here.

The tension seeped out of her. She was quite safe.

The passerby was likely a servant summoned from belowstairs for some purpose. Perhaps he was delivering a decanter of brandy to the duke. Or hot water for washing.

But even as it seemed the man was about to proceed on past, the footsteps stopped outside the archives. The door handle rattled slightly as if he'd grasped hold of it.

Alarm seized Bella. She quickly pinched out the single candle flame with her thumb and forefinger. The room plunged into darkness just as the door swung open.

Chapter 16

The unknown man entered the archives room. A moment of silence reigned in which Bella hardly dared to breathe. Then his firm tread advanced toward the back section where the mummies were located. He was carrying a candle, for its glow cast wavering shadows on the high ceiling.

She sat very still on the floor. The faint scent of melted wax hung in the air. Thank heavens she had chosen the last row of cabinetry in which to examine the sketches. With any luck, he wouldn't notice her in the gloom.

She could hear his every footfall, slow and steady now, as if he were taking the time to peer into every nook and cranny. His steps seemed to turn toward the mummy on the table. The shadows shifted suddenly, an indication that he must have raised his candle to better light the area.

Who was he?

Surely not the duke; fate couldn't play such a cruel trick on her twice. Perhaps Hasani had come to utter

another chant over the mummy. Perhaps Mr. Banbury-Davis needed to fetch a forgotten notebook. Perhaps the robed apparition had actually been a thief who was prowling through the house, looking for items to steal . . .

She reached stealthily for the dagger in her pocket. Then something moved into the opening at the end of the cabinetry.

A dark hulking beast.

Her fingers closed around the shaft of the knife just as the fiend lifted his candle. In the pale light, he transformed into a man clad in dark trousers and a loose white shirt, the sleeves rolled to his elbows. The flame held high in his hand cast shadows on his harsh features.

Miles.

Bella's heart did a somersault. Torn between relief and dismay, she left the dagger in her pocket. How guilty she must look, she realized, cowering against the cabinet with her legs tucked beneath her, the purloined sketches in her lap.

"I knew I'd seen the glimmer of a candle in here," he said. "This room is visible from the window of my study."

Oh, drat. She should have thought to close the draperies. Since the archives room faced the back gardens, it had never occurred to Bella that someone might spot her. But it did make horrible sense. Aylwin House was built in the shape of an *H,* with the two wings extending beyond the central portion. His study was in the west wing and looked out over the gardens, too.

She swallowed, her mouth so bone-dry that her voice came out a croak. "Good evening, Your Grace. What a surprise to see you."

He fixed her with the Ducal Stare. "What the devil are you doing in here so late?"

"I'm working. I didn't realize this room was off limits, too."

"I never said that it was." He stalked toward her. "Why are you sitting in the dark?"

"A draft of air blew out my candle. I was just about to leave when you came in and frightened me half to death."

He stopped in front of her. One corner of his mouth tilted in an ironic grin that eased his severe expression. "Nonsense. You pinched it out when you heard me touch the door handle. Go on, admit it."

He knew. A flush crept into her cheeks. Oh, why had she been so foolish? She ought to have kept the candle burning. In retrospect, it looked far more suspicious to have snuffed it.

He towered over her, and she was forced to tilt up her chin to look at him. "So what if I did?" she said brashly. "I knew it might be you out there. And given your recent bout of ill temper, I had no wish to risk another encounter."

Beyond cocking an eyebrow, he let that go without a challenge. "What are you looking for in here?

"Records that describe the artifacts in the drawing room. Hasani gave me some lists, but they weren't quite complete." That was a fib. She didn't know if they were complete or not. She'd done little more than glance through the papers before leaving them in her bedchamber.

Miles lowered the candle so that the light fell upon the sketches. "Those don't look like lists in your lap."

"Oh, these?" She affected a laugh. "I happened upon them in one of the drawers, that's all. I was very curious to view more pictures of Egypt. One of them—this one on top—made me remember seeing such a scene."

"You had another memory from when you were a little girl?"

"Yes, I was trying to catch a frog, but it hopped into the water and vanished." She lightly traced her fingers over the frog perched on the flat stone. "I must have been present when this sketch was drawn."

"I wouldn't be so sure. Frogs are commonplace along the Nile. You'd probably chased scores of them."

She glanced up at him. "Do you know who the artist was?"

His expression went blank. "My father. Which is precisely why I doubt you were there when he drew that. He did not suffer prattling brats." Miles held out his hand. "Come."

Bella automatically placed her hand in the duke's. According to the servants, his father had been a cold, autocratic man. Miles had been in awe of him. A happy boy when he'd gone off to Egypt, he'd returned forever changed. It was as if he'd inherited his father's stern disposition along with the title. Was there any part of that carefree nature still hidden inside him? Every once in a while, she caught a glimpse . . .

His strong fingers wrapped warmly around hers as he pulled her to her feet. The brief touch was enough to scatter her thoughts when she needed to focus on the conversation.

"Come where?" she asked.

"To my study. And bring along the sketches. I want to see what else you might remember."

A few minutes later, Miles ushered Bella into his private sanctum. Anticipation thrummed in his veins as he guided her to one of the chairs by the hearth, where a fire burned on the grate. "Pray sit down. I'll fetch you

something to drink before we look through those illustrations."

Leaving her, he went to the sideboard to grab a glass and then proceeded to a linen-draped table by the window. There, he poured a measure of burgundy wine from the decanter beside his dinner tray.

He could scarcely believe he had her all to himself. The evening had turned out to be far more interesting than he'd planned. On an ordinary night, his routine consisted of eating here in his study while working on his hieroglyphics dictionary, often until midnight. But a short while ago, as a footman had delivered the tray of food, Miles had stepped to the window to peer out at the darkened garden.

That was when he'd spied the faint glow in the archives, which was situated perpendicular to his study.

His first thought had been that Banbury-Davis had left a candle burning. Concerned that such carelessness could cause a fire, Miles had gone there to check, only to find the room pitch-dark. Immediately, he'd had the uncanny sense that someone was hiding nearby.

He should have known the culprit would be Bella.

The guilt on her face had spoken volumes. She had snuffed her candle in order to conceal her presence. And he didn't believe her excuse of wanting to avoid him. She must have been searching for something in the files. What the devil could it be?

Was that also the reason he'd caught her here in his study two nights ago, poking through the papyri storeroom? That incident suddenly seemed more suspicious, too.

Why didn't she just ask him for whatever paperwork she sought? He knew the contents of every last file in those cabinets, right down to the most insignificant bill

of sale. There was nothing private or hush-hush about the papers. He had personally seen to it that all the records from the expedition had been organized for future reference, from his father's notes and illustrations to the official purchase documents from the Egyptian government for each artifact.

Miles wanted to demand an answer from her. But Bella was a strong-willed woman, and he doubted that she'd surrender her secrets on command. He would have to watch and listen, perhaps trick or coax her into revealing her purpose.

Yes, *coax*. He could think of an infinite variety of ways to charm her into trusting him . . .

Holding the wine glass, he turned to find Bella standing directly behind him. So much for expecting her to heed his request to sit by the fire. She didn't seem to know the meaning of the word "obey." Yet perhaps that was part of her allure; she had a free spirit that refused to bow to his control.

Even now, she seemed oblivious to him. Her full attention was focused on a shelf on which stood a painted funeral mask from the New Kingdom. "How beautiful," she murmured.

She was beautiful in the candlelight, a few strands of brown hair curling around her face, drawing his attention to those kissable lips. The blue fabric of her gown clung to her womanly contours and made him fantasize about the pleasure of disrobing her. Who would have thought that a high-necked, long-sleeved dress could be so seductive?

"Yes," he murmured. "Very lovely, indeed."

She turned to him and her lapis lazuli eyes widened with the realization of his compliment. As a pretty blush spread over her cheeks, he pressed the glass into her hand. "Wine?"

"Thank you." Her gaze strayed to the table where a silver dome covered the tray of food. "Oh, I'm sorry! Have I interrupted your dinner?"

"It's no matter." Miles paused, considering, calculating. If he hoped to relax her guard, this might be a way to do it. "I'd be happy to share. Cook always sends far too much for one person. I've given up trying to convince her to do otherwise."

Bella sank her teeth into her lower lip. She was likely debating whether or not dining with him constituted something more intimate than paging through a pile of sketches. "I really shouldn't . . ."

"On the contrary, you should." He plucked off the silver dome and revealed several plates heaped with bread and cheese, cold beef and chicken, fruit and cakes. "There. How can you resist such a feast?"

Her hungry gaze flitted over the food. "Well . . . I didn't eat much of my dinner tonight."

"Excellent. I'll ring for another plate and silverware."

"Please don't. I'll use my fingers." Sitting down, she broke off a piece of bread, dabbed it in a dish of softened butter, and then added a crumble of cheddar. "It's how the natives eat in Persia—and Egypt, too, I'm sure. Don't you remember?"

Miles sat down opposite her. He watched, fascinated, as she popped a bite into her mouth. "I do, though I was never permitted to follow suit," he said. "Even while living in tents in the desert, my father insisted that every meal be served with fine linens and silver as if we were at a formal dinner back in England."

As he passed her a starched white serviette, she observed, "I see that you've carried on the practice."

"It is the way things have always been done at Aylwin House." Miles poured himself a generous splash

of wine. "The servants would be aghast if I were to change any of the traditions."

Watching him pick up his silverware, she said, "Then I dare you to do so. Right now."

"Do what?"

"Put down that fork and knife, and eat with your fingers like me." A mischievous smile on her face, she plucked a ripe strawberry from a bowl and nibbled on it. It was clear she didn't expect he'd really comply.

Miles slowly laid down the implements. He could scarcely tear his gaze from her lips, reddened from berry juice. He wanted to forget about the damn food, take her straight to his bed, and feast on the delicacy of her mouth—along with other delectable parts of her body.

Instead, he wrapped a slice of roast beef in bread and concentrated on eating with his fingers. It felt oddly liberating to shun the rules of a lifetime. Who would have thought he could be tempted into doing so by the irksome little imp who'd once tagged after him in Egypt?

"Why didn't you finish your dinner?" he asked. "Was it not to your liking?"

She flicked a cautious look at him from beneath her lashes. Had she been in a rush to get to the archives room?

Then she surprised him by saying, "Please don't think me ungrateful, Your Grace, but English food is . . . rather bland. It isn't anything like what I was accustomed to eating in Persia."

"And what would that be?"

She picked up a chicken leg and tore off a bite, then licked her fingers. "Fresh fruit like figs and dates and pomegranates. Spices like mint and lemon and pepper. Cakes made with honey instead of sugar."

Bella leaned forward, and his gaze irresistibly followed the shape of her blue-covered bosom against the white linen tablecloth. In a confiding tone, she went on, "If you promise not to tell, I'll let you in on a secret. It's something that no society lady would ever admit to doing."

His mind raced over a dozen possibilities, all of them involving naked bodies and scented oils, or succulent bits of fruit tucked in forbidden places. He took a swig of wine to ease his dry throat. "Go on."

"Well, then, allow me to confess that I'm an excellent cook," she said. "Perhaps sometime I could make my favorite dinner for you, *khoresht-e bademjan*, a lamb stew with aubergine and turmeric. And for dessert, an ice cream with saffron and pistachios. Though I'm not quite certain where one might find such ingredients in London. I used to buy them from vendors in the bazaar."

Miles wanted that look of dreamy longing on her face to be for him, not cookery. "Do you miss living in Persia?"

Sipping from her wine glass, she glanced out the darkened window. "In some ways, yes. Yet in many others, no, not at all. We only had one servant, so quite a lot of the daily drudgery of housework fell to me. Of course, when my s—" Bella broke off, her wide-eyed gaze cutting back to him as if she'd said something wrong.

"When what?" he prompted.

She shaped her lips into a polite smile. "Nothing. That life is behind me now, Your Grace, and I shan't bore you by dwelling upon it. But pray be assured that I feel quite pampered at Aylwin House. I have my own maid to fetch hot water, to light the fire, and to make up the bed. I fear I shall be quite spoiled by the time I leave here!"

Miles didn't want to consider her departure. He was fast growing accustomed to her presence in his house—though surely sexual frustration had to be the root cause of his fascination with her. Hell, he'd make up her bed himself if only she'd let him into it.

Not, of course, that *that* would ever happen. She had made clear her opinion of his seduction by holding a dagger to his throat.

As he ate, he kept a shrewd eye on her. He still needed to determine why Sir Seymour had left Egypt so precipitously. And that meant persuading her to talk about him. "If you were so busy with chores, how did you find the time to work with your father?"

"In the evenings I would help him with his journals. And once in a while I was able to go with him to the excavation site at Persepolis."

"Why only once in a while? If you had a servant and lived in a small hut, there can't have been all that much housework for just you and your father."

Her gaze turned cool and oddly secretive. "Clearly, *you* have never run a household, Your Grace," she said, then pushed back her chair. "Now, it's getting rather late, and I mustn't keep you. Shall we look at those sketches?"

Miles suspected she wasn't telling him everything about her life in Persia. Putting up a barrier to further questions was a tactic he knew well since he'd done the same himself many times. But he decided to let it go for the moment. Better he should encourage her to feel as relaxed and open as she'd been earlier. That way, she might be enticed into confessing her real purpose to lurking in the archives.

And she might lower her guard and flirt with him. He might have another chance to hold her beautiful

body in his arms. The very thought sent blood rushing to his loins.

He shifted the candelabra to the edge of the desk where it would shed more light onto them. Then he handed her the stack of sketches as she sat down. Instead of taking the opposite chair, Miles pulled over an ottoman. It allowed him to sit as close as possible to her under the guise of viewing the drawings.

"You remembered the scene in the topmost one," he said. "You were chasing a frog."

"Yes, but it was only a fragment of memory, nothing helpful." After an initial wary glance at him, she became absorbed in turning the pages, studying each pen-and-ink sketch in turn: a whirling dervish in his flying robes, an oasis surrounded by palm trees, a temple with a headless statue of the warrior Pharaoh Ramses II.

Bella passed over those images and a number of others without comment until she arrived at the final drawing in the stack. Her eyes widened. "Look at all the boys riding on camels. Goodness, there are so many of them!"

"It was a race." Memory transported Miles back to the blinding sun, the hot sand, the exuberant yells of the youths. As if it were yesterday, he could feel the tug of frustrated yearning inside himself. "I remember wanting very badly to join those Bedouin lads."

"But your father wouldn't permit you?" Bella guessed.

Her direct gaze made him uncomfortable, as if she could see straight into his soul. He didn't want her to realize just how much his father's curt order had crushed him.

He glanced back at the sketch. "Aylwin was right to

do so. As I'd never ridden a camel, I'd likely have broken my neck."

Bella raised an eyebrow. "You called him Aylwin? Not . . . Papa?"

"Of course. He deserved my respect. He—" Miles clenched his teeth. How had she turned this into a discussion of *his* past? "But enough about me. Don't *you* remember anything of that day? You were present in the crowd, watching the race with your parents."

She slowly shook her head. "I'm sorry, it's all a blank to me. I don't recall anything about it."

"You're certain of that."

"Yes." Without warning, she placed her hand on his bare forearm. "I do wish you could have ridden in that race, Miles. But your father surely denied your request out of love. You were his only child and he must have feared to lose you."

A glut of emotions crowded his throat. Aylwin had feared to lose him, yes. But love? He had been valued as the heir and nothing more.

The warmth of her hand penetrated his skin. It made him want to blurt out things he'd never told anyone. Things best left unsaid. "It doesn't matter. It was a long time ago."

"Of course it matters. A father always has a lasting influence on a child's life. Even a father who is stern and authoritative."

He stiffened. "I don't recall describing him that way."

At his chilly tone, she withdrew her hand. "But you mentioned earlier that he didn't care much for children. Your exact words were 'he didn't suffer prattling brats.' Did that include you? Did you have angry words with him when he forbade you to join the camel race?"

"No! I told you, I respected him."

She frowned slightly. "So you'd *never* quarreled with him? Not ever?"

Her meddlesome questions resurrected the buried memory. Little did she know, he had not dared to stand up to his father except for one fateful time. Now, bitter regret welled up in his chest to choke him. If he hadn't rebelled, if he'd just been a dutiful son, Aylwin would never have died . . .

Miles surged to his feet and aimed an icy scowl down at her. "Enough of this inquisition. Since you don't seem to remember anything useful, this is a waste of my time."

Her expression rueful, Bella gazed up at him. "Forgive me for prying, Your Grace. I suppose I deserve the Ducal Stare this time."

"What?"

"The Ducal Stare. You often use it to intimidate people." Looking not in the least bit intimidated herself, she rose gracefully from the chair. "Might I borrow a candle? I seem to have left mine in the archives."

Stifling his explosive temper, Miles turned on his heel and stalked to his desk. He cast an irritated glance around the study, but could only lay his hand on the candelabrum. Bollocks! Why the devil were there no more candlesticks within sight? There ought to be at least half a dozen of them!

He stomped back to her side. "I'll have to walk you to your bedchamber."

As he started toward the door, she trotted alongside him. "If we go to the archives, I can fetch my own candle and then you won't need to escort me."

"No!" He'd be damned if he let her dictate even the smallest matter to him. "I said that I would walk you back, and that's that. You oughtn't be wandering the house alone at night, anyway."

"Why not?"

Their footsteps echoed in the shadowed corridor, hers light and quick as she kept up with his long strides. "You could trip on your skirts and fall down the stairs," he said darkly. "You could break your neck and no one would even know until morning."

"Are you accusing me of being clumsy, Your Grace?"

A thread of amusement underlay her words, and her flippancy only fed his ill humor. "Yes, I am," he snapped. "You dropped a piece of stone on your foot just the other day, did you not?"

She fell silent at that, thank God. He'd had enough of her chatter for one night. He didn't want to hear another syllable out of her. She might have the softest, sweetest lips he'd ever tasted, but there was nothing soft or sweet about the words she spoke. Every one was tart and impudent and too bold by half.

The Ducal Stare, indeed! He wouldn't need to use intimidation if Isabella Jones had the sense to keep her nose out of his private affairs. But she always poked and pried until she'd ripped the scab off old wounds. To think that he'd purported to *like* her presence in his house.

Yet he did. In spite of everything, he wanted her here with him. There was a vitality about Bella that he craved, a warmth that reached to the cold places in his soul. The notion of returning alone to his solitary study held very little appeal.

As they started up the marble steps to the east wing, he cast a sidelong glance at her. She was frowning, her gaze turned downward as if she were lost in thought. Why was she being so quiet?

Had he hurt her feelings?

Remorse edged out his ill temper. He had spoken

sharply to her, perhaps too sharply. Since she didn't know the truth about that fateful event in Egypt, she couldn't have intended to touch a raw place in him.

"How *is* your foot?" he asked in a conciliatory tone. "You seem to be walking well enough."

"My foot? Oh. It's a little bruised, that's all."

She sounded distracted, as if he'd intruded on the mysterious workings of her mind. Since she didn't seem interested in conversation, Miles had to wonder what occupied her thoughts so thoroughly. It couldn't be him. Because then she would be smiling at him, flirting like other women or using witty repartee to amuse him.

Instead, Bella seemed oblivious to his presence. Why *wasn't* she thinking about him, dammit? It was disconcerting to be ignored. Here they were, alone together at night, in a setting ripe for romance.

But he had no intention of seducing her, Miles reminded himself. He had decided that on the night she'd threatened him with her dagger. Perhaps he should be grateful that she did nothing to tempt him now. He could ill afford to encourage any closeness between them.

After all, he intended to oust her from this house once he found out key information about her father's departure from Egypt.

Reaching the top of the stairs, they proceeded down the gloomy corridor with its many unoccupied guest chambers. Miles held up the candelabrum, and the light cast a pale nimbus over Bella's profile, the well-defined cheekbones, the pert little nose, the stubborn chin. And those soft, soft lips that he craved to taste again . . .

Toward the end of the passageway, she stopped at a closed door. Her bedchamber. He half expected her to

go inside without so much as a farewell. After all, she hadn't uttered a word to him for at least five minutes. It was as if he had ceased to exist for her.

Suddenly she swung to face him. Rich and blue, her eyes lifted to his and held firm. He felt the force of her gaze like a bolt of energy. In that moment he knew that she hadn't forgotten him at all.

She laced her fingers together in an oddly nervous gesture. Her bosom lifted as she drew a deep breath. "Your Grace, I've a confession to make. And I warn you, it won't be to your liking."

Chapter 17

So, Bella thought, she had said it. There was no going back. She would have to tell him now.

Without a doubt Miles would be furious. He jealously guarded his privacy, and he would not be happy to learn what she had done. Nevertheless, she must not quail. She knew of no other way to accomplish her objective of persuading him to talk to her about the past.

He cocked a dark eyebrow. At least his mood seemed to have mellowed, she judged. He no longer exhibited the cold anger he'd shown earlier in regard to her impetuous questions about his father. He might rant and rail, but he would overcome his fury about this, too.

She hoped.

With one hand, he held the candelabrum. He placed the other hand high on the door frame, effectively blocking her in the narrow indentation of the door. "A confession," he mused, studying her face. "Does this have to do with your poking through my files tonight?"

He'd struck close to the mark. But not close enough.

Bella swallowed. "Not tonight. Two nights ago. I borrowed something from you."

"Borrowed? I know about your dagger." He frowned. "And I should hope you wouldn't be so careless as to take a piece of papyrus."

"Of course not! I know it's fragile." He stood close, too close. The hard panel of the door pressed into her spine. "The truth is . . . I happened upon a packet of letters. I recognized my father's penmanship on the outside. They were addressed to the Marquess of Ramsgate."

All amiability vanished from his face. In the candlelight, his expression became as stiff and unforgiving as a funeral mask. "So you took my personal letters, by God. And no doubt you read them, too."

"Yes. Though I didn't realize at first that *you* were Ramsgate. It was only later that I figured it out." Bella bit her lip. Perhaps an emotional plea could wipe the coldness from his expression. "Please do try to understand, Your Grace. I lost my father less than a year ago, and I couldn't resist the chance to read his words. I thought the letters might reveal a clue as to why he never told me about our time in Egypt. I didn't mean any harm."

"No harm." Contempt in his tone, Miles walked a few steps away and then turned to face her again. He ran his fingers through his hair, mussing the dark strands. His eyes had never looked so stony. "Those letters were private. Do you ever think before you act?"

His accusatory tone only made her feel worse. On the walk here, she had fretted over the prospect of telling him the truth, arguing with herself, turning coward several times before rallying her courage. She could have kept quiet. He likely wouldn't have discov-

ered the letters were missing until long after she'd left Aylwin House.

But he deserved to know what had happened. And she hoped it might give her an opening to ask more questions. She sensed an inner pain in him, something connected to his father—and hers. Something that had festered in him all these years. Something more than the fact that Papa had abandoned him in Egypt.

Whatever it was, she yearned to help Miles resolve it. Otherwise, he would spend the rest of his life hating Papa.

"That isn't the worst of it," she admitted. "You see, the letters have vanished. I can't find them anywhere."

His jaw clenched. "The devil you say!"

"I'm very sorry, Your Grace." Bella had hoped the confession would lift a burden from her, but instead she felt small and miserable. "I put them in my bedside table for safekeeping. But when I looked for them earlier, to return them to the storeroom, they were gone."

"You misplaced them."

She shook her head emphatically. "No, I distinctly recall securing them in the drawer. I've searched throughout my bedchamber and they're nowhere to be found."

"They can't have walked away on their own." He strode toward her. "Blast it, move aside. I want to look for myself."

Bella turned around, opened the door, and preceded him into the bedchamber. Clearly Miles doubted her word, and she felt compelled to prove herself.

Thick shadows cloaked the corners of the room, veiling the chairs by the hearth and the large four-poster bed. The draperies had been drawn over the

tall windows. The only light came from the dying embers of the fire—at least until Miles strode inside with the candelabrum.

She hastened to the bedside table and opened the drawer. "See? There's nothing here. The letters are gone."

He came closer so that the candlelight spilled into the empty space. "You're certain this is where they were."

"Absolutely. I was reading them in bed before I went to sleep. Then I tied them up with string and put them away here."

Miles leaned forward to glance behind the table. "Who would have taken them? I presume no one comes into this room but your maid."

Bella considered telling him about the ghostly robed figure she'd spied at the end of the corridor. That had been a person, she was sure of it. But in his present fit of temper, Miles likely would accuse her of being irrational.

She watched as he set the candelabrum on the table and then hunkered down to peer under the bed. Gazing down at his broad back, she felt anxious to win back his goodwill. If only he could be as relaxed and charming again as he'd been over dinner . . . "I questioned Nan, but she swore that she never saw any letters. She wouldn't have looked in this drawer, anyway. I've no reason to doubt her word—"

"Here they are."

Miles reached under the bed and withdrew the packet of letters. He brushed off a few wisps of dust that clung to the edges.

Bella blinked, scarcely able to believe her eyes. "How in the world did they get under there?"

He rose to his feet. "Perhaps you only thought you

put the letters into the drawer. If you went to sleep with them, they could have slipped out of your fingers and fallen beneath the bed."

Stunned, she took the little packet from him and turned it over in her hands. All of the letters appeared to be present. But the explanation didn't fit her memory. She hadn't gone immediately to sleep after putting the letters away. She'd sat up against the pillows, puzzling over the identity of the Marquess of Ramsgate and reminiscing about her father . . .

All of a sudden, Bella noticed something odd. "I tied a bow in the string," she said. "But this one is knotted."

Miles gave a dismissive shake of his head. "If you were weary enough to fall asleep with them, then you can't be so certain how you secured them."

But she *was* certain. She'd taught Lila and Cyrus always to tie loops since knots could be difficult to undo. Was it possible that someone *had* taken the letters? And after reading them, had placed the packet under the bed to fool her into thinking she'd dropped it there?

Yes, it was conceivable. But who would have done so?

Hasani?

The Egyptian might have been the robed figure. Yet having worked in this house for many years, he'd have had ample opportunity to read the letters. It made no sense for him to wait until now to do so. And why would he have been poking around in her bedchamber, anyway?

Bella kept those uneasy speculations to herself. Miles still looked angry, his mouth compressed and his eyebrows lowered. He was already provoked by her for having borrowed the letters. She certainly didn't

wish to add fuel to the fire by voicing suspicions of his longtime valet.

She clutched the small packet to her bosom. He was no longer the warm, appealing man who'd shared a meal with her; he had reverted to being the chilly, remote Duke of Aylwin. She ached to restore the camaraderie between them. If only she knew how.

"I'm sorry for taking the letters without your permission, Your Grace. I swear I had no idea at the time that Papa had written them to *you*." Taking a few steps, she stopped directly in front of him. "I suppose you'll be wanting them back now."

She held out the packet, but he made no move to take it. He gazed down at her with an intensity that made the very air come alive. "Keep them," he said. "They mean more to you than they do to me."

"But you've saved them all these years. You surely must have done so for a reason."

"Whatever the reason, it no longer matters." His gaze dipped to her bosom. "Especially when I've more important things on my mind."

A thrill skittered over her skin, as if he had reached inside her bodice to caress her bare flesh. His eyes held a raw desire that called to her deepest feminine yearnings. In a silken growl, he added, "I shouldn't be here, you know. It isn't proper. You surely must realize how unseemly it is to invite a man into your bedchamber."

Out of the corner of her eye, Bella could see the large bed, the pillows plumped and the covers turned down invitingly. What would it be like to shed her clothing and lie naked in his arms? To let him do with her as he willed? To engage in all manner of wicked acts?

A flush suffused her. She mustn't wonder, she mustn't even *think* such forbidden thoughts. "I don't re-

call inviting you," she said tartly. "Rather, you barged in here without my permission."

"Ah, but *you* opened the door. And that is an invitation to tempt even the most scrupulous of gentlemen." He brushed his forefinger over her lips, making them tingle. "However, I've no wish to face your dagger again. So I'll bid you good night."

Leaving her all atremble, he started toward the bedside table to fetch the candelabrum. Just as swiftly, Bella realized his trick. Miles had skillfully employed seductiveness as a distraction. He had done so to stop her talking about the letters.

She couldn't allow him to get away with it. Not when the letters provided her with the perfect excuse to delve more deeply into his past.

She darted to him. "Your Grace, wait, please."

He turned, one eyebrow cocked in a cool expression. He appeared impatient to be away. To return to his isolated cell where he could guard his secrets like the artifacts that he hoarded.

Bella caught hold of his wrist. Before he could do more than frown, she pressed the packet into his large hand, folded his fingers around it, and held them closed.

"You *must* take these letters," she insisted, tilting her head back to meet his gaze. "It's clear from reading them that Papa was very important in your life at one time. And he *did* love you, Miles. Else he wouldn't have taken the time to answer your questions, to give you advice, to speak up for you."

His eyes looked as black and hard as obsidian. "You know nothing about it."

"I know what I read in these letters. Papa cared enough to convince your father to let you go on the expedition. He did his best to help you whenever he

could. Please don't let your resentment of him poison those memories."

A muscle clenched in his jaw as he glowered at her. The resurgence of his anger swirled between them like a dark entity. Only the faint ticking of the clock on the mantel broke the silence.

He abruptly wrenched away from her and stalked across the bedchamber. His steps sounded sharp, wrathful. He proceeded straight to the fireplace.

In a flash of horror, she comprehended his purpose. He intended to burn the letters.

With an anguished cry, Bella darted after him. Too late. He hurled the packet down onto the grate. Tiny flames flared up from the embers to lick at the folded seams of paper.

She didn't stop to think. She flung herself to her knees and plucked the letters from the fire. The string-tied packet tumbled onto the marble hearth. Hot orange teeth chewed at the edges of the letters. With the hem of her gown, she beat at the blaze, desperate to extinguish every trace of it.

A hand seized hold of her upper arm. *His* hand. "For God's sake, Bella! Your gown will catch fire."

She shoved him away. "Leave me be! What is *wrong* with you? These are Papa's letters!"

A ragged sob caught in her throat. Sitting back on her heels, she frantically examined the packet. The edges were blackened with soot, as were her fingers. But the letters were mostly intact. She had saved this precious link to her late father.

Without warning, a shudder shook her from head to toe. It racked her with the horrid need to break down and weep. She wouldn't do it, not in front of *him*. She gritted her teeth to stop the tears that seared her eyes.

The warmth of a supporting arm came around her

back, and she flinched. "Go," she said, refusing even to look at the duke. "Get out. You shouldn't be here anyway."

"I won't touch the letters if they mean so much to you," he said in a tone of quiet command. "But come, you may have burned yourself."

All of a sudden, Bella felt too drained to quarrel. Clutching the charred packet, she allowed him to help her to her feet. His arm encircled her waist as he guided her into the darkened dressing room.

While he took the candelabrum and set it near the washstand, Bella tucked the letters into her pocket. If the duke noticed, he made no comment. His touch was impersonal as he picked up her soot-blackened hands, one at a time, and examined them in the light of the candles.

He no longer appeared angry, only somber and unsmiling. A lock of dark hair had tumbled onto his brow, and she wanted to reach up and brush it back. She despised the urge—no, she despised *him*.

"The letters are mine now," she snapped. "You've forfeited any right to them."

His dark gaze flicked to hers, then back to her hand. "Yes."

Of course he would concur, she thought bitterly. He hadn't wanted them anyway. She had been too naïve to accept that, too intent on making him open up and talk to her.

As if he ever would.

He picked up the pitcher that Nan had left earlier and poured water into the china bowl. "I don't see any blisters," he said, "but I'll need to wash off the ash to be certain."

"I'm perfectly well. Nothing hurts." Nothing except her very soul, which smarted from his odious action.

Attempting to burn the letters had been despicable. It had been a knife thrust aimed at her papa.

Miles loathed her father. And now she finally knew it was hopeless to convince him otherwise.

"Put your hands in the water," he said. "Please."

Bella complied. She needed to clean off the soot anyway, and she felt too heartsore to resist. As she dipped her fingers, the cool liquid soothed her skin. There was something calming about the simple act of washing up.

She reached for the cake of lavender soap, but the duke took hold of it first. He lathered his own hands, then caught one of hers and began to cleanse her fingers, one at a time, gently rubbing away the blackness. "Tell me if you feel any pain."

Bella compressed her lips and averted her gaze to the dressing table where she pinned up her hair each morning in front of the oval mirror. She had no wish to speak to him any further. Let him play nursemaid if he liked. It would not soften her animosity toward him. She had learned tonight just how intractable he could be.

If she was pained by anything, it was the need to depart this house. He had made it intolerable to stay here even one more night. But there was the missing map to consider. The map that Papa had told her about on his deathbed.

Find Aylwin. Find the map. You have half the pharaoh's treasure.

For her father's sake, she must be steadfast in her efforts to claim the pharaoh's treasure. Hasani had mentioned the search for a lost tomb rumored to contain fabulous riches, gold, and jewels. Once she located the map, she and her siblings might have to travel to Egypt to unearth the treasure.

If so, she would find a way to do it without the Duke of Aylwin. She welcomed the prospect of never seeing him again.

He washed her other hand, and then used a linen towel to pat it dry. Turning her palm over, he examined the pads of her fingers. The sensation of his light touch on her skin lit an unwanted spark of pleasure deep within her womb. It was so profound, so startling that for a moment she couldn't breathe.

She wrested her hand free. "Stop fussing. It isn't necessary."

With that, Bella stalked past him and left the dressing room. She wanted him gone. Gone so that she could snuggle in bed and hug the pillow in the hopes of banishing the empty ache inside herself. It was foolish to feel distraught over his ill opinion of her father. The Duke of Aylwin meant nothing to her. Nothing at all.

He followed her into the bedchamber, placed the candelabrum back on the bedside table, and then folded his arms across his chest. His solemn gaze bored into her. "I'm sorry, Bella," he said in a gravelly tone. "What I did was wrong. I should never have tried to destroy your father's letters."

"No, you shouldn't have. But it's over with and done. So you might as well depart."

But he didn't depart. In a somewhat agitated fashion, he frowned and went on, "My conduct was childish. I behaved like an angry thirteen-year-old. Probably because my animosity toward your father is rooted in my childhood."

Bella said nothing. How could she argue with that? It was true.

Casting a moody look at her, he planted his hands on his hips and began to pace back and forth. "As you

gleaned from the letters, I didn't always despise Sir Seymour. For a time, he was more a father to me than my own sire. He gave me the attention, the guidance, and—and yes, the *love* that a boy needs from a father. He was always ready to listen, even to the most trivial questions, without the constant criticism that I received from Aylwin."

His candid words tugged at Bella's heart. Miles was talking to her. Without her prodding him. She had not thought him capable of doing so.

But she wasn't ready to soften. She leaned against the bedpost, reaching behind to grip her fingers around the carved wood. "That's the way Papa was," she said. "Always cheerful, always helpful. It's hurtful when you denigrate him."

"Of course. Yet . . . do try to see it from my perspective. He departed when I needed him most, when I was grieving over the murder of my father. I was left to sort it all out with a near-stranger . . ."

"William Banbury-Davis?"

"Yes." With a grimace, Miles glanced away. "The man was competent enough, but I scarcely knew him. It was a difficult time in my life."

Bella reluctantly imagined him as an adolescent, younger than Cyrus, forced to face circumstances that would be strenuous even for an adult. It must have been a huge undertaking to decide which artifacts to purchase, and to make arrangements to ship them back to England. All the while, he'd had to cope with the loss of his father.

And hers.

She released the remnants of her anger in a sigh. There was no denying her father's culpability in the matter. "I don't know why Papa did what he did. We'll likely never know." She softened her tone. "But Miles,

you really must forgive him. Otherwise, the ghosts of the past will continue to haunt you."

He stared at her, his eyes opaque, hiding his thoughts. "If only it were so simple," he muttered. "It's myself I can't forgive."

"What do you mean?"

Miles didn't enlighten her. He strode to the wall of windows and pushed aside the draperies. Flattening his palms on the sill, he stood there in silence, staring out into the blackness of night.

As if he had forgotten her presence.

Chapter 18

Bella told herself to leave him be. Let him keep his secrets. They were none of her concern. Yet the turmoil she sensed in him called to her heart. She crossed the bedchamber and stopped a short distance from him. Then she folded her arms and waited to see if he would speak.

His face in shadow, he cast a slight glance her way. "It's not just your father's disappearance that has weighed on me all these years," he said roughly. "There's something else, too. Something I've never told anyone."

"Oh?" she murmured.

She warned herself not to expect any confidences. There was no reason why he should share his secrets with her. She'd read his private letters without permission. She'd been caught twice poking through his papers. Worst of all, she was the daughter of the man he despised.

And if she'd learned anything tonight, it was that the Duke of Aylwin was not a man to be forced, persuaded, or cajoled. By his own admission, he'd never spoken

of the secret to which he referred. That meant he trusted no one at all.

Not Hasani. Not Banbury-Davis. Not his cousin, Oscar Grayson.

Miles kept his thoughts and emotions tightly locked inside the surly façade of a beast. And like a caged beast, he snarled at anyone who dared to venture close to him.

Why? What could be so terrible as to make him withdraw from life? She wanted to know, but wouldn't ask. He would either tell her—or not.

He hissed out a breath. "You asked me earlier if I'd ever quarreled with my father. I did, just once. After I'd been in Egypt for nearly a year, he decided it was time for me to return to England to attend Eton College. I objected quite vigorously."

"Of course. You were studying real history on-site instead of reading it from a textbook."

The ghost of a chuckle came from the darkness that shrouded him. "That was precisely my argument, too. I was vehement in my protests. For the first time in my life, I'd found the courage to stand up to Aylwin. I wanted to stay in Egypt, I told him, I *intended* to stay. I'd never seen my father so furious as he was that evening."

Miles stopped abruptly as if he'd been sucked into the vortex of memory. A minute ticked by as Bella waited for him to finish. The rigidity in his stance gave testament to his inner tension.

She couldn't stop herself from asking, "What happened?"

He stood in the gloom, his face averted from her. "Aylwin said . . ." The words surfaced from him slowly, as if dredged from a deep, dark place. "He said he was angry enough to throttle me. Then he stormed out of

the tent. It was dark already, but he took a lamp and . . . he went alone to the excavation site." Miles paused before adding in a heavy tone, "That was the last time I ever saw him alive."

Bella put her hand to her mouth to stop a gasp. The source of his torment was now clear to her. The quarrel had transpired on the night of the attack. And Miles blamed himself for the death of his father.

She could see exactly how he'd arrived at that conclusion. If not for that quarrel, his father would never have left the camp. He would never have died at the hands of grave robbers.

Hardly conscious of moving, she went straight to Miles. She slid her arms around his waist and laid her head on his shoulder, aware of only the need to give him comfort. No wonder he'd come back from Egypt inexorably changed from the sunny boy he'd once been. All these years, he had borne an awful weight of guilt. Alone. Without ever confiding in anyone. Remorse over his father's death had eaten away at him, making him irascible and hostile toward others.

And perhaps as a form of reparation, he had devoted himself to the preservation of his father's legacy. He had buried himself in this great mausoleum of a house and spent all of his time studying the artifacts that his father had excavated from the tombs of ancient pharaohs.

His warm breath stirred her hair. Miles had wrapped his arms around her, too, and held tightly so that the heat of his body intermingled with hers. Nothing had ever felt more right than this embrace. Bella felt stunned and grateful that he'd let down his guard with her. Perhaps the confession might ease his long-held pain.

But first he had to realize that the burden he'd shouldered all these years was wrong. So very wrong.

She drew back slightly to tilt her head up at him, and the faint candlelight played upon a certain wariness in his expression. Did he fear she might denounce him for his self-imposed sin?

She kept her arms firmly around his waist, her hands tracing patterns over his broad back. "Oh, Miles. It wasn't your fault. You couldn't possibly have known that brigands would attack that night."

He gave an impatient shake of his head. "That doesn't matter. I'm still responsible for his death."

"Bah! You were only thirteen. Your father was the adult. One could just as easily claim that he chose his own fate."

"The devil you say—"

He made as if to draw away, but she took hold of his upper arms to stop him, feeling the tension in his muscles. "Listen to me. Aylwin didn't *have* to quarrel with you. He could have heeded your objections and spoken rationally. He didn't have to storm out, either. He could have stayed and discussed the matter. But instead, he *chose* to go to the work site at night. He alone was accountable for his actions."

Miles stared at her, his face fierce with resistance. "You don't understand. I provoked him. I should have been a dutiful son as I'd always been."

Bella understood more than he could imagine. She had struggled with Cyrus asserting himself. Her brother was impatient to procure a job and provide for the family instead of tending to his schoolwork.

"By standing up for yourself, you were learning how to be a man," she said, willing Miles to see the truth in that. "It's a natural step for a boy of thirteen.

Your father should have realized that and reasoned with you, instead of attempting to impose his iron will."

Miles glanced away before returning his moody gaze to her. "My behavior was unconscionable. I don't see how you can excuse it."

She reached up and stroked his cheek, and his skin felt as bristly as his temperament. "I see a man who has suffered from guilt for so long that he's become a hermit, shunning all others from his life. Yes, your father's death was a terrible event. But you can't punish yourself forever. It's time to banish this incident to the past, where it belongs."

His eyes narrowed slightly as if he were looking inward, grappling with the hardened beliefs of a lifetime. She didn't expect he could change his way of thinking with the snap of a finger. But perhaps she'd given him a fresh perspective to ponder. Perhaps if he could overcome his stubborn view of that long-ago event, he could eventually make his peace with it. He could cease insulating himself against the outside world. He could find happiness with other people again. He might even fall in love and marry . . .

The notion caused a wrench in Bella's breast. She didn't like to think of him with another woman. A woman suitable to his high rank. A young, biddable debutante who would bear him children and stay out of his way and who would never draw a knife on him when he kissed her.

She let her hand drop to his broad shoulder. Of course, she herself would be long gone from his life by then. Soon they would go their separate ways, and he would never know of the wildly improper passion that burned inside of her . . .

She noticed Miles was gazing down at her with a

gleam in his dark eyes. One corner of his mouth lifted in an almost-smile. "So I'm a hermit, am I? I never realized that hermits were allowed to hold a beautiful woman in their arms."

Bella knew herself to be merely ordinary in appearance. But his compliment caused a rush of pleasure nonetheless. They were still locked in a close embrace, her hips pressed to his, her breasts joined to his solid chest. His open palm rested at the small of her back as if prepared to stop her from any attempt at escape.

Little did he realize, she had no wish to leave. It felt perfectly right and natural to be held by him. As if somehow he was her other half.

Yet she wasn't foolish enough to succumb to flattery. Despite his often surly manner, Miles knew well how to employ flirtatiousness to his advantage. At the moment, he was merely using her as a distraction to forget that he'd just bared his soul to her.

She busied herself with straightening his collar. "Flattery will get you nowhere," she countered. "I'm perfectly mindful that the bloom of my youth has faded."

A slight frown furrowed his brow, and he brought his hand up to caress her cheek. "You truly don't see yourself as beautiful?"

"Of course not," she said on a feigned laugh. "I'm hardly a girl anymore. At nine-and-twenty, I'm a well-established spinster."

"It's a bit premature to consign yourself to a rocking chair." He bent his face closer, so close she could feel the warmth of his breath. "When I look at you, I see lovely blue eyes that sparkle with life. Soft skin that turns pink when you blush. And the prettiest lips I've ever kissed." His gaze dipped to her mouth and just as her heart fluttered with forbidden longing, he straightened up and

gave her a sardonic look. "But I suppose you'll accuse me of being a liar if I dare to go on."

Her legs felt unsteady from the melting heat of desire. She ought to step away, but lacked the willpower to do so. "Yes, do stop, Your Grace. You're being quite outrageous."

"Miles," he corrected. "I've noticed you only address me formally when you're trying to hold me at arm's length."

"Bosh. I'm *in* your arms right now."

"So you are," he said, his hands drifting idly over her waist and hips as if to familiarize himself with her feminine curves. His eyelids lowered slightly in a hooded look, he went on, "Now is when you should order me to depart your bedchamber. If I stay any longer, you'll be in danger of having your reputation tarnished."

The prospect of his departure pained Bella. Despite all logic and reason, she couldn't bear to end their closeness. Miles had awakened her to the intense pleasure of a man's kiss. Yet she'd only enjoyed a small taste of forbidden fruit, just enough to stir a riotous curiosity inside her. There was so much more that he could teach her of passion. She might never have another chance like this—and if she turned coward now, she surely would regret it for the rest of her life.

She looped her arms around his neck and refused to think beyond the moment. "Don't go," she murmured in his ear. "I should very much like for you to tarnish my reputation."

He drew back to frown at her. "What?"

"The other day," she murmured, "you told me that if ever I wanted you, I would have to do . . . something. You never finished saying what it was."

"I was teasing you." He fixed her with the Ducal Stare. "As you're teasing me right now."

"Am I?" she asked with a coy smile. "I've given considerable thought to what you meant to say, Miles. I believe that you meant for *me* to initiate our next kiss." To make her shameless desires clear, she went on, "And after I do so, I would like for you to come to my bed."

Miles gripped her slender waist as she traced his lips with her finger. He could scarcely believe that Bella was seducing him. Only a short while ago, he'd feared he had destroyed her goodwill forever. Nothing else could have induced him to spill his guts to her. He'd been desperate to convince her that the darkness in him hadn't been caused just by her father.

Afterward, awash in a disquieting relief, he had craved her smile and the reassurance that he could still arouse her desires. But he hadn't been angling for an invitation to initiate her in bodily pleasures. He had come to think too highly of Bella to despoil her like one of his whores.

Now, however, she had yanked the rug out from under him. Although he'd fantasized about this moment—far too often over the past few days—he had never expected her to yield in actuality. Especially not after their quarrel and then the exposure of his black-hearted secret.

Yes, he was black-hearted, no matter what she said to the contrary. Black-hearted enough to take the pleasure she offered.

She arched up on tiptoes, her curvaceous body sliding against him and igniting a blaze in his groin. Her eyelids drifted shut, and the warmth of her breath bathed his lips in the moment before she touched her mouth to his.

That light, virginal kiss nearly undid him. He tightened his arms around her, running his hands up and

down her womanly form. He needed to touch her to ground himself in reality, for she was a dream come true. But he held himself in check, allowing her to explore him at her leisure. She sipped at his mouth in tender little pecks before the tip of her tongue slipped out to trace the seam of his lips.

A groan emanated from deep in his chest. Craving a deeper drink of her sweetness, he splayed his fingers across the back of her head and proceeded to plunder her mouth with ravenous purpose. His tongue found hers waiting to parry with him, and her mouth tasted of dark secrets and decadent promises. He burned to brand Bella as his own, to awaken the fullness of her passion, to make her need him as desperately as he needed her.

When they were both panting with arousal, he drew back slightly to catch his breath. "Tell me this isn't some trick," he muttered against her brow. "Where is that blasted dagger, anyway?"

"In my pocket." She rubbed her cheek against his, and he could feel her smile. "But it would be out of my reach if you were to divest me of my gown."

A gravelly chuckle rose in his throat. Ah, Bella. She was hardly the dried-up spinster of her imagination. She was a mature woman ripe for a night of pleasure. He craved to make her realize just how beautiful she was inside and out.

He turned her around to release the buttons down the back of her gown. First one, then another and another. Each loosening exposed a bit more warm flesh for him to taste with his tongue. As he lowered the top half of her gown, Bella rolled her shoulders to slide her arms out of the long tight sleeves. He had undressed many other women, but never one all trussed up in spinster garb. Odd how this unveiling felt far more tit-

illating than any disrobing performed by a skilled courtesan.

Letting the bodice fall just to her waist, he untied her corset strings and then slid his hands inside her linen chemise to cup her bare breasts. She leaned back against him, tilting her head onto his shoulder, breathing his name in a ragged sigh. Her eyes were drowsy with pleasure as he weighed the perfect globes in his palms. The tips beaded at a stroke of his thumbs and she moved her hips, her bottom brushing his hardness.

He gritted his teeth to keep from taking her right there on the floor. Bella was too naïve to realize how her instinctive movements affected him. In an effort to control himself, he drew his hands from the warm delights of her bosom and turned her to face him again. He intended to do this slowly, so she could revel in every moment of her deflowering.

As she murmured a protest, he soothed her with a tender kiss. "There's no need to hurry. You'll like it better if I linger."

"All right, but I want to learn everything . . . *quickly.*"

A chuckle surprised him. When was the last time he'd laughed during sex? Never. Bella had a way of making him view things in a new and unexpected manner.

He dropped to one knee before her. Working her dress downward over the curve of her hips, he spied the charred spot at her hem where she had smothered the burning letters. Miles knew he ought to be sorry, for he had hurt Bella. But his angry action also had propelled them to this point—though he didn't quite understand how they could be at each other's throats one moment, and kissing madly the next.

He had considered himself well versed in the art of

lovemaking. But he was fast learning that seducing Bella was outside the realm of his experience. Being accustomed to light-skirts trained to please a man, he had never bedded a respectable woman. A woman who shared his passion for ancient civilizations, who bedeviled him at every turn, who thought nothing of challenging his long-held beliefs.

A woman who drove him wild with desire.

As the gown slithered to the floor, he lent Bella a hand to help her step out of it and her petticoat. She tugged off the loosened corset and dropped it onto the heap of her gown. "Englishwomen should rebel against such a contraption," she said with a wry grimace. "I daresay a man invented that whalebone cage."

Still on one knee, Miles could only stare up at her in mesmerized attention. The chemise skimmed her feminine form, and he feasted his eyes on the jut of her breasts and the dark shadow at the apex of her thighs. He struggled to keep his mind on her words. "You . . . didn't wear corsets in Persia?"

"No, I dressed in the traditional costume of the women, a belted robe and jacket." She sighed. "Now, there is something that I *do* miss."

With that allusion to their dinner conversation, she gracefully lifted her arms to pluck the pins from her prudish bun. Then she shook her head and the luxurious brown locks cascaded around her shoulders and rippled down to her hips. The natural sensuality of her movements held him transfixed. So did the curls that fell around her breasts, where the strands played peek-a-boo with her nipples.

Her gaze flitted to him and a charming blush pinked her cheeks. She smiled, a warm yet uncertain look. "I'll just . . . put these pins away. In the dressing room."

Even as she turned to go, Miles leaped to his feet.

"Permit me." He emptied the pins from her hand into his. Then he put his arm around her slender waist, walked her to the four-poster, and dropped the pins onto the bedside table.

Maybe it was irrational, but he didn't want to let Bella out of his sight. Despite her boldness, she had to be feeling somewhat skittish. She might yet change her mind and retract the decision to give herself to a ne'er-do-well with a dark sin staining his soul.

He mustn't allow her time to think.

Drawing her flush against him, he kissed her deeply, thoroughly, caressing her bosom until she was melting in his arms again. He loved the way she responded to him with zeal and fire. He loved her lips, rosy and soft. He loved her full breasts and her slim legs and her rounded bottom.

Not *love* in the sense of poetry and forever. That road had no place in the life he had chosen for himself long ago.

No, what he felt was merely infatuation, a fascination with the novelty of Bella Jones. She had offered him the gift of her virtue, and in return he hungered to make her happy. To erase the memory of seeing her teary-eyed over the half-burned letters and her distraught voice crying out, *What are you doing?*

That had been the moment when he'd recognized that the malice inside himself had the power to hurt her deeply. The moment when he'd known he would do anything necessary to restore the closeness that had sprung up between them so swiftly and unexpectedly. The moment when he'd decided to confess all.

He had never expected to be rewarded like this.

Miles lowered her to the bed. Rather than lie down, she perched on the edge, drew the wealth of her hair over one shoulder, and combed her fingers through the

long strands. He remained standing a moment to strip off his shirt. After drawing it over his head, he noticed by her deft movements that she was braiding her hair.

He flung away the shirt, sat down beside her, and caught hold of her wrists. "Don't."

Those candid blue eyes widened on him. "I always plait my hair at night. Otherwise it becomes tangled."

"I like it free. It's too beautiful to hide."

She arched an eyebrow, and the corners of her mouth curved up, as well. "On the day I arrived here, you scorned it as a middling brown."

Miles caught a lock of her hair, letting the soft strands sift through his fingers. Gold glinted like filaments of fire hidden among the darker tresses. "I hadn't seen it in the candlelight. Nor had I seen it loose, spilling around your shoulders, framing your bosom."

He slipped his fingers beneath the curtain of hair to stroke her breasts over the chemise. Bella's eyes went hazy. Abandoning the braid, she angled herself toward him, put her arms around his neck, and tucked her head into the lee of his shoulder. The soft, swift exhalations of her breath against his skin fed his passions.

He pressed her back against the bed, and she made an erotic portrait reclining against the pillows, the nimbus of dark hair spilling all around her, the hem of her chemise riding halfway up her stocking-clad thighs. He could just glimpse the tantalizing thatch that guarded her womanhood, and the sight sent molten lava coursing through his veins. How he burned to drive into her heated depths and take his pleasure without further ado.

But this night was about her, not him.

Delaying his gratification was a new and torturous circumstance. He'd never needed to do so with his

other women. In an effort to distract himself, he turned his gaze downward. She still wore her shoes, and those sparkly garnet slippers seemed more suited to a lady in a ballroom than a scholar who worked with dusty artifacts.

He eased off one of the slippers. "Where did you get these shoes?"

"What? Oh, they're . . ." Her eyes rounded on him, and then she glanced away, her lashes lowered halfway. "I . . . I don't really remember. Does it matter?"

The shoes likely had come from a secondhand store, or perhaps a jumble sale at a church. She must be too proud to admit it, and that fact struck him deeply. Bella would never want for anything ever again, he vowed silently. He would make certain of it.

Even when she left his house for good.

"*You* matter," he said in a gravelly tone. "I'm curious to know everything about you." He removed her other shoe and dropped it to the floor. "First and foremost, I want to know the taste and feel of your bare skin."

A sigh of assent rippled from her as he slid his hands back up to her thighs to undo the garters holding her white silk stockings. She reached down to aid him with the fastenings, her fingers clumsy as she tried to hurry. "Oh, Miles. I want you, too. So very much."

His chest tightened into a knot, though he didn't quite know why. Women often gushed such nonsense during sex. Perhaps the difference was Bella herself, her lack of artifice.

Bracing one hand on the mattress, he stretched up to brush his lips over hers, savoring a hint of the wine they'd drunk at dinner. "Soon I'll satisfy you," he whispered. "I promise."

He rolled down one stocking and then the other,

leaving them where they fell. Turning his attention to her lower leg, he nuzzled the circlet of dainty tattoos around one ankle. How exciting she was, the perfect blend of sweet and exotic. In the quiet darkness lit by only the dim candlelight, they might have been the only two people in the world.

He kissed a path up her bare leg. "Tell me what you like," he murmured. "I want to know what feeds the fire inside you."

Moving restlessly on the bed, she curled her fingers into his hair. "Everything, Miles. Everything you do makes me burn. I never dreamed it was possible to feel this way."

When she looked at him like that, with wonder and desire in her big blue eyes, he ached to give her the stars and the moon on a silver platter. And if that meant denying himself for her sake, then so be it. He kicked off his shoes, but left on his trousers to stop himself from succumbing too soon to the urging of his hot blood.

Leaning over her, Miles caught the hem of her chemise and tugged it upward. She shifted position without hesitation, undulating her hips and raising her arms to allow him to remove the last barrier to her nakedness. Then he feasted himself on the sight of her in the candlelight: the perfect breasts, the graceful curve of her waist, the dark furring at the jointure of her legs.

Settling down on the bed, he gathered her close, fitting her body against his and cradling her cheek in his hand. "My beautiful Bella," he murmured against her brow. "You are so very lovely. Never doubt that."

She splayed her fingers over his bare chest and shoulders, tracing his muscles, a keen look of fascination on her face. "And you, as well. You could be a model for a sculptor."

A raspy chuckle broke from him. "I'd sooner study statues than pose for them."

"I mean it, Miles. You're . . . perfection."

As she touched her lips to his throat in a soft kiss, he again felt that peculiar ache in his chest. Her admiration pleased him far more than practiced compliments uttered by paid companions. Bella spoke from the heart. There could be no pretense, given her lack of experience in the art of lovemaking.

All conversation melted away as he began to pay homage to every inch of her body, the slender arms, the tender dip at her throat, the delightful globes of her breasts. She embarked upon her own exploration of him, as well, seeming to delight in his muscles, the flat nipples embedded in the mat of hair on his chest, the hard lines of his ribs. At last he could resist no longer. Sliding his hand down over the flatness of her belly, he began to play with her in feathery strokes.

Bella caught a sharp breath. Her hands stilled on him and her eyelids drifted shut as if to focus on the glorious new sensations. Watching the display of pleasure across her expressive face, he delved deeper into her folds to find her secret pearl. She was already hot and wet, ready for him.

Her hips moved instinctively, brushing the erection that strained against the buttons of his trousers. *Wait,* he ordered himself. *Wait.* If it killed him, he would have her pleasure before his. He would make her first time memorable.

He deepened his rhythmic strokes, and she opened her legs wider, uttering small sounds of delight against his throat. He whispered that she was beautiful, intriguing, alluring, the perfect woman. All at once, more quickly than he'd anticipated, her hips arched and she

cried out, her body shuddering with the force of her release.

Miles held her tightly, his heart drumming in his chest, as he allowed her a moment to recover. Her swift responsiveness fed the fire of his own reckless need. Laying her back against the pillows, he sat up unsteadily to wrest open his pants. His fingers were clumsy and her hands came down to grip his. He glanced over to see her half sitting, dreamy-eyed and smiling softly at him.

"May I?" she asked.

He gave up the task to her. Bella leaned close, her tangled hair draping her bare body as she applied herself to the buttons, one by one. Opening the placket to free his tumescence, she lightly traced the length of him and swirled her fingertip in the moisture that glistened at the tip.

Miles groaned from a stab of intense pleasure. *Wait. Wait.* He removed her hand at once, lacing his fingers with hers while he wrestled his desires under control. He wouldn't explode like a green boy with his first girl.

"Did I do something wrong?" she asked quickly.

He could scarcely manage a hoarse chuckle. "No," he rasped. "That felt far *too* good . . . but I want to be inside you . . . *now.*"

He shucked off the trousers and then covered her with his body, nestling himself in the cradle of her thighs. She parted her legs at once and he pushed slowly into her hot tight channel, her slickness easing his entry. As he met a barrier and thrust through it, she tensed, her hands clutching at him.

He paused, contrite in the midst of being blissfully sheathed inside her. "Bella," he muttered, kissing her brow. "I've hurt you."

Her eyes were closed as if in a trance. Then her

lashes lifted. As their gazes met, a rapt smile lent a glow to her face. She touched his cheek. "Oh, my love . . . this is heaven."

My love. The words flowed over him like a heady balm. He could form no reply. His brain refused to function. He knew only that this coupling had a depth and a richness beyond his experience. Joining his mouth to hers, he let the tenderness of his kiss answer her. He and Bella were a perfect fit, as if they were meant for each other. Nothing in his life had ever felt better than this moment.

Those scattered impressions vanished into the intense pleasure of moving within her, thrusting deeper and harder each time. His entire being was focused on the allure of her femininity, the joy of being one with her. She lifted her hips, panting and fervent, as together they strained in unison toward the ultimate pinnacle.

Wait. Wait.

Yet the powerful tide of rapture could not be stopped this time. It rushed over him in a drowning roar that enveloped him completely. He hoarsely uttered her name, and in perfect synchrony, she too cried out, her body trembling. As the last waves carried him into a place of pure satisfaction, he lay over her for timeless moments. His harsh breathing grew steady again, his sanity intruding all too soon.

My love. The echo of her soft words made him never want to leave her bed.

Yet neither did he have any right to stay. Bella needed more than a man who had vowed long ago to dedicate himself to his solitary work. He could never give her the care and affection that she richly deserved.

Holding her close, he knew too that she had mistaken passion for love. It was understandable given her inexperience. Nothing could ever come of their liaison.

He must not take further advantage of her—no matter how enticing the prospect of an affair might be.

Blissful and relaxed, Bella relished the heavy weight of him. She had never imagined that the act of physical coupling could be so gratifying in body and soul. No wonder parents protected their daughters so strictly. One taste of that bliss, and she would want to experience it again and again . . .

Miles abruptly rolled off her and sat up on the edge of the bed. Opening her eyes, Bella lifted an indolent hand to touch his bare thigh. It was rough with hairs and damp with sweat. Why had he drawn away?

"Miles?" Her voice sounded low and husky to her ears.

He turned to meet her gaze. In the candlelight, his eyes were very dark and inscrutable. He brushed back the tangle of her hair and bent down to touch his mouth to her brow. It was the sort of tender peck she'd often given to her brother or sister.

Bella parted her lips in anticipation of a proper kiss. One that would stir those exciting emotions inside her again. One that would lead to another bout of love-making. Was it possible to join their bodies more than once in a night? Oh, she hoped so.

But Miles didn't kiss her.

Even as she lifted her arms to draw him close, the mattress dipped as he rose to his feet. He disappeared into the dressing room, returning a moment later. She rolled onto her side to watch him. How magnificent he looked in his nakedness, with his sculpted muscles and lean waist, his male member lying in its nest of dark hair. How thoroughly he had used it to pleasure her. The mere sight made her body hum with desire.

Bella had not known such joy existed. She still felt

stunned by the occurrence of that startling release. And keen to do it all over again.

Miles sat down on the edge of the bed. He held a damp cloth in his hand and he cleansed her between her legs. An unexpected shyness crept over her. Why was he being so silent?

Then he spoke. "Luckily one of your stockings was caught beneath us. There won't be any stain for your maid to notice."

As he picked it up, she saw the rusty smear on the white silk. But that wasn't what chilled her.

It was the indifference of his observation. He might have been noticing a spot of dust on the floor rather than the proof of her virginity.

The coldness crept deeper into her core. She had always been somewhat impulsive, acting at times without thinking, letting her emotions overrule logic. But never before in her life had she behaved with such utter abandon. How could she have forgotten herself so completely tonight? With a man of such exalted stature?

A man who was known to visit concubines.

In her desire to lie with him, she had forgotten that vile truth. Perhaps his experience with those females explained why he now seemed so aloof. Perhaps she meant nothing more to the Duke of Aylwin than a receptacle to be used and discarded. Those lovely, exciting words he had uttered to her—he might have voiced them to all of his women.

His large hand came down over hers. She looked up to see him gazing somberly at her. As if he had something unpleasant on his mind.

Her throat tightened as it struck her that Miles was also her employer. He might use her unchaste behavior as an excuse to eject her from this house. By her

own reckless folly, she could lose her chance to find the treasure map.

He compressed his lips as if he were trying to find the right words to dismiss her. "Bella, I—"

"Let me say something first." She pulled up the covers to her chin, then drew a deep breath to ease the tangle of panic and distress inside her. "I enjoyed this . . . our little encounter. But I'm sure we can both agree that it must never happen again."

He gave her a penetrating stare. "Indeed."

"Yes, Your Grace." Feeling miserable inside, she contrived a cool look to counter his emotionless mask. "It would be best if we forgot this night entirely. Then we can go on as before. There's no need for us to speak of it ever again."

Chapter 19

Late the following afternoon, Bella stepped through the open doorway to the archives. She had spent most of the day in the drawing room, moving artifacts here and there while accomplishing next to nothing in her distracted state. She'd continued the pretense of work until it seemed the walls were closing in on her and a change of scene became crucial to her sanity.

As if to underscore her unsettled mood, the weather had turned damp and dreary, and the leaden skies cast a pall over the archives. Raindrops tapped on the windowpanes, and the only other sound was a tuneless humming that came from the far end of the room where the mummies were stored.

Bella hesitated by the open door. She didn't recognize the humming. Surely it had to be William Banbury-Davis. But . . . what if it was Miles? Did he ever hum while he worked?

She had no idea.

Since issuing her ultimatum to him the previous evening, she had not encountered him anywhere in the house. Perhaps that was only to be expected. He'd been

agreeable to her request that they behave as if the passionate interlude had never occurred. All too swiftly, he had donned his clothes and departed her bedchamber with only a cursory farewell. Alone in her bed, she had lain awake gazing into the darkness, inhaling the trace of his scent on the pillows, remembering the bliss of their lovemaking, and wishing it had never come to an end.

Now, the thought of seeing Miles flustered her. She almost turned around and walked out. But he was her employer and she would have to face him sooner or later. She couldn't run away every time.

And why should she run, anyway? Yes, they'd lain naked in bed together and had enjoyed an amazing ecstasy, but she had to keep in mind that the experience was nothing new to *him*. According to her maid, the Duke of Aylwin visited a bawdy house on a regular basis. He'd likely engaged in that intimate act with hundreds of women over the years.

Their joining held far less significance to him than to her. If he'd given it a second thought at all today, he likely was relieved to have escaped her bedchamber without the deflowered virgin making weepy demands upon him.

The dirty dog.

No.

No, she mustn't blame him, no matter how much her heart ached. She had *invited* Miles into her bed. He had made her no promises other than to satisfy her desires, a promise that he had fulfilled beyond her wildest dreams. And she did not need anything more from him, anyway. She had a map to find and a mission to complete—which was why she had come here to the archives.

Armed with that resolve, Bella stepped briskly for-

ward. Her footsteps tapped on the dusty parquet floor
in an echo of the pitter-patter of raindrops on the windows. She walked past the rows of polished wood filing cabinets and emerged into the far end of the room
where the shelves held numerous wrapped mummies.

The tuneless humming came from the man bending
over the half-exposed mummy on the long table. A
man in a wrinkled dark green coat and baggy trousers,
with a fringe of brown hair edging his balding pate.

A sense of reprieve eddied through her. All that
soul-searching had been for naught. "Good afternoon,
Mr. Banbury-Davis."

The humming stopped abruptly. He spun around, a
sharp, bladelike implement clutched in his hand. His
bulldog features tightened into a sneer as he looked her
up and down. "Miss Jones."

He looked as grumpy as ever. So much for hoping
the humming might indicate an improvement in his
disposition. He did not like her in the duke's employ;
he'd made that clear in their first meeting. According
to Hasani, William Banbury-Davis had wanted to be
a part of the expedition to Egypt, but the duke had chosen Sir Seymour instead. Now, it seemed the man had
transferred his resentment of her father to her.

"Well?" he prodded. "Why have you interrupted me?
As you can see, I'm a busy man."

"I merely wanted you to know that I'll be looking
through a few of the files. So that you wouldn't wonder who was here."

His scowl deepened. "Must you do so now? My work
requires much delicacy and concentration. Your presence will disturb me."

"I'll endeavor to be as quiet as possible, sir. If you'll
excuse me."

Giving him no further chance to harangue her, Bella

spun around and proceeded to the row of file cabinets as far from him as possible. She opened the top drawer and drew out a sheaf of papers. The sooner she found the treasure map, the sooner she could depart.

She flipped through a stack of official bills of sale bearing the stamp of the Egyptian government. They were written in three languages: English, French, and Arabic. The prices were quite steep on some of the items, and she presumed that Banbury-Davis had negotiated them on behalf of Miles. The new duke had been only thirteen years old at the time and mourning the death of his father.

A death he still blamed on himself.

In spite of all that had happened, her heart ached for him. Had Miles reflected any further on what she had said? Could he ever accept that he was not at fault for Aylwin's violent murder at the hands of grave robbers? Would he ever marry and sire a family? Or would he continue to roam this house like a caged beast for the remainder of his life, snarling at anyone who crossed his path?

Oh, she hoped not. Miles had so much to offer a wife. He could be warm and attentive, exciting and sensual, especially in the bedchamber. Any woman would be thrilled to lie with him each night, to enjoy the skilled touch of his hands, to see his face soften with love . . .

Could he fall in love?

Before yesterday, Bella wouldn't have thought it possible. He was a proud man, arrogant to a fault, and prone to using the Ducal Stare on those who dared to thwart him. Yet if he could lower his guard as he had the previous night, if he could allow his wife a glimpse into his heart, then perhaps he could unbend enough to have a happy marriage.

If only *she* could be his wife.

The impossible thought popped unbidden into Bella's mind. She rejected it at once. How absurd. She wasn't one to succumb to silly, romantic dreams. Despite her noble blood, the Duke of Aylwin was far above her station in life. If ever he wed, he would choose someone younger and more suitable, more biddable, too. He would take her to his bed and arouse her in all those wickedly wonderful ways . . .

The heavy tread of footsteps broke into her reverie. She looked over to see Banbury-Davis advancing toward her. "Just as I suspected, you're not working," he accused. "You're staring into space."

"I was concentrating on a problem," she said, repeating his own words back to him. "And you have interrupted me."

The man very nearly cracked a smile. "Touché, Miss Jones. What are you seeking here, anyway? I'll help you find it, then you can run along and leave me be."

Bella stood her ground, resolute in her intent to continue the search on her own. "Thank you, but I've been very careful not to make any noise."

"You're turning pages," he said, scowling again. "I can hear it and it's bothersome."

"Why don't you resume your humming, then? It will cover any slight sound that I might make."

He thrust his hands onto his stocky hips and raised his voice a notch. "The very fact of your presence here, Miss Jones, is disturbing to my attentiveness. Now, I am asking you again to—"

His words broke off as the sound of footsteps entered the doorway. Not one, but *two* sets of footsteps. The tall file cabinets hid the newcomers from view, and Bella again braced herself to face Miles.

But it was Hasani who rounded the corner, clad in his pale robes and bearing a medium-sized wicker basket in his arms. Behind him trailed Helen Grayson, looking elegant as always in a lilac gown that enhanced her stylishly arranged blond hair.

"Good God!" Banbury-Davis exclaimed. "Can't a man have any peace around here? One would think I was hosting a blasted party!"

Hasani ignored the scholar, proceeding straight to Bella. He dipped his head in a slight bow. "Miss Jones, pardon the interruption, but I heard your name spoken as I was passing by on my way to the drawing room. I was instructed to deliver this to you."

Bella blinked at the basket with its closed lid. "To *me*?"

"It's from Miles," Helen said with a hint of testiness. "I caught Hasani coming out of the west wing, but he has refused to let me take so much as a little peek inside the basket."

The Egyptian valet glowered at her. "As I have already explained, His Grace requested that I give this directly to Miss Jones."

"Is it a gift?" Helen persisted. "It shouldn't be. She's merely an employee."

"I do not question the orders of my master." Clearly irked by the woman, Hasani held out the basket to Bella. "For you, miss."

Bella hurriedly stashed the papers back into the file drawer and then took hold of the container. It was somewhat heavy, with a heft rather like the picnic hamper she would fill for Lila and Cyrus when, as children, they'd begged to eat their luncheon on the hillside.

Now, three sets of eyes stared at Bella. She hesitated to lift the lid in front of this trio of watchers. What on

earth would Miles have given her? Some sort of peace offering to atone for his abrupt departure from her bed? An alarming thought occurred to her. What if it was something intimate that might embarrass her?

Feeling the rise of a blush, she edged past the group. "It's likely an artifact to display in the drawing room. I'll take it there at once. If you'll excuse me—"

"Oh, just open it, for pity's sake!" Helen snapped.

Her nimble fingers flashed out, undid the fastening, and whipped up the lid. Hasani made haste to block her—too late. The contents of the basket had already been exposed.

Banbury-Davis and Helen crowded in for a closer look.

Bella scarcely noticed them; she was too busy staring downward at a cornucopia of fruit and other edibles. She had not seen such varieties in many months. A pile of plump brown dates. An array of ruby pomegranates. An assortment of greenish figs with the stems still attached. A small burlap sack of pistachios. Several little folded packets of paper were tucked along the inner edges of the basket.

Bella lifted one packet and inhaled its pungent aroma. Saffron.

Her heart filled with a rush of delight. At dinner the previous night, she'd listed some of her favorite foods from Persia that she missed. Miles had remembered. And he'd endeavored to find them for her.

Her throat felt taut. Never in her life had anyone given her a more generous, thoughtful, considerate gift. It made her eyes prickle with incipient tears, and she blinked to dispel the moisture.

To hide her reaction, she picked up another packet and sniffed the mustardlike aroma.

Helen stood watching, a disgruntled expression

marring her pretty features. "What is that you're smell-ing?"

"Turmeric. It's a spice often used in the East."

"Whatever could you want with *that*? And what are all those . . . those other things?"

"Dates, for one," Banbury-Davis said, eyeing them rather greedily. "We ate quite a lot of them in Egypt."

Helen stared suspiciously at Bella. "Why would Miles give you fruit and spices?"

Avoiding the question, Bella closed the lid. "More to the point, where did he find them?" She looked at Hasani, who had a very slight smile on his impassive features. "*You* know, don't you?"

He spread his hands wide. "His Grace had business this morning at an estate he owns some three hours' ride to the west. There, his gardeners grow a number of exotic plants in greenhouses."

Bella hardly knew what to make of it. Had he truly had business there? Or had he ridden so far from London to fetch these fruits for her? The possibility made her entire body dissolve with hope.

"Well!" Helen said dismissingly. "*I* would be of-fended to receive such an odd gift. Good day!" Her lilac skirt flared as she spun around and marched out the door.

Hasani bowed. "Shall I deliver the basket to your chamber?"

Bella didn't want to let the precious cargo out of her sight. "Thank you, but it isn't so very heavy. I can manage it myself."

As the Egyptian valet took his leave and van-ished, Bella found herself alone with William Banbury-Davis. He stood watching her with his hands on his thickset hips. His narrow-eyed stare made her uneasy.

"It's your lucky day," she said lightly. "I believe I'll leave you to your work, after all."

As she started to go, the basket in her arms, he snarled, "It's clear that Aylwin has his eye on you, Miss Jones."

Bella stopped, then turned back. In her iciest tone, she said, "I beg your pardon?"

"The duke is toying with you. That's the real reason why he hired you instead of me. He knows you're no scholar."

"Quite the contrary, he's charged me with organizing a roomful of artifacts."

"It's a sop to win you over, just like that basket of fruit." He took a step closer. "What Aylwin really wants is to take revenge on that ne'er-do-well Sir Seymour—by seducing his daughter."

Bella could scarcely draw a breath. "You'd dare insult me so."

"I'm merely giving you fair warning." A smirk on his broad features, Banbury-Davis looked her up and down. "If you've any scruples at all, you'll leave this house at once. Or mark my words, he *will* make you his mistress."

Bella marched straight to the drawing room, set down the basket, and slammed the door shut. The sound echoed out in the corridor. She paced back and forth between the piles of artifacts, trying to rein in her runaway anger.

How dare that awful man insult her so. She hated Banbury-Davis for belittling her as a mere pawn in the duke's game. She hated that he'd planted doubts in her mind, too. Most of all, she hated that he'd made her wonder if Miles really *was* using her for some sort of twisted revenge.

After a time, she plopped down on a crate and stabbed her dagger into a fig, wishing it was Banbury-Davis's black heart. She sliced the fig in half and then ate the delicious fruit.

As she licked the sticky juice from her fingers, she felt calmer, able to think rationally. She mustn't believe a word of his rubbish. If only Banbury-Davis knew, she and the duke had already shared a bed. Miles had *not* asked her to become his mistress. Rather, *she* had initiated the seduction. And he had walked away without a backward glance.

A hollow ache throbbed in her breast.

But if Miles cared nothing for her, why had he sent her the basket? Did he hope to woo himself back into her good graces? Would he knock on her door tonight and attempt to charm his way back in her bed?

Her body grew soft and heated at the mere thought. But she wouldn't allow him. She mustn't allow him. No matter how much she yearned for his embrace, nothing mattered but her mission here. An affair was far, far too risky.

Twilight was falling as she picked up the basket and headed to her bedchamber. The house was quiet as a tomb, and she passed no one in the echoing corridors. Yet as she trudged toward the marble staircase, passing many shadowed rooms, Bella had the oddest sense of being watched.

It was likely her agitated emotions that made her overly sensitive, she decided. The encounter with Banbury-Davis had jangled her nerves. She would not spare another thought for his nasty innuendos. Let the rat think what he willed; his spite would have no effect on her.

A pox on all men, Bella thought as she started up the staircase. *She* would have *her* revenge when she

located the missing map and claimed the pharaoh's treasure. Perhaps she would even return to the archives later tonight to continue her search. This time, she'd be sure to draw the draperies so that Miles wouldn't spy the glow of her candle—

A distant screech broke the silence.

Startled, she stopped halfway up the stairs. The shriek seemed to have originated from the upper corridor where the guest bedrooms lay. From the vicinity of her bedchamber, in fact.

Was it Nan? Had she suffered an accident?

Clutching the basket, Bella took the remainder of the steps at a sprint and then made haste down the long, dim-lit passageway. Dusk shrouded the way, but she could still see well enough to avoid stumbling.

The door to her bedchamber stood wide open. Hurrying inside, she found the room lit only by a fire that burned merrily on the grate. The rest of the chamber lay in murky shadows, the four-poster bed and the desk by the curtained windows.

To her alarm, Nan sat sobbing loudly on a footstool by the hearth. Mrs. Helen Grayson hovered over the maid, alternately scolding her and waving a handkerchief at the girl's face.

Bella set down the basket of fruit on a chair by the door, then scurried toward them. "What happened? Have you hurt yourself, Nan?"

The maid turned up a frightened, tearstained face. Her mobcap hung askew, allowing several hanks of rusty-red hair to come loose. "Oh, miss! 'Twas a phantom! Right here in yer bedchamber!"

Bella crouched down before the girl. "Here? What do you mean?"

"I was in yer dressin' room when I heard noises. Thinkin' 'twas ye, miss, I peeked out to say hello. All

the candles was blown out. That's when I saw it—a ghost hoverin' by the door. It loosed a fearful moanin'. Oh, it sent cold chills down me spine, it did!"

"Silly girl," Helen pronounced. "Ghost, indeed! That screech of yours sent chills down *my* spine!"

Bella rose to her feet and stared at the woman. "What are *you* doing on this floor so late?"

"I had just finished inventorying the linen closet around the corner. One cannot trust the servants with these matters."

Bella found that highly suspicious. "You? I shouldn't think you would take an interest in such work."

Helen lifted her chin and looked down her dainty nose. "When I am Duchess of Aylwin someday, this house and all its contents will be mine. Until then, I shall make certain that nothing goes missing."

The explanation was just barely plausible. Was it possible that Helen was the one playing the ghost? She certainly seemed to resent Bella's presence in the house. "Show me where you were."

"Well! If you insist."

In high dudgeon, Helen snatched up a candlestick, lit the wick at the fire, and marched out the door. As Bella followed, Nan jumped up, keeping close to Bella's side. "I saw it, miss," she said in a shaky whisper. "I know what I saw."

Bella patted that cold, work-chapped hand. "It's all right, my love. I believe you."

She *did* believe. Because she'd glimpsed the spectral figure with her own eyes only a few nights ago. But this evening's incident was far more disturbing. Because this time, someone had actually entered her bedchamber with the purpose of frightening Nan.

Or perhaps Bella herself.

They proceeded around the corner and to an open

door. All three of them stepped inside. The small room had long shelves filled with numerous neat stacks of linens, and the smell of starch hung in the air.

Holding the candlestick, Helen pointed to a pile of tumbled cloth on the floor. "I dropped those pillow coverings at the sound of your scream. Pick them up, girl. It's your fault they're lying there."

Nan scurried to do the woman's bidding, refolding and placing them on a shelf. Meanwhile, Bella glanced into the gloomy area outside where her own sighting had occurred.

This short corridor bisected the end of the main passageway. The figure she'd seen had materialized from somewhere near here, perhaps had hidden in this very linen cupboard, then had made its appearance just as she was trudging to her bedchamber after a long day's work.

That time, the phantom had vanished through the door at the end of the short corridor. The servants' staircase.

Helen could have set up the scene, dropped the linens on the floor, and stolen into the bedchamber. But if she'd been wearing a robe, where was it? Everything on the shelves here looked neat as a pin. And so did Helen herself. If she'd flung some sort of ghostly garment over her head, surely her appearance would be rumpled.

But her coiffure looked as perfect as it had been in the archives, not a single golden hair out of place.

Was the perpetrator someone else, then? Had this other person frightened Nan, then dashed into one of the vacant bedchambers before Helen had come around the corner?

Bella couldn't imagine.

"What a lot of bother about nothing," Helen said

disparagingly as they stepped back out into the corridor. She lifted the candle. "Why, you look rather somber, Miss Jones. Do *you* believe in spirits, too? It's rumored that this wing is haunted."

Nan shivered, clutching at Bella's arm. "Oh, Mrs. Grayson! Don't say such things!"

"Stop frightening the poor girl," Bella said. "I'm sure there's a logical explanation. Sometimes, one's eyes can play tricks, especially in the dark."

"But miss . . ." Nan began.

Squeezing the girl's hand, Bella gave her a silencing look. Nan lowered her gaze to the floor at once. To Helen, Bella said, "Thank you for your help, but you're no longer needed here."

"Well!" Muttering about rude employees, the woman turned on her heel and marched away down the corridor, her hips swaying.

Since she'd taken the candlestick, leaving them in gloom, Bella quickly ushered Nan back into the bedchamber. She pressed the girl down into a comfortable chair by the hearth, then lit several candles to create a cheerful glow.

Returning, she sat on the footstool and rubbed Nan's cold hands between hers. "Now, I should like for you to relate every detail you can remember about this wraith."

The maid gazed wanly at her. "You do believe me, then?"

"Of course. I was only trying to get rid of that dreadful woman. Tell me, did the phantom seem tall or short? Thin or heavy?"

Nan's rusty eyebrows drew together in a frown of concentration. "Medium height, not too tall. And . . . and a bit on the stout side, I think. Oh, miss! Do ye think it could've been a real *person*?"

"Indeed so. Pray don't repeat a word of this, but someone may be trying to play a trick on me, that's all."

"But why?"

"Oh, just to frighten me as a jest. And I think perhaps that person believed *I* was present in the room." She patted the girl's hand. "There, you see? It's nothing for you to fret about. Just leave the matter to me."

Looking relieved, Nan hopped up to finish her duties in the dressing room. Bella remained seated on the footstool. She thought long and hard about who would have done such a thing.

Helen didn't want her here, neither did William Banbury-Davis. Bella tried to imagine the scholar draped in robes and flitting through the shadows. But why would he sneak into her bedchamber and take those letters? Why would he read them and then toss the packet under her bed? The answer remained a mystery.

She couldn't discount Hasani, either. Although he seemed friendly enough, there had been times when he'd stirred a faint disquiet in her. She'd felt it in particular when he had leaned down to pray over the mummy, the eye tattoo visible at the back of his neck . . .

A light rapping came from the closed door, and she jumped. That sound had not been made by a spirit. Had Miles come, after all? Would he use the basket of fruit as an excuse to call on her?

Leaping to her feet, Bella patted her hair and smoothed her gown as she hurried to answer the summons. Her gaze cut to the dressing room. How would she explain his presence to Nan?

But upon opening the door, she faced the tall

stooped figure of Pinkerton. The butler held a silver salver on which lay a folded paper. "A messenger boy brought this for you just now to the service entrance." His rheumy eyes fastened on her in a keen stare. "I thought I should deliver it myself."

Mystified, she took the note. "Thank you."

As he bowed and departed, Bella closed the door and walked to the candle on the bedside table. She broke the red wax seal and scanned the brief message.

Her legs went weak. Unable to believe her eyes, she sank down onto the edge of the bed to read the note again.

Chapter 20

Miles left the ballroom only after dusk fell and the room went so dark that he could scarcely pick his way through the shadowy maze of Egyptian statues. His strides echoed down the long corridor with its crimson runner. Here, candles flickered in sconces, the pale light gleaming over the white pillars that stood at intervals along the walls.

Of their own accord, his footsteps veered to the blue drawing room. A glance into the darkened doorway told him that Bella was no longer working among the gloomy piles of artifacts. He hadn't really expected to find her there. If truth be told, he had been avoiding her all day.

He'd awoken at the crack of dawn from an erotic dream of her. Miles had not felt so randy since he was a boy on the cusp of manhood, furtively using his hand under the covers to alleviate his passions. He'd resorted to that ploy today, too. But the release had been perfunctory in comparison to the bliss he'd experienced inside Bella.

I'm sure we can both agree it must never happen again.

He stalked toward the west wing, his solitary footsteps the only sound in the vast reaches of the house. As a rule, he did not show favor toward any particular woman. Why should he when they were all alike in the dark?

Except for Bella. With her, once had not been enough.

As a rule, he did not act on whims, either. He planned out his days, deciding ahead of time the artifacts he wanted to study or which hieroglyphs needed to be deciphered for the dictionary he was compiling.

Except for this morning. Before full light, he had impulsively set out on horseback for Turnstead Oaks, an estate he owned in the hills of Berkshire. The hard ride had invigorated him, the cool damp air whisking the cobwebs from his mind.

I'm sure we can both agree it must never happen again.

Blast it, that was supposed to be *his* line, not hers. It was what he'd been planning to say to her before she'd interrupted him. He should be pleased she shared his view.

And he *was,* dammit.

Upon arriving at his estate, he had taken a walk through the manor house. It was a lovely place, comfortably decorated, more a real home than the museum-like mansion in London. Turnstead Oaks had been his mother's favorite residence, where she'd recovered from her many miscarriages. Miles often had stayed here as a boy. How long had it been since his last visit? A year? Two years? Three? By the astonishment of the servants, perhaps even longer than that.

Bella would like it here. He saw himself making love to her in the big bed upstairs, the windows open to birdsong and summer breezes . . .

Immediately, he dismissed the fantasy. She had made it clear she would not be his mistress—and that was just as well because an affair carried the risk of pregnancy. Bella was no seasoned whore who knew tricks to prevent conception. And he could not, would not marry her. It was out of the question. She deserved better than a man who knew nothing of love, a man whose sole purpose in life was the study of ancient Egypt.

Better he should focus on extracting more information about Sir Seymour from the lockbox of Bella's memory. Then, when she was of no further use to him, he could dismiss her from his employ.

Edgy and unsettled, he had proceeded to the greenhouses. That had been his real reason for making the journey to Berkshire. He'd chatted with the old gardener, a familiar face from his boyhood days, while selecting a variety of exotic fruits for Bella.

He wondered now if she had liked the basket. Had her face lit up with that warm, open smile of hers? By pleasing her, Miles hoped to unravel the tension knotting his gut. She was a lady by birth and he had taken her virginity. A gentleman would have offered her marriage.

But he could not.

He had vowed long ago to devote himself to the ancient artifacts, to preserve them for posterity, to decode the pictorial language, as his father had wanted to do. Miles had no room in his regimented life for a wife. Only through dedication and hard work could he atone for the sin of causing his father's premature death.

It wasn't your fault. You couldn't possibly have known that brigands would attack that night.

Bella's soft words tugged at him. He'd thought long and hard about her views on the ride into Berkshire and back. Her arguments had been logical and persuasive, and talking to her had somehow lightened the heavy weight inside him. Yet the stone of guilt still lodged in his gut. Perhaps he had carried it so long it had become a part of him, like calcified tentacles wrapping his core.

Only in her arms had he felt freed of that burden. Only in her arms had he experienced a closeness that reached deep into his depths, as if to root out that tangled knot. Only in her arms had he felt loved.

My love. How sweet those words had sounded on her lips. How perfect she had felt sheathed around him. Yet once they'd achieved euphoria together, she had withdrawn into the cool, efficient employee.

It would be best if we forgot this night entirely. Then we can go on as before. There's no need for us to speak of it ever again.

Miles stalked into his dim-lit study and slammed the door. A fire burned low on the hearth, and he seized the poker to jab savagely at the coals. Tongues of flame leaped up like the blaze inside of him that had not been quenched.

He should be thankful that Bella had no intention of making demands on him. Even though she'd been the one to invite him into her bed, she would have been within her rights to demand a marriage offer. But Bella was not like other ladies. She had gifted him with both her virtue and his freedom. They had shared a highly enjoyable evening together. He had been lucky to escape without any entanglements.

So why was he so troubled?

Fraught with frustration, he walked to the window to fetch a candle from the table. He would ring for his supper and then distract himself with work. The papers on his desk had been sorely neglected these past few nights . . .

Even as his fingers closed around the silver candlestick, he glimpsed a movement out in the darkness of the garden. A shadowed figure slipped from tree to tree. The rain had stopped, and the pale moonlight shone for an instant on that slender figure.

Bella.

A jolt sizzled through him. Why the devil was she walking outside? It must be damp and chilly after the rain, and she'd catch her death. Yet a certain furtiveness about her actions pricked his attention.

Releasing the candlestick, Miles moved back out of sight. He didn't want her to glance up and see him silhouetted by the firelight. Instead, he shifted the draperies slightly and peered out through the crack, curious to know her purpose.

He found out soon enough.

As she neared the back wall, another figure emerged from the black depths of the shadows. A man, tall and lanky. The moonlight touched briefly on his fair hair and angular features.

Bella went straight to him and took his hands in hers.

Miles gripped his fingers around the draperies. Who the devil was that fellow? Why was Bella meeting him in the garden—and in such a clandestine manner?

She'd arrived recently from abroad. She'd claimed not to know anyone in London other than that antiquarian friend of her father's, Smithers. But the intruder out there didn't appear to be an old man.

One thing was certain. If he was anyone legitimate,

he'd have come to the front door instead of sneaking in from the mews.

All of a sudden, she lifted her arms and hugged the man. He did the same to her, too, drawing her close to his body.

That tight, heartfelt embrace was a punch to Miles's gut. It drove the breath from his lungs. In the next instant, a flood of fury sent him sprinting out of the study, striding swiftly down the corridor to the antechamber that led into his private apartments.

A fire burned on the marble hearth in the ducal bedchamber. The covers had been turned down on the massive, four-poster bed. With a look of surprise, Hasani stood with an armload of linen in the middle of the rug. "Your Grace! Have you decided on an early night—"

"Go," Miles snapped. "I won't need you tonight."

He stalked past the servant and went to the row of glass doors that led out to the garden. Wresting one open, he proceeded out onto a covered stone terrace. The damp chill of the night air restored a measure of his senses. He slowed his stampede down the steps to the garden path. He didn't want to alert Bella to his presence.

At least not yet.

He advanced swiftly, stealthily through the shadows toward the place where they stood, by the gate to the mews. The scent of early roses mingled with the fecund heaviness of wet loam. All the while, his mind worked feverishly.

This furtive meeting cast a new, sinister light on Bella's other actions. He'd caught her poking through his study, then the archives. She had been searching for something in particular, he felt certain of that. What? Could it have something to do with this man?

Was he a thief?

Miles clenched his jaw. Perhaps he'd been wrong about Isabella Jones. What did he know of her, really? She'd come to him out of the blue, purporting to need a job, the daughter of a man who'd broken his trust to Miles. What if she had inveigled her way into Aylwin House in order to rob him? What if that was why she'd held him at arm's length after their lovemaking?

What if she was playing him for a fool?

No. He didn't want to believe it. He couldn't believe it. Yet on the very next night after seducing him, she'd crept out to the garden and embraced a stranger. Whoever the bastard was, she'd hidden his identity from Miles. At the very least, she had been less than honest.

Keeping to the concealment of a boxwood hedge, he neared the couple. They stood in the gloom of an elm tree. They were no longer embracing, though Bella was gripping the man's arms, her head tilted up as she spoke earnestly to him.

Miles couldn't discern their whispered conversation. But they seemed to be having a disagreement. Her companion shook his head and appeared to be pleading with her. Then he put his hands on her shoulders as if to embrace her again.

And Miles saw red.

He surged forward, making no attempt at stealth this time, his swift steps crunching on the gravel path. Just as they started to turn toward him, Miles seized the man by the scruff of his neck and jerked him away from Bella.

"Hey!" cried his squirming prisoner. "Lemme go!"

A wild fist swung out, but Miles easily deflected it by grabbing that skinny wrist and twisting his arm behind his back.

Bella gasped, her face stark in the moonlight. She came charging toward him. "Miles! For pity's sake, release him at once! He's just a boy."

"Am not," the stranger objected in an adolescent's sullen tone. "I'm as full grown as any man."

Miles dragged him out of the shadows. The moonlight fell on a young man's face that looked as if he hadn't quite grown into its angular contours. He had sandy hair and Bella's blue eyes. He was barely old enough to sprout a beard.

Taken aback, Miles released his captive's arm and scowled at Bella, then the boy. "What the devil—" he bit out. "Who are you?"

"Sir Cyrus Jones," he declared, puffing out his bony chest while rubbing his arm. "And I shall report you to the magistrate for attacking me."

"*You* could be the one tossed behind bars for trespassing," Bella scolded him. Defiance firmed her expression as she turned her eyes to Miles. "Your Grace, may I introduce my younger brother, Cyrus."

For once, Bella was glad to see the cool mask descend over Miles's face. His fury had been a sight to behold. When he'd come charging at them from out of the darkness, she had been stunned by the feral harshness of his countenance.

He had looked fit to kill.

A quiver snaked down her spine. She shuddered to imagine what he'd thought, seeing her skulking in the garden with a stranger. Any fledgling trust that had blossomed between them had been damaged. But what was she to do upon receiving that note from Cyrus, asking her to meet him at the garden gate? She could hardly have ignored it.

Oh, she was in terrible trouble now, judging by the

coldness on Miles's face. He knew that she had lied to him, if not in fact, then by omission. She had led him to believe she was alone in the world, and now she could only hope to rectify matters by confessing all.

Except in regard to her search for the treasure map. Not even Cyrus or Lila knew about that.

She continued the introduction. "Cyrus, this is the Duke of Aylwin. You'll address him as Aylwin or Your Grace."

"*You* called him Miles," her brother pointed out.

The burn of heat rose from the collar of her gown. How was she to explain her informal usage of her employer's name after so short an acquaintance? She'd sooner cut out her tongue than admit to what she and Miles had done in her bed the previous night.

As if sensing her discomfort, Miles said sternly, "Since your sister is my colleague, I've granted her special permission in addressing me. You, on the other hand, will treat me with proper respect. Is that clear?"

Cyrus gave him a wary, mistrustful stare until Bella poked him in the ribs. He said quickly, "Yes . . . Your Grace."

Miles eyed the boy's lanky form for a long moment, and Bella feared the duke might toss her brother out into the mews. Unlike the warm lover who had shown her ecstasy, Miles now wore the stony, autocratic guise of Aylwin. She curled her fingers into fists at her sides. Cyrus had been horribly wrong to disobey her order to stay in Oxford, but now that he was here, she would fight for him. Even if it meant defying the duke and putting her mission in jeopardy.

"I was always hungry at your age," Miles said abruptly. "Come."

He turned on his heel and strode toward the house without a backward glance.

Bella caught her brother's arm as they started after Miles down the winding gravel path. Cyrus loped alongside her, saying in a rather excited whisper, "I thought the duke would be a doddering old fellow with white hair and a cane. But he's strong—and taller than me. I'll wager Aylwin could knock down even the stoutest ruffian in a fight."

Bella had mixed feelings about seeing her brother's sullenness transform into hero worship. On the one hand, she was relieved that he wouldn't misbehave and cause her more trouble than she was already in. On the other, she didn't want Cyrus to try to wheedle Miles into letting him stay here in London.

"You're too young to wager anything," she hissed. "Just remember, His Grace is a very important man and you should count yourself lucky he didn't throw you out into the gutter!"

She had no time to say more because they'd arrived at the service entrance, hidden by a screen of boxwoods and down a short flight of steep stone steps. Miles held open the door. Bella couldn't read his impassive features, but at least he wasn't shouting anymore. Her heart raced as she went past him, the narrow entry causing her to brush against him. She might have wilted into a heap at his feet if she hadn't resolved never to make a fool of herself over him again.

He led the way into the kitchen, where several servants sat around the long worktable, drinking their evening tea near the cheery blaze on the hearth. As one, they all gaped at the entering trio. After an instant of shocked silence, china rattled and chair legs scraped as the staff jumped to their feet to pay obeisance to the duke.

It must be a rare event for the master to venture be-

lowstairs, Bella surmised. They all looked astonished by his presence.

Mrs. Witheridge hurried forward, wiping her hands on the white apron over her black gown and stout form. She bobbed a curtsy. "Your Grace! What an honor. Is there aught we might do for you?"

Miles placed his hand on Cyrus's bony shoulder. "This is Sir Cyrus Jones, brother to Miss Jones. He'll be staying here tonight."

The housekeeper turned and clapped her hands. "Nan, Susan, run upstairs and prepare the green room at once." She looked at Bella. "'Tis directly across from your bedchamber, if that's aright with you."

A weight lifted from Bella's shoulders. "That would be perfect."

She glanced at Miles to thank him, but he was addressing Cook. "If you'll fetch a plate for the lad, whatever's cold in the larder should be sufficient. There's no need to fuss. It's late and he'll take his supper right here. I will, as well, come to think of it."

If any of the staff found that odd, none dared to show any sign. Servants scurried here and there, Cook to fetch provisions from the cold room, a kitchen maid to slice bread and another to brew a fresh pot of tea on the newfangled stove. At one end of the table, a footman laid a fine white cloth and set three places with silver utensils as if they were dining with the Queen.

In a doorway across the kitchen, Hasani stood sipping his tea, his dark gaze fixed on Cyrus. Like everyone else, the valet must be curious to learn she had a brother, Bella thought wryly. His white robes swirling, the man melted back into the next chamber, most likely to avoid being pulled into the beehive of activity.

Just then, Pinkerton shuffled to Bella and bent his grizzled head close to her. "Brother, heh? I thought I

noted a resemblance when the lad came to the door, on the pretense of being a messenger."

She smiled in fond exasperation at her brother, who was slurping a mug of tea brought to him by a blushing kitchen maid. "Well, I do appreciate you coming at once to fetch me. He told me he walked around London lost for a good many hours."

She caught Miles gazing narrow-eyed at her. That look raised prickles on her skin, and she wasn't certain if it was from an untimely attraction or apprehension over her brother. The duke ushered her into a seat opposite Cyrus and took the head of the table. As man and boy filled their plates from the platters of meat and cheeses and other foodstuffs, Bella noticed the servants had vanished, leaving them alone in the kitchen.

Miles cut up a leg of chicken, watching as Cyrus wolfed down a slab of roast beef wrapped in bread. Uneasiness kept Bella from taking even a bite. She felt beset by the instinct to move, to do something other than sit still in anticipation of the duke's inevitable rebuke. He must be waiting for Cyrus to eat before launching an attack.

"Shall I make you cheese toast?" she asked her brother, even though he didn't deserve his favorite meal after the wrong he'd done.

At his eager nod, Bella jumped to her feet and fetched a frying pan from a hook on the wall. Then she busied herself buttering bread and cutting thin slices from the wheel of cheese. Having no notion of how to operate the elaborate black stove, she carried the pan to the massive hearth and placed it on a trivet just above the flames.

Behind her, Miles addressed Cyrus in a clipped tone. "From where do you hail? Are you living here in London?"

"Nay, I traveled from Oxford," Cyrus said, taking a huge swig of tea. "Took the overnight mail coach, then walked around for a good bit trying to find Aylwin House. Did you know there are shops that sell only men's boots? And others that sell just hats? And—"

"I recall now that your father kept a cottage in Oxford," Miles broke in reflectively. "We exchanged letters for a time."

"You knew Papa? But when—how?"

"Quite a long time ago, when I was younger than you. But never mind that. Tell me, what is your purpose in coming here? Are you in some sort of trouble?"

Bella turned her head to see her brother straighten his shoulders and jut out his chin. "It isn't right that my sister has to labor for a living while I stay at home," he declared. "I'm the man of the family now, and it is my duty to provide for us."

"Nonsense," she scolded over her shoulder. "You're underage and I left you explicit instructions to study your schoolwork in my absence. Besides, what sort of post can you fill without a proper education?"

The sizzle of frying bread yanked her attention back to the fire, and she deftly flipped the cheese toast to the other side. The rich aroma of butter smelled heavenly even to her distracted senses.

Behind her, Cyrus said defiantly, "I can drive a coach or run errands or work on a printing press. I can be a salesman in a shop or a plowman on a farm. I can—"

"You can do nothing of the sort," Miles snapped. "As a gentleman, your first duty is to educate yourself in order to take your rightful place as a leader in society. That is precisely what my father told *me* at the age of thirteen."

Crouched by the hearth, Bella went still. Miles must

be referring to the quarrel he'd had with his father on that fateful night in Egypt. The very fact that he could mention it aloud gave her hope that perhaps he was finally coming to grips with his father's death. Then the scent of well-done toast caught her attention, and she pulled the pan from the fire, bringing it to the table. As she transferred the concoction to a white china plate, Miles kept his attention fully on her brother.

"By the by, how old *are* you?"

"Fifteen," Cyrus said, his mouth turning down rather sullenly. "And it isn't fair to make me stay in Oxford with Lila. She's just a girl."

"Lila?" Miles asked with an ominous frown at Bella.

"Lila is his twin sister." Striving for calm, Bella sliced the perfectly browned bread in half so that the cheese oozed out onto the plate. "Would *you* care for a cheese toast, too, Your Grace? I can make more for both of you, if you like."

Without awaiting his assent, she transferred half onto his plate as a peace offering.

Miles picked it up—with his fingers, she noted. He took a bite and chewed appreciatively for a moment, though his stare remained stern. "Are there any other family members you've concealed from me?"

"None. Only the twins." Because an explanation seemed in order, she added lamely, "Perhaps I should have said something, but they're my responsibility and I didn't wish to burden you with the matter."

Miles glared at her another moment, as if trying to decide whether or not to believe her words. Then he shifted his frown to Cyrus. "So you abandoned your underage sister in Oxford. You left her alone in order to come to London on this fool's mission."

Cyrus shifted uneasily in his chair as his defiant ex-

pression turned into that of a guilty little boy. "Lila isn't alone. Mrs. Norris is watching over her."

"Who the devil is Mrs. Norris?"

"A neighbor," Bella said as she buttered more bread for the frying pan. "The widow of a vicar and a very respectable guardian. Cyrus, I presume you didn't ask her permission to come to London. She'd never have allowed you."

"But I left her a note—and one for Lila, too!"

Miles uttered a growl in his throat. "That is hardly the act of a responsible gentleman. They're likely worried to death about you. If I were your father, I'd thrash you for running off like that."

Seeing her brother's dejected features, Bella went to him and put her arm around his shoulders. She brushed back a lock of dark brown hair from his brow. "His Grace is quite right to chastise you, my love. Your duty was to watch out for your sister."

Miles abruptly gave her a piercing stare. She felt the force of it penetrate to her bones. What was he thinking behind that flinty mask? Was he just surprised that she would agree with him?

He turned his gaze to Cyrus, who hung his head, his fingers tearing at the cheese toast on his plate. "Sorry," the boy mumbled. "But I was stuck at the cottage with nothing to do but study. It wasn't fair!"

Miles pushed back his chair and stood up. "A man always fulfills his obligations. Fairness has nothing to do with it. Tomorrow, I shall see to it that you return to Oxford. Be ready to depart at first light."

With one last intent look at Bella, he walked out of the kitchen.

Her heart twisted into a painful knot. She wanted to run after him, to thank him for the basket of fruit and for giving fatherly counsel to her brother. Most of

all, she wanted to throw her arms around him and lose herself in the joy of his passionate kisses.

But she herself had put a stop to all intimacy between them. They had mutually agreed to end their impulsive affair. *It would be best if we forgot this night entirely. Then we can go on as before. There's no need for us to speak of it ever again.*

By her own declaration, she was no longer the duke's confidante and lover. She was merely his employee again. And now that Miles had caught her withholding the truth about her family, he had no reason to trust her ever again.

Chapter 21

Mounted on horseback, Miles rode beside the black coach along the narrow, rutted lane. It was high noon and the sun shone down from a clear blue sky washed clean by yesterday's rain. They had reached the outskirts of Oxford at last. The journey from London had taken more than six hours with one brief stop for refreshment at a posting inn.

Bella and her brother had come to the stables at the crack of dawn. While she'd issued directions to the coachman, Cyrus had peered enviously at the glossy black gelding being saddled for Miles. Despite the boy's hopeful query about borrowing a horse for himself, Miles bade him ride in the coach with Bella. The scamp deserved no rewards for abandoning his twin sister.

Miles still could scarcely believe Bella had two younger siblings. He had presumed her to be an only child like himself. Why had she never spoken of them? She'd had the perfect opportunity when they had discussed his father's death. *By standing up for*

yourself, you were learning how to be a man. It's a natural step for a boy of thirteen.

Bella could have explained that she'd had ample experience with adolescent boys. Instead, she had led Miles to believe she was alone in the world. It displeased him mightily to learn the extent to which she had shut him out of her private life.

Yet what right did he have to expect her confidences? Aside from that long-ago sojourn in Egypt, they had known each other less than a fortnight. That was hardly enough time for them to have grown close—even if they had shared the most spectacular night of his life.

Small houses lined the lane, the front gardens a riot of colorful spring flowers. A long-ago memory came to him of Sir Seymour laughing with his wife about how he'd been able to afford only a tiny cottage on his academic salary. Even in youth, Miles had been struck by how adoringly Lady Hannah had gazed at her husband. It had made such a stark contrast to his own parents, his mother frail and morose, his father cold and authoritarian.

Now, in his mind, the blue-eyed, brown-haired image of Lady Hannah transformed into that of her daughter. Miles wanted Bella to gaze at *him* with such adoration. For a brief time he'd believed she had formed an intense attachment to him.

My love. She had called him that in the heat of their joining, and he had thought—hoped—that she felt a true affection. A fierce longing had taken root in him, a weakness that continued to bedevil him even though yesterday she'd uttered those same two words to her brother.

Miles felt like a damned fool. "My love" was nothing more than a casual endearment to her. She'd probably said it to numerous people over the years, family

and friends alike. It meant little to her, just a tender phrase tossed out during a highly charged moment.

Nevertheless, he had half expected her to come after him when he'd left the kitchen. He'd wanted to steal a moment alone with her, to hold her in his arms and unleash his frustrations in a fervent kiss. But Bella had no interest in further intimacy. Any closeness of mind and spirit had been an illusion. She clearly did not trust him enough to divulge the details of her private life.

Logic told him to dissociate himself from her. There was no point to torturing himself with false hopes. Yet he had volunteered to come on this journey. He had given up a day's work in order to escort her brother back to Oxford. Perhaps because Bella made him feel alive, as if he'd awakened from a long sleep. One night of love had not been enough to satisfy him—it would never be enough.

Impatient with himself, Miles shut down the rise of lust. Fantasy accomplished nothing. He would not press his attentions on an unwilling woman, and that was that.

The coachman drew the team of horses to a halt outside a quaint cottage with a roof in sad need of repair, judging by the holes in the thatch. The stone chimney was crumbling, and the garden had reverted to a wild weedy tangle. A few yellow roses straggled up the walls along with a choking blanket of ivy.

A female face peered out of one of the mullioned windows, her features made indistinct by the old wavy glass. An instant later, the cottage door flew open at the same moment as Bella flung open the coach door at the footman, who had been reaching for the handle.

A remarkably pretty girl darted down the path. Like a fairy princess, she had golden-brown hair tied back

with a pink ribbon that matched her gown, and Miles presumed her to be fifteen-year-old Lila.

Bella hopped out without even waiting for the step to be lowered. Clad in the bronze silk gown that she'd worn at their first meeting, she hastened to greet her sister at the garden gate. There, the two hugged each other tightly, and when Cyrus came trudging up to them, they brought him into their little circle.

Miles swung down from the gelding, scarcely aware of the footman taking the reins from him. A sense of isolation settled over him, the knowledge that he did not belong here. Bella and her siblings shared a close-ness that he had never known in his own life—except perhaps to a small degree with their father, Sir Sey-mour.

But that had been a very long time ago.

Peeling off his riding gloves, Miles hesitated to in-trude on the private reunion. Perhaps he should wait here by the coach and allow Bella to visit with her family. He could give them an hour or two together before it would be time for him and Bella to return to London.

Then a discordant sight caught his attention.

Lila began to wring her hands. When she spoke, her young voice held a trill of anxiety. "Oh, Bella, I'm so glad you're home. You won't believe what happened last night! Someone broke into the cottage!"

Miles crossed the rutted lane in two steps. To hell with propriety. He had to hear what the girl had to say. As he drew near, Bella and her brother both spoke at once.

"A thief—here?" Cyrus began.

"Oh, no!" Bella cried out, glancing over her sister as if to seek injuries. "Are you all right?"

Lila sniffled. "Of course! I frightened him away."

"Was Mrs. Norris present? Do tell me you weren't alone."

"She was sound asleep upstairs," Lila said, her voice breaking. "It was dreadful. I—I heard a noise and . . . and . . ."

Bella slid her arm around her sister's shoulders. "Come inside, my love. You can tell me all about it over a cup of tea."

Bella's deep blue gaze flitted to Miles, and the distress there cut straight to his heart. Then she directed Lila up the walk and into the cottage. Cyrus followed, his posture hunched as if he held the weight of the world on his shoulders. Clearly, the young man understood now that he should never have left his sister unguarded.

Miles grimly took up the rear. Although this pleasant little neighborhood didn't appear to be crime-ridden, thieves could be anywhere, looking for an easy mark. Perhaps Cyrus's absence had been noticed, and the villain had broken in believing that only a fifteen-year-old girl had been home. Miles clenched his jaw to think of what might have happened to Lila at the hands of a brute.

As they entered the cottage, a matronly woman with gray sausage curls and a green gown waited in the tiny entryway. She greeted Bella with great warmth and wagged a scolding finger at Cyrus before sweeping him into a hug. Bella introduced Miles, first to Lila, who turned frankly curious blue eyes on him, and then to Mrs. Norris, who bobbed a deep curtsy upon learning he was the Duke of Aylwin.

All aflutter, Mrs. Norris hastened down a narrow passage to fetch tea from the kitchen. The cottage had a cozy feel, he noted, from the steep staircase to the low ceiling and the miniature rooms. Bella started to

lead her sister into a sitting room to the right, but Miles stepped through a doorway to the left. There, a blizzard of books and papers had been flung haphazardly over the dining table and bare wood floor.

"What happened here?" he asked.

Gliding with ethereal grace, Lila approached him. "This is where I found the thief, Your Grace. I heard a noise—a thump as if a book had been dropped. So I crept downstairs in the darkness to see what it was."

Miles raised a stern eyebrow. "Was that wise? Oughtn't you have awakened your guardian?"

"Oh, Mrs. Norris can sleep through a crashing thunderstorm! And I was quite safe since I had my knife—"

"Your knife."

"Why, yes." Lila dug into the pocket of her pink gown and withdrew a small dagger much like her sister's. "Papa taught me how to use it in Persia."

"Mmm." Miles glanced at Bella, who met his gaze, her lips tilted in a slight smile. He could not help but appreciate that Sir Seymour had raised two such capable daughters. "Tell me what transpired."

"I came upon the man right here"—Lila nodded at the dining chamber—"poking through those crates in the corner by the light of a candle."

"Did you get a good look at him?"

She ruefully shook her head. "I'm afraid he wore dark clothes and had a hat pulled low on his head. When I screamed, he nipped out the candle at once and surged straight at me. That's when I slashed him." Her dainty features turning fierce, she reenacted the scene by plunging the knife through the air.

"Did you hurt him?" Cyrus asked with avid interest.

"Yes," Lila said. "There was blood on the blade,

though I doubt I did any more harm than to gouge his arm, more's the pity! He went flying past me and out the back door and that was that."

Miles revised his opinion of Lila as a delicate fairy princess. It seemed she was as plucky as her sister.

He stepped into the dining chamber to examine the mess. "Was anything else disturbed besides this room? Anything stolen?"

"Nothing is missing. I looked around, but we've really very little to steal, anyway." A tremor ran through Lila as she pocketed the dagger. "I was just now composing a letter to you, Bella, to beg you to come home—and to see if Cyrus had found you. Then I heard the coach outside and you arrived—like magic!"

As Bella comforted her sister with a kiss on the brow, Miles picked up one of the many scattered notebooks. Opening it, he experienced a jolt of recognition. That untidy scrawl belonged to Sir Seymour. Miles looked through several more of the notebooks, then went to peer into the half-empty crate in the corner. It contained more books and papers. There were two other unopened crates, as well.

He caught Bella's eye and frowned, and in a flash she appeared to comprehend his meaning. She shooed her sister and brother toward the kitchen, instructing them to assist Mrs. Norris with the tea. When they were gone, she hurried closer, saying, "These crates hold Papa's life's work. I cannot fathom what a thief would want with any of this."

Miles couldn't imagine, either. Yet he had a bad feeling in his gut, an uneasiness he could not shake. Most robbers sought valuables like jewelry or coins. Was it possible this was no ordinary thief?

But what significance could there be in these old papers?

Her troubled gaze on him, Bella rubbed her arms. She went on in a somber tone, "You might as well return to London without me, Your Grace. I'm afraid I shall have to beg leave from my post and remain here in Oxford."

Her words struck a hard blow to his chest. Miles stared at her familiar features, the entrancing blue eyes and the pert chin, the soft lips that could utter an impudent remark or seduce him with a kiss. For a moment he could scarcely breathe as everything in him rejected the prospect of never seeing her again. "The fortnight that you promised me is not quite up."

"I'm sorry, but surely you can see that fulfilling our agreement is no longer possible." She walked to the window to stare out, her fingers gripping the sill. "I was wrong to leave here from the start. Wrong to travel so far from my family. Only think of what could have happened to Lila."

Seeing Bella shudder, Miles wrestled with the need to enfold her in the safety of his arms, to offer his protection. But how could he? As her temporary employer, he did not have any real claim on her. And she herself had shunned any hope of further intimacy between them.

He stepped nearer, anyway, stopping just short of touching her. "And what of yourself?" he asked roughly. "Think of what could happen to *you* if I were to leave you here. What if that thief returns?"

She whirled to face him, all fire and brimstone. "What other course of action do I have? Shall I abandon my brother and sister to fend for themselves again? I won't do it!"

Those fierce lapis lazuli eyes caught at his heart. He made a snap decision, a decision that felt absolutely right. Perfect, in fact. "You do have another choice. All

three of you will pack up your belongings at once and
come back to London with me."

"I've never been in a palace before," Lila said in awe
as they stepped into the foyer of Aylwin House with
its cream marble floor and the grand staircase soaring
upward to branch off in two directions. Her head tilted
back, a bandbox of belongings in her hand, she slowly
twirled around to view every aspect of the massive
hall.

Bella imagined the impressive sight through her
sister's eyes. Ornate pillars soared to the ceiling. The
walls displayed huge murals of mythological scenes on
panels framed by elaborate gilding. In the center of the
room, an obelisk rose like a needle to point at the high
glass-domed roof, now dark from nightfall.

"I wonder if my voice will echo." Cyrus cupped his
hands around his mouth. "Hallo!"

A faint *hallo* ricocheted back to him.

The twins shared a laugh.

Miles handed his riding gloves and hat to a white-
wigged footman in crimson livery. Another footman
took the bandbox from Lila, along with their outer
wraps. Not a hint of a smile cracked the solemn faces
of the servants, although Bella thought she spied a
twinkle in their eyes. There would be an animated
discussion of the new arrivals tonight in the servants'
hall, she surmised. Perhaps nothing so unusual had
happened in this mansion since the newly minted Duke
of Aylwin had returned from Egypt with many ship-
loads of artifacts over twenty years ago.

Yet she herself still suffered grave misgivings about
bringing her siblings here. Although the duke's offer
was a godsend, Bella disliked imposing on his hospitality, for it made her feel beholden to him. She felt

guilty, as well, for in return for his benevolence, she was tricking him about her true mission in finding the treasure map.

How was she to search, anyway, if she had to monitor her brother and sister? Or tend to her duty of organizing the artifacts in the blue drawing room? And what if the twins interrupted Miles? He was accustomed to working in solitude, and she doubted that he realized just how lively two adolescents could be.

If only Mrs. Norris had been able to come to London, too. But the widow had a son and grandchildren in Oxford and could not be persuaded to part from them.

Bella had given her siblings a stern lecture on the long ride back to London in the sumptuous coach, but already they seemed to have forgotten her instructions about proper behavior in a ducal residence. Now, Cyrus grabbed Lila's hand, and against her laughing protests, he tugged her toward the marble staircase.

Bella made haste to intercept them. "There'll be no exploring tonight," she warned in an undertone. "Tomorrow is soon enough for a tour."

Cyrus eyed the long balcony on either side of the stairs. "But I only want to go up there and see if my voice echoes—"

"You'll heed your sister's command," Miles said firmly, stepping to Bella's side. "In a moment, you'll both be assigned bedchambers. And there you'll stay until the morning. Any insubordination will be reported directly to me."

He aimed the Ducal Stare at them, and the twins lapsed into meek silence. Bella hid a twist of amusement, for they could have no inkling of the kindness that Miles hid behind his brusque exterior. But she knew. No matter how he might scowl and scold, he was

a considerate man underneath it all. He'd offered his protection to all of them, when it surely would be an inconvenience to him. He had even assisted them in packing up their meager belongings, including Papa's papers.

Had he done so for her sake? Was it possible that he harbored an affection for her after their night together?

With all her heart, Bella wanted to believe that. She herself felt a decided warmth toward him, and a mad desire to see his face soften with love when he looked at her. But it wouldn't do to dwell on impossible dreams. She must remember that her stay here was only temporary. Miles was a confirmed bachelor, a dedicated scholar, and a nobleman far beyond her reach.

If he felt anything at all for her, it could only be lust.

A quiver stirred deep within her womb. How she longed to satisfy her own hunger for him. But she must never act upon her desires again, especially not now, with her brother and sister so close at hand.

Pinkerton came hobbling from the rear of the house, Mrs. Witheridge at his side. As Miles introduced Lila to them, Bella could see the curiosity in their eyes. How surprised they must be that the master would treat the brother and sister of an employee as honored guests.

Cyrus would occupy the same chamber as the previous night, while Lila would be installed in the bedroom next to Bella's. In short order, the housekeeper led the twins toward the grand staircase, while Pinkerton headed back down to the servants' hall to issue the appropriate instructions to the staff.

As Bella made to follow, Miles stopped her with a brief touch to her arm. All of her senses sprang to alert

as he bent his head closer. "If you're agreeable," he said in an undertone, "I would like to keep your father's papers locked in the storage room next to my study. You have my word that I won't touch them without your permission."

Why did he wish to keep Papa's effects locked up?

Struck by a knell of uneasiness, she searched his sober features. She thought of the missing letters, the ghostly figure that both she and Nan had glimpsed. Miles knew nothing about that intruder. Yet he too must have been disturbed by the peculiarity of the break-in at her cottage. Was it possible there was a connection?

Bella needed time alone to think about it all.

"I'd like to check the crates to see if anything is missing, perhaps sometime in the next day or two," she said. "But you've forbidden me access to your study."

One corner of his mouth lifted in an attractive half smile that turned her knees to softened butter. "Then a new rule is in order," he said in a husky murmur meant for her ears alone. "You may enter any room in the west wing at any time . . . day or night."

Just like that, a spark kindled between them, the air shimmering with heat. She felt its warmth all the way down to her toes. Was he suggesting that she slip into his bedchamber in the dark of night?

The prospect sounded so very tempting—and so very reckless. She had a duty to her siblings, a job to finish, a map to find. Yet when his gaze dipped to her mouth, Bella had the wild urge to throw her arms around him, to join their lips in an ardent kiss, no matter that a footman stood on duty across the vast hall.

On impulse, she reached out to grasp Miles's hand. He immediately laced his fingers through hers, too, his grip firm and strong. His eyes were dark and intent on

her. A powerful surge of emotion washed through her, a swell of passion and gratitude and affection, with hidden depths that she dared not explore.

Was it love? Surely she could not be so unwise as to give her heart to the almighty Duke of Aylwin.

It seemed safest to focus on appreciation. "I never had a chance to thank you, Miles. For the fruit basket . . . for allowing me to stay here . . . for taking all of us into your home. You've been far, far too kind."

Before she could disgrace herself by begging for his love, she tugged her hand free and escaped up the staircase.

Chapter 22

The following morning, Bella took her brother and sister on a tour of Aylwin House. They tramped up and down the many staircases, peeking into rooms crammed with statues and into other chambers that were unused, the furniture draped in dustcovers. She sketched them each a map to carry, too, in case they became lost. The twins were on their best behavior, having been suitably awed the previous evening by the warning from Miles.

The Ducal Stare had its good uses.

At midday, they ventured down into the kitchen and enjoyed a simple meal of shepherd's pie at the long table, amid the bustle of the kitchen staff preparing the master's luncheon. Bella wondered if Miles would eat alone in his study where they'd shared a cold supper, smiling and talking, on the night they'd made love.

Beset by wistful longing, she reminded herself it was best to lock away the memory of that forbidden intimacy. Best, too, to stay out of his path by avoiding the ballroom where he often worked. Best not to think about him at all.

After luncheon, she intended to settle her brother and sister in the huge library. They were both avid readers and she could trust them to do their lessons there and then entertain themselves with the many books on display. But first, she escorted them to the blue drawing room so they could see how she was organizing the jumble of broken artifacts.

Cyrus exhibited a keen interest in the task. He asked scores of intelligent questions, some of which she couldn't answer, while helping her lay out the scarabs on a table draped in the white silk that Miles had provided.

Lila wandered to a pile in the corner that Bella had not yet sorted and plucked out an item. It was a flat round implement made of dented bronze with an ornate handle. "Do you suppose this is a mirror?" she asked, bringing it to them.

"I don't know," Bella said in surprise. "It might be."

"Maybe I could polish away the tarnish. Then we can see if it shows our reflection." Lila snatched up a rag and began to rub hard on the bronze surface.

Bella smiled. She could see Papa's influence on her brother and sister, for he had conveyed to them his love for bygone eras. Many an evening, they'd gathered around the fire in their stone hut to examine items he'd unearthed that day, or to discuss how people lived in the ancient world. A lump formed in her throat. How dearly she missed her father . . .

The sound of footsteps yanked her out of the memory, and she turned just as Helen and Oscar Grayson sauntered through the doorway.

The moment of nostalgia fading, Bella braced herself to deflect their snide commentary. She had felt a particular distaste for them ever since that vicious incident when Helen had trod upon Bella's foot.

The couple looked as if they belonged at a fancy party, fair-haired Helen resplendent in an aqua gown with sea-foam-green trimmings, and Oscar the quintessential gentleman in a claret coat with gray pinstripe trousers and a rose-pink waistcoat. His muttonchop whiskers had been neatly trimmed beneath an artful mop of dark wavy hair.

Bella wasn't fooled by their fine appearances. These two could only be up to no good.

Helen glided past the stacks of artifacts, her disdainful gaze flicking to the twins and then back to Bella. "Miss Jones!" she uttered. "My maid heard gossip that you'd moved your family into Aylwin House. I simply could not believe that you would dare to impose so greatly on the duke's charity."

Bella gritted her teeth behind a pleasant smile. As much as she'd like to utter a biting retort, she must not lose her temper in front of her siblings. "Mrs. Grayson, Mr. Grayson, allow me to present my sister and brother. Lila, Cyrus, Mr. Grayson is the duke's cousin."

"And heir, don't forget," Oscar added with a nasty smirk.

Oblivious to any undercurrents, Cyrus bowed in a desultory manner, then returned to his study of the scarabs. Laying down the bronze mirror, Lila dipped a graceful curtsy, all the while staring in wide-eyed innocence at Helen. "Oh, what a perfectly gorgeous gown, Mrs. Grayson. I've never seen anything so pretty in my life."

Helen preened. "I employ the finest modiste in London. Though I daresay, a girl of your foreign upbringing can have little experience in matters of style."

Lila took an earnest step closer. "I've studied the fashion journals, madam. And I am quite skilled in sewing my own dresses. See?" She twirled around,

spinning the dark gold skirt of the gown that she had reworked from her former Persian robes.

Bella thought Lila with her golden-brown hair far more lovely than Helen who had amber feline eyes and a superior tilt to her chin. Then Bella noticed Oscar leaning on his cane and staring with an avid expression at the young girl.

Nothing could have been better designed to stir her protective instincts. She could not tolerate another moment in the company of these two miscreants.

"I'm afraid you've come at an inconvenient time," she said tightly. "His Grace requested that I take my brother and sister for a tour of the statuary in the ballroom. If we don't leave now, we'll be late."

"You never told me that," Cyrus said, glancing up from the scarabs.

"Aylwin sent me a message earlier," she fibbed. "And we dare not disobey his command." Taking Lila and Cyrus each by the hand, she stepped toward the couple. "If you'll excuse us."

Oscar and Helen retreated in a huff, though not without bending their heads together to mutter back and forth about uppity servants and their deplorable manners. As the pair went out the door, and Bella towed her siblings in the other direction, she distinctly heard Oscar's voice echo down the vast corridor.

"Miss Jones looks much older than those two," he said with a snigger. "Can we be certain they're not *her* whelps?"

Bella very nearly turned around and marched back to give him a well-deserved tongue-lashing. Instead, she pulled her brother and sister onward down the passageway with the tall white pillars along the walls.

Perhaps she *was* old enough to be their mother. There was nothing wrong with that. She had raised

them from the time of Mama's death, shortly after their birth, when Bella had been fourteen. She had cooked for them, bandaged their scrapes, taught them their lessons, nursed them through childhood illnesses.

But being nearly thirty years of age didn't make her a withered crone. Miles certainly hadn't found her too old to arouse his lusts. He had been more than happy to . . .

"Ouch, must you squeeze so hard?" Cyrus said.

"And pray don't walk *quite* so fast," Lila added rather breathlessly.

Bella released their hands and slowed her pace to a stroll. "Sorry, darlings, I must have been lost in thought."

Lila cast an astute glance back over her shoulder. "Those two made you angry, didn't they? *I* didn't like them very much, either, to be honest. They were rather snobbish." She paused, her face growing wistful. "Though I do covet Mrs. Grayson's gown."

Bella laughed, her wrath easing along with the tension in her limbs. "Perhaps one morning we'll go out to the shops," she said impulsively. "Even if we haven't the means to purchase anything, there's no harm in looking at fabric and trimmings."

Her face alight, Lila clapped her hands. "Oh, yes, please! Can it be tomorrow?"

"At the end of the week. And then only if your schoolwork is properly completed."

"I'm staying right here," Cyrus declared. "I need a new pair of boots, but what's the point if I haven't any funds to buy them?"

Lila disagreed, and the twins launched into a spirited squabble about the merits of browsing versus buying.

They'd arrived at the arched doorway to the ball-

room, and Bella tried to shush them, fearing their voices would carry to Miles. "That's quite enough, both of you," she murmured. "It's time to go to the library for your lessons."

When she took hold of their arms to steer them in the opposite direction, Cyrus balked. The massive doors to the ballroom stood open, and he craned his neck to peer at the rows of Egyptian sculptures. "Wait! You told the Graysons that the duke is expecting us. You said he wanted to show us those statues—and I do want to see them."

Bella had taught her siblings never to lie, so she sought a tactful way to explain that she'd invented the appointment. "I'm sorry, but you see, I was too busy to chat with them today, and I needed an excuse . . ."

The words died in her throat as Miles stepped into the doorway.

He looked as he always did on a workday, the white shirt stretched over his muscular shoulders, the sleeves rolled to the elbows, the black trousers defining his long legs. Yet every part of her body heated up with tingly awareness. She could have stood there for hours, drinking in his appearance. His hair was slightly mussed, as if he'd run his fingers through it multiple times while trying to solve a difficult hieroglyph. The slight, very attractive smile on his lips caused a hitch in her heartbeat.

He withdrew a gold watch from his pocket and flicked it open to check the time. "I presume you've come for our appointment. May I commend you on your promptness . . . especially if you were delayed by my cousin and his wife."

The twinkle of humor in his dark eyes made her dizzy with relief. He had overheard her awkward

explanation and he had covered for her. And blessing of blessings, he didn't appear to mind the interruption.

"Thank you for inviting us here, Your Grace," Cyrus said, peering past Miles. "I say, is that a coffin?"

Her brother loped eagerly into the ballroom. Though most of the room was filled with a maze of statues, he went straight to a long, rectangular structure fashioned from granite, the sides chiseled with the images of Egyptian gods and goddesses.

Miles strolled to one end of the massive box. "It's called a sarcophagus. It would have been placed inside the burial tomb and the pharaoh laid to rest in here."

"It's enormous! And it must weigh tons. How did you ever transport it here all the way from Egypt?"

Cyrus hung on every word as Miles launched into a technical description of the system of pulleys and winches and manpower required to convey stone monoliths aboard ships. Without even being aware of walking closer, Bella took up a stance alongside the duke and let his deep voice roll through her. It was an excuse to breathe in his masculine scent, to savor a trace of his body heat. If only she had the right to slide her arm around his lean waist, to tuck her head into the shelter of his shoulder, to feel his strong heartbeat. How she wished he would look at her with the warmth of true love in his eyes . . .

Lila wandered to a nearby statue of a robed Egyptian wearing a tall crown decorated by a serpent. Even as she tilted her head back, her mind was clearly on other matters. "Have you been to the shops already, Bella?"

"I'm afraid I haven't had the time."

"Then how will we know which ones are the best?" Lila snapped her fingers. "I have an idea! Lady Milford

dresses beautifully. We can call on her and ask her advice."

Miles stopped in mid-sentence. He pivoted on his heel to aim a hard stare at Lila. "Who did you say?"

Bella's pulse jumped. Why did he look so angry all of a sudden? The relaxed man of a moment ago had vanished behind a rigid mask.

Then a sick sensation assailed the pit of her stomach as she remembered that Lady Milford had issued a warning to Bella. *You must never mention my name to Aylwin. The duke is a proud, reclusive man who dislikes being maneuvered.*

But it was too late to shush her naïve sister.

"Lady Milford," Lila repeated. "She came to our cottage shortly before Bella left for London. Do you know her, Your Grace?"

A thunderous expression darkened his eyes. "We've met."

Lila blinked warily at his sharp tone, and when she parted her lips as if to question him further, Bella said quickly, "I'm afraid this tour will have to be delayed. I've just remembered that His Grace and I have an important business matter to discuss."

She shooed her grumbling brother and sister out the door of the ballroom. "The library is straight along the passage and down the stairs. Use your maps if necessary."

Bella pulled the heavy doors shut and turned to face the duke. Her palms felt damp, and her heart thudded against her rib cage.

His eyes were narrowed in a cold suspicion she hadn't seen since their first meeting, when he had caught her sneaking through the grand corridor and hiding behind a pillar. At that time, he'd believed her to be a husband hunter on the prowl.

But she couldn't quite fathom the depth of his wrath this time. Was there some sort of feud between himself and Lady Milford? An unresolved quarrel that the woman had neglected to mention?

Even if he'd guessed that Lady Milford had made behind-the-scenes arrangements so that Bella would have a better chance to be hired, was that really so dreadful a sin? She had wanted to provide for her brother and sister. Now that Miles had met Lila and Cyrus, surely he could be made to see reason.

Of course, he needn't know the part about her search for the treasure map. That had nothing to do with Lady Milford.

He took a menacing step closer, his hands planted on his lean hips. "You claimed to have known only that Smithers fellow when you moved back to England. You never said a word about Lady Milford."

Bella swallowed hard. Smithers was the antiquarian who supposedly had purchased artifacts from her father overseas. But she herself had never met the man. The ruse had been entirely Lady Milford's concoction, and Bella had been so anxious for an excuse to live at Aylwin House that she'd dutifully repeated the story.

"I was only slightly acquainted with her ladyship," Bella said, tightly gripping her fingers together to stop them from trembling. "A few weeks ago, she came to the cottage in Oxford, hoping to find my father. They had once been friends, you see. When she learned that Papa was . . . dead, and that I needed to earn a living, she suggested that I apply to you for a position. She thought you might hire me since your father and mine were once business partners."

"You said that Smithers told you about the position."

"I . . . yes, but I only did so on Lady Milford's recommendation. She cautioned me not to mention her

name. She said you were a very private man and might be upset to learn that she'd been meddling."

"*Upset?* I'm livid." His furious gaze raked her up and down. "You entered my house under false pretenses, you lied to me about being alone in the world, you concealed the truth at every turn. It seems you're nothing more than an accomplished actress."

A painful knot pulled taut in Bella's breast. She deserved his censure. Yet he seemed far angrier than the situation warranted.

She put out her hands, palms up in supplication. "Please try to understand, Miles, I needed to earn a living so that I could feed my brother and sister. Lady Milford only meant to help me."

"Bollocks." Throwing her a contemptuous look, he paced back and forth in front of the sarcophagus. "I can guess precisely how that woman helped you—by instructing you in how to charm me. You pretended to be coy, you lured me into your bed and then pushed me away, you led me on and tormented me day and night—" He savagely bit off his words and jabbed his forefinger at her. "From the moment you set foot in my house, you've been plotting to entrap me."

Tears blurred her eyes at the viciousness of his accusations. "Entrap you?"

"Don't pretend ignorance. Everyone in London knows about Lady Milford and her schemes."

Bella shook her head in bewilderment. "I-I truly don't know what you mean."

He plunged his fingers through his hair, tangling the black strands. "Good God, Bella! I'm speaking of marriage. The woman is a damned matchmaker!"

Chapter 23

Miles grabbed hold of the brass knocker and rapped hard on the door of the town house. He had a strong urge to kick in the door. But that would only attract attention from the passersby on the street and spark speculation that he was Lady Milford's latest dupe.

In an effort to take the edge off his temper, he sucked in a lungful of cool afternoon air. He could not erase the image of Bella's stricken face as he'd accused her of trying to hoax him into wedlock. She'd claimed not to have known of Lady Milford's avocation. He had been too enraged to accept Bella's word before he'd stormed off on this mission.

Yet in retrospect, he had to concede that even the most seasoned actress could not have fabricated her look of shock. It was very likely that Bella had been hoodwinked as well as himself.

The mastermind of the heinous ruse resided in this town house.

He raised his fist, intending to batter the heavy wood panel again. Then the door opened abruptly. A butler

with cropped white hair and a sober black suit stood there.

Miles frowned, momentarily distracted by a vague familiarity about the servant's weathered features. But he had never been to this house before. He didn't socialize, either, so it was unlikely he'd encountered the fellow at a different residence.

The butler regarded him impassively. "May I help you, sir?"

"I wish to see Lady Milford." Miles shouldered his way past the servant and into an airy foyer. "At once."

Not a muscle moved in that stoic face. "I shall check if her ladyship is at home. Have you a calling card?"

"Blast it, no. Just tell her that Aylwin is here."

On hearing the venerable name, the butler inclined his head in a bow. "Certainly, Your Grace."

As the man turned, something in the harsh lines of his face struck a stronger chord of recognition. This time, the pieces fell into place. Those now pale cheeks could have been enhanced by rouge, the white hair and eyebrows darkened with soot . . .

A cold sword of certainty pierced Miles. He grabbed the man's arm and spun him back around. "You! You're Smithers."

One grizzled eyebrow lifted in inquiry. "The name is Hargrove, Your Grace. Might you be mistaking me for another servant?"

Hargrove's pale blue eyes were steady. A liar would be inclined to shift his gaze away. Unless, of course, he was extremely skillful at artifice. And a master of disguise.

The antiquarian who had come to Aylwin House had been the virtual opposite of this man. Mr. Smithers had been a flashy windbag in a checkered green

coat who had spouted glib nonsense like a common street-seller while he'd attempted to convince Miles to purchase a box of cheap scarabs. Smithers also had expressed keen interest in the fact that Miles worked alone. The fellow had listed all the advantages of hiring a curator to assist him.

Not three days later, Bella had arrived with her tale of having known Smithers overseas. She'd said that he had told her of the position of curator. Today, she'd admitted that she'd never met the man.

Lady Milford had orchestrated the scheme with the assistance of Hargrove. The bastard was loyal to his mistress and would not admit to his role in the scam. It would give Miles great satisfaction to plant a hard right hook into the man's square jaw.

But Hargrove was merely an underling. Miles craved to confront the main player, the spider spinning her web of deceit.

Fueled by cold fury, he stalked to the staircase and started up the marble steps, taking them two at a time.

Hargrove hurried after him. "Your Grace! Her ladyship is dressing for a drive in the park and cannot be disturbed."

"Then make haste to warn her. I'll allow you half a minute to announce me."

Miles let the butler take the lead up the flight of stairs and then along a corridor with yellow striped wallpaper and a thick carpet that cushioned their footfalls. Hargrove rapped on a door near the end of the passage. His sober gaze flicked to Miles before someone opened the door and he stepped inside.

Miles prowled back and forth, counting off thirty seconds. At twenty-eight, the door opened again and the butler stood back to allow him entry. Hargrove gave him a hard stare this time. There was nothing

subservient in that look, Miles noted. He was right to think the man devoted to Lady Milford.

As Miles went in, the door behind him closed with a quiet click, and he found himself in a small sitting room attached to a larger bedchamber that was visible through an arched doorway. Here, white-painted bookshelves lined the walls and late afternoon sunshine poured through the double windows. Lady Milford stood there, one hand on the sill, gazing outside. Her coal-black hair was drawn up in a knot, and a lavender silk dressing gown draped her slender form.

She turned to him and smiled cordially as if he were an invited guest. "Aylwin," she said, coming toward him with her hand extended. "What a pleasant surprise."

He took her dainty fingers without thinking, then let go at once. This meeting would not be on her terms.

"There is nothing in the least pleasant about this visit," he snapped. "I have just learned of your deception. You planted Isabella Jones in my house on purpose. You've been scheming to saddle me with a wife ever since you brought that other brainless chit to Aylwin House a few months ago."

How well he remembered being subject to another of her matchmaking ploys. To his great misfortune, he had been crossing through the entrance hall at the moment the woman and her protégée had come to call. Lady Milford had been an acquaintance of his mother's, and he'd felt compelled to show them basic courtesy. But he'd never spent a more irritating half hour, listening to the girl prattle about nonsense. When she had proposed moving the Egyptian relics into storage and redecorating Aylwin House, that had been the final straw to his patience, and he'd sent them on their way.

"The *chit,* as you describe her, was Lady Beatrice Stratham, daughter of the Earl of Pennington," Lady Milford said. "And you're quite right, she isn't nearly as quick-witted or bright as Miss Jones. Would you care to take a seat?"

She settled herself in one of a pair of pale green chairs by the fireplace and folded her hands in her lap, looking far too serene for a woman confronted by an enraged duke.

Miles had too much pent-up rage to sit. He roamed the confines of the room with its feminine accoutrements and felt the need to hurl one of the china figurines onto the marble hearth.

Instead, he swung toward his nemesis. "So when you failed with the vacuous debutante," he said darkly, "you set your sights on another type of female. You plotted and conspired and came up with Sir Seymour's daughter. You even had your butler don a disguise and pretend to be an antiquarian in order to convince me that I needed to hire a damned assistant!"

Lady Milford denied none of his accusations. "I'm pleased that you were kind enough to give Miss Jones a position. Sir Seymour left her only a tiny cottage and no means of subsistence. She struck me as a very intelligent and capable young woman, someone who could be helpful to you in cataloguing and organizing. *Has* she been helpful?"

"That is irrelevant!" Miles roared, jamming his hands on his hips to keep from throttling the woman. "You meddled in my affairs. You connived behind my back and against my will. All for the purpose of trapping me into marriage!"

A wry smile touched her lips. "I very much doubt that any mere woman could trap *you* into marriage, Your Grace. You are far too fixed against the institu-

tion and a confirmed bachelor of many years. I will confess, nevertheless, to hoping that you might fall in love with Miss Jones. Have you?"

The barefaced question flummoxed Miles. He had not been expecting it. His mind went blank to all but the image of Bella's face, smiling tenderly at him, whispering "*my love*" while he'd been buried deeply inside her body. Then just yesterday evening, on their return from Oxford, she had taken hold of his hand and he had hoped . . .

He snapped out of the fantasy. Love? That was just a pretty word used by poets to describe raw, pounding lust.

Only a damned fool would be deceived into thinking otherwise.

Pacing back and forth, he scowled at Lady Milford. "I assure you, madam, I am *not* in love. Nor shall I fall prey to your baited snare of wedlock. You have no right to interfere in my life."

Her shrewd gaze softened. "I was once a dear friend of your parents. Before the duchess died, she asked me to watch over you."

"The hell you say. You weren't present at her deathbed."

Miles shied from the decade-old memory of those long, torturous hours of listening to his mother's labored breathing. It had been so very wrenching to wait alone for her to slip away . . .

"She wrote to me shortly before she passed on." Rising, Lady Milford walked to a small desk and opened a drawer. She rummaged through some papers and brought forth a folded missive, which she handed to him. "She told me that her fondest hope was for you to fall in love and marry someday. You may read it if you like."

Miles recognized his mother's neat penmanship. His fingers gripped the paper tightly for a moment before he shoved it back at Lady Milford. The constriction in his chest threatened to squeeze out his righteous anger.

He fixed her with what Bella termed the Ducal Stare. "I don't give a damn what my mother told you. I alone will dictate the course of my life—with no intrusion from a blasted matchmaker!"

Lady Milford released a small sigh as she replaced the letter in the desk. "Then it seems I must beg forgiveness, Your Grace. It's just that . . . I've sometimes wondered if your mother might be the very reason why you've never married."

"What?"

"As a young boy, you saw the duchess confined to her bed after many miscarriages. She was too delicate for pregnancy. It was quite difficult for her—and for you to witness her pain. Perhaps you fear putting a wife through that arduous experience."

Lady Milford could not have been more off the mark. Yes, he'd felt panicked by the prospect of impregnating Bella—only because he would feel compelled to offer for her. But it was penitence over Aylwin's death that had required Miles to live alone. At a young age, he had vowed to devote himself to preserving his father's legacy.

This woman had no way of knowing that. Bella was the only other living soul who knew his darkest secret.

"You are mistaken," he stated coldly. "I'm dedicated to my work—and that will never change. A wife and a family would be a millstone around my neck."

Her violet eyes turned cool as she regarded him for a moment. "I see. I presume you will be releasing Miss Jones from your employ, then. She is innocent in this

matter, and I will not permit you to toss her into the street. Send her here and I shall assist her in finding another post."

Once again, Lady Milford had managed to dig her claws under his skin. Discharge Bella? Banish her from Aylwin House? Let her go to work for some other man?

No.

Miles clenched his jaw. Everything in him rebelled at the notion of never seeing Bella again. He wanted her to remain under his protection. Then a ghastly thought struck him. He'd chastised her without mercy, made cruel allegations against her character, hurt her intolerably by accusing her of abetting in the plot to ensnare him.

What if she had already packed up and departed?

After the quarrel with Miles, Bella had escaped to her bedchamber. She'd turned the key in the lock, buried her face in the feather pillows of the canopied bed, and indulged in a bout of cathartic weeping. It was completely unlike her to fall apart. She had always been the strong one in the family, the organizer, the healer, the voice of reason. But never in her life had she felt so desolate as she did now.

She loved Miles. The sentiment had tiptoed into her heart so quietly that she could not point to one particular incident that had won her over. Perhaps it was his rare smile or the way he hid his kind heart behind the façade of a beast. But she had known in the moment that his eyes had turned to ice that she'd wanted his face to soften with love.

When every last tear had been drained, she forced herself to get up and walk woodenly into the dressing chamber. There, she splashed cool water on her face to ease the redness of her eyes. In the mirror, she

appeared pallid and ordinary and she couldn't imagine why a highborn duke had ever deigned to lust for her.

She wasn't a refined lady. She had grown up in foreign lands and had peculiar tattoos around her ankles. She looked nothing like the femme fatale that he had accused her of playing.

His furious reproaches echoed in her mind. He believed her to be a party to Lady Milford's plot to lure him into matrimony. He thought she had come to Aylwin House under false pretenses in order to *marry* him.

Nothing could be further from the truth. He didn't know it, but her purpose had been the treasure map, the one that she had yet to find. The one that she would *never* find now because Miles very likely would expel her from his home. He had stalked out of the ballroom in a rage, and she had no idea where he'd gone.

Taking a ragged breath, Bella went back out into the quiet of her bedchamber. She ought to depart now and save herself the humiliation of being tossed out in the street. But it was late afternoon already, she had no funds, and there were her brother and sister to consider. Not only that, but Miles had three crates of Papa's papers locked in his study, and she would not, she *could* not leave them in his possession.

Rubbing her cold arms, she paced to the windows and looked out over the garden with its geometric paths among the rosebushes. No, she must remain here for the moment, brace herself to confront Miles again, and request the small salary that he owed her. It might be enough to pay for their return to Oxford. Then she must make arrangements for the crates to be shipped back, as well.

With any luck, she and her siblings could depart on the morrow.

A lump lodged in her throat. Lila and Cyrus would be devastated to leave here. They had arrived only yesterday and had barely had time to explore the mansion. Everything was new and exciting to them, a welcome change from their routine of schoolwork. It would be a huge disappointment to them to be forced to return to the little cottage.

And for her, as well. Bella had enjoyed her work with the relics, studying about ancient Egypt, and putting the artifacts in order. She'd been genuinely happy here, and a great deal of that pleasure had been due to Miles himself. She had relished talking with him, being in his company, coaxing him out of his beastly moods and making him smile. He in turn had shown a true generosity of spirit by welcoming her brother and sister into his home. She had even dared to hope it meant that he felt a strong affection for her, and not merely lust.

Then Lila had mentioned Lady Milford's name and the whole world had come crashing down. For as long as she lived, Bella would never forget the bitter chill that had hardened Miles's face.

Lady Milford, a matchmaker! The news had caught Bella utterly by surprise. She had never associated with polite society, so how could she have known? And why had the lady chosen her, of all women, to entice the reclusive Duke of Aylwin into giving up his bachelorhood?

Granted, Papa had been employed by Miles's father. But Bella knew she was no great beauty and Lady Milford had met her only once. The woman had come to the cottage and decided right then and there that Bella

possessed the ability to tame a snarling beast like Aylwin.

How had she known they were well suited?

Amazingly, she and Miles had felt a mutual attraction at once, a powerful bond that had culminated in one exhilarating night of love. Glancing at the bed, Bella felt a keen sense of loss. Although they both had agreed it must not be repeated, she had reason to believe that he still desired her more than ever. It had been clear in the intent look of his eyes, in the way he had helped her family, in the firmness of his fingers around hers by the stairs the previous evening.

If Miles did harbor deep feelings for her, that would explain why he had exploded in anger, because he'd felt duped and betrayed. But he now scorned her as a clever, calculating husband hunter. And Bella had no idea how to convince him otherwise.

An upsurge of anger washed through her pain. Blast him! Why should she care what he thought of her, anyway? He had shown no abiding faith in their closeness, for he had been quick to believe the worst of her.

The basket of dates and pomegranates still sat on the table by the door. Loathing the reminder of him, she picked up the gift and carried it across the corridor to her brother's empty bedchamber. Let Cyrus enjoy it as a bedtime snack. She herself would only choke on it.

Late afternoon sunlight slanted through the windows. Her brother had scattered a few of his belongings on the writing desk, including their father's quill pen and inkpot. A couple of his favorite books sat on the bedside table. Already Cyrus had made this place his home. Bella's heart ached at the notion of uprooting him and his sister yet again.

Her siblings presumably were still in the library,

tending to their schoolwork. She would go downstairs and check on them, give them a few more assignments to keep them busy, and order a tea tray to occupy them until after dark.

Once they were settled, she had one very important task to do. The identity of the phantom had been weighing on her mind, and she had a good notion as to who had been trying to frighten her.

Although she intended to depart Aylwin House, the ghost didn't know that. Bella had a strong suspicion there might very well be another haunting planned for this evening.

Maybe it was foolish to bother with revenge since she was leaving tomorrow. Yet she intended to lie in wait, anyway. In her present ill humor, it would give her great satisfaction to give the culprit a taste of his own medicine.

Chapter 24

Miles returned from the visit to Lady Milford in a state of unease.

Leaving his mount in the stables, he strode through the rose garden, his boot heels crunching on the gravel path. Dusk was already beginning to spread shadows beneath the trees. He was late, much later than he'd intended.

A carriage had broken its axle and crashed in the street, the mishap occurring right in front of him, and he'd stopped to assist the aging pair inside, the old man dazed and the woman having suffered a bleeding wound to her head. They'd been frightened tourists who knew no one in London, and Miles had waited with them while a doctor had been summoned and a team of workmen had come to haul away the wrecked vehicle. Then he'd arranged for a hackney to convey the old couple to their hotel.

Now, a knot of tension twisted his gut. He had meant to come home much sooner. Many hours had passed since his quarrel with Bella after luncheon, when he had barely allowed her the chance to speak. Then,

when she *had* spoken in her own defense, he had refused to believe her. Instead, he had berated her without mercy. In light of those violent rebukes, he feared she might already have packed up her belongings and departed Aylwin House with her siblings.

Miles glanced up at the gray monolith of the east wing, but saw no light or movement in the windows of her bedchamber. It was not yet dark and maybe she was still at work in the blue drawing room.

If she was here at all.

He yanked open a side door that led into the main body of the house. His footfalls echoed in the long marble passageway. No servant lurked nearby so that he could inquire as to the whereabouts of Miss Jones. Aside from his own swift steps, the place was as silent as a tomb.

That was the way it had always been in this house. Cold, quiet, sepulchral. He remembered such solitude even as a boy. Loneliness had been as familiar to him as a comfortable old boot. Then Bella had taken up residence here and he had found himself listening for her voice in the corridor, watching for her to breeze through the doorway, and feeling a rush of pleasure when she did.

An incipient panic clutched at his chest. He wanted her to remain here under his roof. If she was gone already . . .

As he neared the entry to the west wing, someone stepped out of the doorway to the archives. It was the bulldog figure of William Banbury-Davis, who was carrying an armload of books as he turned to shut the door behind him.

Giving Miles a curt nod of greeting, the man said in an aggrieved tone, "There you are, Aylwin. I've been looking all over for you. I thought you should know

that . . ." He paused, squinting his eyes in the dimness of the corridor. "I say, is that blood on your cheek?"

Miles lifted his hand to swipe at his face. His fingers came away sticky. Impatient, he took out his handkerchief and wiped them. "I stopped to help with an accident on the street. What is it you wished to say? Be quick about it."

"When I went to fetch some research books from the library, those two rascally youngsters were in there. Did you give them permission to play with the pieces of your Senet board? That game is a rare Egyptian relic!"

Miles felt a jump in his pulse. Lila and Cyrus were in the library?

He took a step closer to the man. "When?" he demanded. "When exactly did you see them there?"

Banbury-Davis frowned at him. "I don't know. Perhaps . . . half an hour ago."

Half an hour. Bella would never have left the house without her brother and sister. And if those two were in the middle of a game, they hadn't been packing, either.

A sense of jubilation tugged up the corners of his mouth. "Brilliant," he said, clapping the man on the shoulder. "Thank you."

Miles turned to go. Now that he knew Bella was still in residence, he decided to clean up first before he sought her out. He owed her an abject apology and it wouldn't help his case to look like an unkempt vagrant.

"Is that *all* you have to say?" Banbury-Davis snapped. "Don't you care that they might lose some of the pieces to the set?"

Miles felt a jab of irritation. The man had never overcome his resentment toward Bella's father, and Miles wanted him to realize once and for all that such

nonsense would no longer be tolerated. "On the contrary, I'm sure they have a great respect for ancient artifacts. After all, they were taught by none other than the esteemed Sir Seymour Jones."

He left Banbury-Davis glowering in the corridor.

A spring in his step, Miles headed through the arched doorway and into the west wing. It was a great relief to know that he wouldn't have to go haring after Bella all the way to Oxford in order to coax her to return. Yet he still would have to proceed with caution.

He had behaved like an unbridled jackass. He had not listened to her explanations or considered her desperation to find a position, even though he had seen for himself the ramshackle condition of her cottage. She had been left without a stipend to support her siblings. No wonder she had fallen easily into Lady Milford's ploy.

Yet his own pain and anger had goaded him to hurt Bella. He had been furious to think that she had come here under false pretenses. That all of her sparkling smiles and tender kisses had been based on lies.

Entering the ducal bedchamber with its gold and blue décor, he untied his starched cravat. He strode through another doorway and into the dressing room. Here, the walls held floor-to-ceiling mahogany wardrobes that were only sparsely filled since Miles did not require a wide variety of garments for social events. As he shed his charcoal-gray coat and flung it over a chair, he noticed Hasani sitting on a stool in the corner and polishing a pair of black boots.

Miles was glad to see the valet back at work, for he had taken ill the previous day. One of the footmen had filled in for him. Hasani had been an unobtrusive part of Miles's life ever since those long-ago days in Egypt. The servant was always there in the background,

dutiful and deferential, anticipating his master's every need. They'd shared an easy camaraderie, for the man had an uncanny sense of when to speak and when Miles preferred silence.

Hasani sprang up, his white robes swaying. His dark eyes widened as he eyed Miles's face. "Your Grace!" he said. "Have you suffered an injury?"

Miles briefly explained about the accident, and then proceeded to the washstand to soap his hands and face. He had no wish for further conversation. His mind was too caught up in contemplating what to say to Bella. Maybe she would refuse to speak to him at all. He had hurt her deeply and he must not expect her to absolve him of guilt at once. It might take time for her to learn to trust him again.

If he hadn't done irreparable damage to their friendship.

Miles grimaced. He disliked this cloud of disquiet, this sense of being cast adrift into uncharted territory. He was accustomed to resolving problems by ducal decree. Never in his life had he needed to win back the favor of any woman. His carnal relationships had always been shallow and brief, rather like business arrangements.

But what he felt for Bella was deep and steadfast. He didn't know quite how it had happened or what to do about this unrelenting desire to keep her in his life. Especially since he had managed to make such a muddle of things by losing his temper.

As Miles grabbed a linen towel to dry himself, he saw that Hasani had laid out the coat on the clothespress. The man was leaning over it, the tattooed eye visible at the back of his neck as he employed a bristled brush to clean the superfine cloth. Miles had seen him perform that task hundreds of times over the years.

Yet something about the valet's slow, irregular strokes struck him as odd. Perhaps Hasani was still feeling unwell.

The Egyptian glanced up with an enigmatic look. "Will you be working in your study this evening, Your Grace?"

Miles's thoughts returned to Bella and his keen hope for a reconciliation. If he could entice her to his study on a pretext, he would need privacy in order to woo her. He'd give up the dukedom to see her smile at him again. "Yes, I shall be. You may take the night off and rest. Pray see to it that no one disturbs me."

A short while later, spruced up and refreshed, Miles failed to find Bella working in the blue drawing room. Nor was she in the library with her brother and sister, where the sound of bright laughter had drawn him like a lodestone.

Stepping through the doorway, he spied Lila and Cyrus seated at a round table near the blazing fire. The carved alabaster pieces of the Senet game were spread over the mahogany surface. Their good-natured argument ended abruptly as they caught sight of him.

Lila hopped to her feet and dipped a charming curtsy. She frowned at her brother, who then rose to make his bow. Both gazed rather warily at Miles. "Good evening, Your Grace," they recited.

When Lila edged in front of the table as if to hide their activities, Miles concealed his amusement behind a stern look. "I heard a rumor that you two had found my Senet game on the shelf."

"We've been extremely careful with it," Cyrus hastened to say.

"We aren't reckless children," Lila added. "No matter what Mr. Banbury-Davis might have told you."

That earnest tilt of her chin reminded Miles of Bella. Bella, who was more a mother to the twins than a sister. He had an even greater respect for her now, knowing that she had raised them well despite the hardships of living in a foreign country with only one servant and a father who was too often away on an archaeological dig.

"You're perfectly welcome to use the set." Miles strolled closer to eye the rectangular box with its thirty squares on top, some with carved symbols, and the four sticks and the little carved crowns. "Have you figured out how to play yet?"

"No, but we've been trying out different rules," Cyrus said eagerly. "I don't suppose *you* might be able to teach us, Your Grace?"

"I'm afraid no one has ever found the instructions for the game. So your endeavor here actually could be a helpful contribution to history." At their obvious delight, he allowed a grin. "Now, I was looking for your sister. Have you seen her?"

"She joined us at teatime," Lila said. "Then she bade us wait here until she came to fetch us for dinner."

"I do wish she would hurry back," Cyrus added. "I've a mind to go and look for her."

Miles wanted no such interference. "Actually, there has been a change in plans. Bella and I shall be busy tonight going through your father's papers." At least he hoped so. He pointed to the brocaded rope that hung from the ceiling near the fireplace. "If you would like to have your dinner served right here, you've only to pull that cord. A servant will come to take your request."

"Oh, famous!" Lila said. "May I pull it now, please?"

Miles chuckled, remembering how he had liked doing that as a youth. "As you wish."

She rushed toward the fireplace, and Cyrus dogged her heels. "How does the mechanism work?" he asked over his shoulder. "It must be connected by wires in the walls . . . down to the kitchen, perhaps?"

"Yes, I'll show you tomorrow morning," Miles said. "Now, you may stay up for an hour after you've finished your dinner. Then both of you must take yourselves off to bed. Is that clear?"

They nodded. "Tell Bella not to worry about us," Cyrus said.

"She forgets that we're fifteen already," Lila added. "We can take care of ourselves!"

"So I see," Miles said in some amusement. "Well, I must go now and find your sister. If you'll excuse me."

Anxious to resume his quest, he strode out of the library. The house was dim with only an occasional wall sconce to light the vast passageways. The only other logical place that Bella might have gone was up to her bedchamber. Had she been there ever since leaving her siblings at teatime? His chest tightened. He hoped to God he hadn't driven her to tears over his cruel reproaches.

He hastened up the grand staircase, the echo of his footsteps as hollow as his heart. She didn't deserve to suffer a moment longer. Somehow, he had to make things right between them. Even if he had to get down on his knees and grovel.

Evening had cast deep shadows throughout the east wing. As he headed into the gloom of the upstairs corridor, he cursed himself for not bringing a candle. He could just barely see the way to her bedchamber.

Abruptly, a commotion broke out at the end of the passage.

Disbelieving, he narrowed his eyes. Two figures grappled in the darkness, one a ghostly white form, the

other murky and indistinct. He could make no sense of the scene. What the devil . . . ?

Then came a sharp cry. A yelp. And Bella's upraised voice.

Spurred by alarm, he sprinted down the long corridor. An intruder had seized hold of her. She appeared to be struggling with him.

Miles lunged, yanking the assailant away from her. A man, judging by his size and build. He stripped away the pale sheet that draped the fellow.

Then he swung his fist into her attacker's jaw, connecting with a satisfying crack. Uttering a strangled cry, the man staggered backward and fell, then cowered on the floor, whimpering. In a fury, Miles reached down to grab him and stopped in shock. Through the darkness, he recognized those frightened features.

He was gazing at his cousin, Oscar Grayson.

Chapter 25

Bella gripped the dagger that she had been holding to Oscar's throat when the duke had appeared from out of nowhere. "For heaven's sake, Miles! What are *you* doing here?"

"More to the point, why is he here?" Miles growled, standing guard over his cousin. "And why was he covered in a sheet while attacking you?"

"He wasn't attacking me," she said irritably. "*I* had attacked *him* in order to stop him from trying to frighten me."

She had been hiding in the linen closet for the better part of an hour, peering out the narrow opening of the door and waiting for the specter to make an appearance. Right about the time she normally came upstairs after work, the figure had stepped out of the servants' staircase and glided toward her bedchamber.

Bella had crept out and pounced on him from behind. When she had put the knife to his throat, he'd yelped in alarm. She had warned him not to move lest he die a bloody death. That was when Miles had come barreling out of the darkness to ruin her capture.

"Frighten you?" Miles asked in a sharp tone of confusion. "For what purpose?"

Bella told him about the sightings she and Nan had had of a wraithlike form. "I believe he and Mrs. Grayson had hoped to scare me into leaving Aylwin House."

"The devil you say!" Reaching down, Miles seized his cousin by the scruff of the neck. "Come," he snapped. "We need to have a talk in a place where there's light."

"Ouch!" Oscar sniveled. "That hurts!"

All of a sudden, another ghostly figure came swooping out of the darkness of the servants' staircase. It was Helen, her pale aqua skirts rustling. "Release him at once," she cried out. "You have no right to manhandle my husband."

"Count yourself fortunate that I don't manhandle you, as well," Miles retorted.

Ignoring her outraged huff, he marched Oscar forward, and Bella darted ahead to open the door to her bedchamber. "In here," she said. "The fire is lit."

She had sent Nan away a while ago, not wanting the servant girl to witness the altercation out in the corridor. Miles dragged his cousin inside, grabbed a straight-backed chair and planted it in the middle of the rug, then thrust Oscar down onto it.

Helen scurried to her husband's side, sinking down to croon over him. His wavy dark hair was a wild mess from the sheet he'd worn. A trickle of blood dripped from the side of his mouth and she dabbed it with her handkerchief.

Bella slipped the dagger back into the pocket of her gown. Then she lit the wick of a candle at the fire and went around the room, lighting all the tapers. She was rather irritated at the turn of events, for she had not

meant to trigger a family squabble. She had only wanted to give Oscar a severe warning that would make him regret the phony hauntings that had terrified her maidservant.

"You struck him!" Helen accused, glaring up at Miles from her crouched position beside Oscar's chair. "Your own cousin and heir!"

"He deserved that and more for what he did to Bella," Miles asserted. "Though I would venture to guess it was *you* who came up with this harebrained scheme for him to play a ghost."

Helen pursed her lips. "Miss Jones doesn't belong in the household of a duke. She's a foreigner and a conniver and I warned you from the start that she was maneuvering you for her own enrichment."

"And better *you* should maneuver me?" Miles asked in an ironic tone. "That's what this is all about. You're afraid that I might wed Bella and sire a son, thus thwarting your chance to become a duchess."

"What about me?" Oscar put in, glaring up at Miles. "*I* deserve to be the sixth duke. It is my right!"

Miles snorted. "Bollocks. No scheme of yours could ever stop me from marrying whomever I choose."

Bella wasn't fooled by his insinuation that he might offer for her. Miles was merely using her as a pawn to hammer Oscar and Helen. And she'd had quite enough of being discussed as if she weren't even present in the room.

"No one is marrying anyone," she stated. "In fact, it should make all of you happy to learn that I shall be departing from Aylwin House on the morrow. As soon as His Grace pays me the salary that I am owed."

Everyone's attention swung to her. Oscar wore a nasty grin on his battered face, Helen a triumphant smile, and Miles an intense, unreadable stare. The

duke opened his mouth as if to voice a response, than set his jaw and remained silent.

Bella felt a twist of pain that he would not even protest her announcement. But of course, Miles believed her to be a husband hunter, too, just as Helen did. He had made his views on the matter perfectly clear only a few hours ago.

She turned to Helen. "You took a packet of letters out of my bedside table several days ago. After you read them, you tossed them beneath my bed to make me think that I'd dropped them there."

Helen laughed. "Nonsense. You've no proof of that."

That superior, gloating smile convinced Bella that she was right. Helen was exactly the sort who would read stolen letters in the hopes of gaining fodder for her schemes. The idea of her nosing through this private bedchamber made Bella feel violated.

His expression hard, Miles took a step toward Helen and Oscar. "Did either of you go to Bella's cottage in Oxford and search through her father's papers?"

This time, Helen looked blank. "Oxford? Why would we travel to such a provincial place in the midst of the season?"

"And to a cottage, no less!" Oscar added with a rusty chortle. "I must say, it is not surprising to learn that Miss Jones would spring from such a rough abode. She's a savage who drew a knife on me—"

"That is quite enough," Miles barked. "You've insulted Bella for the last time. I want you two out of here at once."

"We've only tried to protect you, Miles," Helen said, rising to her feet and putting her hand on her husband's shoulder. "And in return, you struck poor Oscar in such an unsporting manner."

Oscar endeavored to appear woebegone by putting a hand to his injured face and moaning.

"Get out this instant," Miles thundered, pointing at the door. "If either of you dares to set foot in Aylwin House again without my express permission, I'll cut off your allowance entirely."

Abandoning the wounded act, Oscar hopped up from the chair. "Come, my darling. We needn't stay and be insulted."

He and Helen linked arms, and with a disgruntled glance at Bella, they marched out of the bedchamber. Miles stalked after them, stopping in the doorway with his hands on his hips to watch their retreat down the darkened corridor.

As he came back inside and shut the door, Bella felt a rush of untimely desire heat her insides. She had only ever seen the duke wearing informal work attire. Tonight, he looked extraordinarily handsome in a dark blue coat over a white shirt and starched cravat.

Surely he wouldn't have dressed up just to visit *her*.

"Are you going out?" she asked coolly. "Don't let me keep you."

He stopped in the middle of the rug, his gaze concentrated on her. "I've no plans for the evening other than to speak to you."

Her heartbeat lurched at the husky note in his voice. She was keenly aware that they were alone. Miles seemed larger, more intimidating than ever, yet she wanted to fly straight into his arms and rest her head in the crook of his neck, to let his strength ease the pain that tangled her insides.

But that would only confirm his mistaken belief that she had come to Aylwin House to trap him into marriage. He would think she was trying to bamboozle him.

He took a step closer. "Those two won't bother you ever again," he said. "But blast it, Bella, you should have told me they were playing a trick on you. I'm responsible for whatever happens under this roof."

"I wasn't entirely certain it was them," she countered. "Besides, I was handling the situation quite well on my own. There was no need for you to rescue me."

He looked as if ready to argue the point, then his expression eased, his mouth twisting wryly. "You're a very capable woman, especially with that dagger. Nevertheless, I would hardly be a man if I didn't protect you from harm. Surely you wouldn't want me to stand back and do nothing if I thought you were under attack."

Incensed, she crossed her arms. "Odd that you should say so, Your Grace, when you yourself verbally attacked me this afternoon."

Miles glanced away before returning his gaze to her. He braced his hands on the back of the chair that his cousin had occupied. "I came here to apologize for that, Bella. I'm terribly sorry for all those things I said to you. I was wrong to make such vile accusations. Can you ever forgive me?"

His contrition caught her off guard. For a moment she could only gape at him in stupefaction. Unlike the cold, hateful mask he'd worn in the ballroom, now he looked remorseful and sincere. Why? What had happened to alter his harsh denunciation of her?

Those vile words still rubbed raw deep inside of her. *You pretended to be coy, you lured me into your bed and then pushed me away, you led me on and tormented me day and night . . .*

Bella walked stiffly away to the fireplace and

whirled to face him. "I never tried to tempt you to the altar. That was completely unfair of you to imply that I did. Have you forgotten that it was *I* who told you we could not continue with . . . this?" She gestured at the bed, unable to speak the word "lovemaking." Love had had nothing to do with their coupling, not even for her. It had been glorious, forbidden lust—and in spite of everything, she wanted it again.

His gaze held steady. "I was too overcome by shock to think clearly. The evidence seemed to point toward the fact that you had duped me. But I quickly realized my mistake after I stormed out of the house. I knew it even as I knocked on Lady Milford's door."

"You went to see her ladyship?"

"Yes. I was furious at her for interfering in my life. It wasn't the first time she'd done so." Releasing his hold on the chair, he paced closer to Bella. "She confirmed what I'd already surmised. That you had no knowledge of the ruse. It had been entirely her doing."

Her legs weak, Bella sank down onto the chair by the hearth. Miles really meant it. He no longer blamed her. Yet the canker of his angry words still lodged beneath her breastbone. "What do you mean, she'd done this to you before?"

He stopped in front of her, ran his fingers through his hair. "As I told you at our first meeting, matchmaking is a particular sore point to me. A few months ago, Lady Milford brought her protégée here, a Lady Beatrice, an insipid girl right out of the schoolroom who was full of empty chatter about redecorating Aylwin House. Since Lady Beatrice was clearly aware of the woman's matchmaking skills, I presumed you must be, too."

Bella reluctantly saw his point. He had committed

his life to his work with the Egyptian artifacts, yet many ladies couldn't understand the depth of his dedication. When they looked at Miles, they only saw the prestige of his title and the prospect of becoming mistress of this grand house. Even Lady Milford had done so on behalf of Lady Beatrice.

Bella, too, secretly thought he would benefit from the tender affections of a wife, but not for the shallow reasons of those society women. Miles was a fine man beneath all his bluster and he deserved to be loved. But she didn't dare tell him so—or admit that she herself harbored foolish feelings for him.

He sank down onto one knee in front of her chair and took hold of her hand, rubbing it gently. "Bella, please don't leave here tomorrow, I beg of you. I want you to stay. You and Lila and Cyrus. For as long as you like."

Her throat tightened. The feel of his warm fingers on hers almost did her in. She was astonished that he would kneel before her, the almighty Duke of Aylwin, pleading for her forgiveness. She couldn't imagine he'd done so for many women.

Yet *why* did he want her to stay? That was the question to which she craved an answer. Miles had a strong sense of duty and an adherence to gentlemanly conduct. Did he only feel compelled to right the wrong that he'd done to his employee?

Or had he set his mind on seduction?

The notion ignited a fire deep inside of her. But they had no real future together. He would never marry her. He had made his disdain for the institution very clear. And she could not engage in a carnal affair because her brother and sister would be sullied by association.

Bella drew back her hand and gave him a cool look that hid the knot of pain and confusion in her heart. "I

don't think that would be wise, Your Grace. It would be best if I return to Oxford."

He frowned slightly and glanced away for a moment, the harsh lines of his face etched with frustration. Then his gaze sought hers again. "Will you at least consider a delay? We have yet to go through your father's papers. In fact, tonight might be an excellent time to start."

"I promised to join Lila and Cyrus for dinner."

A faint smile touched his mouth. "I'm afraid you're too late. When I stopped in the library earlier, they seemed hungry, so I allowed them to pull the bell rope and order whatever they liked."

"But I'd planned to spend the evening with them."

"They're busy trying to figure out the rules to an ancient Egyptian game. And they're fifteen, after all. Quite old enough to keep themselves entertained. They even promised to take themselves off to bed at a reasonable hour." Miles stood up and held out his hand to her. "Come with me, please. It's time for us to determine what that intruder was seeking in those crates."

His gaze was dark and steady on her. He had swept away all of her excuses. And she couldn't deny that the prospect of an evening in his company made her pulse beat faster.

Bella drew a deep breath. Truly, she could not resist him when he looked at her with such warmth. With trepidation in her heart, she placed her hand in his.

Half an hour later, they sat side by side near the blazing fire in his study. Miles had unlocked the storeroom and pulled out one of the crates, and they were now examining the contents. Although the task would have gone faster if they could have split the work, he had logically stated that only Bella would know if something

was missing. So he had placed an ottoman close to her chair and perched on it while they looked through the papers and journals together.

Bella had a difficult time concentrating, for his nearness kept intruding on her attention. She was acutely aware of the brush of his hand against hers, the spicy allure of his scent, the enticing heat of his body. More than anything, she yearned to lay aside their work and cuddle in his arms instead.

Nothing could be more impossible. She knew the danger of succumbing to his charm. It would only bring her more heartache. Better to get this task over with and done. Then she would be free to go.

She flipped through the pages of a notebook, seeing the drawings of various artifacts that her father had found at the site in Persia, and the scrawl of his descriptions. These were his most recent writings, from the crate the intruder had been poking through when Lila had come downstairs and surprised him.

"Did you pack all of these journals yourself?" Miles asked. "Or did your brother and sister help with the task?"

"Actually, Papa put them away. He would store each notebook as he filled the pages and then start a new one." She paused, struggling to fathom why anyone would be interested in the journals. "What if this is a wild-goose chase, Miles? What if the intruder didn't care about Papa's papers at all? What if he merely thought there were valuables inside the crates?"

Miles cocked an eyebrow. "We won't know until we look through them all. And I just have a gut feeling about this. I suspect you do, too."

"Pardon?"

He took her hands in his and held them firmly as if to demand her undivided attention. The sudden grav-

ity of his gaze should have been a warning. "You've been poking through the papers from the expedition to Egypt," he said. "First the papyri in the storeroom, and then the records in the archives. It's high time you told me exactly what it is that you're seeking."

Chapter 26

The command came from out of the blue. For a moment Bella couldn't breathe from the constriction in her lungs. His dark eyes were so direct and piercing that she feared he could see straight into her mind and hear her father's words.

Find Aylwin. Find the map. You have half the pharaoh's treasure.

She lowered her gaze to the open journal in her lap. "I was merely curious to learn more about my past," she fibbed. "Although I was there in Egypt as a child, I have very few memories of that time."

Miles grasped hold of her chin and tipped it up so that she had to meet his unwavering regard. "Don't prevaricate," he said. "You've been looking for something and so was that intruder. There may be a connection."

"I already considered that, but—" She broke off, realizing her slip. She'd just admitted to conducting a search, after all.

"Tell me," he urged softly. "Whatever it is, perhaps I can help."

Unable to look away, Bella bit her lip. His brown eyes were warm, reassuring, and she felt a sudden, aching need to unburden herself. No one else knew of her father's deathbed revelation, not even her brother and sister. And how could she expect Miles to trust her if she refused to be honest?

Oh, she did long to clear the air between them. To never again have to concoct a story to hide her true purpose here. To know that there were no secrets between them.

Yet would he condemn her for deceiving him? Would he react with fury as he'd done when he'd found out about Lady Milford?

Bella swallowed the dryness in her throat. "I'll tell you under one condition. You must promise you won't get angry and shout at me."

A slight dip of his eyelashes implied regret for his earlier outburst. "You have my word."

She hoped he meant it. He might despise her again, and that would be difficult to bear. Yet she felt compelled to confess, anyway. "You were right to think that I came to Aylwin House under false pretenses. I did. But only because on his deathbed, my father told me to return to England and find you."

"To find *me*?"

"Yes, though I didn't know who you were at the time, not until Lady Milford came to visit me. You see, Papa fell very ill. On the night before he died, he had a moment of lucidity." Her throat caught as she remembered sitting by his bedside, seeing his blue eyes open and focus on her. "He reached for my hand. And he said very clearly, 'Return to Oxford. Promise me. Find Aylwin. Find the map. You have half . . . the pharaoh's treasure.' "

Miles said nothing. Only the hissing of the fire

disturbed the silence as Bella waited tensely for him to react. Maybe he would think her real purpose was far worse than plotting to entrap him into marriage. Maybe he would brand her a thief.

She forced herself to continue. "I came here hoping to find the map and the treasure. Not to enrich myself, but so that I could provide for Lila and Cyrus. At the time, I didn't know you, Miles. I feared that you would try to stop me from claiming our inheritance."

A frown furrowed his brow. He pushed to his feet and towered over her. "So all this time, you've been searching for a treasure map?"

"Yes, but I never found it." Her fingers dug into the arms of the chair. "When you forbade me to enter the storeroom with the papyri, I thought I might as well look in the archives, to see if the map might have been misfiled with the other documents."

He began to pace back and forth in front of the desk. "A pharaoh's treasure . . . that doesn't even make sense. My father funded the entire expedition. Since he had to pay the Egyptian government dearly for every artifact he sent back to England, he would never have promised half the contents of a burial chamber to your father, who was merely an employee."

Bella hadn't considered that. Had she come to Aylwin House on a fool's errand? "All I know is what Papa told me. There must be *some* explanation."

As if lost in thought, Miles frowned into the fire. "I assisted every day at the excavation site. I never heard any mention of a treasure map. Are you certain that Sir Seymour wasn't delusional from the fever?"

"I—I don't believe so. Papa seemed very determined that I would understand him. I told him we'd talk further in the morning. But he passed away dur-

ing the night. I never had a chance to ask him for more information."

Bella blinked to clear the mistiness from her eyes. Not for the world did she intend to succumb to tears. Now that she'd made her confession, it was too important to find out what Miles might know.

Which didn't appear to be much of anything.

Too restless to sit, she rose from the chair and watched him pace. "Hasani mentioned that your father originally went to Egypt with the purpose of finding the burial site of a young pharaoh. According to legend, it was untouched by grave robbers and full of many gold artifacts. But Aylwin never located that particular tomb."

"Tutankhamen. But those stories of a vast treasure trove were merely hearsay. There was no actual proof to back up the rumors."

Bella refused to let her dream fizzle to nothingness. It would be too devastating to fail to fulfill her father's last wishes. Yet she could see by Miles's expression that he was genuinely puzzled.

She stopped his pacing with a touch to his wrist. "Is it possible that your father might have discovered such a map and didn't tell you? Could it be among your collection of papyri?"

Miles slowly shook his head. "I'm familiar with every one of those ancient documents. They're all written in hieroglyphs. I've never seen a geographical map . . ." Then an arrested expression came over his face and he turned to her, catching hold of her arms. "What did your father say again? Tell me exactly."

She dutifully repeated, " 'Return to Oxford. Promise me. Find Aylwin. Find the map. You have half the pharaoh's treasure.' "

His fingers tightened on her arms. "That isn't the way you said it the first time. 'Find the map. You have half . . .' Then you paused before adding, 'the pharaoh's treasure.' "

"Papa *did* pause there," Bella said, remembering. "I thought he was just having difficulty speaking. He was very weak. Are you suggesting that he stopped on purpose?"

"Indeed. 'Find the map. You have half.' He may have been trying to convey that *you* have half the map."

The notion stunned her. "That can't be. Where is it, then?"

"Perhaps in one of the crates or stuck in one of his journals. But if you have half, then that means *I* must have the other half, which is why Sir Seymour insisted that you return to England and find me."

"How incredible. Do you truly think so?"

"Yes," he said in a galvanized tone. "Especially since I have a fragment of a papyrus document that has never made any sense to me. Come, I'll show you."

Miles turned on his heel, picked up a branch of candles, and strode into the storeroom adjacent to the study. Bella followed closely behind. Excitement bubbled in her. Could his theory really be true? Oh, she hoped so. Nothing else made sense.

The tall cabinets of drawers looked the same as on the night when he had caught her snooping in here, the night when he had pulled her into his arms and kissed her for the first time, awakening her deepest feminine desires. That memory alone caused a flush of longing in her.

But she mustn't think such thoughts. Not now, not ever. Even if she decided to remain at Aylwin House for a time, her stay could only be temporary. Any lon-

ger, and it would be too tempting to give herself to Miles again even though he had made plain his aversion to marriage.

He proceeded to the far end of the small room and handed her the candelabrum. "Hold this, if you will."

She grasped the ornate silver base while he opened the topmost drawer of a cabinet and withdrew a single, thin sheet of papyrus about the size of his palm. He carried it back out to his desk, where he laid it down carefully atop the polished mahogany. Bella set the candelabrum nearby so that the light of the candles illuminated the fragile sheet.

Hieroglyphic pictures in faded ink covered the scrap of papyrus. There were little holes here and there, and she could see the fiber of the reeds that had been used to make the paper. Much to her disappointment, however, she saw no roads or other topographical illustrations.

Miles picked up his gold spectacles from the desk and put them on to examine the papyrus closely. He pointed to one side. "See that ragged edge? It appears as if it was torn, perhaps in half."

"But it doesn't look at all like a map."

"True, but the words and phrases seem to be directions. Left and right, with references to specific landmarks. I would have to sit down and study the hieroglyphs more closely. But I do believe this papyrus could very well be what your father would call a map."

The possibility was so amazing that Bella caught hold of his arm. "Oh, Miles. So the treasure map really does exist, after all."

He removed his spectacles, tossed them aside, and

smiled, his eyes softening as he brushed his fingers over her cheek. "Yes. But it's worthless without both pieces. Now we shall have to look for your half."

An hour later, they had pulled out all three crates and searched fruitlessly through dozens of leather-bound journals and other papers. There was no scrap of papyrus anywhere, even though they carefully checked the individual pages of each notebook to see if it could have been tucked in between them.

While they worked, they'd speculated on what must have happened. Either Aylwin or her father had discovered the papyrus, perhaps in the tomb they'd been excavating. Recognizing that it gave directions to an undiscovered treasure trove, they had torn it in half, each man keeping a piece as a safeguard against thievery.

As he opened the last crate, Bella had a disquieting thought. "Miles, could this map have had something to do with your father's death? Do you suppose he might have been killed by someone who'd wanted to steal his half of it?"

Miles glanced up, his eyes meeting hers. His face had hardened into a bleak expression. "The likelihood had occurred to me, yes."

A bone-deep horror gripped Bella. She forgot the notebook lying open in her lap as her mind grappled with the revelation. "Then perhaps that would also explain why Papa left Egypt so swiftly. He feared for his own life. So he took Mama and me away in the night." She paused, feeling sick. "But Miles, he left *you* without protection. How could he have done so if he'd suspected there was a murderer on the loose?"

Miles stroked her arm reassuringly. "You needn't look so aghast. By escaping with his half of the map,

Sir Seymour rendered my half utterly useless. So I was perfectly safe."

"But he should have brought you with us."

"Quite the contrary. Upon my father's death, I became Duke of Aylwin. If Sir Seymour had kidnapped an underage peer, the full force of the law would have been after him."

Bella digested that for a moment. Perhaps Miles was right, her father had taken the best course of action under the circumstances. "Do you suppose the intruder was also looking for Papa's half of the map? And what if he's already found it?"

"It's possible," Miles said rather grimly, as he took another leather-bound journal out of the crate. "That's why I do wish you'd told me about this map sooner. We're dealing with someone who may have already killed once."

Bella couldn't have told him before now. She'd been too determined to find the treasure map on her own, too afraid that he would try to thwart her. It had taken her decision to leave Aylwin House to realize that she had nothing more to lose.

So she merely said, "Do you think the culprit might be William Banbury-Davis? He was in Egypt, too. Maybe he'd heard a rumor about the map and wanted it for himself. He very much resented my father for being chosen to go on the expedition instead of him. Perhaps he wanted the glory of discovering a lost tomb full of treasure."

"I'm aware of all that." Miles set down the journal and slid his fingers through hers. "Bella, you're to leave this investigation to me. If the map does indeed give directions to a trove of ancient treasure, there are those who would do great harm to get their hands on it. I won't have you putting yourself in danger."

"I'm perfectly capable of taking care of myself."

A faint smile touched his lips. "Yes, you are." Then his fingers tightened around hers, his thumb stroking her palm. He looked very serious again. "But do listen to me, please. You've come to mean the world to me. If anything ever happened to you, I honestly don't know how I could go on living."

Her heart turned over at the rough note of emotion in his voice. His eyes were steady on her, resolute and candid. The world faded away to just the two of them, alone in his study while the rest of the house slept. She could only think of how close they sat, how very much she yearned for him. Nothing else mattered to her but Miles, not the map, not the treasure, not even their quarrel. Could she truly mean so much to him? It seemed an impossible dream . . .

"Oh, Miles," she murmured on a thread of longing.

She couldn't have said who made the first move. But then they were in each other's arms, and he was kissing her so deeply and tenderly that all resistance melted from her body. In some part of herself, she knew she ought not allow him, yet it felt so right to be held in his embrace that all of her objections faded into nothingness.

His hands roved up and down her back, playing with her hair, brushing her neck and ears with a light touch. She indulged her own need to stroke him, too, to reassure herself that he was real. Her fingers slipped beneath his coat to memorize his lean waist and the hard contours of his chest. A fever beat in her blood. How was it that he could stir her so completely, as if like the map, they were two parts that joined to become a whole? Her life would be bleak without him. And yet how could it be otherwise? Their situations

were just too different, his station being so exalted, and hers so ordinary.

Miles drew back slightly, dropping gentle kisses over her brow, as if he were reluctant to give full vent to his desires. He caught her face in his palms so that she looked into his ardent dark eyes. "God help me, Bella, I do love you. I intend to marry you. I *need* to marry you."

She trembled. He couldn't be serious. "It's only lust that makes you say so."

"Yes, I do lust for you. How could I not?" He traced his thumb over her damp lips. "But that can't explain why you haunt me day and night. Or why I can scarcely bear to be apart from you. Or why you can twist my heart into knots with just a look or a word." He gave her a fierce look as if to convince her by force alone. "You *will* be my wife."

She had to be dreaming. How could he have changed his ironclad view of marriage so drastically in the space of a few hours?

She tried to make light of it. "Oh, Miles. Do you think to bully me with the Ducal Stare?"

"I'll do whatever it takes to coax you to say yes." He kissed her lips tenderly. "Say it, my love. Please. I need you with me, always."

A wistful sigh eddied from her as she touched his dear face, his jaw raspy with stubble. "I can't be a duchess. I don't know how."

"Then I shall relinquish the dukedom," he declared. "But one way or another, I *shall* wed you. And I'll devote myself to winning your heart. You'll come to love me, too, in time."

She blinked in surprise. "Do you think that I don't—"

He placed his finger over her lips. "You said 'my love' to me when we were in bed. I hoped then that you might—but when you also spoke the same to your brother, I realized it was merely a term of endearment." Miles gave her a fervent look. "Marry me, darling, for I've enough love for both of us."

Bella could no longer hold back the emotion that spilled from her heart, and she threw her arms around him. "Miles, of course I love you. You're my *dearest* love. And you needn't change anything about yourself. I adore you exactly as you are. Except—if I am to be your wife, you may *never* visit a bawdy house ever again!"

He chuckled. "You're my one and only. I promise you that."

An exultant smile lightened his face before he kissed her again, even more feverishly this time, until she felt drunk from the pleasure of it. Then he stood, sweeping her up into his arms.

Looping her arms around his neck, Bella laughed. "What are you doing?"

His eyes gleamed with promise. "I can't properly make love to you here. It's high time you were introduced to the ducal bedchamber, where you'll be spending every night for the rest of our lives."

A sparkle of excitement filled the evening, and she clung to him, nuzzling his neck as he carried her out into the corridor, his footsteps firm and strong. She could scarcely believe this moment was real and that Miles loved her. He passed through a doorway, kicking the door shut with his foot, and then walked into a large chamber lit by a lamp on the bedside table and the glowing embers on the hearth.

Miles set her down by the large canopied bed and they kissed and caressed while shedding themselves

of the layers of their clothing. Then he laid her down on the cool sheets, and when she reached for him, he ordered, "Wait. You will allow me to please you first."

For once she submitted to his command. It was just too impossible to resist the delight of his touch, for he had begun to stroke her all over, breasts, belly, thighs, moving down her legs to kiss the delicate tattoos that encircled her ankles. He worked his way back up to caress her everywhere, from the crook of her elbow to the valley of her bosom to the triangle of hair between her legs. He parted her there, plying her with his finger and then his tongue, so that she quivered with a fire that swiftly burned out of control.

Even as the rapture burst in her, he came down over her and she felt the pressure of him filling her. Instinctively she arched her hips to draw him in deeply and completely, for nothing had ever felt more right than being joined with Miles. He paused, breathing hard while gazing down into her slumberous eyes, a look of unguarded adoration on his face, an expression so tender that she feared again that she must be dreaming. "Bella," he muttered. "You're mine. Forever."

She tiptoed her fingers over the familiar contours of his face. "My dearest, dearest love."

She couldn't form any more words as he began to thrust into her, slowly at first as she clutched his back and lifted herself to his rhythm, then harder and faster until she shattered around him, the waves of bliss spreading out and lapping every part of her body, while he groaned from his own release, voicing her name on a sharp cry.

In the aftermath, they lay in a sweaty tangle that felt like heaven. She loved the heaviness of him atop her and murmured a protest when he shifted position to take his weight from her. He chuckled deep in his chest

and settled her close to the length of his body, tucking her head under his chin and planting a kiss in her tousled hair.

They whispered and talked about inconsequential matters. By unspoken agreement, they avoided the mystery of the missing map piece, for Bella wasn't yet ready to allow the outside world to intrude upon their idyll. Miles also revealed more about his visit to Lady Milford, admitting that he'd stubbornly proclaimed that he had no interest in marriage and then jesting that now he would have to allow the woman to gloat. "She had the temerity to say that she hoped I would fall in love with you. I blasted her with a denial in no uncertain terms." He gave Bella a wry smile. "Yet her comment forced me to realize the truth—that I *do* love you. And the very thought that I could have driven you away filled me with dread."

Bella rested her head on his shoulder, her hand idly stroking his chest. "I'm amazed that you could alter the beliefs of a lifetime."

"Once I realized that I loved you, there was no turning back. I had to make you mine by marriage vows." He tilted up her chin. "The sooner the better. I'll begin making the arrangements tomorrow."

A swell of love and exhilaration expanded in her, along with a sense of rightness. They belonged together. "Oh, Miles, I do want to be your wife. So very much."

She melted into him and they made love again, slowly and tenderly, relishing the beauty of it until they were both sated and drowsy. Miles fell asleep in her arms and she enjoyed the feel of him snuggled against her. He looked much younger and more relaxed with his eyes closed, the fan of his dark lashes lying against his cheeks. He'd had a lonely childhood with a stern

father and an invalid mother, and Bella fiercely vowed
to make him feel loved for the rest of their lives.

It occurred to her, then, that she had come here to
Aylwin House looking for a missing map that would
guide her to riches. Instead, she had found Miles. He
was the real treasure, more precious to her than any
tomb piled high with jewels and gold.

Yet the cold whisper of reality intruded on her bliss.
Someone was looking for that map. And in the heat of
their lust, she and Miles had left the papyrus fragment
lying unguarded in the study.

Chapter 27

Bella tiptoed out of the ducal bedchamber, pausing in the doorway to take one last look at Miles. A deep, enduring love filled her heart. Sound asleep in the big shadowed bed, he lay on his side, the covers drawn up to his lean waist. He had stirred slightly when she had arisen, but he hadn't awakened. She had dressed silently, resisting the temptation to linger.

She dared not fall asleep and be discovered here in the morning by a maid coming to light the fire or Hasani gliding in to awaken his master. Such a circumstance would cause talk among the staff, and the gossip might spread to other households. If her reputation was tainted, it would reflect badly not only on Miles but her sister and brother, as well.

Yes, it was wise to depart now. But she didn't have to like it.

Resolutely, Bella turned and went out into the corridor. The hollow tapping of her footsteps sounded eerie in the darkness of the marble passageway. Before retiring to her own bed, she must secure the

papyrus and lock her father's papers in the storeroom as a precaution.

Was William Banbury-Davis the culprit? Could he have killed Miles's father in a quest to claim the map? The notion made her shudder. But if that was true, why had he never stolen the piece that belonged to Miles? After all, Banbury-Davis had acted as Miles's guardian in Egypt after her father had fled, and he'd have had ample opportunity to take it.

Was it possible the man didn't realize the map had been torn in two? Perhaps all this time, he'd believed that Bella's father had run off with the entire map.

The theory held merit, and she would have to tell Miles about it in the morning. He would decide upon a course of action, for he had the authority to see to it that Banbury-Davis was arrested for murder.

Bella entered the study to find the scene exactly as they'd left it, the fragment of papyrus lying on the mahogany desk, the branch of candles still burning. The bonging of the casement clock startled her, and she glanced up to check the time.

How surprising that it was only midnight. She felt as if she'd lived a lifetime in only a few short hours. An irrepressible smile curved her lips. Her circumstances had changed in a way she had never dreamed possible. Only this past afternoon, she had been miserable and hurting from Miles's furious denunciation of her. She had resolved to depart Aylwin House in the morning.

Instead, this grand mansion would now be her permanent home. She would marry Miles, become his duchess, bear his children. Her hand slipped over her midsection. Was it possible she had already conceived? Oh, how she yearned to present him with a son or

daughter, to give Miles the happy family that he'd never known.

The thought put her in a cheerful state of mind, and she hummed tunelessly as she went to the third crate, the one they hadn't finished going through before love had distracted them. She decided to take a few of her father's journals to her bedchamber to examine before going to sleep. Reaching inside, Bella drew out several of the notebooks. As she did so, something slid out of the bottommost one.

She picked up a sealed, folded sheet and turned it over. A letter? On the front, written in her father's scrawling penmanship, were two names, first *The Marquess of Ramsgate*. That had been crossed out and *The Duke of Aylwin* written below it.

Her surroundings faded away and she saw herself as a little girl standing behind her father, watching him sprinkle sand on the ink and tapping it away. Then Papa had uttered an irritated sound, dipped his pen back into the inkwell, and crossed out the name, the quill scratching. There had been a hot breeze blowing through the tent, an impression of shimmering sunlight outside . . .

Bella blinked and the snippet of memory vanished. She was standing in the study, staring down at the folded missive, sealed with a circle of red wax. *Ramsgate*. No wonder the name had sounded so familiar to her. It wasn't just that she'd heard Miles called by the title in Egypt. She had also seen it inscribed on this very letter.

Why had her father never sent it? And when had he written it? Had it had been right after the fourth duke's death? That would make sense, for Papa had automatically used the name by which he was accustomed to

addressing Miles. Only then had he realized his mistake, crossed it out, and penned Miles's new title.

Bella sat down and opened the journal from which the letter had fallen. She scanned the cramped, scribbled writing and in a rush of excitement, realized that it was the missing notebook that detailed her father's sojourn in Egypt. There was no time now to read all the daily notes from the excavation site.

Instead, she quickly turned the pages, looking for the fragment of papyrus that would match the one belonging to Miles. But it wasn't there. Frustration nipped at her. Surely this notebook would be the one place where her father would have put his half of the treasure map.

Was it perhaps tucked inside the letter to Miles?

Bella held the folded paper up to the candlelight, but couldn't see through it. Should she awaken Miles? Or just put it away until morning?

It was then that she noticed something odd about the notebook in her lap. The stitching of the leather binding was irregular and loose at the top corner. She worked at it with her fingers, pulling the thread until she could look inside. With a gasp, she spied a piece of papyrus.

Working feverishly, she separated the rest of the stitching, taking care not to damage the ancient paper. She slid it out, and much to her jubilation, it appeared to be a perfect match for the other piece.

Just to be certain, Bella hopped up and ran to the desk. With trembling fingers, she fitted the two pieces together and gazed down at the time-faded ink of the hieroglyphs. There were pictographs, with people and animals, even a tiny eye at the top like the one on the back of Hasani's neck.

An exultant smile lifted her spirits. She had found the map at last! Miles would be thrilled, for now he could decipher the entire message. Soon they would know if the directions led to the secret burial site of the Pharaoh Tutankhamen and the fabled treasure trove.

She couldn't wait until morning. Miles needed to know at once. He deserved to share in her elation that the mystery had been solved.

But even as she started to turn, a flicker of movement from behind startled her. A sharp pain exploded at the back of her head.

The world went black.

Miles awakened to find himself alone in the large bed. He pushed up on one elbow to scan the dim-lit chamber with its dark lumps of furniture and the glowing embers on the hearth. In his dream, he had heard a distant pounding—but it must have been the thud of his own heartbeat. Bella was gone, as were her clothes from the floor. She must have decided to return to her own chamber.

He lay back down, folded his arms behind his head, and stared up at the shadowed canopy. It was irrational to feel uneasy. Bella had been prudent to avoid being found in his bed. Nevertheless, he didn't like letting her out of his sight.

Not until the mystery was solved.

She thought herself a strong, capable woman. But she had not seen the body of his father with his throat slit. After killing him at the excavation site, the gang of robed bandits had ridden through the encampment, creating havoc and setting some of the tents on fire. Miles himself had pulled six-year-old Bella out of her parents' burning tent.

He'd long wondered if someone had paid those renegade tribesmen to kill his father. Though Miles had never been able to prove it, his chief suspect had been Sir Seymour Jones, who had taken his family and vanished. It had been the act of a guilty man.

But now Miles finally understood what had happened. Fearing for his life, Sir Seymour had escaped with his half of the treasure map.

That meant the culprit had to have been someone else. Someone who'd wanted that map. The question was, who? He could think of only two possible suspects, two men who had been in Egypt at the time: William Banbury-Davis and Hasani.

Banbury-Davis, he could understand, for the man had been resentful of not being included in the expedition. He would have been eager to seize the fame of discovering a fabled tomb. But Hasani? The Egyptian had been a faithful servant to Miles for many years, and before that, had served Miles's father. Miles had never had reason to question the man's loyalty.

Yet he had a tense knot in his gut. There was no danger to Bella, he assured himself. She was safe in her bedchamber.

Although someone had broken into her cottage looking for the map, the intruder couldn't know that Bella was even aware of the map's existence. She had told no one but Miles himself of her quest.

He was just being overly cautious, wanting her here in his arms. He wouldn't be content until she wore his ring upon her finger, until they had spoken their vows and recorded their names in the church register. For too long he had locked himself in a regimented life out of duty to his father. Bella had helped him realize how wrong he'd been, though it had been a shock to fall so

deeply in love with her. But his decision to wed her felt right, good. Perfect, in fact.

He closed his eyes and tried to sleep, to no avail. Thoughts of that damned map kept intruding on his mind. He wished Bella had told him of it sooner. Yet he could understand why she had not. Until tonight, he had given her no reason to trust him.

Throwing back the covers, Miles rolled out of bed and reached for his trousers from the floor. He had not locked the study. He couldn't risk the chance of the map being stolen.

And his mind kept returning to Hasani. There was something about the man that continued to bedevil Miles. Hasani had been ill the previous day. He had not been present on the morning that they had traveled to Oxford to learn that an intruder had broken into the cottage overnight and had rifled through Sir Seymour's papers.

Could that burglar have been Hasani? Had his illness been a ploy to explain his absence?

Earlier this evening, the valet had used oddly jerky movements to brush Miles's coat. Miles had been too intent on composing his apology to Bella at the time to determine why. But now the answer hit him.

Hasani was right-handed. Yet he'd been wielding the brush with his left hand, which accounted for his awkward strokes.

The sense of unease deepened in Miles. Lila had slashed her knife at the intruder. There had been blood on the blade afterward, she'd said. Had Hasani's right arm been wounded by her?

There was only one way to find out.

Miles yanked on his shirt and stalked out of the bedchamber. The moment he stepped into the corridor,

he heard a sound that alarmed him. The distant shatter of glass.

Bella came to with an awareness of total darkness. At first she could not fathom why she lay sprawled out on the hard floor, a dull throbbing pain at the back of her head. Then she remembered being in the study, seeing a flash of movement behind her. After that . . . nothing.

She sat up slowly, struggling to get her bearings. Gingerly, she felt a lump at the back of her skull. Where was she?

Something poked into her spine. Reaching into the gloom, she felt a round knob. As she moved her hands up, she found several more, and her fingertips traced the outline of drawers.

She was in the storeroom adjacent to Miles's study. But where was the door?

The blackness of the windowless room blinded her. If only she could see something. She crawled forward, following the guide of the cabinetry. Then, as she rounded a corner, she spied a faint rectangle of light.

The door.

Bella rose slowly to her feet, her head spinning. She made her way forward and felt for the door handle. When she tried to turn it, however, it refused to budge. Locked!

Clenching her fist, she hammered on the panel, the sound reverberating in her skull. "Miles!"

He had to wake up and free her. But she had shut the bedchamber door upon leaving, and a long stretch of corridor separated the ducal suite from the study. The chances of him hearing her were minimal. Yet what else could she do?

She battered the door again, harder this time, screaming his name.

No sound came from the study. She might have been the only person awake in the house.

Bella rested her forehead against the wood panel. Who had struck her? She had been dragged into this small room and the door locked. Had William Banbury-Davis come back to the house under cover of darkness? Had he already stolen the treasure map?

All of a sudden, she heard footsteps and then a key rattled in the lock. The door swung open and she blinked against the brightness of light. But her rescuer wasn't Miles.

Hasani stood there in his white robes, holding up an oil lamp with a flame inside a glass chimney. "Miss Jones!" he said, a look of concern on his dusky features. "I heard you pounding. Are you all right?"

"Someone hit me over the head and then locked me in here." Bella brushed past him and hastened to the desk, but the two pieces of papyrus had vanished. "Oh, no! Have you seen Mr. Banbury-Davis? I must waken Miles at once."

"There is no need," Hasani said reassuringly. "His Grace has the situation well in hand."

"In hand?"

"Yes, you see a short while ago, the duke discovered Mr. Banbury-Davis prowling here in the study and chased him down to the wine cellar. His Grace dispatched me to fetch the map. That's when I heard you pounding on the door."

"Oh. *You* have the two pieces of papyrus?"

Hasani patted his robes at his side. "The map is right here in my pocket. Come, I'll escort you to His Grace and we'll give it to him."

Carrying the oil lamp, the Egyptian led the way out

of the study and down the corridor to the main part of the house. Bella had to proceed slowly, for her head still ached and she felt woozy.

Hasani seemed impatient, walking with energetic steps a little ahead of her, turning back now and then to urge her to hurry. She glimpsed the tattooed eye at the back of his neck, and suddenly recalled seeing one just like it on her portion of the map. What did it mean?

As they turned a corner and went down another long corridor, she asked, "What did His Grace tell you about the map?"

Hasani glanced back at her, the lamp throwing harsh shadows over his face. "Only that the ancient hieroglyphs give directions to the lost tomb of the Pharaoh Tutankhamen. The burial site has been covered by desert sands for many thousands of years."

Bella found that peculiar. Miles had told her he couldn't be certain of the map's meaning until he'd had time to study the symbols. "You mentioned once that His Grace's father had been looking for the tomb. But . . . how did Mr. Banbury-Davis find out about the map?"

Hasani's face darkened. "That one is driven by greed, always poking and prying, never showing respect to the dead. He wishes to break into the tomb and disturb the pharaoh's rest, to steal the items the boy-king needs for the afterlife. Tutankhamen's tomb must never be looted by English swine."

The depth of loathing in his voice sent a shiver over her skin. She had witnessed the animosity between the two men once before, when Banbury-Davis had been working on one of the mummies. Hasani had insisted upon uttering a ritual prayer over the withered body. He had reminded her of an ancient Egyptian priest . . .

Hasani stopped at a door in the wall. He gave Bella

a veiled stare. "I daresay it would have been best if you had not brought the other half of the papyrus back to England. Tutankhamen's resting place must be left undisturbed."

How had Hasani known that her father had taken half of the map? Had Miles told him?

Even as she puzzled over that, the Egyptian reached out to open the door. His loose sleeve fell back and she caught sight of a linen strip that bound his right forearm.

He motioned to her to precede him down a narrow flight of wooden stairs and into the cellars. "Go ahead, Miss Jones," he said. "His Grace is holding Banbury-Davis captive and we mustn't keep him waiting."

A chill froze Bella in place. That wrapping. Was it a bandage?

Lila had stabbed the intruder. And Bella suddenly knew with sickening certainty she had been wrong to think the culprit had been Banbury-Davis.

It was Hasani.

Miles wasn't in the wine cellar. This was merely a ploy. But two could play that game.

Putting her hand to her brow, she leaned against the wall. "I'm afraid I can't manage the stairs. That knock on my head has made me quite dizzy. You go on down without me."

Surreptitiously, she groped the side of her skirts with her other hand for her dagger. But the pocket was empty. He must have taken the weapon while she was unconscious.

"Come," he asserted forcefully. "I will assist you down the steps."

As he made a move toward her, Bella lashed out with her fist. She struck him hard on his injured right forearm.

Hasani howled with pain. The oil lamp in his other hand went flying. The glass chimney shattered, spilling a stream of oil that caught fire like a flaming tail across the marble floor.

Bella turned to run, but Hasani seized hold of her with his good arm and wrestled her toward the open doorway. He was surprisingly strong and muscular. In horror, she knew he meant to kill her. To thrust her down the steep stairs.

Miles would think it an accident. He would believe that she had tripped while going back to her bedchamber and had tumbled down into the cellar.

She screamed, her voice echoing in the corridor. Fighting and wriggling, she kicked at Hasani, her movements hampered by her skirts. By brute force, he inched her closer and closer to the doorway. His face was cold and twisted with effort.

Then abruptly his weight lifted from her. Light from the burning oil flickered on the hulking form of a beast.

Miles!

With a fierce growl, he spun Hasani around and hit him hard in the jaw. The Egyptian stumbled backward and hit the wall. He bent over, moaning. Miles allowed him no quarter. He rushed at Hasani and grabbed him by the front of his robes. "You killed my father. Admit it!"

In the eerie light, Hasani's face reflected a perverted pride. "His Grace intended to open the tomb of Tutankhamen—son of the god Ra. It could not be allowed. Not ever!"

"Damn you. And damn that bloody treasure!"

Miles swung his fist again, but Hasani blocked it with his good arm. As the two men grappled, fighting for dominance, the Egyptian whipped out a dagger, the blade glinting.

"Miles, watch out!" Bella cried.

Miles ducked, knocking the knife so that it went skittering across the floor. Bella darted to snatch up her dagger. Even as she turned back, her fingers tight around the hilt, she saw that Hasani had managed to break away from Miles.

The Egyptian ran toward the fire. He flung out his arm and two bits of paper fluttered onto the burning oil.

The map!

Even as Bella took a step, it was too late. The pieces of papyrus touched the flames and flared bright for an instant, then darkened to ashes.

But in his haste, Hasani had tripped on his robes. He staggered sideways, teetering in the doorway, his arms wheeling. Then he fell backward through the opening and plunged down the stairs into the darkness.

Bella heard the sickening thud of his body strike the cellar floor.

Miles hastened downstairs into the gloom and came back up a few moments later. He hauled Bella into his arms and pressed his lips into her hair, his heart thudding in heavy strokes. "It's over," he muttered, tilting her face up. "He can't hurt you anymore."

A shudder shook her. She dropped the dagger and clung to him, her arms encircling his waist as she reveled in his warmth. "Oh, Miles, he meant to kill me— and you. He wanted to stop us from finding the treasure."

He tightened his embrace. "Thank God I found you in time. When I heard you scream, I feared I'd be too late."

Laying her hands on his hard chest, she looked up at him in distress. "Did you see? He burned the map. It's gone!"

Miles glanced at the patch of flaming oil on the marble floor, then back at her. He looked remarkably

calm as he tenderly brushed a lock of hair from her cheek. "I can't say that I'm sorry. That map caused entirely too much misery and grief. The death of my father—and you and Sir Seymour being forced into exile for all those years."

"But . . . you're a scholar. That tomb would have been the discovery of a lifetime!"

He cupped her face in his large hands. The look of adoration in his dark eyes made her warm all over. "Bella, my love. Your safety means more to me than any pharaoh's trove. Don't you know that? As far as I'm concerned, the treasure can remain hidden for the ages—so long as I have you."

Chapter 28

The following morning, Bella found Miles in the library with her brother and sister. They were gathered around a globe of the world on a pedestal. Lila and Cyrus were showing him where they had grown up in the mountains of southern Persia. In turn, he pointed out the place in Egypt where the artifacts had been found in the Valley of the Kings.

Bella's heart turned over at the sight of them together, the three people she loved most in all the world. Lila, so sweet and delicate in her yellow gown. Cyrus tall and gangly, his shoulders thrown back as if to mimic Miles's proud posture. And Miles himself, his dark hair slightly tousled as always, his chest broad and muscled beneath his white shirt, his face relaxed and happy.

Joining them, she boldly slid her arm around Miles's waist. Lila and Cyrus regarded her action in utter astonishment. Seldom had Bella ever rendered them speechless.

She glanced up at Miles. "Have you told them our news, my love?"

His mouth curved in a smile that made him melt-ingly attractive. "I was waiting for you, darling." To Lila and Cyrus, he announced, "Your sister has done me the great honor of agreeing to be my wife. We're to be married as soon as I can make the arrangements."

Silence reigned for a moment as the twins stared, goggle-eyed, from Miles to Bella. Then a clamor of questions burst forth.

"Will there be a wedding party?" Lila said, her blue eyes alight. "Will you wear a fancy gown, Bella? Will *I* wear a fancy gown?"

"Does that mean we'll be living here for good?" Cyrus asked. "This will be our home? May I ring for food anytime I like?"

"Yes to all," Miles said on a laugh, clapping the boy on the shoulder. "And now I must beg a moment alone with your sister, for there's something I need to show her."

Threading his fingers through Bella's, he drew her out of the library and down the corridor to a nearby chamber. This one was grand as well, with gilded chairs and couches. She remembered being left here to wait on her first visit to Aylwin House, but instead she had surreptitiously followed the footman upstairs to see Miles.

Now, she noticed the numerous Egyptian artifacts on display, fine statues of gods and goddesses. But Miles didn't stop at any of those. Instead, he took her to the fireplace, where a huge painting hung above the marble mantel.

It was the portrait of a proud, dark-haired man in a crimson cape with an ermine collar. He was holding a sword in one hand and a scepter in the other. His harsh, unsmiling expression held a haunting reminder of the Ducal Stare.

She turned to Miles. "He looks familiar. This is your father?"

"Yes. The fourth Duke of Aylwin." Miles gazed up at the image for a moment, his face showing a hint of regret and sorrow. "For so many years I blamed myself for his death."

Bella laid her cheek on his shoulder. "It wasn't your fault. Surely you can accept that now. It was all about that map—and Hasani's determination to stop your father from finding the hidden tomb. I think Hasani fancied himself a priest of the ancient Egyptian religion."

Miles's expression darkened. "I can scarcely believe that my father's murderer was right here in this house all these years. And that the bastard would dare to attack you—" He bit off the words and then gently touched the back of her hair. "How is your head this morning, darling? Still hurting?"

"Not at all. I'm just glad everything turned out well."

His arm came around her waist, drawing her closer. "I have you to thank for exposing the truth. You freed me from that burden of guilt. Now I can see my father as a man to be loved and admired, and not merely as a source of pain and guilt."

Bella reached into her pocket and drew out the letter. She hoped and prayed that it contained a message that would help Miles find peace. "I nearly forgot. I found this letter last night tucked into one of the journals. I believe Papa wrote it to you on the day after your father died. I don't know why he never sent it."

Miles stared down at the two names, *The Marquess of Ramsgate* scratched out and *The Duke of Aylwin* added beneath it. Then he slowly turned it over and broke the seal with his thumb.

Bella would have moved away to give him a mo-

ment alone, but he held her close. "I don't have my spectacles. Will you read it to me?" He led her to a settee, where they sat side by side, their bodies touching, as he unfolded the letter and handed it to her.

A lump in her throat, she gave voice to her father's words.

To my Lord Ramsgate—

Words cannot express my sorrow at the loss of Aylwin. He was a fine man who loved you greatly, though he was too proud to show tender sentiment. He believed it his sacred duty to behave according to the strictures of his high rank, to teach you how to conduct yourself properly, to present himself as the model of a strong, principled leader. Pray know that your keen intellect and enthusiasm for scholarly pursuits was a point of vast pleasure and pride to him.

Yet I must confess that Aylwin's death weighs heavily on my shoulders. Last week, I made a discovery at the worksite, a papyrus map known only to your father and me, for it would stir greed in the hearts of the wicked. We divided the map in half for safekeeping. Yet someone did find out, and I dare not explain more for fear that you yourself might be endangered. I beg only that you understand I must leave your service at once and take my family far away along with my half of the map. Only then will you be safe from harm.

Yrs. with my everlasting affection & regard,
Sir Seymour Jones

Bella looked up at Miles to see his eyes glossy with tears. He glanced away, and she held him close, rubbing a soothing pattern over his back. "Papa must have ^ decided that it was too dangerous for you to know anything at all about the map," she murmured. "That's why he never sent the letter. If you'd known, you might have tried to track down who murdered your father. You might have been killed yourself."

Miles drew back and gazed solemnly at her. "Actually, I suspected foul play all along. And now it is my turn to beg that you not be angry if I make a confession."

"Angry?"

He set aside the letter and took her hands in his. "Bella, for a very long time I feared that the murderer was your father. I didn't want to believe it, but what else could I think when he disappeared? Then when you came here, out of the blue, I allowed you to stay because I felt compelled to uncover the truth." He raised her hands and kissed them. "Can you ever forgive me?"

Bella could only smile tenderly at him. "No wonder you asked me all those questions about Papa."

"And you don't despise me for suspecting him?"

She emphatically shook her head. "All of that is in the past, my love. It doesn't matter anymore. I'm only glad that you finally know the whole truth now. You know that Papa truly did love you—as did your own father. They merely wanted the best for you."

Smiling, Miles pulled her close, tucking her into his side. "Speaking of the best, if only I'd known when I caught you sneaking through the corridor that it would be the best thing that had ever happened to me."

"You gave me the Ducal Stare."

"And you were not intimidated." He stroked the

bare skin of her neck in a way that released a flood of warmth in her. "That was the moment that I began to fall in love with you."

Nothing in the world could match the joy of seeing the softness of love on his face. She snuggled closer, relishing the swift beating of his heart against her bosom. "For me, it was the first time you took me in your arms and kissed me in your study. Never in my life had I known such feelings existed. Oh, Miles, I do love you. So very much."

"Then I shall endeavor to make you love me even more," he said, a wicked gleam in his dark eyes. "Every night for the rest of our lives."